THE COMPANIONS

THE COMPANIONS

AGE OF ARTHUR · BOOK ONE

JOHNFITZAUTHOR.COM

John Fitz

This is a work of fiction inspired by historical and legendary figures. While some names, characters, places, and events are drawn from history and mythology, they have been interpreted and adapted for creative purposes. All other characters and incidents are products of the author's imagination.

Cover and Interior Design by We Got You Covered Book Design
WWW.WEGOTYOUCOVEREDBOOKDESIGN.COM

ISBN: 979-8-9939785-0-5 (paperback)
ISBN: 979-8-9939785-1-2 (hardcover)

THE COMPANIONS

THE AGE OF ARTHUR • BOOK ONE

JOHN FITZ

SCOTI TRIBES
LUGUVALLIUM
INSULA MANAVIA

DUN GUAIRE
PICT TRIBES
HADRIAN'S WALL
EBORACUM

INTRODUCTION TO THE AGE OF ARTHUR

It was around 500 AD, the darkest of ages. Rome had abandoned Britannia, leaving behind an urbanized people wearing togas, drinking wine, going to the baths, many of them embracing the new religion of Christianity. The Welsh-speaking Britons had once been part of a global empire, trading goods from around the world, using coins, and writing in Latin. With the legions gone, barbarian invaders from northern Germany now occupied much of the island, the Romano-British barely hanging on in the west. Their world was on the verge of collapse as dozens of competing kingdoms and warlords dotted the landscape. Lawlessness and chaos reigned as the native Britons desperately tried to keep civilization alive. This was the Age of Arthur, when the legends were born.

This is their story.

CHAPTER ONE

The forests of the Weald had never been kind to prey, and today the quarry had no fearsome teeth, horns, or claws; instead of sporting feathers or fur, this prey ran on two legs. But this quarry could fight back. Arturius, one of the hunted, was only certain of one thing: he would never be enslaved again. The dense foliage of the primeval forest created a perpetual gloom. Sunlight rarely graced the forest floor in this place untrammeled by man, a refuge in southeastern Britannia once used by the Romans Empire for sport. Poachers of game faced a brutal death if caught, and though the empire had left Britannia years ago, locals still avoided the evil spirits and banshees that dwelt there.

The ground felt damp beneath his body as he remained motionless. Arturius could smell the musky odor of earth and decaying leaves as he lay beneath the carpet of rotting vegetation, trying not to think about the insect that was slowly crawling up his left leg. Fear clinched his gut as he felt the creature moving its way up, yet he knew he had to remain still. One move, one twitch, and he could be spotted and killed. He concentrated upon the fleeting images of a Saxon warrior stalking him, his eyes narrowed so the whites of his eyes were camouflaged. If a bird could be spooked by that, then so could this fur-clad bastard.

His mouth was dry as he kept his breathing measured. Concentrating on his breathing would calm him, as when he held his breath, he could feel his heart beating, willing it to slow down. It was not the first time he had felt fear like this, but long ago he had learned how to control his fear so he could function. If he failed now, he knew the icy clasp of panic would be the last thing he would feel before he died. *But I am not going to die today,* he thought.

The sweaty-palmed dread he was experiencing now was mixed with a sense of anger and a desire for revenge. The Saxon warrior searching for him had a name: Holt, an evil bastard who haunted his dreams, his nightmares of that yellow-toothed bastard smiling at him as he tormented him. Helpless rage would startle him out of his sleep, but he was not sleeping now. This was real. This was no dream.

He and his friends had tasted freedom for only a few days, but already it felt like a lifetime. Arturius and his two teenaged companions had made a pact to die rather than be captured again, but Arturius was confident that if he could perform with the skill he possessed, they would survive. He visualized himself striking the pose of a slinger with perfect rhythm and balance, flinging his projectile towards the Saxon hunter with speed and accuracy.

The sling consisted of two pieces of braided rope about eighteen inches long, linked together by a leather pouch, the projectile being a lead pellet. Thralls would never be allowed to touch a real weapon, but to the Saxons, the unassembled sling looked like innocuous pieces of rope and leather. Arturius could assemble it into a deadly weapon in just a few minutes, able to cave in a skull with a well-placed throw.

Saxons regarded their thralls as less than human, cursed by Woden and Thunor to be wretched Nithings fated to serve at the feet of their Saxon masters. Slaves who ran away were destined to die as a lesson for daring to seek freedom. He almost gagged, recalling one such recaptured thrall, disemboweled and burnt in the fires, the smell of charred pork and shite still fresh in his mind. He and his friends had sworn they would never let that happen to them.

The Norse believe their thralls had lost the favor of the gods; luck and fortune having deserted them and, in their world, luck was everything. The Norns, the three blind witches that weaved one's life's thread on their looms of fate, were no doubt cackling in mirth at his plight. Arturius and his friends were once Romano-British nobility, ones who had ordered servants about their entire lives until they had been thrown into thralldom by the treachery of King Aelle of the South Saxons.

Finally, the bowman stepped into a spot on the trail where the trees thinned out enough to give Arturius an unobstructed view. He had a clear shot now. Ever so slowly, he rose out of the leaves, an easy shot, or so he hoped. His bollocks started to ache as they always did when he felt threatened. He wondered if that ever happened to anyone else. Suddenly, a youth stepped out from behind a massive oak farther down the trail, and the Saxon's head snapped around at the sight.

It was Caradoc, one of his companions. They were committed now, and there was no going back. His friend was curly-haired and stocky, wearing a ragged- looking tunic that only a thrall would touch. Even from this distance, Arturius could see Caradoc's startling blue eyes that contrasted with his dark complexion and hair. A beam of sunlight flashed off the iron collar of a thrall around his neck as he darted from tree to tree.

"Hey, Holt," Caradoc called out in the guttural Saxon tongue, "I bet you cannot hit me, you Svien Hund!"

Holt's full attention was on Caradoc, and his back was turned. The Saxon drew back his bow with the intent to kill, taking his time to get a clear shot at his tormenter. Fully upright now, taking care to make as little noise as possible. Arturius settled his body into his well-practiced firing position. Caradoc was risking his life to act as a decoy for Arturius to spring the ambush, and Arturius only had time for one shot.

He crouched, the sling hanging down as he took a cleansing breath and relaxed his shoulders. He swung the sling backwards like a pendulum, bringing it back in a circle. Once, twice, three times, and release! His arm ended up pointing at the back of Holt, eyes fixed upon his target. The almond-shaped lead missile hummed like a bee as it headed for the back of Holt's head.

Whirrrrrrr, Smack!

The Saxon stood still for a moment, stunned, then the stricken warrior's body collapsed forward, as if his legs had been transformed from stout supporting structures into wet ropes. Arturius stood still, transfixed for an instant, then he scampered to where the fallen bowman lay. He kicked the weapon away from the prostrate man's hand, then he grabbed Holt's seax, the Saxon's short sword, from a scabbard. Once Holt was disarmed, Arturius let out his breath in a whoosh. *By Jupiter,* he thought, *I was holding my breath the whole time. Is he dead?*

Arturius fell back to one knee, suddenly drained of strength. Relief flooded though him as everything around him seemed sharper, brighter, and more vivid. *By all the gods, I am alive,* he thought. He felt weak as a kitten, feeling a strange mix of pride in his skill and revulsion at the results as he gazed down upon the slack-jawed face of Holt, the tongue lolling out, saliva drooling from his unmoving lips. The Saxon's loose breeches were stained yellow with urine, overwhelming the normal stench of body odor and rotten teeth that Holt was known for.

Holt certainly looked like he was dead. If so, Arturius had just killed a man, his first. He was surprised over how little remorse he felt. Arturius had hunted and killed countless times before, but those were innocent animals. He had always felt a sense of regret whenever he had dispatched one of those unfortunate creatures, but for this man, he had none. Arturius wondered what his mother would think of him now. He had been raised in a Christian household, as the official religion of Rome still had many adherents in Britannia, and she was one of the faithful. Would she be disappointed in him for what he had just done?

His stepfather had been a Roman pagan, and he would have had no problem with this act of violence, as he was a member of the mystery cult of Mithras that Roman legionaries followed. Those who admired Mithras valued strength and honor, and the protection of family and friends. War was killing, and they accepted that. The followers of the Christos believed killing was a sin, and Arturius thought it odd he did not feel more guilt. *Am I a murderer,* he thought. *Do I possess no compassion for my fellow man?*

He felt he had no choice but to dispatch Holt to save himself and his friends, but the killing of this bastard seemed almost too easy as he reveled in the sense of accomplishment and relief. He had crossed his own personal Rubicon, killing a man to defend himself and his friends, more of a rite of passage than the old-fashioned Roman ceremony when he had received his virilis toga at the age of fourteen. He did not feel like a man then, but now he knew that he would never be the same again.

"A head shot," stammered Caradoc, who ran up and joined him next to the fallen figure. "That was an amazing throw! Is he dead?"

"I do not know yet," he said.

Arturius found the projectile that had hit the Saxon lying in the grass at the man's feet. Arturius put the object into his pouch by his side, and then he slowly reached up to Holt's head. He felt the neck for a pulse. It was there, but it was weak and thready. Then he gingerly pressed upon the spot where the missile had struck, feeling a warm wetness where the skull was deeply indented, with pieces of bone grating under his fingers. He pulled his hand back in disgust.

"I was aiming for the center of his back," Arturius muttered, "a lucky shot, but unlucky for him. He still lives, but probably not for long. If he does awaken, he will not remember his own name."

His reverie was broken by the sound of the distant baying of the hounds down the path that Holt had come from as farther up the trail, a tousled blonde head popped out from behind a gnarled tree. It was Cerdic, his other companion.

Cerdic hissed, "We are in a pile of shite now, we have got to move!"

Arturius shook his head and motioned for Cerdic to join them.

"Come over here," Arturius said. "You remember the little present he gave us the night when Holt made us slaves? Well, let's give him that same gift back."

Cerdic smiled, then once he joined them, they all gave Holt their offering, a stream of fresh urine that splashed over the prostrate Saxon. They quickly stripped him of his Holt of his possessions, nervously glancing down the trail. Arturius reached out and placed a reassuring hand on each of their shoulders.

"Cerdic, Caradoc, remember what we talked about. If we maintain a steady pace and keep moving, we can stay ahead of them. Those dogs cannot run long and steady like we can."

Arturius cracked a smile.

"Remember the story of Pheidippides at Marathon in ancient Greece? He ran one hundred and fifty miles in two days, to Athens and Sparta both before and after the battle."

"Arturius, he died," Cerdic said, rolling his eyes.

"Well, we'll just skip that part."

Arturius was trying to look more confident than he felt, but he had to keep their hopes up.

"It is only fifty miles or so to Caleva," he said.

"And then it is fifty miles to Glevum," Cerdic replied.

Then all three recited the plan aloud in unison.

"And it's only fifty miles to Venta Silurum."

"Well," Cerdic said as he sulked, "I am not going to run that in two days, I can tell you."

"Okay, let's get started," he said."

Then it dawned on him. It had been one year since he and his friends had been enthralled, and tomorrow he would be turning eighteen. *Will I be alive to see my birthday,* he wondered.

CHAPTER TWO

They started at a slow and steady pace along the woodland trail with Caradoc in the lead. He had the most knowledge of the woods, and he was the one who had marked their trail. This was the third day after their escape from the rolling pasturelands to the southeast, the farms and villages now controlled by the South Saxons. The boys were in the portion of the forest that was more level and easily traveled, not so dominated by the hills and steep valleys so characteristic of the eastern stretches of the Weald.

They were headed northwest, or so Arturius hoped, though it was so gloomy, he had no idea what direction they were going. He thought back of how they had gotten here in the first place. They never would have successfully escaped except for the help of a party of Jutes living in Aelle's lands that had taken pity on them and had helped them to escape. The Jutes had been offended by Aelle, who had broken three of the nine virtues the Norse valued when they had been enthralled, that of hospitality, truth, and honor. *For so-called barbarians,* he ruminated, *some of these northerners have more honor than my own people.*

If not for Caradoc, he knew they never would have gotten this far. Their Saxon masters could not wield a bow like Caradoc could, so they had allowed him to hunt for venison on occasion. On those hunting expeditions, Caradoc had been always guarded, but there were times when his watchers were inattentive, and he had surreptitiously left bits of cloth to mark a trail for them to follow when they made their escape. The problem was these strips of cloth had blended in with the vegetation, and now Caradoc was struggling to find them.

Arturius might be tired and hungry now, but his current hardships were not unlike the trials he had endured as a youth. He remembered being almost faint with hunger, trying to hit the targeted pole with a river-smoothed stone as his stepfather looked on impassively. "I can be here all night if I must," he remembered Cato saying as the old Spaniard feasted on wine and cheese while Arturius struggled to complete his task of hitting the target pole a dozen times before he could to share in the food. He had almost hated the ancient slinger then, but now he knew why he had been so hard on him. Today he silently thanked his stepfather; he and his friends were alive because of the relentless training he had endured.

The farther they traveled, the darker and deeper the woods became, the path barely perceptible in the omnipresent gloom. The bases of the trees were covered in green moss, shaggy green giants with dark limbs overhanging them, and the sun invisible as an occasional drip of water fell from the leaves above, making the forest feel even more oppressive. Would the darkness ever end? Suddenly, Caradoc stopped. He had come to a barely perceptible fork in the path, scanning the path to find the marker he had previously placed. He looked lost.

"What is the matter?" asked Cerdic.

Arturius and Cerdic exchanged an anxious glance. His heart sank; this was no time to get off track. Arturius tried to still his sense of panic and frustration as Caradoc continued to search for his marker. *Jupiter Optimus Maximus,* he prayed, *help him find that bloody thing.*

"This way," the phlegmatic Caradoc announced.

Off they went. Arturius was still concerned they were still off-course, but now at least they were on the move. Regardless, they were committed to go where Caradoc led. *Remember the teachings of Marcus Aurelius,* he thought, *try to say something positive.*

Arturius panted out as they ran, "I don't hear the hounds anymore. We lost them. You are doing well, Caradoc. We would have never gotten this far if it was not for you."

His friend turned his head and repaid his compliment with a brief smile. They continued until they came to a large opening in the forest, and Caradoc came to a stop, again looking perplexed. Arturius continued to try to look impassive, but inwardly he was seething. *By Hercules' bollocks*, he fumed, *how could Caradoc lose a marker again.* He thought of old Cato and his teachings on how to be a leader, and the need for him to have the courage that those who honored Mithras possessed. He heard his stepfather's voice; *tell your men you believe in them, and do not show panic.* Arturius hoped that he was appearing calm, even though his gut was knotted in fear.

"My friends," Caradoc glumly croaked out, "wait here. I need to gather my bearings."

Caradoc started to inspect the entrance to each of the several trails that led from the clearing. After many minutes of impatient searching, he returned to the other two, despair written on his face.

"I cannot find my marker. It is either blended in with the trees, or it is missing. It should be here somewhere. I do not know which path to take."

"By Woden's missing eye," Cerdic loudly groaned, "are you telling us that we are lost?"

The Jute looked at the dark-haired boy in disgust. Caradoc angrily gazed back at him.

"Cerdic, I swear___"

Arturius placed a hand on both Caradoc's and Cerdic's shoulder as he had done earlier.

"Stop it, both of you. No battle plan survives intact once combat begins, and our escape is no different. Think of this as a war against Aelle. Our victory for now will be just to survive, but someday, we will return to kill that one-eyed cur. Do not get discouraged. We can find game to kill and water to drink. If we cannot get out of the Weald tonight, then that is okay, we just need to adapt and change the plan."

Suddenly, a disembodied voice called out from across the clearing.

"Do not move, boys, we have a dozen archers covering you. Lower your weapons, and you won't be hurt."

Arturius's heart sank as a cold chill ran down his spine, but then cold, pure logic overrode his fear. He would look for a way to escape, to fight back, and not let the panic overwhelm him. Arturius looked around to see where that voice had come from. Shadowy figures emerged from the clearing surrounding them, slowly stalking towards them from all sides. The three of them huddled together, back-to-back, facing outwards and weapons out and ready to fight.

"Do as they say," Arturius whispered. "That warning was in British, not Saxon. Let's try to talk our way out of this, but we will not become slaves again. We die first. Agreed?"

The two others nodded. As the shadowy figures emerged, their images became clearer, the approaching wearing a mishmash of different types of clothing, armor, and weapons. Most had spears, and only a couple had bows.

"So much for a dozen archers," muttered Caradoc.

One man came closer to them than the others, dressed in a long, brown robe tied with a dirty white rope. Unlike his companions, he carried no weapon, only a long wooden staff in his hand. He was very tall, with piercing green eyes, his thin face dominated by a nose that bore a patrician's hump, classic to the Mediterranean world. The front part of his head had been completely shaved, forming a semicircle from one ear to the other, the tonsure of a British Christian monk. *What is a priest doing here in the middle of the wilderness?* Arturius wondered.

"Who are you, and what are you doing here?" the stranger asked.

The boys nervously glanced around for a few moments before Arturius broke the silence

"We mean you no harm. We are just passing through the woods to Caleva."

"Well," the man replied, "you three are a curious mix with the iron collar of a thrall around your necks. You two look like Britons, but that third one who was mentioning something about Woden's eye looks like a barbarian Saxon to me."

"I am a Jute, not a mangy Saxon," Cerdic quietly hissed.

"Well," Arturius muttered, "your mother may think you are a Jute, but your father was British, and you do have a British name."

"Cerdic," Caradoc whispered, "you know that Jutes and Angles and Saxons all look the same to us."

"Well," Cerdic said, pouting, "they are not the same."

"Shh," Arturius said. "Let me talk."

Arturius opened his arms wide as he called out to the man in the brown robe.

"First, we like to know who you are, brother."

"Alright," the man replied. "My name is Brother Petrus. I am the leader of a place of refuge here in the Weald for the free men and women of Britannia. We serve no masters or lords, and here in the Weald, we are safe from Saxon and British warlords alike. And who might you be?"

The three boys looked at each other in silence for a moment, then Arturius spoke up.

"This is Caradoc, a prince of the Silures. And this other one is Cerdic, whose father was the leader of the confederation of the Catuvellauni and the West Saxons. As for myself, I am Arturius, from Tintagel, land of the Dumnonai.

"So, what in the name of the Christos are you three doing here? Can we trust you to be the people you claim to be?"

Silence reigned for a few moments. A flood of emotions erupted in Arturius' mind as the memories of his life up to now jostled around in his head. His excitement at being an honored guest of the Saxons had been crushed after he was betrayed and thrust into slavery. There had been a time when he had almost given up hope, but the strength of his friends had sustained him. Now hope had returned, but were they about to be enslaved again after being so close to freedom? Arturius inwardly sighed. *Jupiter Optimus Maximus,* he prayed, *give me strength.*

"So, Brother Petrus," Arturius called out, "trust goes both ways. We may not look like nobles, but you don't look so reputable yourself. And if you are a priest instead of a common brigand, then you must be an educated man. So, let us see if you can recite the lord's prayer for me. In Greek."

Brother Petrus raised his brow with a frown, but then his face broke into an awkward grin.

"A reasonable request," the priest said, "and easily fulfilled."

The priest folded his hands together as he started his prayer.

"O Pateras, mas pou einai ston paradeiso___."

The priest droned on, reciting the prayer in passable Greek in a cultured Latin accent. This was no common thief. Arturius remembered some rumors about there being a refuge like this in the wilderness. Could he trust this man? *He does not look dangerous,* he thought, *but what are brigands supposed to look like?* The man had a kindly face. Once the prayer was completed, Arturius decided to take a chance.

"Thank you for that, Brother," Arturius said as he opened his arms wide. "I believe you are who you say, so I will tell you about us. Over a year ago, my companions and I were sent to Aelle as part of a hostage exchange, to help ensure the peace between the British and the Saxons. We were to learn of their culture and function as goodwill ambassadors, while three of his sons were exchanged for the same purpose."

"Well," Petrus retorted, "hostage exchange is a common Roman practice. It may work well with civilized people, but that didn't work out very well with these bloody barbarians, now, did it?"

The three young men nodded as Petrus shot Arturius a steely look.

"If your friends are some sort of noble blood, then why are you with these other two? Oh, wait a minute. Arturius, eh? I may have heard about you. You're related to that idiot Vortigern then, aren't you? You are not his son, though. A grandson or nephew, perhaps?"

Arturius hung his head, his cheeks burning bright with shame and anger.

"Yes, I share his blood through my father, whom I do not remember. He was Vortigern's brother, Uther the Pendragon. My mother's side is Roman, and not British at all. As for Vortigern, I reject him as he has rejected all Britons."

"Even if you are what you claim to be, why did the Saxons not just kill you three along with the other British leaders on *The Night of the Long Knives*?"

"We do not really know why we were spared," he said, shrugging. "Perhaps they valued us as translators. We all know common British, of course, and we all can read and write in Latin as well. Caradoc can speak the language of the Silures, and I know the dialect of the Dumnonai."

"And my mother was a Jutish princess," Cerdic chimed in, "so I still had value as a hostage to Aelle. Please, my good Brother, leave us alone and let us move on. We are just trying to go through Caleva to the land of the Silures. We wish you no harm."

Brother Petrus scoffed.

"So, you three are thinking that you can wander into Caleva and then go on your merry way back home? Bah, you will not stand a chance! Rogues are everywhere, and they might give you back to gain Aelle's favor in a heartbeat. None of you look so noble to me. How do I know you are not spies sent by Aelle to find our camp?"

Arturius glanced at the other two boys for a moment, then thoughtfully replied.

"No one would teach a slave how to wield a weapon with skill. Do you agree, sir?"

"I suppose so, yes."

"Sir," Arturius said as he pointed to Caradoc, "if you would allow my Silurian friend here to show you his skill with a bow, and if I show you what I can do with a sling, perhaps you might be swayed."

Brother Petrus laughed.

"A sling? Really? No Saxon has ever stooped so low as to use such a weapon. They would think that as unmanly, I believe, so you would not learn that art from them. And no Saxon would let a thrall even touch a bow, much less shoot one. Fine. Do you see that fat oak across the clearing, the one with the split trunk? That looks to be fifty paces or so. Let us see if either of you can come close to that."

Caradoc bent down to retrieve his bow, as the warriors that surrounded them made it clear that any false move could be his last. He strung the weapon and tested its draw strength a few times. Caradoc gave Arturius a worried look, murmuring under his breath as he strung the bow.

"Thank you for volunteering me for the demonstration, Arturius. I have never shot this bow before. I may not be able to hit a barn with this thing."

Arturius gazed nervously as Caradoc fastened the leather bracer he had taken from Holt. He could not tell if Caradoc was being sarcastic or if he was genuinely angry. *I should have asked him first,* he thought. *By Jupiter, I can be such an idiot sometimes.* Caradoc notched his bow as he assumed a classic archer's stance and fired. The arrow arched toward the tree, barely missing it to the left. The archer turned to Brother Petrus.

"Grant me another chance," he said. "Compared to our longer bows back home, this weapon is a piece of shite!"

He then selected a new arrow, notched it, and let it fly.

Thwack!

It struck the tree with a well- centered blow, just below the split in the trunk. He looked at Arturius with a sigh of relief; now it was his turn. His mouth went dry again as all eyes turned to him. His gut clenched, and then his balls started to ache as they always did when he got nervous. *Oh shite,* he thought, *a sling is not as accurate as a bow from here. What was I thinking?*

Arturius pulled out a new lead projectile, placing it into the pouch of the sling as he stared at the tree. Never averting his gaze, he repeated his breathing routine to calm himself, assuming the classic slinger's pose once more. The missile in the pouch swung forward in a fluid movement, and then he released the projectile.

Whirrrrrrr, thunk!

It not only hit the tree, but it shattered the arrow that Caradoc had just shot. Brother Petrus and his men looked at him with amazement as Arturius wore a sheepish expression.

"Slings are not really that accurate," he said. "I am happy to just hit that tree, but hitting the arrow? I could try that a hundred times and not pull that off again."

"Lucky for you maybe, but not for me," muttered Caradoc. "That was my best arrow."

"Well," Brother Petrus said, chuckling, "I have been known to say I would rather be lucky than good. In this case, I think you may be both."

He then looked thoughtfully at the three boys.

"Come with us then, back to our home. You are welcome to stay with us. Indeed, we had heard that Aelle had some noble hostages, and you must be those fellows."

The three young men looked at each other, stunned by their good fortune. Then Arturius spoke up.

"We need some privacy to discuss your offer, Brother. Give us a moment."

He and his two friends huddled together to talk amongst themselves.

Arturius whispered, "I had heard some of the other slaves talk of this Petrus and his refuge. I thought it was a rumor, but it sounds like this may be real. Cerdic, Caradoc, what say you? It seems to me our best option is to accept their hospitality. Do you agree?"

Caradoc looked grimly at the men surrounding them and muttered,

"I will not be a thrall again. I would rather fight and die now than to surrender myself."

Cerdic replied with a sly grin.

"I also heard of these escaped thralls, but that doesn't mean they won't kill or enslave us either. But we have no food, no water, no women, and no shelter, and I could really do with an ale right now. I say we go with them, so long as we keep our weapons."

"I have heard these same rumors," Caradoc muttered. "They might kill us, but we won't be their slaves. I heard they had banned slavery there, but how can people live without slaves? I am not sure I believe it."

By Hercules bollocks, Arturius thought, *a land without slaves. I want to see how this place works.* How did they function without servants? He thought it was worth the chance just to see a place like that.

"Who knows," Arturius said, "maybe they have some books with them as well. Keep your weapons handy, and stick together if they prove false, but I think we can trust them. If they wanted us dead, it would have happened by now. Do you both agree?"

Caradoc displayed a glum smile while Cerdic chuckled. Then he nodded in assent.

"I don't give a tinker's fart about books," Cerdic snorted, "but by Thunor's beard, they bloody well better have some ale. I say let's do it."

"Okay then, we are of one mind then," whispered Arturius.

He broke away from the huddle and walked up to Petrus and smiled as he held out his hand. "We will come if you agree that we are regarded as guests, not captives. We keep our weapons and will be free to leave if we choose. What say you to that?"

Brother Petrus made the sign of the cross, and then he shook his hand.

"Excellent," Brother Petrus said. "I swear that by grace of the Christos, our lord and savior, that I agree to those terms."

Petrus turned to a grizzled man bearing a bow.

"Lucanus, lead us back to the settlement, please, I don't have a clue how to get back."

The man replied in a grunt and then muttered, "Follow me, Brother," and off down another murky trail the group went.

As they walked along, the priest put his hand on the slinger's shoulder.

"Arturius, have you ever tried to teach others to use one? One does not need a grown man's strength to be deadly with that weapon."

"If you can throw a rock well, you can be a good slinger," Arturius said as he smiled. "I have been doing this all my life, and it is harder than it looks. But yes, even boys and women can be good slingers if they work at it."

"How did you learn how to wield the sling," Petrus queried. "That skill seems rare in this land."

"I was raised by a retired legionary from the Balearic Islands. He married my mother after my father died. When my mother remarried, her new husband was the only father I ever remember. My real father may have been related to Vortigern, but I hate that bastard and all he stands for."

"That Vortigern is a sneaky wanker, isn't he?" Brother Petrus said.

"That is the patrician Roman blood in him," Arturius said, laughing. "Those fellows will kill their own mothers to get a purple stripe on their togas. And I must say, you have a salty tongue for a man who claims he is a priest. How is it that a man of the cloth leads this group?"

Brother Petrus grinned.

"As my brothers here can surely attest, I am not your typical man of the cloth, and the story of how I came to lead this merry little band will come out in due time. Come. Let us continue to move on."

CHAPTER THREE

The three boys and their escorts continued their trek through the primeval forest on the narrow trail, and it was eerily quiet. The only sounds Arturius could hear were the breathing of the men and the calling of the wild birds around them as they seemed to walk for hours deeper into the forest. The sun had set long ago. Arturius felt overwhelmed by foreboding blackness. If he wandered off the path by a few feet, he could be lost forever. As they plodded along, Arturius reflected to when he joined the South Saxons and just how naive he had been.

He wanted adventure and to see the world, but he never imagined the circumstances that were now his reality. As a boy he daydreamed about living a life like Julius Caesar, being kidnapped by pirates and then escaping, and then returning to kill the bandits, winning fortune and fame along the way. *I found adventure all right,* he thought, *but none like the fantasies of my youth.*

The reality of being enslaved had been an awful experience, something he would not wish upon his worst enemy, but his leaving home was not all negative, either. Before his enslavement, his time with the Norse had been the most carefree of his life, and he had come to respect them and their culture, and he had found the best two friends that anyone could ask for.

They were his brothers now.

He remembered his mother reminding him of his good fortune to be growing up in western Britannia and receiving a nobleman's training. He could hear his mother now: "*Be thankful you are not like those starving boys in Rome, conquered by those blue-eyed Goths. You do not know how lucky you are to receive a good meal and proper education!*" At first, he had lived as an honored guest of the South Saxons, but then he had become a thrall, grateful for any scraps the stray dogs had left behind. *My mother was right*, he thought. *How galling.*

Still, Arturius knew he was happier now than he ever would have been at home. Ever since his older brother had drowned in a boating accident, his mother had never been the same. She was overly protective, always telling him to be careful, and his primary memories of her were of her sadly lying in bed and complaining about everything. His memories of being called into her chambers *"to have a little talk"* still filled him with dread. How thrilled he was to get out of that little port town of Tintagel, that little speck of civilization perched on the edge of southwestern Britannia.

Leaving home had given him the opportunity to get away from his mother's smothering, so he had jumped at the chance. Arturius still did not know why King Constatine had selected him to be exchanged for a Saxon boy, but he suspected that the ruler thought him expendable. Having an uncle who was a brother to the king of the Ordovices made him valuable in the eyes of the Saxons. Little did the South Saxons know he was not in line for anybody's throne. His stepfather, the only real father he had ever known, had died from what the medicus called a bad heart right after he left to join Aelle's tribe, and so now he felt no reason to return.

Arturius was conflicted about his feelings about the Norse. It had been a family of Jutes who had risked their lives to help them escape, all on a matter of honor. He was certain no Briton would have helped them like that. That was how he thought of the Saxons: they were humanity at both its best and its worst. When he was younger, Arturius had thought of them as ignorant barbarians, but once he had joined them as an honored guest, he was surprised at the splendor of their world. Their stories and songs and poems were wonderfully complex and rich.

Being a free Saxon was certainly a different life than being trained as a Roman noble. Instead of learning about Homer and Cicero, Arturius discovered how to become a warrior. He chuckled to himself as he thought of what Cerdic called it, the school of the four F's: fighting, feasting, fornication, and farting. *Cerdic certainly has a way with words,* he thought. It had been the worst of the Northmen who had enthralled him, and it had been the best of them who had set them free. *And it was the Norse Gods that helped us to escape*, he thought. He would make a proper sacrifice to them soon to give them thanks.

Then his mind came back to the present. Onward they moved in a single file through the forest. The smell of damp vegetation made him nervous, but it also made him feel alive, enjoying the solitude of their traipse through these woods. Finally, he saw the light of some fires in the distance as they approached a large encampment, the oppressive forest opening into a large clearing that was revealed in the glory of the full moon that night. Once the trees opened, he could see a village that was surrounded by an earthen rampart and a ditch in front, with sharpened stakes in front of the walls.

Instead of the haphazard chaos of the typical British settlements he was used to seeing, this community was laid out in a very regular grid pattern resembling those Roman military encampments that he had read about. Instead of Roman military tents, most of the dwellings were the round huts that were so common in Britannia. The traveling group was broken up, as the men splitting into different directions once in the camp. Brother Petrus directed the three boys to follow him.

"What about our pursuers?" he heard Cerdic ask. "Aren't you worried the Saxons will discover where we are going?"

"Not to worry," replied Brother Petrus. "Our trackers changed the markers your friend here left once we moved past the clearing to a different trail. If they were following those bits of cloth, they would get lost. We also left meat on the trails laced with nightshade; those dogs will not bother us."

Arturius and the others all started to talk at once, peppering Petrus with questions when he shushed them as they approached the main dwelling in the center of the compound.

"My dear sirs, I am sure you are all curious about our community here. Your questions will be answered once we are sitting down, and I could use a draught of ale right now myself."

"Sounds good to me," chortled Cerdic, "I'll take two."

They entered a large British style roundhouse, ducking in under a low-slung door to be greeted by a cheery fire in the middle of the hut illuminating the house, its smoke curling up through the roof. It always amazed Arturius when he was in these traditional British homes to see the smoke wafting through the thatch ceiling, even though the same structure could keep the never-ending rains of this island from seeping in. It was so different from the rectangular masonry buildings so typical of Roman structures, yet this felt to be such a welcoming place, as if he were coming home.

Once they had entered, two girls ran up to Brother Petrus with shrieks of joy and pounced on him to give him an enthusiastic hug, followed by a kiss hello. The oldest looked to him to be about their age, while the other girl appeared to be a bit younger. An older woman stood behind them, and Arturius supposed she was the wife of Petrus. She gave her husband a kiss on both cheeks as she greeted him, while she gave him and his friends a small bow.

"Boys. I would like to introduce you to my wife, Sister Brigid. She is the deaconess of our community here, and the two of us are the spiritual and political leaders of our little refuge here in the wilderness.

"Hello there, boys," the matron said with a brilliant smile. "Welcome to our home."

Sister Brigid was petite and vivacious, with graceful movements that were quick and decisive. Her head was covered by an apostonik, a symbol that she was a woman of the Christian faith. He could not see her hair, but with her auburn eyebrows, she appeared to be redheaded, her face covered in a mass of freckles. Her teeth were a bit crooked, and her large nose was not quite straight. She would never be accused of being beautiful, but her winning smile made her seem like a ray of sunshine on a cloudy day.

"Girls," the matron said with a Hibernian lilt, "thank you for welcoming Brother Petrus back. Now you must take care of our young guests here!"

The two girls settled down and introduced themselves.

"I am Senna, and this is Lucilia, my younger sister. Brother Petrus and Sister Brigid are our guardians, and our new family. We welcome you to the community of the Weald!"

With that, they both kissed him and the boys on the cheeks and then ran out to get food for the returned travelers. He looked at his friends in amazement, not sure what to think of being kissed by two beautiful strangers. As soon as the duo scurried out, the wife of Petrus spoke up.

"You may call me Sister Brigid. It is a pleasure to finally meet you, but do not get any ideas, gentlemen. These two young women were raised in a family that honored traditional Roman culture, aristocrats that stayed on here in Britannia. That Roman kiss was ceremonial, but it is a little surprising if you are not expecting it."

"I hate to disappoint you three boys," Petrus said, laughing, "but they were being polite, not lecherous."

After everyone sat down at the table, the matron served them some tankards of ale as promised. Introductions were made all around as he started to relax with the toasty fire in the hearth with drinks they had not tasted for a year. The home seemed such a welcoming place. The girls returned with food, and Arturius had a delightful dinner with the talk at the table dominated by the girls chatting about their oasis in the Weald. Then Lucilia and Senna were sent off to bed while the boys sat by the fire in animated conversation with their hosts, lubricated by even more ale.

"So," Arturius asked as he tried to suppress his grin, "tell us about those two young girls that we just met. What are they doing here? And how old are they?"

Sister Brigid responded with a laugh.

"Please remember that this is a Christian household," she said. "We do not marry off our young girls at the instant of puberty like those pagan Romans liked to do. They might be considered a marriageable age for some elderly patrician in Italia, but we are civilized here, and those young women will make their own decisions about when and whom they marry. They are too young to be courted at present, so remember that."

"Well, none of us are ready for marriage," Cerdic said, grinning. "I just want to get to know them better."

She touched Cerdic gently on the shoulder as she replied.

"Dearie," she said sweetly, "if any of you lay a hand with them before they are ready, I will cut your bollocks off and serve them to the pigs for their breakfast."

Petrus and his wife laughed uproariously while the three youths gave each other nervous looks.

As the laughter died down, Cerdic muttered to Petrus, "She is kidding, right?"

Brother Petrus continued to chuckle.

"I do not know, dear," Petrus muttered, "are you being serious?"

"Well, my dearest husband, there is only one way for our new guests to find out."

As the conversations went on, he and his friends began talking about their adventures so far. The more they conversed, the more Arturius was impressed with Sister Brigid. He had not been sure what to think of her at first, but it was soon apparent she was just blustering in her earlier threat. Sister Brigid had an advanced sense of humor for sure. She talked tough, but she did it with a smile. She asked probing questions without judgement, and she had charmed them all into telling their life stories without hesitation. She even got Caradoc to talk, practically a miracle in his eyes.

Arturius and his friends told their stories about their escape, their lives before coming to the Weald, and the trauma they felt during their servitude. She charmed them all, but at times she would use language that would make a sailor blush. Whenever she talked to him, she made him feel the world only revolved around him, and she was doing the same to his companions. Sometimes she would gently touch their shoulders when making a point to make them feel at ease. Arturius liked her; she was like an older sister that he never had. After the boys had spoken of their ordeals, they started to pepper their hosts with questions about their refuge in the wilderness.

Arturius asked, "So how did you start this place?"

"Petrus and I were the ministers of a Christian congregation at the town of Novomagus Regini. We were worried about the Saxons attacking us, so we built this camp and stocked it with supplies in case we needed to escape. You only had to see what was going on further east of us to be worried. Sure enough, when Aelle and his scoundrels landed nearby, we came here. That was how we became guardians of these two girls, as they accompanied us."

"What about the rest of their family?" Arturius queried.

Sister Brigid sighed with a haunted look in her eyes.

"Their father is a military man, off somewhere in the north with the remnants of the provincial army fighting pagans, while his wife and three daughters lived in Novomagus. Their mother and their sister, a beautiful young lady named Ria, chose not to come with us, and they did not make it out."

"So, these two survived and their mother and sister did not?" Arturius quietly asked. "How did that happen?"

Brigid spread her hands open.

"It is a bit of a story. Before the Saxons destroyed Novomagus, there were two Christian communities serving the community, and our congregation fled when Aelle landed. Vortigern told us we had nothing to fear from the Saxons, but we did not believe it. The other priest in town, a very earnest and devout young man, was also worried, but he decided to remain in the belief that faith and prayer would deliver them from evil. His congregation went to his church to pray for a miracle from the Christos."

Petrus added, "The mother of the girls allowed Senna and Lucillia to come with us, but she was strong minded, believing the priest's talk of miracles, so the mother and Ria stayed."

Sister Brigid sighed as she shook her head. She wiped a tear from her eyes as she paused a moment to gather herself.

"My husband and I believe that prayer is important, but we do not rely on miracles. Sure enough, Saxons sacked the city. Those people deemed unsuitable for slavery were locked in the church, and it was burned to the ground while they were still inside while the priest was used as target practice for their archers. Apparently, the girls' mother was raped and killed."

Brother Petrus rubbed his chin as if in thought.

"As for their remaining sister," Petrus said, "we pray that she is in heaven with her mother, but we fear that she may be still alive and is enduring the tortures of the damned while still here on earth. It is not a pleasant fate for a young woman captured by rampaging Northmen. So, we have become the guardians of these two sisters until they are united with their father."

"We have no idea where he is," Brigid said with a sight. "But at some point, we will move community to a safer location in the west. Hopefully then, we can track him down and deliver them to him, unless they meet the right man and start their own families. And let me assure you, that would not be any of you young gentlemen."

But as the fire continued to cast its cheery glow in the room, the boys learned why they were being welcomed so warmly. The community had few warriors to defend them, and they were being asked to lend their skills in the training of the people there to defend themselves. As young noblemen, they had been educated in the martial arts, and Petrus and Brigid asked them that night to help the refuges to learn how to fight. Arturius could see the desperation in his hosts' faces, and they all agreed to help. He felt like he had no choice; these were good people, and it was the ethical thing to do. The details of their agreement occupied the rest of the night.

Finally, the conversation petered out; it had been a long day for all of them. They were led out of the house to one of the smaller round huts nearby, their living quarters for their immediate future, and the two other boys collapsed onto their mats and fell asleep almost immediately. Arturius took a while to drift off. His mind swirled with images of his day, the most eventful of his life up to now.

Slavery, he thought. Certainly, the night he was enslaved was something he would never forget. Arturius had servants his entire life, servants who waited on him and his family hand and foot. Once he accepted slavery as the natural order, but now the lash had taught him otherwise. From what Brigid and Petrus were saying tonight, they preached that the faithful were all equal in the eyes of the Christos, and their hosts confirmed that this refuge in the Weald did not allow such servitude.

It did not mean that he wanted to be a Christian himself. All gods were capricious, even the Christian one, though he still favored the Roman ones. He was a stoic, a lover of philosophy, not of religion. The Christians could be exasperating, but at least the Christos seemed to be on their side; Arturius respected that. Not so with the Roman pantheon, as his own gods were both respected and feared. You could not rely on a pagan god to be on your side. You made sacrifices to placate them, but one never knew what tricks they would play on you.

His personal dream was to enjoy life, to read books and meet witty friends, and to discuss philosophy and art and all the wonders of the world. That luxury was an option that was denied to him. The circumstances of today's world had left him no choice. It was clear from tonight's conversation that Petrus and Brigid wanted him and his friends to be soldiers to help defend them from the chaos of this world. His life was heading in only one direction, fighting to keep civilization from collapsing around him. *The life I dream of will not happen for me,* he thought, *but perhaps my children can have the life of an intellectual that will be denied to me.*

The Roman legionaries had a code: demonstrate strength and honor, take care of your fellow legionaries as your family, respect your superiors, obey your orders, and be ready to die to protect your brother soldiers. The legions defended the weak and innocent from the barbarians; a thin, red-cloaked line that kept civilization from destruction. Now he was being asked to do the same. He thought of the two girls he had just met, and the tragedies that had befallen them. *People like that deserve to be protected,* he thought. *It is a noble calling.*

This was to be his new home. Even though he had found his mother annoying, he still missed her, and he wondered if he would ever see her again. He loved her, but she drove him crazy. He wondered if he was the only son who felt that way, if there was something wrong with himself, but he could not help how he felt.

He was finally able to calm his mind, dreaming of the next battle he would set up with his miniature legionaries like he used to play with as a child. It was calming, though he knew a real battle was anything but. That seemed to help, harking back a time when life seemed safe and secure. He had a purpose now. He had pride in what he was being tasked to do, to safeguard these people who were carving out a new life for themselves. And he was free. He would never take freedom for granted again. Off in the distance he heard the baying of wolves or wild dogs; or were those Saxon Hounds?

CHAPTER FOUR

Amid the forest clearing, Arturius was startled by a snarling Saxon berserker, bursting out of the woods and charging straight at him. The advancing warrior bellowed out his blood-curdling war cry as he advanced, his weapon poised high above him to deliver the mortal blow. Arturius was frozen, his legs paralyzed in terror, unable to move. Arturius tried to load his sling, but in his haste the stone slipped out, falling to the ground with a thud. *Something is wrong with me,* he thought. He was moving like a man underwater, clumsy and glacially slow, fumbling to load his sling.

As he struggled, icy fear gripped him as he tasted the bitter bile of impending death rising in his stomach. The Saxon drew nearer, his face in a grimace of hate. He could hear the battle cry of the warrior growing louder, the piercing sound reverberating in his skull. Arturius could almost smell his body odor and see the black rot in his teeth. His panic was almost overwhelming him. His hands were too awkward, and now it was too late. He looked on in terror as the sunlight glinted off the cruel blade as the axe descended towards his head. Arturius tried to scream, but no sound came out as an explosion of light overwhelmed him.

Then his eyes opened. The door of the hut had been thrown open, with brilliant sunshine flooding into the room. Arturius sat up, cold sweat dripping from his brow. He was alive. *Thank the Gods that was only a dream*, he thought. His two companions were lying in their beds, gazing at the doorway with sleepy eyes. The head of a grizzled old man had appeared, silhouetted in the daylight. The light was hurting his eyes, and he still felt groggy, but he knew that this was no morning to sleep late.

"All right," the old fellow barked out, "Get up, you lazy shites, we have work to do."

Arturius blinked again at the harsh morning light, dismayed that he kept having these nightmares. Would his mind ever shed the iron collar of a thrall? *Will I have these dreams forever?* he wondered. He kept his worries to himself as he and his friends tumbled out of bed. It was their first day in this forest refuge, and apparently it was time to go to work.

The old man beyond the doorway glared at them balefully, with one hand on his hips and the other holding a three-foot-long stick. Arturius looked at the wooden club warily; it looked to be a centurion's Vitus, similar to the one Cato had used to whack him with when he was in trouble. The old codger may have had a Vitus, but he did not look like a centurion, dressed in a simple linen shirt, overlaid with a battered breast plate of boiled and hardened leather. On his head was a brimless skull cap made of felt. He wore trousers, with his lower leggings made of strips of leather and linen. He was short and wiry, with an erect posture that suggested he was physically more capable than one would guess by looking at his wrinkled and careworn face.

"My name is Macro," he said grumpily, "and I am about the only person who has been trained in the art of war in this little paradise of ours. Well, at least until your lot showed up. Now help me to understand this. You three dodgy blokes are to help us train the worthless rabble out there how to defend themselves? You three look like you just stopped feeding from your mama's teats. You do not look like trained warriors and men to me."

The three of them gave him a shocked look. Finally, Arturius spoke up.

"We may be young, but all of us are of noble blood and have been trained to take our place in the battlefield."

"Oh," Macro spat out as he raised his brow, "pardon me, my noble sirs. Bah! That claim of noble blood will not buy you a sack of dung at the market. Patricians and Equestrians, Bah! You won't find any toffs like that around here, my young sirs. This place is a collection of ownerless slaves and landless peasants. Brother Petrus and Sister Brigid are the only noble ones in this shite-hole. Those two were the only educated ones that did not slink off to the mainland in fear."

Macros rolled his eyes, as he put his hands on his hips.

"They have given me the pleasure of training this illustrious group, and there is not enough of me to go around, but Brother Petrus has assured me you three can help me in my trials of Hercules to get this group to know the difference between the arse end of a spear and the pointy end. And I am thinking you might not know how to wipe your own bottoms, much less handle a weapon."

"We all three have different skills," Cerdic scoffed, "but I have no doubt that any one of us could dispatch you in less time than it takes to piss out last night's ale. Of course, looking at how old you are, it might take a long time for you to empty your wrinkled old bladder."

"There is no need for us to get into a pissing match," Arturius interjected, keeping his voice even. "But we do have martial skills, I can assure you. We have not been properly introduced, I believe. I am Arturius from the land of the Dumnonai."

Then Arturius pointed to each of his friends as he spoke

"This is Cerdic, of the Catuvellauni and West Saxons, and that one is Caradoc of the Silures."

Arturius grasped the man's forearm in a Roman handshake, remembering the phrase that Cato had told him that legionnaires used to say to each other.

"We greet you with strength and honor," he said.

The old man's scowl softened as the handshake was returned. Was that the hint of a smile?

"Well, then, I am Macro, from the tribe of nobody. I only answer to Brother Petrus, Sister Brigid, and the Christos for the preservation of his faith from the heathen barbarians. And I am about the only one here who has had training in the legions."

Macro looked at them with a scowl.

"So," he sniffed, "what martial skills do you three whelps possess?"

"Arturius here is an excellent slinger," Cerdic said with a confident tone, "and Caradoc an expert with the bow."

"Cerdic here has experience in the Saxon ways of war," Caradoc said, proudly. "He is skilled with the sword, the spear, and has trained in the shield wall. He can even ride a horse."

Macro looked at Cerdic appraisingly.

"You have been in a shield wall? Really? A puppy like you? How did that mistake happen?"

Cerdic's face flushed red.

"I have trained with my people, but I have not yet been in a proper battle."

Macro studied Cerdic for a long time.

"Cerdic, my boy, there is a big difference between training and an actual battle. I have seen more than one hero on the practice grounds turn into a cringing child in an actual fight."

"I am not worried. The men from Germania are the best fighters in the world."

"Cerdic," Macro scoffed, "you should know it was us Romans that taught those smelly Germans how to fight."

Cerdic grinned.

"That may be true, but we are much bigger than you Romans. And we are not afraid to die."

"Every man fears death," Macro said as he shook his head, "but we teach our men the courage to risk death to protect our comrades. And you know it used to be the Saxons fought much like your natives did here in Britain, challenging us to a one-on-one duels, screaming war cries and tossing spears about, and then they would all charge like a disorganized mob. But after a few centuries of having their bollocks cut up by a disciplined Roman legion, the Saxons have learned the Roman way of war."

"We learn how to fight one-on-one all right, better than any Roman," Cerdic said, smirking, "but that is not the focus of our training. We use teamwork, attacking and defending as a group behind a wall of shields, not seeking individual glory, but instead fighting for victory."

Macro rolled his eyes again.

"Well, guess where those smelly barbarians learned that from? Us Romans, that is who! But at least the feckin' eejits have enough sense to wear clothes, unlike your British ancestors who fought naked, all tattooed up and painted blue."

Macro motioned to them to follow him.

"Boys, let us join the motley crew you are supposed to supervise. I will give you assignments to help train these people. You may not know much, but whatever knowledge you have, it is more than the peasants here possess."

As they walked towards the open gates, Arturius glanced at the busting village, ignoring the curious stares directed their way as they entered a large meadow where some men were impatiently waiting for them at the far side. The grass of the meadow was beaten down, showing hard use, but the spears were farm tools, their shields mere planks, not the polished gear of his youth. Still, they looked to be grown men, some twice his age or more. How would they receive him? He must look like a child to some of them. *By Hercules's bollocks, my head hurts,* he thought. *I drank too much ale last night! I hope I do not throw up.*

Macro put his hand on Cerdic's shoulder.

"Cerdic, young man, you will stick with me. The biggest and strongest are being trained in the shield wall. You can help me there. The second training group will go with you, Caradoc. Pick anyone with archery experience. That will be damn few, but select the stocky ones with the arm strength to pull a war bow. As for you, Arturius, you get the ones who look like you. You know, the ones who are too skinny and short to do anything else."

They all laughed as Macro moved his hand off Cerdic's shoulder to wag his finger.

"And Arturius, I think you should go back and pick out some of the stronger women and children as well. If someone can throw a rock a reasonable distance, you might make a slinger out of them, and I am not joking about that. So, how was it that you three come to join us?"

Arturius replied, "We were made slaves to Aelle on *The Night of the Long Knives*. Then we escaped and ended up here."

Macro said in disgust, "That Aelle is a treacherous, bloodthirsty gobshite. Why didn't he just kill you all when he and that spineless Vortigern held that so-called council of peace? We lost a lot of good leaders that night. Vortigern helped strengthen his own kingdom by betraying the rest of us. The tribes never should have selected that slimy bastard to lead all of Britannia, and that was how he repaid us."

They fell silent again, plodding towards the waiting throng. Arturius became lost in thought as he recalled that awful evening when he and his friends were enslaved. Over a year ago he and his two friends had been assigned to watch the horses of the guests at Aelle's hall when the various leaders of all of Britannia had arrived. The night was pitch black as a severe storm hit that night. Gusty winds and stinging rain had pelted them as they gathered the beasts together. The thunder and lightning rumbled through the sky as if Thunor himself had come down from the black clouds to smite them.

They had been soaked to the bone. Their oilskins were of little use in the wind and rain. The horses were almost unmanageable, with their eyes rolling up in fear as they pranced about. The boys helped gather the animals with some of Aelle's men, but then Arturius had gone back towards the barn with two of their helpers when without warning the men grabbed him. The horses ran away, snorting in fear.

Pinning him down, they tied him up and gagged him, dragging him inside the barn where he was unceremoniously dumped into a stall. It was that bastard Holt who had held a spear at his throat as he shivered on the ground in the corner of the barn. Holt had leaned back, snorted up a huge wad of phlegm, and then spit it on his face. The warm spittle had landed on his forehead, then it slowly oozed down towards his mouth. He remembered Holt's words like it had happened just yesterday.

"Better eat that up, boy," Holt had said with an evil grin, "it might be the last food you get for a long time."

Soon after, Caradoc and Cerdic joined him, both trussed and gagged like him. Now they all three lay there, miserable, wet, and scared. He remembered the smell of wet hay and horse manure filling his nostrils as flies landed on them, unable to brush them away. Arturius flushed with shame at the memory of Holt standing over him, his shriveled little cock in his hand as he pissed all over his bound captives. He would never forget the smell of hot, fresh urine mixed with the other barnyard smells had made him vomit, and he had almost choked to death as Holt watched and laughed.

"You ain't princes no more, boys," Holt had cackled to the three of them. "You are thralls now! Scum. Worthless slaves. Now I wanted to slit your feckin' throats and feed you to the hogs while you were still alive, but Aelle has other plans for your lot. I need to keep you alive for now, but it don't mean alive and well. You will do as you are told. If I say you are to lick the shite off my arse, you are going to do it and do it well."

He remembered being disgusted by the fetid blackened stumps in his mouth as Holt grinned, his face only inches from theirs.

"You have seen how we treat our Welsh slaves. Well, you are going to be *their* slaves, so any shite detail they don't want to do, you will do. Any beating they deserve, you will take. Any hope you may have, died with your fathers and your other Welsh leaders this night. You might think your souls belong to that nailed dead god of yours, but by Thunor's hammer, your bodies belong to me."

Welsh. It was the first time he had heard it used. It would not be the last. It was an insulting Saxon word for a despised foreigner, never mind that the Britons had been there for centuries before the Saxons had shown up. The memory of that night would forever be seared into his brain. Arturius shivered for a moment before his mind came back to the present, then he smiled at the thought that Holt was lying dead on the forest floor. *It served that gobshite bastard right*, he thought. Then he heard Macro shout out to the men before him.

"All right, you poxy goat-buggering arse-wipes, listen up. These three men with me have been educated in the art of war, unlike the rest of you wankers. You will do what they tell you to do, or by the Christos I will put your bollocks in a sling and beat them with my Vitis. Now line up!"

CHAPTER FIVE

From the neighboring field, Sister Brigid listened to the sounds of men training to become warriors echoing across the fields. She smiled for a moment; Macro's curses were amusingly creative if you were not on the receiving end of them. The three recently arrived young men were chatting animatedly with Macro, and she wondered what abuses they had suffered before they had arrived here. It could not have been anything worse than she herself had experienced, having been enslaved earlier in her own life.

The three were privileged nobles once, but now they had all experienced life on the other side, and she had no doubt the arrogance of the nobility had been beaten out of them. But one thing the nobles did better than anyone else was fight, and now they were imparting those skills to the commoners here at the Weald. It was poetic justice; she just hoped this would work. Training innocent young men to kill other young men was not her interest in life, though as a woman, she knew she needed good strong men to protect her from the other kinds of men.

She weighed less than a hundred pounds soaking wet, so she knew she would not last two seconds in a shield wall, but she could match verbal barbs with the best of them. In a battle of wits, she thought, most men came to the fight unarmed. Not her dear Petrus, though; he was intellectually brilliant, and he did not have a mean bone in his body. She loved him for that. But she was also grateful for those well-muscled men who were willing to die to protect her and the ones she loved.

Today she was involved in a more peaceful endeavor, thrilled to have these two boys with her today. They were new to the community, and they were helping her with her dirty work, including the capturing of wild bees. The one hive they found was way up in a tree, needing a ladder to get to them, and she was happy she didn't have to climb it herself.

One of the lads was already on top of the ladder while the other was holding it still. She did not know how the lad at the top was doing it, but there he was, some fifteen paces above her, using the hand saw to cut a quivering branch off the juniper tree. The tree was a spindly thing and was not overly blessed with stout branches, so she was worried the ladder would fall off to one side or the other any second now. She just prayed the beehive was to come down before the lad fell off.

"Be careful not to drop the hive and hurt the bees," she admonished the boy.

"Yes, Sister," the lad muttered under his breath as he continued to hack away at the limb.

She observed the struggling boys with amusement, her mind wandering. Brigid loved nature, and the healing of the sick was another part of her mission in life. Besides reading and spreading the word of the Christos according to her mentor, Pelagius, she was an herbalist. She would gather plants of both medicinal and culinary interest and would help the healers and the cooks accordingly, but her favorite aspect of nature was the gift of bees. They were such fascinating creatures, and everyone coveted honey, the collection of which was her true specialty.

Looking at the bee box she had built brought her back to the memories the ancient Druid who had taught her the art of beekeeping. As a girl in Hibernia, she had learned how to construct the wooden boxes with a removable top, with slats that were suspended to allow the bees to form their honeycomb. Brigid knew how to remove honeycomb without irrevocably damaging the hive, and other tricks to keep a hive healthy and producing year after year, something the Romanized Christians did not know how to do.

It was not until later that she devoted her life to the Christos, but she had continued the art of honeybee husbandry. She remembered the negative reception that she had received from the other Christian priest in Novomagus when he heard of her hobby. The sanctimonious bastard called it a pagan practice, claiming she was committing a sin against the Christos. *That priest was such an intolerant idiot*, she thought.

Unfortunately, he was not the only cleric appalled by bee husbandry, and with the Druids almost gone here in Britannia, she feared someday their knowledge of the natural world would be forever lost. Only the Christian priests could read and write, and the old beekeeper had told her that writing things down was a Roman skill that no self-respecting Druid would ever do. She thought it was a shame. *How much of the knowledge of the natural world would fade away if nothing is ever written down*, she thought. The art of beekeeping could be forgotten if all the Christian priests in Britannia were as intolerant as that dunderhead, and the world would be much the worse for it.

The golden hum of the bees was a world away from the sounds of Macro training the men to be warriors. She was proud of her role in the community, much like the one the queen played, as the hive could not survive without her. And the big-eyed drones? Well, the males had their uses to entertain the queen, but when the fall came, the Druids said that the males would get shoved outside the hive to die. The queen was the one who ruled the hive, and the other females did all the work, so no males were needed. She laughed to herself. *Too bad people did not do that,* she thought.

But she loved her husband, Petrus. He was such a kind soul. Overly idealistic, socially awkward at times, but kind-hearted and sincere. If only all men were like him. She enjoyed the company of most men, but the professional warriors scared her. In her mind, they were just trained murderers. She needed to make sure that the warriors of the Weald, the lads like Cerdic and Caradoc and Arturius, were civilized, protectors of the weak and innocent. Brigid worked hard to make sure the defenders of the Weald had souls as well as spears.

Finally, the lad started back down the ladder holding the newly- cut branch as far away from himself as he could as the bees were swarming around him. He brought the branch with the ball of bees to the large wooden box that would be their new home and gingerly laid it inside. Brigid then used a bellows-like device to waft the smoke into the box to stupefy the creatures. Her oiled beekeeper's suit protected from the stinging insects, but her helpers were not so protected, and now the other poor lad who held the ladder sported welts all over his body.

"Those bloody bees stung me all over," he wailed.

"They never stung me," the taller boy said as he chuckled. The Christos protected me. Maybe that means you will go to hell someday."

Brigid curled her lips in dismay. She wished she had a bee suit for everyone, but she only had one of those exotic suits.

"Now boys, the Christos has nothing to do with that. It is true that the bees attack some people and not others, but it matters not what gods that you believe in. Some of the pagans who had taught me about the bees never got stung themselves, just like you did not get stung today."

Once she had closed the box with the bees and had moved herself and the boys away from the stinging insects, she took off the suit and wiped the perspiration from her brow. Unfortunately, the young man who had held the ladder was still hopping up and down, complaining that he was being stung, even though no bees were anywhere nearby.

"Take off your shirt and let's have a look at you," Brigid commanded. "There may be stingers still on you."

The boy looked askance at her until the other boy chimed in.

"Come on now, mate. It's not like she has never seen a man without a shirt on. Get on with it."

The boy took off the shirt reluctantly as he muttered, "Well, she is old enough to be my mother."

Brigid rolled her eyes in annoyance, but then she gasped in horror as she looked at the boy's back. There were a few stingers there alright, but the disturbing sight was the angry mass of crisscrossed scars that were visible. He had clearly been whipped, probably until the bones showed through, and more than once. Her own scars itched at the thought.

"I am sorry, Sister Brigid. I know those marks show me to have been a disobedient slave. Don't think less of me because of that. That is why I came here, so I would not get whipped as much, and I am happy to say that since I have been here, no one has laid my back open yet. But I am a hard worker, and___"

"Shush, young man. I was a slave once myself. No one deserves to be punished like that, and no one thinks less of you because you bear the scars of having a cruel master. It was that person's fault, not yours."

She removed all the stingers that she could find as the memories of her own enslavement came flooding back to that terrible moment when raiders had come to her family's hillfort in Hibernia. These brigands from their rival clan had killed her father and brothers and raped her mother and sisters and even herself, although she was not yet a woman then. She was sure it was because of that physical abuse that she could not bear children. It was such a shame, as she knew that Petrus would have made such a wonderful father.

Secretly, she mourned the fact that motherhood had been denied to her. Even now, not a day went by that she did not wish she could be fertile. Prior to that horrible episode, she remembered seeing nothing wrong with having slaves to wait on her. It was how the world was. But once she and her sisters were abused and then sold into slavery, she was able to experience firsthand how the other side of the coin looked, and what a dirty and degrading side of the coin that was. Finally, the last of the stingers were gone.

"Alright, boys, we are done here now," she said, suppressing her emotions of her past. "Let us head back to the mess hall and get yourselves something to drink. That was hot work. I will head back to my hut. Thank you again for your help. You both were excellent workers."

As they walked back, the tallest with the scars on his back looked at Brigid sheepishly.

"Sister Brigid, I did not know that you and Brother Petrus were enslaved. I always thought you we both nobles."

"Oh no, young man. Petrus received a wonderful education as a young man because his father was a prominent cleric, but he was never enslaved. But he was as poor as a church mouse. On the other hand, I was a member of a noble household in Hibernia, but a rival tribe killed my parents and then those buggering arse wipers sold me into slavery. "

"How did you escape slavery, Sister?"

"That is a long story," she muttered.

"Well, we have a long walk ahead of us. We have time, don't you think?"

Sister Brigid sighed, and she reluctantly decided to share her past with the lad.

"After I was captured, I was sold to a rich woman in the south of Hibernia. When the King of Munster became the first great Hibernian king crowned as a Christian monarch, a big gathering was assembled for that. My uncle had been looking for me the entire time, and once we bumped into each other at the ceremony, I was recognized and set free."

Brigid smiled now when she thought of her rescue and the kindly priest named Patrick who preached that Christians should not own other Christians as slaves. He had been the one to convince her domina to set her free, and now she owed the Christos her life. Then her jaw clinched. *Not all Christians are so charitable,* she thought. She had heard of a new bishop from Rome who had recently arrived in Britannia, preaching that slavery was part of the natural order of life. She hoped that the gobshite would go somewhere else.

"Wow, that is quite a story! So, you were a noblewoman once. I knew it!"

She shook her head at the memory.

"I did not feel so noble," she said, trying to keep the sadness out of her voice. "I was freed for the price of a handshake and a cow. It was galling that I was viewed equal to a beast of burden. I remember my uncle thought that was a generous price for a slave.

"How did you meet Brother Petrus?"

Brigid's lips curled up into the hint of a smile at the memory.

"Once I was freed, I stayed in the compound called the Rock of Cashel, the place where Saint Patrick and his colleagues instructed new priests and priestesses in the mysteries of the Christos. It was there I learned how to read and write, and it was also there that I met Petrus."

She thought back to the first time she saw him. Petrus may have been tall, skinny, pimple-faced, and socially awkward, but he was also the charming youth who had come to steal her heart. It was love at first sight. No hairy-chested warrior for her, she wanted a man who could muster up a conversation. He was intelligent and was blessed with a good sense of humor and a positive outlook on life, and he truly cared about other people. His social graces were lacking, he had no wardrobe and barely a penny to his name, but she did not care. Unfortunately for Brigid, her uncle did not share her enthusiasm.

"So how did you and Brother Petrus come here to Britannia?" the boy asked.

Sister Brigid laughed.

"Well, of course we fell in love. My family did not want us to marry, as he had no money, so we eloped. Well, we ran away. In fact, we had to steal two horses to do it, but I did leave a note for my uncle with some jewelry for the pilfered nags, but still, we left without permission. So, we went to the east coast, sold the horses, and caught the first trading vessel we could find to sail away from Hibernia. The first place that the ship came to was Novomagus Reginorum. We got off there and started a church, and the rest you know."

Some things about those days she could never talk about. There was much more to Petrus than met the eye, and that included his ancestorial lineage; she was sworn to secrecy about that. The boy looked up at her shyly.

"My mother and I are so grateful to you and Brother Petrus giving us a place to live in freedom. Thank you again. This place you and Brother Petrus have built has been a miracle for me and my family."

"You are welcome, as is your family."

The boy hesitated as his eyes dropped to the ground in embarrassment.

"My mother thinks you are a saint. She wanted me to ask you for a lock of your hair that we may keep as a relic for us to offer our prayers to."

"That would be a feckin' eejit thing to do, dearie. I can assure you that I'm no bloody saint."

The boy blushed in embarrassment.

"I have never heard a woman talk like you," the boy said. "My mother would put my head on a stake if she heard me say something like that."

"Well, dearie, do not tell her that I know how to say charming phrases like that in five languages. She might have a stroke."

The young man chuckled.

"I will not tell her. But do not worry; she thinks it is fine that you talk like that. She said you must use rough language that so that the men will listen to you."

"Well, dearie, she is correct," she snorted. "You have no idea."

She and the two boys then stopped inside the entrance to the compound, and she bade them thanks for their help. She rushed off for another one of her meetings. She mused to herself as she scurried away. *No, young man,* she thought, *you do not have any bloody idea.* She had to look and sound tough to lead people, especially the men. Sometimes she had to smack them around to get them to listen and hope they did not smack her back. She had to be strong for all of them.

It was truly a pain in the arse for her, and it was not just the men that were the problem. As she walked along, she heard the tinkling conversations of women as they were doing laundry in the nearby creek. Brigid felt a pang of longing as she felt that she could not have any women friends, or it could create jealousy over perceptions of favoritism. After all, she was a deaconess, and in the British tradition, able to administer all the sacraments, a role had given her the gravatas to be a leader. She felt lucky. The Roman styled Christians did not allow women to have such leadership roles, but being a leader of the community was still a lonely existence.

In a way, she thought it was fortunate that she was not considered to be very pretty; otherwise, the men would all being trying to bed her while the women would want to scratch her eyes out. *It must have been the plan of the Christos in the beginning,* she thought. The only females that she felt she could talk to were Senna and Lucilia, and they were still too young to hear many of the things Brigid needed to get off her chest. But she was thankful to the Christos for her dearest Petrus. He was her best and only true friend.

Brigid sighed; more meetings to attend, so it was going to be another long day. She prayed to the Christos that the three new boys and Macro and the rest were up to the task. A person needed to live in safety to develop a more just world. She and her husband had built a new society, one with social justice for the poor and formerly enslaved. For instance, she knew of no place in the world where slavery did not exist. Not even the ancient philosophers, such as the utopia in Plato's book *The Republic,* could envision a world without it.

She was grateful that Patrick of Hibernia had promoted the idea that Christians should not enslave other Christians, and many in Rome felt the same. Still, some disagreed, including Gildas, the new bishop from Rome. She and Brother Petrus followed the teachings of a cleric named Pelagius, a radical in other ways besides the issue of slavery, and rumors were the boy-buggering bishop was sent here into the hinterlands by the church leaders to stamp out heresy. She prayed he would just go back to Rome. She fretted about everyone's safety. Her people were undoubtedly despised by other Briton kingdoms, the bishop, and the barbarians, so the priority for now was to just stay alive.

CHAPTER SIX

Arturius sat on a tree stump by the blazing bonfire, his mind aswirl with his experiences these past few weeks. The fire was mesmerizing, its red embers glowing in the dark, the warmth and flickering lights somehow comforting him. It was Saturday night, and the refugee camp in the Weald was in the mood to celebrate. He spied Cerdic off in the distance, talking to a couple of attractive girls, while he could hear Caradoc playing some music on those awful bagpipes of his. Scores of young people were running around laughing and drinking, but not him. He just wanted to be by himself.

His first few weeks here in the camp had been busy, training and marching, and everyone was expected to pitch in on the community activities, such as tending to the fields and building huts. He was tired. He was also fascinated by this community, impressed with the culture that Petrus and Brigid had put together. He wondered how they could take in all refugees arriving from all over Britannia, and he worried that the Saxons would someday overcome their superstitious fear of these woodlands and come in to wipe them out.

Arturius now was painfully aware of how naive he had been regarding the troubles in the rest of the Britannia. Tintagel still had trading connections with the rest of the world, though decreased from what the old folks said it had been in the past, but still his homeland was largely unaffected by the calamities the rest of Britannia had experienced. He knew that the political situation had not been good once the legions had left, but he hadn't known just how bad it was.

The stories the refugees were telling him were bone chilling. Economic activity in the rest of Britannia had ground to a halt, as no one minted coins anymore, and the roads were beset by bandits. Raiding parties were everywhere, pillaging and burning and killing everything in their path. And it was not just the Saxons; Britannia had been a place of chaos before the Romans came with some thirty tribes constantly fighting each other, and once the hand of Rome had been removed, the island had reverted to those same tribes fighting tooth and nail against each other once again.

For people with no tribal affiliations, Britannia was a dangerous place. People from all over the known world had settled here, and now they were being preyed upon by Saxons and British tribes alike. Everyone with money had already fled to settle on the Amorica peninsula in Gaul, what they now called Little Britain, or Britttany. The poor, the landless, and the slaves were the only ones left behind, preyed upon by everyone else. Entire cities had been abandoned, farms were left fallow, and starvation and misery stalked the island.

Growing up in his protected cocoon in Tintagel, Arturius had no idea things had been this bad. The Western Roman empire was on its knees to the barbarian hordes, and Britannia was no exception. Arturius felt like he belonged nowhere. He was still sitting on the log in contemplation, when out of the darkness, a smiling Brother Petrus and Sister Brigid emerged, holding hands as they approached him. *They are quite a couple,* he thought as they drew closer. They had been married forever, yet they looked like moonstruck teenagers, still obviously in love. He hoped he would be that lucky someday.

"Greetings, Arturius," Petrus said as the two of them sat down on the log beside him. "You look a bit lonely out here all by yourself. How are you feeling?"

"I am just a little overwhelmed, that is all. This town you have built here in the wilderness is quite impressive. I never imagined a place like this existed."

Brigid's eyes twinkled in the firelight as she laughed.

"Well, you are right," Petrus said. "We are giving the common people a new way to live, with a democratically elected republic. Actual laws should govern us, not the whim of some warlord. It is a lot to take in."

"Where did you two come up with these ideas?"

Brigid clapped her hands together and she tilted her head as she spoke.

"An excellent question! We are followers of the teachings of Brother Pelagius, a British cleric who believed that social justice was part of the teachings of the Christos."

"I have heard of Pelagius, Arturius replied, "but wasn't he burned at the stake as a heretic in Rome?"

Tears welled up in Brigid's eyes as Petrus spoke.

"Yes. But his teachings live on. More than one clergyman and deaconess here in Britannia feel Pelagius was correct, and that it was the church authorities in Rome who were in error. In my mind, Brother Pelagius was a martyr to the true teachings of the Christos."

Brigid grabbed a stick as she angrily stoked the fire for a moment.

"Error, my arse," Brigid spat out. "Those gobshites in Rome deserve to burn in hell!"

Arturius looked at first to Brigid and then to Petrus with sadness etched upon their faces.

"I am so sorry to hear that," Arturius said.

Brigid dried her tears as she spoke.

"You are right, Arturius. Brother Pelagius advocated other more controversial things besides just the issue of ending enslavement. He taught that in the eyes of the Christos, all people were equal, that aristocrats were not selected by the Christos to rule, that our leaders, both men and women should be selected based on merit, not one's station in life."

That was dangerous talk. Arturius reflexively touched his sling, as if he were about to defend himself, glancing around to make sure no one else was listening, as such ideas could get someone killed. Then he relaxed, as no one threatened them here, and the idea *was* intriguing.

"Well," Arturius said, nodding, "I must admit I had never heard of such a thing before. Is that written in your gospels?"

"No," Brigid firmly said. "But it is clearly in the spirit of what the Christos said."

"Then why don't all your Christian clergy say this? Where did Pelagius get his ideas from?"

Brigid and her husband glanced at each other, then Petrus nodded before he spoke.

"Pelagius came from the small island between here and Hibernia, Insula Manavia. The people there are called the Manx, and are of ancient stock, the ones who had built the great stone circles you see all over Britannia. They were here long before our own ancestors arrived, and now they survive only on that small island. He had been captured and enslaved as a boy, his owner a priest who had recognized he possessed a great intellect and freed him. Pelagius became a priest himself so he could go back to his homeland and covert the people there, but he decided it was the Roman Christians who really needed saving."

"Poor fellow," Arturius said. "No wonder he was killed. The ruling class would despise him."

"Yes," Brigid replied as she nodded. "He believed that the best form of government was where the people ruled, not a king or emperor, much like the old Roman Republic. And that is what we are building here, a democratically elected republic. In time, we hope that all of Britannia, and maybe even Rome someday, will join us in creating a more just society."

"I don't know; that Roman Republic was a disaster in the end," Arturius said as he shook his head. "They had endless civil wars until Caesar Augustus became emperor. Neither Romans nor Britons would want anything to do with a republic anymore."

"Don't forget," Petrus said as he wagged his finger, "the Roman Republic functioned well for five hundred years. What caused the old republic to collapse were the generals with their private armies, like Julius Caesar, and widespread corruption. But Pelagius recommended some improvements to the old model. For instance, in the old republic, only the rich could run for office. They would build temples and put on gladiator games to sway the voters, and in return for being elected, they blatantly accepted bribes while in office to enrich themselves."

"Of course, that is just how politics works," Arturius said with a shrug.

Brigid's eyes narrowed.

"No," she firmly said, "we can do better than that. In our model, it will be ordinary people that get elected, and they will be paid well instead of having to take bribes. Taxes would be equally shared, and we will have a functioning legal system, loyal to the republic instead of a king. No one would be above the law."

"That won't stop the civil wars from occurring," Arturius muttered in an incredulous tone. "In times like these, it is tyrants who rule, and the man with the most spearman by his side becomes the king."

Brigid opened her arms as she smiled.

"Why not have a world where there should be no king at all," she said. "We want three branches of government, with an elected assembly that makes the laws, and an independent judiciary, and an elected civilian leader who enacts and implements the laws of the land. The civilian leader must periodically face reelection, and that could be anyone with talent."

There was silence for a moment as the embers of the fire glowed. Could something like this actually succeed?

"So, who would control the army?" Arturius snorted.

"The soldiers would swear an oath to the republic, not to a king or general, and generals cannot become an elected government leader. Once a politicians' term of office had been served, they cannot run again."

There was another prolonged silence as Arturius took it all in. Brother Petrus put his hand on Arturius's shoulder, his voice growing more impassioned.

"The supreme leader would be given the same title Caesar Augustus used," Petrus said. "We would call him the Princeps, our leading citizen. And our laws the legislature passes will apply to him as well as everyone else. No children will be able to inherit any titles, including his. Our leaders should be selected on merit, not by who your family is."

Arturius tried to suppress his laughter.

"You cannot be serious. And you want to do this for all of Britannia, not just here?"

"Yes," they both chimed in together as he shot them an incredulous look.

"Well, it sounds like you need a general who does not want to be king."

"Exactly," they both said at once.

Petrus and Brigid looked at each other and laughed as Arturius crossed his arms, frowning. Then a sly smile crept across his face.

"In everywhere else I have ever heard of, the king and the commander of the army are the same man."

"That was not true for Caesar Augustus, now, was it," Petrus said, a wistful look in his eyes.

Petrus removed his hand from the shoulder of Arturius as he gave Brigid a loving look. Brigid used her stick to stir the fire again, a shower of sparks spiraling into the air. There was beauty in that, the destruction of a piece of wood creating something new. But those sparks would never last for more than a moment. This entire conversation reminded him of a fire, mesmerizing and beautiful, but something that could never last.

"It makes sense that ruler should not be the head of the army," Petrus said as the fire blazed up, "or you lose the rule of law. And that is not all that Pelagius advocated. For instance, he felt anyone could run for office, that women could rule as well as men could. Even someone like my lovely bride here could become the leader."

Arturius's eyes opened round as he blew out his cheeks.

"My, my, that is ambitious."

"The Romans never did like us women to have any power," Brigid sweetly said. "Unlike the Romans, the British had many famous queens. Among Pelagius's people, women were often leaders. There was no overall chieftain. One person who was the best farmer oversaw that, the best sailor was the admiral, and the best soldier headed the army, and so forth. With the Manx people, there was no overall king in charge."

"So Arturius," Petrus said as he continued to stir the fire, "we are building a radically new community here. This could be the nidus for the dispossessed of Britannia to flock to, a just society that no one has ever seen before. Surely, we can do better than just return to the tribal chaos that once was the norm Britannia before the Romans came. And we will."

The conversation paused as he contemplated the world these two were trying to create. Arturius shook his head in wonder. *A world without slavery,* he thought. *No kings or tyrants. Laws that apply to everyone. No bribes and no corruption, a utopia better than Plato ever imagined.* On the mainland, he thought the rich and powerful would crush a place for thinking this way, but they were far from Rome. Why couldn't it happen here? Britannia had no government to overthrow, as the province was in chaos. *Maybe this could work,* he thought.

It seemed to him that it was better to fight for a cause like this rather than just trying to survive, but now they needed not just a general, but one who did not want to be a king. He knew Caradoc and Cerdic would eventually leave for their homes, and both might ascend to the throne; neither would want to be such a general. But they were his oath sworn blood-brothers now, and he was sure they would help protect the people here. *But a general who does not want to be a king,* he thought. *Who could that be?* Macro was a good trainer, but he kept saying he was just a simple soldier. Arturius could not imagine the old centurion in that role.

He admired both Petrus and Brigid, but he was no Christian himself. He honored the philosophy of Stoicism, believing in having wisdom, courage, virtue, and justice. He wanted to achieve eudaimonia, a well-lived life, to read books and drink wine with his friends as he lived a life of moderation in tune with the natural world. Both Petrus and Brigid knew of his beliefs, and they had reassured him they were tolerant of other faiths, that someone like him would always be welcome here. Where else in Britannia could he live this way? Civilization itself seemed to be collapsing everywhere. Where else would it be possible for such a community to arise out of the ashes here in Roman Britannia?

He continued to stare at the glowing embers as he contemplated the conversation they were having. A republic that Petrus and Brigid dreamed of could be like the wood in this fire, brilliant and beautiful, but doomed not to last long. But on the other hand, it *was* a noble idea. *Who knows,* he thought, *maybe I could be that man, preserving civilization in an uncivilized world.* Petrus and Brigid were gazing at him intently, and it sent chills down his spine. His mind churned like the storm-tossed sea; was this why they approached him this evening? He had only been here for a few weeks; it seemed like they barely knew him. But then again, who else did they have? And wouldn't this be a noble endeavor for a stoic to support? *What would a person like Marcus Aurelius do,* he wondered. *Could I be such a man?*

CHAPTER SEVEN

When the games started that morning, Julia had been pleased the arena had attracted more spectators than she had seen in years, but still it was only partially full. Generations ago, it would have been packed, and the games could have gone on for days. Now the crowds were sparser because of the great migrations from Britannia to Gaul, but the stadium itself was still impressive, an oval-shaped earthen mound, built hundreds of years ago before the Romans had flattened the center to create a natural amphitheater.

It had once been a holy place for the bloodthirsty Druids, and Julia shuddered to think of what barbaric rituals and human sacrifices those evil priests had once performed here, but Rome had turned it into a place of honor, though it was a shadow of what it had been in the past. She flashed a disdainful glance at her husband beside her, laughing at the jesters entertaining the crowd between fights. His fleshy jowls quivered as he chortled, causing a sour taste in the back of her throat. *The man is a fat fool,* she thought. *He disgusts me.*

She was going mad with excitement and fear. The amphitheater's attendants had already dragged away the last body and had just finished raking the surface of the arena for the next fight. The crowd was abuzz with the thrill of anticipation. Next up was one of the headliners, a show the crowd had been waiting for, an event she had been dreading for weeks. Her beloved lover Ferox was about to meet a giant nicknamed the famous Egyptian Lion, infamous for being an implacable killing machine.

Her lover was also highly regarded, but today she feared for her dear Ferox's life. Then the entrance gate opened, and the roar of the crowd filled the arena, yet she was annoyed the cheering was offset by a few boos. She knew some of the spectators loathed her gladiator lover for his reputation of cruelty, but Julia knew it was not his true nature. He did what he had to do to survive, but he had a soft side, and that tender heart belonged to her.

Her paramour was a type of fighter called the retiarius, lithe and quick as a leopard, and just as dangerous. The sun gleamed off his skin, his body nearly naked except for the bronze manica protecting his left arm and shoulder. She thought those boos must be coming from the men that envied him. She was certain their wives and daughters all wanted her Adonis. *Sorry girls, he is all mine*, she thought. Ferox was Greek, and he looked like an Olympian with his dark wavy hair, his olive-toned complexion, and his liquid brown eyes. He was bare chested as usual, his rippling muscles accentuated by the oil he was adorned with to enhance his sex appeal to the crowd.

Barefoot and wearing a mere loincloth, he only had three weapons. The one in his right hand was a round fisherman's net, weighted at its periphery and tied to his wrist. Hanging from his right side was his dagger, but his primary weapon was in his left hand, his bronze trident. The long and heavy spear had a large knob on the end, and it flashed in the sunlight as he held it aloft to elicit a roar from the crowd. Julia would have preferred he had more armor, but the protection that Ferox relied upon as a retiarius fighter was his quickness.

A new roar from the crowd intruded into her thoughts. Ferox's opponent had entered the ring, outfitted as a secutor, and he was clearly the favorite of the mob as the noise of celebration was even more enthusiastic than what her beloved Ferox had just received. The Egyptian Lion held his broad-bladed gladius up to the sky, shimmering in the sunlight with lethal promise. As the cheers started to fade, he thrust up his rectangular shield, the mirror of the classic Roman scutum, and once more the frenzied roar of the crowd echoed across the arena.

His name was Nata, the most spectacularly muscled man Julia had ever seen. Bare chested, his naked torso gleamed and rippled in the sun. His scanty loincloth was accented by a broad and intricately designed leather belt. His right arm was covered with a bronze manica, while his left shin was protected by a bronze greave. His helmet was smooth and round so the net could not catch on to it, and it bore tiny round eyeholes to help to protect him from the trident's prongs. The heavy helmet was decorated with scales and fins, symbolizing a fish, while the retiarius was the fisherman.

The cheers of the throng stilled as the chief magistrate called for silence. He let go of a checkered flag, and the instant it hit the sand the mob erupted into a roar. Her heart fluttered. *Jupiter Optimus Maximus*, she prayed, *protect him!* The fight started with Nata slowly advancing, crouched with his curved shield tilted forward. His gladius was poised just behind the right edge of the shield, protected but ready for the killing thrust. He lumbered forward, steadfastly pursuing her darling lover as Ferox danced around, thrusting the trident towards Nata's face to keep the Egyptian at bay.

Suddenly, Ferox tossed his net, and Nata ducked behind the shield as his gladius swept the net to the side; the trident flashed forward, a glancing blow. The shield brushed the trident away as the gladius thrust out, and again the Ferox danced to the side. Now holding the trident with both hands, Ferox stabbed repeatedly at the face of the Secutor as he advanced, his net abandoned on the ground. The cord that attached the net to Ferox's right wrist was long and trailed on the sand, and Ferox tried to use the cord to trip the secutor as they circled.

Somehow the bastard swiped it away, even though she knew Nata could barely see. Ferox kept on the attack with thrust after thrust, the shield blocking the trident as it slashed back and forth. The retiarius darted forward to gather up the net for another throw. The secutor's shield bobbed up and down and then to the side to ward off the blows as the long trident kept the secutor at bay, the heavily- armored man steadily pursuing the darting retiarius. On it went, attack and advance, parry and dance away, and neither man could get the advantage.

Finally, a horn sounded, and the first round was over. Julia breathed a sigh of relief. She had seen her lover in many fights, but Julia had never seen a secutor that was so quick and skillful. In Ferox's previous fights, she could always tell right away that her lover was the better man, but today, she was not so sure. The fighters went to their attendants, the Egyptian Lion taking his heavy helmet off to reveal streaks of sweat pouring off his brow. The combatants took some water and toweled off as their assistants massaged their muscles until the horn blew again.

Back to the center of the amphitheater they went, thrust and parry, circle and dance, back and forth, the fighters slogged away at each other. Each round seemed the same, with Ferox whirling around while the Egyptian Lion chased him. She was used to seeing her lover's opponent tire by the third and fourth round, but not this one, seeming as fresh by round nine as he had at the start, and now Ferox was tiring, sporting a few nicks and cuts, the loss of blood concerning her. She was worried.

The horn blew to start the next to last round. The sweaty gladiators warily approached each other, the secutor steadily moving to attack, the retiarius fending him off with his trident. Once again Ferox tossed the net, but Nata cut away the cord of the net with his sword. A wave of panic enveloped her. *His net is gone,* she thought. Her heart dropped as she saw Ferox run backwards from his foe, stop, and then grab a hand full of sand. The crowd started to lustily boo at the retreat as the referee approached him with his hot poker to push him back into the fight.

But then, holding his trident in front of him, Ferox charged full speed at his heavily armored foe, violently thrusting the points of his weapon into the ground in front of the secutor as he simultaneously threw the sand into his opponent's face. The Egyptian Lion moved his shield up to protect his eyes, and she gasped in amazement as Ferox vaulted over the lumbering giant like a pole vaulter in the Greek Games.

The roar of the crowd was deafening as her heart swelled with pride. *By the gods, I can barely breathe,* she thought. When the beleaguered secutor lowered his shield again, the foe in front of him was gone. Her lips curled up into a wicked smile. A trident quivering in the sand was all that remained of the retiarius who was there just seconds ago. *Won't that big bastard be surprised when he feels that knife in his back*, she thought.

Ferox sprung to his feet behind the surprised secutor, and darted toward Nata, ready to stab him from behind, but the Egyptian Lion showed he was faster than the cat he was named for. Nata darted forward, dropping his shield as he pulled the trident out of the ground before Ferox could strike. Then secutor somersaulted over headfirst, landing in a crouch to face her lover, trident at the ready, his gladius still in his right hand. Ferox was too close to Nata for him to skewer him with the rident, but the gladius was still in play.

The blade slashed down, and her heart almost stopped as the wickedly sharp blade barely missed Ferox as he ducked and brushed the sword away with his knife, tumbling away backwards and grabbing the shield as he rolled. Panting, the two fighters stared at each other as the crowd went wild, her heart beating out of her chest. The fighter's weapons and roles were scrambled up and reversed. Ferox had lost his trident, but he now had a shield and his knife in his other hand. Nata held the trident and his gladius now, and he had tossed his helmet to the ground, his hair plastered with sweat as the beast gave her lover a menacing grin.

The crowd howled with delight at the unexpected development. No one had seen gladiators using this combination of weapons before. Nata charged, a blur of speed and slashing weapons, and Julia could not believe that a man so large could move that fast. The spear went low while simultaneously the sword went high as he ran past Ferox, attacking both sides of his body as once, but Nata was not the only one who was quick. Seemingly without effort, Ferox parried both strikes to the delight of the crowd.

Nata skidded to a halt, took a couple of breaths, and then charged again. The slashing weapons flashed in the sun with lightning speed, but Ferox was equal to the task, again blocking both blows with aplomb. Back and forth the attacks went, Nata sprinting side to side instead of the forward and backward movements she was used to seeing, her lover continually on the defensive with the limited range of his knife.

She was so excited she almost fainted as the horn blew again. This was the last break they would have, and the tenth and final round would be next. Julia could not remember the last time that she had seen a fight go into the final round like this. The crowd was in a frenzy, and she was thrilled to think her lover was putting on such a show.

"Kill that bloody lion!" she screeched as she joined the chants of the cheering mob.

Each man was covered in sweat, still bleeding from the various nicks and cuts that their trainers could not fully staunch, but still they were ready for more. The crowd was abuzz in fascination, and their cheers of approval echoed through the arena. They went out into the sands warily eyeing each other, then Nata, unencumbered by his helmet, attacked in the same pattern he'd used before in the last round, darting side to side as his weapons flashed through the air with blinding speed.

It was Ferox who was the plodder now, weighted down by the heavy shield, his knife too short to mount much of a counterattack. The Egyptian Llion stayed on the offence while her lover displayed his own quickness as each thrust was blocked and parried with skill. The mob was chanting and cheering with glee. The bigger man continued to display a quickness that Julia found incredible as he flashed back and forth with his unusual side-to-side attacking pattern, weapons whirling almost too fast to see with each pass.

It was Ferox that was always on his heels now, and the paltry length of his own knife meant that he was on the defense, but then her heart almost leaped with joy as she saw the four-pointed knife suddenly trap the sword, and the gladius was ripped out of Nata's hand. She knew her lover had the advantage now as her heart fluttered in anticipation. Both men paused for just an instant, then they simultaneously sprinted to the fallen weapon, Ferox smashing the shield against the shoulder of his foe as they scrambled for the sword.

Ferox won the race for the loose weapon as Nata grimaced, holding his shoulder, but as her lover picked up the blade, Nata swung the knobby end of the trident like a club, striking Ferox in the knee. Ferox let out a yelp of pain as he limped away from the blow. The blood drained from Julia's face in shock, but Ferox was still on the move, tumbling away from Nata, and he sheathed his knife, replacing it with the more potent sword. Ferox had the advantage now with both shield and sword, but he could not move well. The Egyptian Llion, still in pain, maintained a rictus of a smile as he waved his only weapon, his trident, at Ferox's face. Her eyes glittered with excitement.

"Go Ferox! Kill that Egyptian harlot's son!"

Her husband continued to ignore her, seemingly just as fascinated as the rest of the crowd by this turn of events. Both men were injured now, Nata with his shoulder and Ferox with his leg. The audience was abuzz as Ferox chased the Egyptian Lion, only able to wield the trident with one arm, but the Egyptian Lion still had fangs as he kept her beloved Ferox at bay, thrusting the long spear at the head and feet of the hobbled retiarius. Ferox staggered after the still nimble Nata until the horn blew the last time, and the final round was done. She clasped her hands together in glee. It was a draw. *Thank you, Mars and Jupiter,* she thought. *My Ferox lives!*

The crowd went berserk. They knew the custom was that if both gladiators had fought valiantly to the end, even in a contest to the death, then both men were considered a victor, and they would live to fight another day. It was a rare event to last the full ten rounds, and everyone in the arena knew they had witnessed something special. Julia breathed a sigh of relief. The exhausted combatants tottered over to the canopied section where the magistrates sat. The fighters saluted the assemblage, and applause continued to fill the air.

The chief magistrate tossed a small purse of coins towards each of the men, and then they were escorted to the infirmary at the ludis to be examined and to have their wounds dressed. Out came the slaves to clean and rake the sand for the next event. Now Julia's heart fluttered even wilder than before. The fight was stressful enough to watch, but that was not the most fearful moment she would be experiencing today. Though the contest was over, her gut clenched, and she was barely able to breathe.

Julia needed Ferox to survive this fight, the first of the promises they had made to each other. Now it was her turn to risk her life. Her mouth went dry as terror gripped her. Swallowing her fear, she muttered to her husband that she was exhausted and would be going home now. He scowled and nodded but never looked her way. She thanked the gods that he had ignored her as he usually did, never seeing her face with the anxiety she thought it must have shone. Her husband was going to stay behind for the final contests, sure to be going out carousing with his friends before coming home blind drunk at dawn.

He would not awaken until the afternoon, so she had time. Her romantic adventure was beginning. Today, she was going to free her lover, then later they would mount the horses her handmaiden had secreted away to ride east to freedom. It could be days or more before her pig-of-a-husband would even know she was gone. She and Ferox were headed to a place of refuge, a place she had heard about hidden in the vast forest called the Weald. There they were to start a new life together.

She marched to the gladiator's quarters alone as her handmaiden had run ahead to her house to fetch the things she needed for their travels. The silent servant joined her as she hurried along, lugging two amphorae along with the jars for the poisoned wine. Julia trusted her personal servant not to speak of her plans, as she had the unfortunate creature's tongue cut out years ago. Regular beatings alone did not guarantee silence and loyalty from her handmaidens in the past, and her mother's idea of preventative mutilation worked wonders. Julia hated chatty slaves, and this solved that problem nicely.

Once her wine containing the powerful emetic was given to the guards at the entrance to the ludis, then she would be irrevocably committed, and there would be no going back. Her mouth was dry, and she felt waves of anxious anticipation course through entire body. She knew it was the fear of being caught, mixed with the joy of finally fleeing with her lover that possessed her, and she had never felt like this before. It was intoxicating. *This must be what warriors feel before combat,* she thought. *No wonder they love it so much.*

Julia plastered a smile on her face as she chatted up the guards as they drank her wine, then she walked straight into the infirmary to the cubicle where the medicus cared for the injured. Her heart leapt with joy to see that Ferox was in the room, and again she shared her wine, this time with the medicus and his guard as she gaily chatted with the harassed-looking surgeon. After a minute, the poison did its magic; both the guard and the medicus bent over, retching uncontrollably. Then she directed the mute slave girl to shatter the other amphora, revealing two long, glittering knives.

She saw Feox's eyes shine with excitement, but she thought it odd that he hadn't said a word. *Is he disappointed with me for some reason,* she wondered. But then Ferox put his hand behind her head as he gently kissed her, her heart melting before him. Her eyes were closed as they embraced. *I have never been so happy,* she thought. The sweetest kiss she had ever known had only lasted for a few seconds before she felt her hair being grabbed from behind, pulling her head back.

Love for her gallant gladiator filled her heart. *Silly boy*, she thought, *we do not have time to make love now.* Her eyes flew open as she felt an unexpectedly sharp pain explode across her throat. An unblinking Ferox stared at her with an odd expression, something she had never seen before, an almost feral gaze that seemed to penetrate her soul. She started to shiver as she felt something warm and wet flowing down her chest, and then she suddenly felt lightheaded. She felt surprised as she noticed the knife in his hand, its blade covered in blood.

She tried to talk to Ferox to ask him what was going on, but try as she might, no words could escape. Her arms were roughly pinned to her side as he abruptly lowered her onto the examination table, and her thinking became muddled and slow. The warm wetness expanded across her chest; *Oh no, my beautiful stola is getting ruined,* she thought. Only then did reality intrude as a wave of indescribable despair flooded her. *By Jupiter,* she despaired, *my Ferox has betrayed me. He was lying to me all along.*

Her eyes fluttered in disbelief as she remained pinioned on her back while Ferox continued to hold her down. She writhed and struggled to move as he stared into her eyes like a feral cat playing with its prey. His smile looked chilling, his eyes cold as a glacier in the candlelight. Her strength started to wane, her brain sluggish, unable to think clearly. *He is enjoying this,* she thought. *How odd.*

A stew of conflicting feelings flooded her body. Anger at his betrayal mixed with her embarrassment of her own stupidity swirled around in her mind. She shivered as she grew colder as she felt her body's strength ebb away. Julia closed her eyes, unable to bear looking at him anymore. She heard a ringing in her ears, and her eyes reluctantly opened again, but she saw nothing but brightness now. Shadowy figures in the background began to move closer to her. She tried to talk, but she couldn't form any words, her mind descending into the white fog.

Mother? You were right. I am such a fool. And then she thought no more.

CHAPTER EIGHT

The blood pooled around his bare feet, hot and sticky, as if he was still in the sands of the arena. Ferox let go of Julia, her eyes glassy and vacant. slowly backing away as he relished in the glow of the demise of his latest victim, a thrill like no other. A gladiator was trained to kill, and it was only in the taking of a life that he felt fully alive. It was the one thing he was truly gifted at doing. He had been the recipient of stunning cruelty his entire life, and nothing thrilled him more than when he gave it back, especially to people who were the privileged ones. Suddenly, the mute slave girl took the other blade from the broken amphora and started to viciously stab away at the torso of the dying woman.

"Stop that," he spat out as he grabbed the knife out of her hand. "The slut needs to be in one piece. Once we complete our escape, then you can hack her up."

He looked around the unadorned cubicle, cold and smelling of fresh blood that shimmered on the floor in the guttering lamplight. It had been once been a place of healing, but now death was in the air. After he had taken the knife from Julia's servant, he walked over to the kneeling and retching guard, grabbed his hair, and sliced his throat just as he had with Julia. Again, he gazed into the eyes of the man as he died, but this kill was not a satisfying as hers had been. This was a common man, a soldier, whereas she had been a selfish and privileged patrician that had driven him mad with her adolescent romantic fantasies. Once he was finished, he glanced up at the servant, annoyed with the pouting glare she was giving him.

"You stupid girl, don't you get it? I need her body to be intact. You might be next if you do not do what you are told."

As Ferox contemplated the mute slave girl, his smile slowly grew, the crucifix around the servant's neck filling him with the disdain for those who believed the idiotic teachings of the Christos. *You might think you are going to be free now;* he thought, *but you will be just exchanging masters. It will be the gladiators that you will call dominus now.* Besides the girl, the only person left still alive in the room was the medicus, still on his knees, retching in misery, his eyes wide with terror. The physician's eyes grew even wider in the flickering light as Ferox put the knife to his throat.

He hissed, "You are to stay in this room. I want to keep you alive, but it does not mean that I won't cut your bollocks off and shove them down your throat. Do not move, and do not make a sound. Understand?"

The physician weakly nodded as he retched again. Ferox tied him up and left the miserable man lying on the floor in a pool of his own vomit and Julia's blood. The doctor was well known to him, and Ferox thought he had been an excellent surgeon for the inevitable injuries he and his comrades had suffered. The man had always been unfailingly polite and kind in his ministrations to him, so he felt a tad of regret when he threatened him, but Ferox knew he had no choice. The medicus had to be subservient for their plan to succeed, and he was a patrician anyway, the class of people he truly despised. He directed the girl to follow him as he headed towards the treatment room next door where King Nata was waiting. Ferox turned to the girl.

"You have the keys, right?"

She nodded and pulled them from a pouch in her tunic and handed them to him. He calmly opened the locked door and greeted the Egyptian, giving him the remaining knife. Ferox and Nata exchanged excited glances as they crept into the gladiator quarters to free the rest of their comrades. *We were the slaves once,* he thought. *Now it is we who will become the masters.* His comrades all smiled and pounded each other on the back as they were released from captivity, but the laughter died away when the Egyptian Lion glared at them.

"All of you, shut up and listen," Nata said. "I regret we could not tell you about our escape until now, but we are all going to be free if you follow my orders."

Nata told them the plans that he and Ferox had concocted, and to a man, they all agreed to the gambit to gain their freedom.

"When we are finally free," Ferox solemnly intoned, "Nata will be my king. I will give him my life to serve him. Then once we have taken the city, I will be making my oath of featly to him, *the Sacrementum Militare,* and *the Gladiatorum,* and those who wish to follow me in my pledges may do the same as I, but there is no pressure for you to do so. Those of our brotherhood who wish to leave may do so without any hard feelings."

Just as he knew they would, to a man raised their fists and proclaimed their fealty to Nata as their leader, and then Nata raised his hands up as he shushed them.

"Thank you for your loyalty," Nata said, tears of gratitude in his eyes. "We will administer the oath once we are done here today, and we will be like Spartacus in *the Great Slave Revolt* centuries ago, forming an army that will instill fear into the hearts of the patricians and kings. Now let us do our jobs, and at the end of the day we will have a kingdom that will know no end. We must finish this while most of these rich and noble toffs are still at the games."

Ferox felt a flush of belonging and love sweep over him, a depth of emotion he had never experienced before. He had never known his father, and his mother, a scurrilous whore herself, had always seemed uneasy around him, more interested in her daughters than him. She had sold him into slavery to keep them fed, and from there he had ended up becoming a gladiator. These men, these brothers of his, were the only family he had ever known. More than once, he had been forced to injure and even kill men he loved, but now that would never happen again. He was free, and now, so were they.

Though he had pity for the medicus who had treated him so kindly, and he felt sympathy for the peasants and those who were enslaved, such as Julia's servant, but those people were not his brothers. People like them, those not in their unique fellowship, were destined to serve him and his fellow gladiators. Nata was his king now, and he would die for him and his friends. Those who were not his brothers were expected to serve them without compunction.

Ferox ordered some men to drag out the medicus and Julia's body while the rest of the men crept outside and quickly dispatched the retching guards stationed at the entrance. They all met up again at the weapons locker, and once he opened the door using the keys they had taken from the guards, various weapons were handed out to the freed gladiators. Then they entered the empty guard's barracks and distributed their uniforms and armor to the men as they split up into two groups.

Nata was in command of the men now wearing their gladiator gear, while the other contingent dressed as guards to be commanded by Ferox. Both groups headed towards the north gate house, Ferox in the lead, where they were met by the mute servant leading the two horses that Julia had sequestered away for her escape. The medicus and Julia's body were unceremoniously dumped on the back of the mounts. Then they split up, with Ferox and his men going first towards the main gate first to act as the hare while Nata's contingent were the hounds. They wanted to deceive the town's garrison into thinking Ferox's men were loyal guards being chased by renegade gladiators.

"Follow me, boys," Ferox announced in a gleeful tone. "Freedom awaits."

Ferox, his face obscured by the side pieces of his guard's helmet, tightly held the reins of the first horse as they approached the gate. The panicked medicus was perched precariously in his saddle, while the body of Julia was stretched over the back of the second mare, her servant holding her body to keep the corpse from falling off. They approached the gate in a trot, the medicus was barely hanging on as he swayed in the saddle. Once they were at the base of the gatehouse, Ferox looked up to the pale and sweating physician.

"You know what to do," he whispered in a menacing tone.

The medicus loudly cried up to the looming gatehouse, "Let us in! Some gladiators have escaped, and my mistress has been wounded! I have brought some guards to help defend the city. Open up now! They are right behind us!"

Ferox felt an uncharacteristic feeling of anxiety sweep over him, as this was the most dangerous part of their caper. If this ruse did not work, then he and the others would be doomed. His senses were tuned to a high pitch as if he were in the arena, his heart racing as he waited for a response from the captain of the entrance. The ploy depended on deception. Would these curs be fooled? The captain of the guard needed to be rushed, to make the decision to open the gates before anyone noticed that the guards surrounding the physician were not men they recognized.

Now the only thing that protected him and his comrades from a deadly fusillade of arrows was how well the cheek pieces of their helmets had hidden their faces. He and the rest kept their heads turned to gaze back towards Nata and his men to help with the deception. *Would that be good enough*, he wondered. The captain of the guardhouse and the medicus continued their exchange as the seconds seemed like hours, and now Nata and his men almost upon them. Then he heard the gates swing open, and his heart soared. It had worked. They were in.

He and his gladiators rushed inside and killed the startled captain, quickly beating the remaining guards into submission. As he always did, Ferox was there to stare into the vacant eyes of the captain moments before he died. *That will be the last mistake you will ever make,* he thought. Nata and the second group sauntered behind them. The main gate was taken, and Ferox was elated: the entire town was theirs now. Nata displayed a huge smile, and then he addressed the group who now controlled the main entrance of Durnovaria.

"My fellow gladiators, let us finish the taking of this town. Ferox and his men and will go and secure the other gates. The rest of you sweep though and bring anyone you can find to the town square, and we will sort them out there. We are not to set fire to the town. Only kill if you are forced to and leave the women alone. We must be quick. I want every person here to be in the square when I address them. Later today, once we are fully secure, then you will make your oath to your brothers and to me. Those of you guarding these gates, sound the horn if you see any relief force coming. Get to it, men!"

As he went on his assignment, Ferox smiled as he heard doors being shattered, windows being smashed, and women and children crying. It was music to his ears, as these were the sounds of victory, the clatter barely detectable over the huge roars still coming from the stadium. The noise of the crowd made him smile, as it meant they were still undiscovered by those rich bastards still watching the games. Once the garrisoning of the gatehouses was completed, they would be safe. While Nata was still in the town square, the other gladiators gathered around him. He and Nata had planned their escape in secret, so it had been a leap of faith for them to have participated in this venture. They crowded around him now to hear what was to happen next.

"Ferox, my brother," said a gladiator from his right. "What is King Nata going to tell these pissed off people still at the games when they finally arrive at the front gates?"

Ferox gazed at the man with a look of confidence.

"They will be told that the town is no longer theirs. Many of the wealthy and privileged who are still out watching the games have left behind their wives and children, and those so-called noble families are being rounded and brought to the gates. They will be our hostages, The others here in town, the peasants and the slaves, will be coming from the square to help us in our rebellion.

"What are we going to do with the peasants?"

Ferox barked out a cruel laugh.

"There should be no love lost by those people for the rich, so Nata will be asking them to join us in the uprising. They have no good option to say no. Nata is telling them that if our rebellion fails and we are captured, then we will claim that some of the slaves and freedmen in the town had participated in our escape."

The gladiator next to him looked puzzled.

"How could they have? Even we did not know you were doing this!"

"Of course, and we did not tell those scum either, my friend," Ferox said with a chuckle. "But that does not matter. All of them, innocent or not, would die if the masters retake the town. Even the peasants know how the Romans react to a slave uprising, so those mother-buggering slave owners out there would never believe their side of the story. Like it or not, the peasants and the slaves we just freed share our fate."

"I see," his comrade said. "But about what about the hostages you speak of. What about them?"

Ferox kept his face emotionless. *This poor fellow is dumb as an ox,* he thought, *but he is also strong as one. It is of no matter. He is still my brother.* Ferox placed his hand on his shoulder as he patiently replied.

"Hostages will be taken up to the walls and they will be tortured and killed if anyone tries to retake the town. Some will become our slaves, while others we might exchange for ransom."

Another gladiator to his left spoke up.

"You say the slaves and townspeople will join us," he asked in a surprised voice. "But does that mean that we going to let these bastards become our brothers also?"

"Of course not," scoffed Ferox. "Most of the slaves living here will become our slaves instead, as that is all they are fit for. We are just not going to tell them about that right now. Those who are strong and ruthless enough may become one of us, but they must be trained as we were. They will have the compassion beaten out of them, just as it was with us."

"What about the gladiators still fighting out there in the arena? What happens to them?"

Ferox chuckled as his arms opened wide.

"They have charioteers from the north out there now, not gladiators from Durnovaria. None of our true brothers are there. We do not care what happens to anyone else but our own."

Some of his comrades looked worried, and at first one spoke up.

"I don't believe they won't try to take their city back," one of them said incredulously.

"They would be fools to try," Ferox spat out. "They have no siege equipment, and these walls are stout. The peasants will fight to the death with us, and we will crucify their families before their eyes if we need to. I am not worried."

Ferox placed an arm on each of the shoulders of the men standing next to him.

"Comrades," he announced in a commanding voice. "The gods have graced us with their favor. It is we who are the masters now. This is our kingdom now, our fortress."

One of the men softly grumbled, "Which gods do you mean? I lost faith in any of them."

"Nata and I do not give a rat's arse what gods you believe in," Ferox scoffed, "or whether you believe in any at all. The Christos will keep the slaves docile, while other gods, be they Roman, British, or Norse, can bugger off. King Nata honors the Egyptian ones, as do I now, and you should do the same. It was his gods that gave us the luck to be free men now."

Then a group of frightened and inexperienced townspeople showed up wielding spears, and he made sure they were spread out along the walls with their lances held high to let the arriving nobles see that the walls were well manned. As he predicted to his comrades, after the roars from the arena stopped, an angry mob arrived. At the main gate an indignant magistrate came forward, threatening severe retribution if he and the rest were not let in, but he fell silent when his wife and children were put on top of the wall with knives to their throats. Eventually the crowd dispersed, the angry eyes of the nobles turning vacant and defeated as they trudged northwards, shorn of their family and belongings. Durnovaria belonged to the gladiators now, and the once powerful patricians were now joining the ranks of penniless refugees.

Once Ferox had made sure that the defenses at his post were secure, he went into the house that Julia had once inhabited after Nata had sent him a message telling him to meet him there. Ferox was the first to arrive, and he promptly went to the rear of the home where the ancestral shrines were located and swept out the busts and death masks of the former occupants. These holy idols of her ancestors, collected over hundreds of years, were unceremoniously dumped in an adjoining alley filled with refuse. He lifted his tunic and emptied the contents of his bladder upon the relics to show his disdain for the family of that whiney wife he had just slain.

Soon after Ferox had anointed Julia's household gods with his urine, Nata arrived to greet him. Nata was usually a taciturn man, but not today; this was the first day of his reign as king. The two embraced, and then the new king reached into a small knapsack on his side and pulled out a battered statuette of Amun-Ra that he had fashioned out of wood years ago as a reminder of his homeland. Amun was the chief deity of the Nile, revered by Egyptians for thousands of years.

The other figurine Nata brought out was the one Ferox told others was an image of his father. It was not. Ferox never really knew who his father was. The figure he had possessed when he was still in servitude represented a god that Nata had told him about, the falcon-headed man, Montu, the Egyptian god of war. Nata placed the two statuettes on the main pedestal in the enclave as Ferox congratulated him.

"Well done, my king. It was a good day. Your plan worked like a charm."

"Ferox, my brother, you do not have to call me king when we are alone."

"As you wish," he said. "But how is your shoulder? I almost had you there in our fight."

"Bah, it is nothing," Nata scoffed. "And how is your leg? I almost killed you there, but I needed you alive to allow us to escape. Otherwise, I would have slain you then and there. The question is, would you have killed me in our fight if you had the chance?"

"Of course. And I almost did, but you were too quick. Your survival was not vital to our plan of escape, you know."

Nata wore a bemused look as Ferox sighed.

"It is what we do. The only people that I have feelings for, the only ones I respect, are my fellow gladiators. And we have learned to kill the people we love. It is the gladiator way."

Nata paused for a moment, inscrutable at first, and then he raised his brow as he smirked.

"You are right."

Then he and Nata got on their knees before the two simple statuettes on the main pedestal, praying and giving offerings of food and wine. After their ceremony of thanks, Nata turned to him.

"This is just the beginning. Our kingdom had started, and we will drive out the British nobility and sweep the Saxon swine into the sea. Bandits and the downtrodden, those who are strong and ruthless, these are the men who will be welcome under the banner of my kingdom. But I have heard disturbing news of late; there is another group like us, an army of the dispossessed forming to the east in a place called the Weald led by a boy named Arturius. They are trying to gather the same type of men that we seek, and this cannot be tolerated."

"I have heard of them as well. They are mainly Christians I think, so they should be easy to kill and enslave for ourselves. Some priest and his woman also lead them, or so I have heard."

Nata touched Ferox on the shoulder.

"You have done well to lead this double life, pretending to care for that wrinkled old bitch that was once our mistress."

"That selfish harlot deserved to die," He snorted. "I practically gagged every time I had to shag her, but I would just close my eyes and think of you. My life had always been a façade, pretending to be something I am not, just to survive. I can only be myself around you."

"Didn't you feel sorry for her?"

"No," he scoffed. "People like that are tools to be used, nothing more. The key is to find their weaknesses and exploit them. You should have seen the horror in her eyes as I cut her throat. It's delicious, watching their eyes as my victims die. There is nothing quite like it."

"You are a merciless fiend," Nata said as he shook his head, "and I love you for it."

Ferox laughed. It was a feeling akin to sexual pleasure whenever he saw the spark of life leave someone as he cut their throats, a taste he had developed from being a gladiator. But with her, to see it in her eyes, her trust so betrayed, it had been more exhilarating than usual. It had reminded him of the early days of his gladiator training, when they were given dogs to be cared for by them for months until the day came when their pet approached them with its tail wagging, and they had been forced to cut their dog's throat and watch the trust in their eyes fade into horror. *My training made me the hardest of men*, he thought, *but it also made me strong."*

"You are right," Nata said. "There is nothing like snuffing out a man's life when you have bested them in combat. That is the best."

Ferox chuckled as an evil grin crossed his face.

"You must know that I especially like to slay the ones who grovel to the Christos."

"Why the Christians?" Nata asked.

"My mother was a whore who loved the Christos. My father could have been anybody with enough silver to get my mother to spread her legs, and it did not take much. After she sold me into slavery to feed her daughters, I served a rich Christian household. I became their dog. I trusted them, and I wagged my tail whenever they gave me scraps. Then their daughter became pregnant thanks to me, and so they whipped me and sold me off to become a gladiator. They thought it merciful, but they just did not have the bollocks to kill me, which is what I would have done. No, they wanted to make my life hell. So, for the memory of my harlot mother and my former masters, I enjoy sending them to their hell instead."

"You know the ways of the Christians then."

"I do."

Nata rubbed his chin in thought for a few moments.

"I have another task for you if you are up for it. I need you to go to the Weald and pretend to be one of those seeking refuge there with the priest and their boy general. Learn their ways, their strengths and weaknesses, and report back. Can you do this?"

Ferox nodded.

"For you my king, I would do anything."

Nata poured two cups of wine from an amphora and held his flagon up to the sky.

"A toast then. To strength and honor. And to our brothers."

Ferox also raised his mug.

"To strength and honor. And to our brothers."

They both downed the wine with gusto. Then Nata put both of his hands on Ferox's shoulders.

"Well, now," he said. "We have some catching up to do!"

They embraced, kissing each other in desperation and lust, and then the two walked hand in hand into the bedroom.

CHAPTER NINE

The people had named it *Sister Brigid's Bibliotheca*, or the Latin library, the name given to the hut that contained the extensive collection of books that the community had accumulated to preserve the written word from the flames of the barbarians. Senna sat in the window box, dutifully copying the ancient Roman papyrus scroll word for word onto the parchment codex to preserve the document for future generations. Sister Brigid knew Senna loved to read, and she had assigned her the task of supervising the conversion of the fragile scrolls into the more compact and durable codex type books made of parchment.

One of the scribes copying a scroll let out a scream, "This is such a pain in the arse!"

Senna was taken aback, but then she replied in a level voice.

"What seems to be the problem, my dear?"

"These scrolls are so cumbersome. There must be thirty or forty sheets glued together so I must unroll it forever. This papyrus stuff is so bloody fragile, it's just falling apart. Why did they make their books like this?"

Senna suppressed her laughter, causing her to pause before she spoke.

"You are right. Years ago, papyrus was cheap, and it is easy to write on, but since trade with the Mediterranean world has dried up, we cannot get it anymore, so now we are using these sheets of thinned cow skin for these new codex books. This library will be relocated to the west someday, and these new books should bear the travel much better. Sister Brigid is trying to preserve the written word for future generations."

"But we already have the bible, which is all we need. The stuff we are copying was moldering away in the attics of those rich Romans, and they are full of pagan thoughts!"

Senna tried to keep the annoyance out of her voice as she replied.

"Knowledge of the wider world is important: law, business, philosophy, the arts, history, mathematics. The Christos gave us those things, too. We have the history of the known world for a thousand years in these scrolls, and they should not go to waste. Even the ideas in the old religions are useful to know to convert those pagans, as it is good to know how they think, don't you agree?"

"I suppose so."

"Now you need to get to copying your book. We can chat about this later."

The girl nodded and resumed her scribbling as Senna tried to appear as if she was still proof reading. Instead, she was daydreaming, trying to figure out a way to escape from the rest of the scribes. She longed to be reading in solitude in her woodland refuge by the river where she kept a shrine to the goddess Isis, a place unknown to others at Weald, even including her sister and her vacuous and flirtatious friends. *I should be more polite to this girl,* she thought, *but all she and her companions do is gossip.* She knew she would never be friends with the other girls here, preferring to discuss events and ideas and not whisper about other people's behavior.

Senna was a pagan herself, but she felt no need to advertise that fact. She was exasperated by the scribe's narrow-mindedness, but then she flashed her sweetest smile towards the scribe, secretly giving thanks to Isis that she was the one in charge of the library. She loved both Brigid and Petrus, but their religion did not touch her spirit like Isis did, the Egyptian goddess who catered to women. She knew the cult of Isis was once one of the leading religious movements in the Roman world, and Christians had tried to stamp it out, but on the fringes of the empire the goddess's appeal persisted. Of all the gods, it was Isis was whom she preferred the most.

It was the slaves and poor who honored the Christos, while the patrician class loved philosophy and polytheism; Christianity had little appeal to educated people such as herself. There were exceptions, of course, like with Brigid and Petrus, but most of the noble families of Rome had been suspicious of this new religion. It was a good thing Senna knew where the more controversial works were stored, or she knew this pretty little creature beside her would lose her mind; the works of Ovid came to her mind.

Socially, she felt isolated from almost everyone at the Weald. She hailed from a family of distinction, people who had worn purple hemmed togas, the symbols of the Roman Magistrates, at least when Rome was in control. Her mother had made it clear to her daughters they were of noble birth. Here in the camp, it seemed like everyone left behind after the exodus to Brittany were peasants or escaped slaves, many of them illiterate, viewing her and her sister with suspicion.

As for herself, she did not bloody well care whom your parents were, as she only had disdain for the stupid ones. *Many of the people here certainly seem intimidated by me*, she thought. Except for her younger sister, who barely counted, she had no friends her age to speak of, and at sixteen, that was quite a burden. If her mother were still here, she could have been engaged to be married about now, but fortunately, Brigid and Petrus thought she had a few years before she needed to think about that.

She had yet to meet anyone she wanted to marry herself, and just finding a friend was enough of a challenge. True, there were adults she was close to, such as Sister Brigid and Brother Petrus, but they were old, probably close to thirty. No friends, at least until those three noble hostages had shown up. Those young men were intriguing. All three were now in their late teens and were steadfast companions, but each boy was so different. Life had certainly gotten more interesting once those three had arrived.

Cerdic, the big-boned blonde from the Catuvellauni tribe located in south-central Britain, was strikingly handsome to be sure. He was gregarious and funny; he hunted, fished, and was reputed to be quite a warrior. Unfortunately, he would not look at a book unless it fell from the sky and hit him on the head. He seemed exceedingly popular among the girls in the camp. Too popular really, as he seemed to have a new girl on his arm every few weeks. He was someone to admire perhaps, but not a person she could call a true friend.

Caradoc hailed from the Silures in the rain-soaked mountains to the west. That tribe was mysterious and feared, known for their skills in archery and the art of the ambush. He was pleasant to look at if he smiled, which was seldom. He was so quiet that she could not get him to talk. He seemed to be reserved and brooding as well, and there was something chilling about those light blue eyes. Well-muscled, his ability with his long bow seemed uncanny. Hunting was a passion, and that was a good thing for keeping the group well fed. He was also quite the musician as well, always playing those bagpipes of his that Senna despised. But he seemed to be in his own world, a world she could not relate to.

Arturius, on the other hand, was someone that she could talk to. Arturius was also a reader. Senna looked at the book she had just finished copying, *Meditations* by the Emperor Marcus Aurelius, written a couple of hundred years ago. The life philosophy of stoicism he espoused was consistent with her own beliefs, more so than the old Romano-British Gods, or the newer Christian and Norse ones. Arturis was funny, self-depreciating, modest, and insatiably curious. All the girls in the camp had eyes for him, and she was pleased that he seemed oblivious to them.

She could not wait to give the book to Arturius to read. He was of somewhat less than average height, dark haired and hazel-eyed, and his physique was thin and wiry. He was not built like a traditional warrior. To compensate for his lack of size, he could run like the wind, and with his sling, he could fell a warrior like Achilles. He walked fast, talked fast, and sometimes seemed to flit from one task to another before fully completing the first one. His skill with a sling was so remarkable that his contribution to the group's larder was as impressive as what Caradoc and his bow could do. And what he lacked in size, he made up for in his mind and personality.

Senna was lithe and golden skinned, and her unruly locks loved to get tangled, unlike her sister's hair, which was thin, straight, and blonde. Her eyes were hazel, while Lucilia's were blue. She was short, while her sibling was taller. She was thin, while her sister was voluptuous. Senna was quiet, while Lucilia was vivacious. Senna was athletic, while her sibling preferred a nap. Lucilla could sing like an angel, while Senna sounded like a frog. Senna was book crazy and kept to herself, while her sister was boy crazy, surrounded by a hoard of friends and admirers. Senna looked like her father, while Lucilia looked like their mother. It was difficult to believe they both had come from the same womb, but despite their differences, they were also best friends.

Cerdic and Caradoc both had girls fawning all over them, but Arturius did not seem interested romantically in anyone. Still, it was clear to her that he liked both her and her sister, but in different ways. She connected with him mentally, as a friend. As for her sister, she was vivacious, entertaining, and funny, a person it was hard not to like. She was lost in her thoughts when the door opened, and a person walked in. *My,* she thought, *look who it is. Arturius!* She beamed a smile that could have melted the glaciers of the world.

"Hello, Senna, it is good to see you. I was hoping you would be here."

"Well, hello to you, too! I was just thinking of you as well."

She blinked once in frustration at her overeager greeting, not like the other young women who threw themselves at him.

"Really," he replied quizzically.

"Why y-yes," she stammered as she attempted to hide her blush with little success.

"Look here, Arturius. We have a velum copy of the book by Marcus Aurelius that we talked about. It is ready to read now, and I thought I would give you the first crack at it."

He flashed a smile that set her heart beating like a captive bird.

"I would love to do that. For once, I have the afternoon free, and I was hoping that book was ready. And well, ___"

Arturius paused for a moment in an awkward silence. She broke the silence with a giggle.

"Well, what?"

He blushed red as he often did; he seemed charmingly awkward around girls, something she thought was an endearing trait.

"Well, I know you have read *Meditations* of course, but I have read only some snippets of passages, but not the whole thing. And I was hoping to borrow that book today and be able to read it, and then we could talk about it together."

"Of course," she said nodding, "I would like that very much."

The news filled her with happiness. It was an opportunity to get to know him better and take the afternoon off herself. A sly grin curved her lips.

"And guess what? We've just found a copy of *Lysistrata* by the Greek playwright Aristophanes that I was wanting to read for myself. I also have the afternoon off, so perhaps we could find a place to read together."

His eyes opened wide with delight.

"Oh, that would be great. I have heard of that play, but I have never read it. What is it about again?"

She successfully suppressed her giggle this time.

"It is a comedy set in the time of the Peloponnesian War. The war was going on forever, and the women got tired of the whole thing, so the wives got together and refused to lay with their husbands until they stopped fighting."

"Now I remember hearing about it. And as I recall, that led to a peace settlement right away. I heard it was quite amusing."

"Oh, now, she said as she pretended to pout, "You ruined the ending for me."

She chuckled as he playfully rolled his eyes.

"I think you knew that already."

She continued to smile.

"You are correct, I did," she said. "I was just teasing you. But wouldn't it be nice if that sort of thing happened in the real world."

"You are absolutely right. I just wish everyone would just get along and no one would have to fight."

"Oh now," she scoffed, "you are trained as a warrior, right? Isn't that why you are here, to teach all the young men to be good killers?"

She resisted the temptation to groan out loud and cover her face in embarrassment. *Why did I just say that?* she thought. He looked like she had hurt his feelings.

"Everyone needs to learn how to fight to defend themselves," he said in a solemn tone. "And I was taught by my stepfather how to be a slinger. It is a fun thing to do if you are just doing target practice. And trying to hunt with a sling is a real challenge, but I feel a little guilty just killing an animal for food. I don't want to be a warrior, really. I would rather spend time in a library and read books and talk about philosophy and drink wine with my friends. I just want a life of peace."

She nodded, still embarrassed and almost unable to speak.

"Good, I am glad to hear that. I think the same way."

She looked at him with fondness; they wanted the same things in life. Then, she gave him a searching look.

"Have you ever killed someone?"

She felt her face grow hot at the audacity of the question. *What is wrong with me?* she thought. *Why did I ask him that?*

"Once. It was a man who was trying to kill me and my friends. As I said, I feel uneasy killing animals because those are innocent creatures, but with that man, I did not feel guilty at all. If it were someone else, I probably would have felt different, but he was far from innocent. He had tortured us when we were captives under Aelle. I did what I had to do."

This was not the kind of conversation she wanted to have. It was time to gracefully move on. She wanted to smooth things over with him, and then she thought of her sanctuary, the shrine of Isis in the woods, a place no one else knew existed. *Perhaps it is time to share that place with a kindred soul,* she thought.

"Arturius, I have an idea. I know a place that is special, where there is a small pond created by beavers who built a dam. It is very peaceful. Would you like to come with me to see it?"

"I'd love that," he gushed.

"Very well. I can leave now. Ready?"

He nodded. They stopped by her house on the way to grab some food and blankets, and then they set off though the woods to the stream that flowed near the camp. She picked out a barely perceptible path near the river's edge going upstream, and after walking for twenty minutes, they came across a pond created by some fallen trees that had been felled by those industrious little rodents. She pointed out to Arturius the beavers' home, a mound of sticks and branches near the water's edge that stuck out a couple of feet above the waterline. Near the beaver lodge was a meadow surrounded by the overhang of some huge old trees. Arturius looked around in wonder.

"This is a lovely setting. I had no idea this even existed."

"I love it here. It is one of my special places."

"I have heard of beavers, of course," he said, "But I have never seen any, nor have I seen a dam like this before."

"It is too early for us to see them right now, but I have spotted them out swimming around in the early evenings. They are such cute little things."

"I won't tell anyone. I do not want some hunter to spoil this place."

"I appreciate that," she said with a smile.

They went back to the clearing and read for a while, the quiet murmuring of the water flowing past the small dam accentuated by the calling of the songbirds that flitted about. She could not think of a more tranquil location. They read for about an hour. Periodically, she would slip him a surreptitious glance. This afternoon was going well, and she decided to was time to show him the shrine that only she knew existed.

"Arturius, there is another special place that I know of that I want to show to you."

"What is it?"

"Have some patience. You will see."

Senna took his hand again and led him along an overgrown path for about two hundred paces upstream from the pond to where a structure seemed to appear out of nowhere. It was like they were in their own private world, the view from behind them was covered with dense foliage. The river was barely visible through the leaves as it flowed nearby. The path had opened to reveal a small open-faced structure, a tiny square-shaped building constructed of finely fitted stones that had a semi-circular opening facing the river.

The floor and the alcove located at the back of the structure looked like it was made of marble, covered with a round roof and faced with a simple Tuscan column on each side. Along the back wall was a curved inset used to support the idols and statuettes that were a part of Roman religious life, empty now except for a figurine of Isis. The statue gleamed, newly polished and proud, and the floor and walls appeared clean from recent use. He glanced around, only able to see the charred bones of a nearby building, buried in a thicket of vines, a once proud dwelling abandoned now for a hundred years or more.

"That is impressive," he said. "It looks like the ancestral shrine of a home, but without the rest of the house. What is that doing out here in the middle of nowhere? "

"I don't know. But I have wandered about the area here to figure that out, and the only sign of habitation I have found are the ancient ruins next to us. I believe this shrine was for those people who lived there.

"It looks like someone is actively using it now."

"Oh, that is my doing."

She nervously laughed, hoping she was not disappointing him with a paltry shrine like this.

"This place was a wreck when I first found it, but then I brought this shrine back to life. No one else knows about this."

Arturius gave her a warm smile.

"This is a very special place for you then. I am honored that you have shared it with me. And I swear to all the gods that I will tell no one else about this."

"Thank you," Senna said as a tear graced her eye.

She laid out the blankets in the alcove, and they sat down in the coolness of the shrine and resumed their reading. She felt at peace. She had never felt so comfortable with a boy before. And here they were, alone together. Arturius had resumed reading his book. He seemed oblivious and absorbed, and she was a little disappointed that he had not attempted to kiss her. She liked it that he wasn't aggressive as some boys were, but had he no interest in her? She pouted. *I am not sure what he is thinking*, she thought.

When Arturius had joined the community at the Weald, she did not know what to make of him at first, a thin and wiry young man, animated with boundless energy. He was funny and talkative and could relate to just about anyone he met, but initially, he was shy around her. They bonded over their mutual love of literature, and they shared similar philosophies about life. In time, she had become his friend. Once Senna discovered that he loved books as much as she did, she was smitten. She sighed. *Do I want him as a friend, or as a lover?* she thought. *And if he becomes the latter, he would be my first. Can't I have both?*

Her mother may not have approved of him, as she felt that people should be like dogs and pigeons, selectively bred for excellence, but Senna believed in the philosophies of Pelagianism espoused by Sister Brigid, that people were born equal, each with their own unique strengths and weaknesses. It was actions that made one noble, not the accident of birth. Romano-British marriages amongst the nobility were normally arranged by the families for political reasons more than anything else, and if her mother still lived, that might have held true.

But her mother was deceased, and father had been gone for years; Petrus and Brigid were her guardians now, giving her free rein to marry whomever she wanted at a time of her choosing. She did not want to settle down just yet, but this young man was someone that she might consider as a long-term partner. She needed to overlook that he did not have a penny to his name, and she was not sure about Arturius being a warrior, but she was certain that she was fond of him. She continued to read as she snuck in glances now and again. He continued to be oblivious to her as he sat beside her, absorbed in reading his book.

Finally, she could stand it no further. She leaned over and gave him an affectionate peck on the cheek. He turned and looked at her in surprise. Much to her annoyance, he did not follow up with a kiss back. She leaned again, this time with a brief closed- mouth lip-on-lip affair of a kiss between close friends, similar to the one the boys received when they first arrived. She pulled back, keeping her face close to him, seeing his eyes widen. He had been shy and a little awkward with her up to now, and she realized that with his recent enthrallment, this might be the first time he had experienced intimacy with a woman.

She wanted more, and a few seconds later, she leaned forward again and proceeded to the Savium, the open-mouthed kiss of Cupid. They embraced as she nibbled and softly sucked on his lips in an erotic, yet playful way. His lips were stiff at first, clearly inexperienced as he was; up to now he had only experienced the lash, not love. He was a quick learner though, and as he relaxed, his breathing became heavier as they continued to kiss. Her breathing quickened as desire for him filled her being. She caressed his upper body as he caressed hers. She felt his hand slide down her tunic to cup her breast in a gentle caress, and she reveled in the feeling of pleasure. *I will just have to make sure things do not get out of hand*; she thought.

Then she felt his hand start to slide down, and once he started to head below her waistline, she reached her hand down and gently pulled it back to her breast. *That is as far as you get to go,* she thought. *I am not ready for anything more right now.* When they first started kissing, his lips were wooden, but he soon caught on to the tender little nibbles and gently soft sucking she did, and he copied her. Then she slipped in a flick of her tongue, and she felt him stiffen as he pulled back for a moment to stop kissing her to look into her eyes.

"Um, I just wanted to let you know," he stammered, "I have never really kissed anyone like this before."

She giggled for a moment as he placed her hands in his.

"I hate to disappoint you," she said with a firm expression, "but I am not about to rut with you in the woods like some slave girl."

"Oh, n-no," he stammered, "I did not mean it like that! I just do not have much experience with kissing."

She sighed as she playfully rolled her eyes.

"It does not hurt to practice."

They spent the rest of the afternoon talking and holding hands like lovers, and even though there were periodic episodes of kissing, that was as far as she let things progress. Sex before marriage was not something a noble Roman woman did, or so she had been taught. They talked about everything, and they talked about nothing, and the rest of the afternoon swept by in a blur. They sat there together for a long time, but to her, it seemed not long at all.

Finally, Arturius sighed as he gave her an anxious look.

"I am having a wonderful time here with you, but I have got to get back. I hate to go, but reality intrudes."

"What do you have to get back for?"

He displayed a sheepish look as he hesitated.

"I had plans to meet someone at sundown, but it is not important now, I___"

"And who was that you were going to meet," she asked in a honeyed voice.

"Well, your sister said I should meet her. She said something about a picnic. And I guess she and the rest of her group of friends are ___ "

"My sister?" she said sharply.

Her thoughts grew cold as she felt a chill cross her spine. She had heard that the young people of the community were having a bonfire tonight, and Lucilia had batted her eyes at her this morning, looking coquettish as she had mentioned she had some special plans that did not involve the group that evening. A cold wash of dread mixed with anger filled her being as the realization dawned on her. *Oh, by the gods,* she fumed, *Lucilia was going to be with Arturius!*

"You are meeting with Lucillia," She snorted. "After we did this?"

Her eyes bored into his with the look of a woman scorned.

"She said it was with a group, and ___"

Lucilia, that flirtatious little vixen, she thought. Her sister could entrap any boy here in the Weald, but her Arturius? She had to know Senna had feelings for him. Rage and humiliation washed over her now like a torrent, her rage unstoppable as the stew of emotions flooded through her body.

"You bloody idiot. It was a picnic with just her, not a group event. Really! How could you!"

With that she sprang up, hurriedly gathering her things to run away back to the village as he stammered on about how he did not know what Lucilia had planned, and that he was sorry.

"Shut up, will you," she hissed, and he fell silent, looking like a forlorn puppy who had just been beaten.

Senna could not hear the words as her head was literally buzzing, her mind mired in a noxious fog. She did not know what to think. She did not want to think at all. This had started out as one of the best days of her life, and now it was the worst. When she hurried away from the shrine, Arturius had looked so sad and lost that she almost felt sorry for him. Almost.

CHAPTER TEN

For early September, it was unseasonably warm, and what a glorious day it was. The sun had heated the air pleasantly as puffy white clouds marched across the sky. Birds chirped a happy tune, bees and other insects buzzed around him in merriment, but nothing of the beauty of nature could lighten Arturius' mood. He staggered across the practice field, hauling a heavy basket to join Cerdic and Caradoc atop a small hill that overlooked the men in training. He and his friends had been in camp for months now, and they had fallen into a now familiar routine. The men of the village were practicing martial skills, and he and his friends were the ones in charge of the training.

Each of them had a role. Caradoc had his archers, and Macro was primarily helping Cerdic, leaving Arturius to supervise the novice slingers on his own, and progress had been slow. A few of his slingers were coming along, but the majority were not getting it, and he knew his two friends were having similar problems. The huge basket he carried seemed as heavy as he was, and in it was something that he hoped would help them all. He struggled up the hillock, glancing at Caradoc and Cerdic as they sat on their haunches as they morosely gazed at some men below.

It was not just problems with his students that bothered him. His head would hurt whenever he thought about the incident with Senna those many weeks ago. He had not even thought about trying to kiss Senna when they went to the river, assuming they were going to read. He just wanted to spend some time with her, but having a romantic interlude had not even crossed his mind. A peck on the cheek would have been fine, and he hadn't even expected that.

But the pleasant afternoon had turned into a disaster, and he had never been so embarrassed in his life. His cheeks burned hot whenever he thought of his own stupidity. Of course, he had apologized to Senna, but she had remained cool towards him ever since. Arturius knew he was clueless when it came to dealing with the opposite sex, and his recent thralldom had not helped him relate to women. It did not dawn on him that Lucilla had romantic designs when she'd invited him to the picnic, naively believing it was a group event with the other young people.

He had gone from having no one interested in him, to having two young women who wanted to be with him at the same time. But they were sisters, and jealousy had reared its ugly head. Now no girl wanted to talk with him, and he thought his reputation in the community had been tarnished forever. Lucilia's scorn did not bother him, but Senna? She had been a friend, and he missed her. *Maybe even my best friend,* he thought, *I told her things I never felt comfortable sharing with anyone else.*

He sighed at the thought; *by Jupiter, women are such trouble.* But he knew he was not getting married anytime soon, and as a soldier, that might not ever occur. He felt he was not a young man to catch a woman's eyes, not like Cerdic or Caradoc, who were big, good-looking burly types. His friends were real nobles, and in his mind, he was almost a Nithing. *What have I got to interest a woman,* he thought. *I am a penniless refugee, and all I am good at is just using a child's toy to throw rocks.*

But self-pity was not going to win any battles, and he hefted the basket higher to join his friends. He was going to show them something he thought they would both be interested in. When he finally joined them, sweating and panting, his friend barely acknowledged his arrival. Caradoc was morosely gazing at his archers as they were practicing, and Cerdic was as doing the same, evaluating his shield men doing their drills. They gave Arturius a mildly curious glance as he plopped down beside them. *By Mithras,* he thought, *this thing was heavy.*

"How is it going?" he said in a cheerful voice.

"How is it going?" Cerdic grumbled. "Well, it is not going. Look at those fellows down there. It is a bleeding mess."

"And my boys cannot hit the side of a barn," Caradoc joined in. "So, it is not going for me, either."

Then Caradoc looked askance at the basket.

"What have you got there?" he muttered.

"Ale, I hope," Cerdic spat out. "I could use an entire keg about now."

"Nah," Caradoc said, smirking. "He probably has a girl tied up in there. That is the only way he can get one to talk to him now."

His two friends laughed while Arturius reddened from embarrassment. Then Caradoc and Cerdic resumed looking morose as they ignored the basket. Arturius knew the big Jute normally tended to be gazing at the world with favor, an ale in one hand and a girl in the other, but that was not the case today. His typical cheerfulness had been rarely seen for the last few weeks. Caradoc always looked a bit grumpy, but today he looked more so than usual. Arturius knew how they felt, because he was feeling the same about his job here in the Weald.

It was well known in the community that they were going to have to move the bulk of their population to the west. The refuge was being inundated with new arrivals. Petrus and Brigid hoped they had enough food for the coming winter, but everyone knew they would need to start fresh somewhere else, a new home that could support a larger population for their long-term survival. The real question now was when and where they were going to go.

And when the migration began, they would be the big, juicy target of every roving band of raiders and bandits along the way, not to mention the Saxons who were always looking for booty and slaves.

The people from the Weald needed to be able to defend themselves, and right now they were far from being ready. He and his friends were responsible for training these men into competent warriors, and many of these people under his tutelage had been hopeless and helpless in learning any skills. He was struggling in teaching the art of slinging, and he knew that similar concerns weighed on the other two as well, but in his basket was a solution to their problems, or so he hoped. Arturius tried to maintain a positive tone as he looked at Cerdic.

"How goes it with those antique swords that your men are using? Are they worth anything?"

Cerdic growled back, "I don't know what to think. Once the blacksmiths cleaned them up, they cut well enough, but they are so bloody short! It's a different style of fighting than I am used to. The gladius is good for a fight in tight quarters, I suppose, but against a real Saxon warrior, who knows? I know that I wouldn't want to use it in a real fight."

Arturius nodded in sympathy.

"We are lucky to have any weapons at all," he said.

"True," Cerdic grumbled. "But we should be trained to fight like a real warrior. Using a short sword is about as good as using a British phallus with a good Jutish woman. It is too small to do much good."

"Those gladii are better than nothing," Arturius said. "It is going to be quite a while before we get much else. And if you do those legionary formations, I think they will work just fine. The Romans conquered most of the known world using those tactics and weapons."

"Who would bury hundreds of swords in a bog like that," Cerdic grumbled.

"Men who expected to dig them up later," Caradoc morosely said. "Whomever put them there must have been killed before they could be used.

At least you *have* swords now. My archers are having to make do with green sticks for bows."

Arturius nodded, knowing that forging an actual sword was a difficult endeavor, much more so than a mere spearhead. They had one blacksmith worthy of the name. Senecio was training people, but they were concentrating on making arrow heads. They were short of iron and trained blacksmiths to turn out spears or anything else. These Roman Gladii had been discovered in some peat bog weeks before they had arrived. The swords numbered several hundred, buried for the gods knew how long. Petrus thought they dated from the early days of the Roman invasion, which would make them more than three hundred years old. Cerdic shook his head as he sighed.

"I would love to teach a few of our men with a good Saxon shield and spear, but with our shortage of weapons, we are concentrating on learning these old-fashioned legionary tactics."

Arturius tried to sound hopeful.

"How are those old Roman training manuals. Do they help?"

Cerdic buried his head in his hands, and then he pointed to a formation of men in the field to the right of them, some eighty strong. Macro was teaching the formation to quickly change from a marching column to a defensive oval. The men were bumping into each other as Macros yelled at them in fury.

"Look at those fellows out there. They are struggling with just the basics of footwork right now. And they have trouble hitting something they are aiming at with their sword against a wooden post, much less forming something like a testudo. Just look at them. Even the basics are a struggle."

"Well, you must like the idea of that new sword that Senecio is making for you," Arturius said brightly, trying to lighten the mood. "Do you have a name for it yet?"

"Not yet. She needs to taste blood first."

Arturius knew that sword was a special one, a new design that could both thrust and slash. The pommel Senecio had built was a narrow half-moon shape instead of a ball like a traditional spatha. Cerdic could still use the hammer grip for a chopping motion, but now he could change the grip to one he might use when cutting food with a knife, a new way to swing a sword that could be a game changer in a fight. The young men fell silent once more as they continued to watch the infantrymen struggle to maintain formation. *By Hercules bollocks,* he thought, *Cerdic's boys down there really are a mess. No wonder he is frustrated.* Arturius turned to Caradoc as he broke the silence once more.

"Are you having better luck with your budding archers?

Caradoc scowled.

"I think that bunch of bumbling oafs down there are doing better at their infantry maneuvers than the people I have. I have a handful that are starting to develop some skills, but the former slaves, particularly the town dwellers, meh. They are awful. Some of them could not hit a barn if they were ten paces from it."

"I have the same problem," Arturius said.

"I think my expectations are too high," Caradoc said dejectedly. "I had been trained in archery all my life. How could they do all of this in a few weeks? And the equipment we have is a big part of the problem. Our issue is the bows. The ones we have are too short and the wood has not been properly aged. It takes at least three years for a stave to be ready to be carved into a proper weapon. And the bows your other tribes in Britannia use are for hunting, not war; they are just too short."

"Don't you have any men who could any be good in a fight?"

"We have a grand total of only four that I could call an archer. But with the rest of these fellows, many of them will never get it."

Caradoc buried his head in his hands, then raised his head up again in disgust.

"Brother, I am at a loss here. But maybe you are having better luck than I am. How is it going with your slingers?"

Arturius shrugged his shoulders.

"Some of my folks are pretty good at getting their stones out there, but accuracy is a problem. You know it is harder to aim a shot from a sling than it is with your archers. Some of my people could hit a group of troops who are bunched up, but there is no guarantee they would hit anything important. So, we are not ready, either."

They all fell silent again as they took in the scene below them. Finally, Cerdic broke the silence.

"You know our plan to escape to the west means we need warriors who know their business, and I do not care how well I train these men as infantry; the Saxons are just too experienced. Our boys will get chewed up. We need another edge. We are going to need missile troops that are competent, or we are done for."

"Some calvary would be nice," Caradoc scoffed, "but that is not going to happen. You need horses and people who know how to ride them."

Arturius looked with pride at his friends. Despite their frustrations, they were obviously still committed to defending the people here in the Weald. In appreciation for the hospitality shown to them all when they arrived, the three of them had promised Brigid and Petrus they would help them get their new settlement established safely. He knew his two friends missed their homes, but an oath was an oath, and they were going to see this through to the end. Once the people here were in a safe place and were well protected, his two friends might try to go home again, but they were all in this together now. That was the quality of person his two friends were, and he loved them for it. *Okay,* he thought, *now is the time to spring this idea.*

"Brothers, I read about something I wanted to share with you. I think you will be interested. Senecio had some of his people make these new weapons for us to try out. I would like your opinions as to whether this could be a solution to some of our problems."

Caradoc's voice dripped with sarcasm.

"Well, Cerdic and I have wondered what you have been up to. It is nice to see you emerge from the cocoon of that amazing library. Of course, you do not have much choice. No girl will ever talk to you again, so you might as well just read books in your spare time."

"I imagine that Senna walks out the back door as soon as you come in," Cerdic said as he continued to look at the infantry struggling in the distance.

Arturius's cheeks burned hot whenever he thought of his stupidity with Senna. Would anyone ever forget? Would she ever forgive him?

"So," Caradoc said as he crossed his arms across his chest, "what is your bright idea? War elephants?"

"We need to try something much easier to learn," Arturius said. "Once we settle in the west, we will have more time to continue to train our people to master the art of the bow and the sling, but for now, how about this? I had a new weapon created for us to try."

Arturius pulled a projectile out of the large basket he was carrying with him.

"Hmm. That is one strange looking arrow, to be sure," Caradoc observed.

Arturius looked down at Senecio's creations with pride. The point was the same barbed head that was typical for arrows, but this looked more like a dart than an arrow. This was much shorter than one typically used in archery, and the butt end of the arrow had a handle that protruded from the back of the fletching. The most peculiar aspect of the shortened arrow was an oblong lump of lead that gave the arrow some weight, located about a third of the way back from the barbed tip.

"So, this looks like a cross between an arrow and a miniature javelin," Cerdic commented. "It is so tiny! Are we supposed to throw this thing?"

"Yes," Arturius replied. "It is called a plumbata. It is basically a lead weighted dart. I read that some legions, especially in Illyria, are using these with great effect. It does not require great skill, and if thrown underhanded, it travels a long way. You can throw it overhanded as well. I think even some of the womenfolk could be lethal with these."

Caradoc raised his brow.

"Now I know why lead is in short supply for your slingers."

Arturius shrugged as he held up the plumbata.

"Well, we put it to good use. I think this could be remarkably effective if we use them as a disciplined group to throw them. It should require little training to use them. Those legionnaires in Illyria also use these in the shield wall, not just the missile troops. You can fasten several of these to the back of a shield instead of using one or two bulky javelins."

The expression on the faces of Cerdic and Caradoc brightened.

"Do you have more?" they both asked at the same time.

"Yes. I had several dozen made that I brought up here in this basket, so with your permission, I will bring them to the practice field. Let us go visit your boys and try this out."

Arturius hauled the heavy basket down the hill as Cerdic and Caradoc gathered their men together to watch the demonstration. Arturius laid the basket on the ground and then backed up a bit as the men crowded around the container. A buzz of conversation filled the air as they looked in the basket to discern its contents. Arturius spoke to the crowd of people around them in a loud voice.

"Caradoc and Cerdic have given me permission to show you these new weighted darts called plumbata. When you throw these, you can get different effects depending on your technique. Let me show you what I mean."

He walked about thirty paces from one of the archery practice butts, holding the dart by the handle located posteriorly to the arrow fletching. He crouched, then he took a few steps forward, and in one fluid motion he whipped the dart upwards with an underhanded throw, flying high into the air, striking the archery butt with a hearty thump once it came down. He turned back to the crowd of men.

"Now, I am going to use two at once."

Arturius heard a buzz of conversation as he approached closer to the archery butts, stopping twenty paces away before releasing another plumbata high. The heads of the crowd followed the missile as it started up, then immediately after releasing the initial dart, Arturius placed another plumbata into an overhand throwing position, tossing the second plumbata toward the target like a spear. The two missiles struck the target simultaneously, the thumps merging into the sound of one. He could hear the crowd of trainees murmuring in surprise and admiration, knowing that any defender would be hard pressed to block a missile attack coming from two directions at once.

"Alright then," exclaimed Arturius," let's get these plumbata distributed, and give it a try."

The group moved with eagerness to the container of missiles that Arturius had brought with them, gathering around the basket and talking excitedly amongst themselves as they handed out the novel devices.

Caradoc whispered to him, "Those things look like fun toys. The question is how much damage those darts can do compared to a real weapon."

"Plenty," he confidently said. "Let's go join the group and we can practice with the rest of them. I sincerely hope we can pick this up quickly. We are all so young, and the only gravitas we have is our knowledge of weaponry. With these things, we will be on the same level as everyone else."

"Oh, I'll be fine, because I will be with you," Cerdic replied, his words colored with sarcasm.

They all laughed as they walked back to join the group. Arturius noted a hint of a smile crossing Caradoc's face. Arturius was happy to see that Cerdic was beaming; having some effective missile troops could keep his infantrymen alive. He decided to have a quiver made for these things so someone could bring even more to the fight besides the plumbata attached behind a shield. That would give them a lot more missiles. *By Mithras,* he marveled, *this just might work.*

As they joined the group surrounding the basket of plumbata, Arturius heard Cerdic mutter, "So, these glorified darts are supposed to keep my boyish arse from being captured and sold to become eunuch slave in Persia. Really?"

Arturius could not keep himself from smiling, and he looked upon the beaming faces of the men who were picking up the plumbata with apparent relish. Arturius felt happy. His friends were being supportive of the idea, and the men were also intrigued, except for one fellow. *That is odd,* he thought. *The new man over there is the only one who is not smiling. Something is unusual about him. What is the name again? Ah yes, Ferox.*

CHAPTER ELEVEN

Cerdic knew this was an important night. It was early spring, and a chill was still in the air. The community council sat on tree stumps and camp chairs around a circle of fire pits, and he and his friends had been given the privilege to join them. The firelight danced across the faces of the various leaders of their refugee band while they discussed the long-term strategic plan of the group. It was a clear evening, with a nearly full moon and a brilliant canopy of stars above them. The glimmering of the moon combined with the flickering lights of the fires, creating a pattern of unusual radiance upon the visage of each person in the group. Their faces were well illuminated, yet they had a ghostly sheen as well. It was as if one could see each other's souls.

The ring of fire around them kept prying eyes and curious ears from intruding on their deliberations. Cerdic felt frustrated. He had been here almost a year now, and the number of new refugees was overwhelming. *There are twice as many of us now,* he thought. *We have got to do something.* They had been preparing for the great trek all winter, and he knew it was time for this community to move to another place. The meeting tonight was to get the ball rolling.

All those whose opinions were most respected in the camp were there in attendance. Among the others was Senecio, the leader of the blacksmiths and armorers of the group. Cerdic looked at him with a smile. He was short, well-muscled, with skin that looked like a weathered leather, wrinkled and red from years in the forge. Senecio was widely respected for his skill in creating weaponry, and Cerdic was thrilled that he was forging him a sword he could call his own. He suppressed his sigh of impatience. He had heard the sword was almost finished, and he could not wait to use it in combat.

The various other representatives and key figures in the council were there as well. This included Lucanus, their guide through the forest, who was representing the hunters and scouts. Tonight, his input would also be important. His visage was even more wrinkled than Senecio's face, which did not look possible. The soft-spoken Lucanus resembled an ill-kempt peasant, but he was known to be judicious in his comments. Sister Brigid started the proceedings off with a prayer, and then her husband began addressing the group.

Petrus stood up with a serious look as he glanced out at each of the people in the circle.

"I have called this group together to discuss our long-term strategy. As you all are aware, we cannot stay indefinitely in the woods of the Weald."

Petrus waved his arms around him.

"We are surrounded on three sides now, an island of Britons surrounded by a sea of Saxons. By winter, we'll either starve or be enslaved. Only to our west do we have Britons that are not at war with us. The question is, do we try to stay here, or do we move our people to the west?"

Then Petrus wandered around the group, asking the opinions of everyone as he pontificated about this and that, and Cerdic had not heard a word after the first few sentences. He tried to look interested in the proceedings, but his mind wandered. *By Thunor's hammer,* he thought *that Petrus just drones on and on.* He reminded Cerdic of his Greek tutor his father had foisted on him who never stopped talking about Demosthenes and Cicero and all these dead people he could care less about, and he would not spare the rod if Cerdic did not pay attention. He rubbed his hands; at least no one was going to rap his knuckles tonight.

During his speech, Petrus had mentioned the Catuvellauni more than once, and thoughts of his home filled him with sadness. *Home, what is my home,* he mused. *What am I?* His father had made sure he knew the world of the Romano-British, and his mother had made sure he was also part of the world of the Saxons and Jutes as well. He was both, and he was neither. Cerdic shook his head as he pondered his paradox. And what was he doing here?

Some in the Weald hated anyone from Germania. Most treated him well enough, but some were clearly uncomfortable with his presence, thinking Saxons and Jutes were all the same, scurrilous barbarians. But he and his friends had given their oaths to Petrus and Brigid to protect these people until they were in their new sanctuary. Cerdic had promised he would not go to his homelands until this job was done. Petrus was a man he had nothing but the greatest respect for, and Sister Brigid was like an older sister he never had. He could not let them down.

Back home, his father's tribe, the Cantullevauni, and his mother's West Saxon tribe had been allies. He had grown up in two worlds, splitting time between both communities. Unlike other British tribes, when a great famine had hit before he was born, his parents made sure their mercenary allies were taken care of, not deprived of food like other British tribes did with their own Germanic auxiliaries. The West Saxons had stayed loyal honoring their oaths as allies because they had been treated fairly.

Some of the other Saxons tribes had faced starvation because their own British allies deceived them, and Saxons being Saxons, they did not die without a fight. Cerdic thought the Saxon rebellion years ago was justified, and that opened the door for the current Saxon invasion. When Petrus had mentioned the Saxons taking Cantullevauni lands, it was the Middle and East Saxons he was talking about, not his own tribe. His West Saxons were still loyal to the Cantullevauni, and no doubt they were fighting against those other tribes from Germania to help their British friends. He hoped so, anyway. *An oath is an oath,* he thought as he fingered the amulet of Thunor's hammer under his tunic, *and by the gods, we keep our oaths.*

He did not know if his mother and his brothers were alive, and he had no way to find out unless he went north though the Saxon and Angle lands to find them. Cerdic knew he could not go alone and expect to survive. Was the alliance his father had organized still working? Would the West Saxons welcome him, or would they view him as a lying Briton? What would the Catuvellauni do now if he just showed up? Just getting home was dangerous enough, as there were too many hostile Saxons between him and home. Then Petrus finally got to the point where Cerdic needed to pay attention.

"Lucanus, what do our scouts say is going on with the British kingdoms to the west?"

Brother Petrus sat down as the grizzled woodsman stood up to address the crowd. He pursed his lips and paused a bit before replying.

"The lands of the Durotriges to the south and west of us have been deserted. There is little there but empty cities and overgrown fields."

Petrus turned to Arturius.

"What about the Dumnonai, Arturius? How do you think they would receive us?"

Arturius stood up.

"I am certain King Constantine would not welcome us in his own kingdom. They will not oppose us if we are between them and the Saxons, but they would not help us, either."

Lucanus nodded, and then he pointed to the north as Arturius sat down.

"I agree. And we need to stay away from British realms northwest of us, such as Glevum, Aqua Sulis, Corinium, and that area. They may not be friendly, either."

"I am afraid you are correct," Sister Brigid said. "I think they would not appreciate us using their lands in competition with them, and they like having their slaves."

Finally, Cerdic could stand it no more.

"What is going on with my tribe, the Catuvellauni?" he asked.

Lucanus gave him a sad look as he replied.

"I don't know. It is total chaos up there. We do know the Cantullevauni lost some of their territory to the East Saxons, and I am not sure if the West Saxons are still allied with them."

Cerdic suppressed his desire to comment. He needed to talk to Lucanus more when this never-ending conference was over.

"So what is our destination when we finally make this great trek?" Caradoc queried.

Lucanus nodded as he replied.

"As I said, areas south and west of us are wide open. I believe we can settle around Venta Belgae, and the Durotriges lands have a fair number of abandoned hill forts. From what I could see, the most promising place was called Camalet. We could move in there and not intrude on the old Roman towns at all, and there are several other hill forts nearby that could be fortified."

"That sounds promising," Sister Brigid said with a smile. "So, what did you hear about Durnovaria? There are rumors of a gladiator revolt there. Is that true?"

"Yes. The town was taken over by a slave revolt. The Durotriges no longer control the town, and the survivors are scattered all over."

"Were you able to find out if the gladiators would be friendly to us or not?" Petrus asked.

"I don't know. They would not talk to us or anyone else. They seem to not be freeing the enslaved but are making new slaves out of free men. The rumors are that if you do not fall in with them, you will be either wear a slave's collar or be brutally killed."

"How illogical for them to treat others like that," Petrus said, surprise etched on his face. "It is important for us to use reason over emotions in our relations with others. Gladiators have been so brutalized, though it is not surprising they lack compassion. We, of course, would welcome any refugees that wish to join us."

That is all we need, thought Cerdic, *more bloody refugees.* He racked his brain to remember the geography of the place. He recalled Camalet was not far from Durnovaria, maybe twenty-five miles or so due north. That could be trouble if the gladiators were as dangerous as they sounded. He thought that the walled town of Venta Belgae would be a better spot, maybe twice as far away from the gladiators, but that was a former British town, and it was certainly nearer to the East and South Saxons. *If it was left up to me,* he ruminated, *I would go to Venta, not Camalet.*

"There is another interesting development," Lucanus said. "The remnants of the united British army under the command of Ambrosius Aurelianus have just arrived at Caleva from the north and are fortifying the place.".

"That is interesting," Arturius said as he stood up. "How does his army look? Were they successful at all?"

Then he sat down as Lucanus turned to him to answer.

"They were campaigning against the Scotti and Picts, and we gather it did not go well for them up there. And that is all what I know."

The crowd started to whisper among themselves as Lucanus sat down.

"I have always admired the fortitude of Ambrosius Aurelianus," Sister Brigid said as she stood up. "In some ways, he seemed to be the last true Roman left on these shores, but now his legacy seems tarnished because he still fights to have the Roman Empire return to our island, but as you know, few agree with that. Lucanus, I assume he has not changed his tune, correct?"

"Quite right, Sister," Lucanus answered. "He still loves the old empire. As for his troops, he has some mounted scouts that are quite skillful. But the rest of his troops are dispirited."

Cerdic tried to keep his face emotionless as he squirmed in his seat. Discussing British politics made his skin itch. His own father had despised Ambrosius, a man he regarded as ruthless and misguided in his desire to bring Britannia back into the fold of the Roman Empire. He had said Ambrosius would sell his own family into slavery to return Rome to its former glory. But it turned out that Ambrosius was right to not trust Hengist and Aelle; that had cost him his father's life. But there was no bloody way Cerdic wanted the Roman Empire back in Britannia, and every Briton he had ever met felt the same. He started to listen again to Lucanus.

"Ambrosius's army was mainly calvary. He can no longer supply those fancy Roman horses for his troops, so they are now infantry, and they ain't happy about it. His army looks to be on its last legs."

Brother Petrus started to pace around the fire as he addressed the group in an animated tone.

"So, it sounds like some lands are just empty for the taking," Brother Petrus said.

Then Brother Petrus turned to Lucanus.

"This Camalet place, do you think that is true that we could settle there? There are no major kingdoms nearby if the Durotriges have all left. It sounds promising."

Lucanus paused a few moments before replying.

"I think so, Brother. And if Ambrosius can hold Caleva, that could function as a buffer between those lands and those mother-buggering Saxon arse-wipes like Hengist and his brother Horsa. Pardon me, Sister, my language was a little ripe there."

Cerdic smiled. *Lucanus,* he thought, *you must spend too much time out in the woods. She curses more than I do.* He looked upon Arturius and Caradoc in amusement as they, too, looked like they were trying not to laugh out loud. Then he saw Sister Brigid stand up with a frown on her face.

"That is alright, Lucanus," she said, her voice becoming louder. "I think calling them mother-buggering arse-wipes is being polite. If ever there were barbarian sounding names, it would be those two brothers, Horsa and Hengist. Sounds like they translate as Horse's ass and Horse's ass licker to me. Those two lead the East and Middle Saxons, don't they? Well, when Vortigern became the leader of the governing council of Roman Britain, who thought he would grovel for the spawn of that pagan Hengist. Rowena, I think that harlot is called. Forty years younger, hair as black as the ravens they worship, and rather busty, I hear."

She snorted as she started pacing about, wagging her finger at the men seated around her.

"It amazes me still what stupid things men do to gain the favor of seeing a pair of teenager's breasts. Lots of slave girls to rut with, but oh no, Vortimer grants the lands of loyal British tribes to be controlled by the former mercenaries, just so he can see what sexual feats pagan girls can do in bed. I did not think a man that age could do any sexual activity, except to dream about it. Men should think with the head that God put on their shoulders, not with the little one dangling between their legs."

Boy, that got her stirred up, he thought. It occurred to him that she may have been just reminding her husband what would happen if he strayed, not that that would ever happen. Petrus was crazy in love with her. As the peals of laughter calmed down, the grizzled old centurion Macro spoke up.

"By Jupiter, you don't talk like any nun I have ever heard, that's for sure!"

"It is talk that you block-headed men can understand and frankly need to hear. And speaking of language, Macro, with that comment about "by Jupiter," we do not need more references about the old Roman gods, either. We have enough trouble with Woden and Thunor and the other bloodthirsty Norse heresies that the British people are adopting wholesale to please their new masters."

Macro's face reddened as he looked sheepishly at his feet and muttered, "Sorry, I didn't mean to offend, but I have been a soldier too long to be in civilized company sometimes."

"You ought to hear him when he is training the men.," Cerdic chuckled.

"I have," she answered. "And there are times I wonder why lightning does not come down from heaven to strike him dead when he is on the practice field. But if the Christos can forgive him, then so can I. And he has taught me some interesting curses. But Macro, try to keep it on the training grounds, not here."

She winked at Macro, and his face turned crimson all over again.

Brother Petrus shrugged.

"Regardless, those who do not want to live under the Saxons are flooding into here, and we must deal with it. I am proposing we evacuate all the women and children, but keep a core of warriors, blacksmiths, and a few others here to keep the iron and weapons manufacturing still active."

"Some of those staying should be women as well," chimed in sister Bridget, "as they are adept at making arrows and plumbata. We do not want the menfolk here too lonely!"

The other leaders spoke up in turn to support the concept of relocation, but much of the discussion concerned the logistics of such a move. The conversations droned on into infinity. He buried his frustration by keeping his face impassive, but inwardly he was seething. *By Thunor's hammer,* he thought, *I despise meetings. Talk, talk, talk, and everyone has an opinion.* He didn't think this was a good way to run a community. They should pick someone to be the king and then trust them to make the decisions. The meeting went, but in time, a consensus was accepted by the group.

"We are in agreement then," Brother Petrus announced. "Let us evacuate the bulk of our women and children to Caleva, then we'll look closely at Camalet as a place to settle. Our people will never be slaves again. We must find a home where we all can live not only in safety but in freedom. We need to arrive in time to sew new crops, so we should leave soon."

"I'll be curious to see how our new tactics work in a real fight," Macro said.

Petrus frowned as he spoke.

"I would prefer to pray for a safe and successful journey. Deaconess Brigid, I give you the honors to lead us in prayer."

As they bowed their heads to pray to the Christos, Cerdic's entreaties were somewhere else, slipping his hand under his tunic to again touch the hidden amulet that symbolized the hammer of Thunor. *If a fight comes*, he prayed, *then All-father Woden, let me be viewed as a worthy warrior by my comrades.* He could not wait for his boys to try out the Roman gladii and their new tactics that they had practiced so diligently for these last few months. Most of all, he vowed to give his new sword a taste of blood so he could name her. He promised to sacrifice a goat as a gift to the gods this very night to make his dreams come true.

CHAPTER TWELVE

After the meeting broke up, the three boys walked out together to head for the woods when Caradoc was surprised to hear Brother Petrus call out for the three of them to stop. After they came to a halt, he and the others turned around and waited for him to join them.

"I want to talk to the three of you in private for a moment," he said as he trotted over. They formed a small circle away from the rest of the attendees who were still heading back to their homes.

"So, what did you all think of the meeting?" Petrus asked as he tried to catch his breath.

"I thought it was good," Arturius said. "At least we know what we are doing now."

"I agree, but it was a long one," Cerdic mumbled. "And did we actually pick the day we are leaving? I don't remember hearing that."

"I think you were asleep during that part," Caradoc muttered with a sly smile.

Petrus smiled as his eyes twinkled. He put his hands on the shoulders of Cerdic and Caradoc.

"I did not detain you all to give you any trouble. I just wanted to talk.

The three of you are nobles with families, and you may choose to go home if you must."

"Of course, we are going with you," Arturius sputtered. "Our oaths bind us all together."

"Well," Petrus said, "All of you have been gone from your homelands for a long time, you know."

That is a good point, Caradoc thought. *I do miss my family.* Caradoc had been in the Weald now almost a year, but in his mind, that did not matter. He had made a blood oath with his three friends to always be there for each other, and once they had all arrived at the Weald, they had agreed to help the people of the forest settle in their new lands. Caradoc could not understand what Petrus was thinking of asking such a question. In his mind, it was simple: he had made a promise, and he was committed to helping these people with their journey.

"First you, Cerdic," Petrus said as his hands dropped back to his side. "I talked to Lucanus and some others of the refugees about your homeland extensively, and I think the Catuvellauni will welcome you home with open arms."

"Well, that is good," his friend said. "But I am seeing this through to the end. I am not going anywhere."

"Don't you see," Petrus said in an earnest tone, "I am releasing you three from your oaths if you really need to go home. They may need you more than we do."

Cerdic smiled as Petrus looked at him searchingly.

"I am not going anywhere until I feel my promise to you here is fulfilled."

"Same for me," Caradoc muttered as he nodded.

"And me as well," Arturius said. "Brother, if we leave to go home now, I am afraid your defenses will suffer. We will not think about leaving you until your fortifications in your new home are ready, and the men are fully trained."

"So, why are you asking us this?" Cerdic asked with a puzzled look on his face.

Brother Petrus clasped his hands together as he sighed.

"I worry about you three being away from your families for so long. As nobles, you have families and opportunities at home. I feel guilty keeping you here."

"Brother, I know I am staying with you long term," Arturius said with a sigh, "and Cerdic and Caradoc will always be our friends, but this is our home for now, and we will make sure everyone is taken care of."

Cerdic looked troubled for a moment.

"I would like to know what is going on with the Catuvellauni and the West Saxons. When the trek is finished, I might head up there to see how things fare. With your permission, of course."

"Certainly, my boy," Petrus said as he nodded. "According to our scouts, there is a new head man over the West Saxons. We hear he's not kindly disposed towards the Catuvellauni, but at least they are not at war with each other, for now anyway. And the Catuvellauni have lost a lot of territory to the East and Middle Saxons. Otherwise, we really do not know what is going on up there, except the Catuvellauni need help."

"Well, at least the Catuvellauni may be happy I am coming home someday. But as I said, I am not leaving you until you all are ready."

Brother Petrus put his hand on Cerdic's shoulder.

"Cerdic, I want to let you know that once we are safe in Camalet, you should go talk to the Catuvellauni about coming to join us. That tribe has a similar problem, being pressured on three sides. Perhaps the best thing for them is to migrate to a safer place just like we are doing."

"You have a point. We'll see, and I thank you for that offer, Brother."

Caradoc could see tears well up in Brother Petrus's eyes as he looked at each of them, one after the other.

"I just wanted to be sure that you all are okay with working with us. I would not blame you if you chose to go home, but I also believe that we may not survive this trek without your assistance. I am profoundly grateful for your help. We all thank you. Now, get some rest. We have a lot to do before we begin our journey."

With that, the priest shook the hand of each of the three young men and walked back to the firepits towards Sister Brigid, who was waiting for him. He felt his own tears starting to form, which he wiped away with his sleeve. *I think Petrus is the most honorable man I have ever known, t*hought Caradoc. He had never met someone as selfless as him.

"That was a strange conversation," Cerdic remarked. "What was that all about?"

"As he said, I think he does feel guilty," Arturius said. "Unlike everyone else here, we do have homes we could go to."

"Well, he shouldn't," Caradoc snorted. "The people helped us when we were in need, and now we are going to help him."

"He is an amazing man," Arturius murmured. "I have never met anyone like him."

You are right, Caradoc thought, *I never have, either.* Petrus was socially awkward at times; he laughed when things weren't funny and was sad when he shouldn't be, and he was all elbows and knees. Caradoc had never met a more uncoordinated man. Brother Petrus was always late and always lost, and he would forget his own head if it was not attached to his shoulders. When the priest got in front of an audience, he didn't know when to shut up, and when he had too much to drink, he would try to sing in a voice that could drive sane people crazy.

His wife was foul mouthed and opinionated, but he never told her what to do, and his love for her knew no bounds. But Caradoc prayed that if he ever got married, he would love his wife as much as Petrus adored Brigid. He was a man who clearly loved the Christos, yet he did not punish those who did not believe as he did. Caradoc never saw him lose his temper. It seemed to him everyone in the Weald loved Petrus, and he and his two friends would be happy to die for him. Another tear welled up. *Since when have I wept like a child?* he thought.

"What I don't understand is why Brother Petrus didn't want anything to do with our military preparations," Cerdic said. "You would think he would be more interested in that."

"He is a man of peace," Arturius said as he rubbed his chin. "He doesn't want anything to do with killing, even in self-defense."

"He has no military duties if we get attacked," Cerdic groused. "What is his role if we get hit? He is all involved with everything else around here. Is he a coward?"

Caradoc raised his eyebrows.

"No, you are wrong," he growled. "I think it takes more courage to not fight sometimes. Petrus is adhering to his convictions. There is nothing wrong with that."

"Enough of this, boys," Arturius said as he threw up his hands. Let's go do what we set out to do. Caradoc, go get your filthy little rabbit, and Cerdic, get your lice-ridden, stinking goat. We have some sacrifices to do tonight, eh? I'll meet you at the Mithraeum when you are done."

With that, the three of them split up to prepare for their tasks for the rest of the evening. Caradoc headed to a grove of ancient oaks to sacrifice his rabbit to the Druid god Lugh, Son of the Spear, as he prayed for a safe journey. There he disemboweled the creature and read the signs that foretold the future when he inspected its organs, and Caradoc was pleased that the liver was clean and the animal healthy. It was a good sign for their coming trip. After his gift was given to his gods, Cerdic met him at that same grove with his baby goat. His friend beheaded the struggling creature and nailed the head to a tree as was the custom of the Norse, and he, too, made an offering.

Then the two of them picked their way through the dark forest trail to meet Arturius down by the stream where they knew there was a cave that had been used as a shrine to Mithras. The mystery cult was a favorite among the Roman legions for hundreds of years, banned in the empire when the

Chistian authorities had outlawed paganism, but there were still adherents who honored Mithras in Britannia. It was the one of the reasons Cato the slinger had been in Britannia, and Macro was secretly an adherent to the cult, even though he was ostensibly a Christian.

The three young men and a handful of others of their brotherhood feasted that night upon the recently slaughtered animals that Caradoc and Cerdic brought with them. Arturius had encouraged his friends to join the community of Mithras soon after the arrival in the Weald, and together with a handful of other followers, they stayed up all night to witness the dawn of that morning to celebrate Sol Invictus, the unconquered sun. The three of them had made their sacrifices and prayers together as Britons, as Romans, and as the Norse, yet they were all bound together as brothers. He felt ready to do his part in this great adventure that lay ahead.

CHAPTER THIRTEEN

It was the ravens that told him they were there. Arturius shivered as he looked at them, their hungry, black, soulless eyes gazing down upon them as the caravan slowly approached the woodlands. The scavengers were looking for a meal, and he was sure they looked upon the procession of Britons as the next course. Suddenly, the evil-looking creatures took flight from the edge of the woods, suggesting that someone, or something, could be moving through the forest. The hair on the back of his neck rose up. Something was wrong. *It had been too easy up to now,* he fretted. *The bastards must be coming for us now.* They had been on the road for several uneventful days, and he had a feeling their good luck was about to end.

"Don your armor," he called out to the slingers behind him. "Spread the word. Get ready for an attack."

As the order passed up and down the caravan, he glanced at one of the slingers under his command; it was Senna, putting on her armor with the rest. That was no accident; he wanted her under his wing so he could watch out for her. Then he looked ahead with trepidation at a few widely separated columns of smoke, and they were not the small tendrils that suggested a hearth fire. These thick black columns meant one thing: homesteads had been burned, the residents killed or enslaved, and the raiders responsible for those events were no doubt nearby.

Arturius slowly exhaled to relieve his tension. *I wish Macro was with us,* he thought. The old warrior claimed his arthritis had flared up, and he was too old to travel. Arturius was not sure about that. The old centurion would rather have fought as a simple soldier rather than bear the burden of command on his shoulders, and so he had refused any request for him to lead the men into battle. That responsibility had fallen on the shoulders of himself and his friends, and it meant it was his responsibility to win this fight if it came to one.

A wave of anxiety came flooding in like a waterfall. The town council had picked him to be in overall command of this expedition. That was a surprise; he could not believe the leadership of the Weald wanted him to do this. Arturius was incredibly nervous; he knew that either of his two friends could have also assumed this role, but the request for him to be the general in command was seconded by both Cerdic and Caradoc, and Petrus and Brigid had also insisted upon. *I am not qualified to do this,* he thought, *but who else is?*

This caravan that he was responsible for was carrying the people of the Weald fleeing to the west. Carts and wagons were filled with supplies and all their belongings, the small children and the elderly riding while the mother and older children trudged alongside on foot. All the able-bodied men were separated into three groups: the head of the column had Arturius and his slingers and plumbata men, the middle of the wagon train had Cerdic with the warriors destined for the shield wall, and Caradoc and his contingent of archers and plumbata throwers made up the rear guard.

Then it happened; a group of men, hundreds it seemed, burst out from the woods on the right, some three hundred paces away. His heart dropped a beat as a wave of panic filled his being. *There they are,* he thought, *Saxons!* Most wore the baggy trousers and clothing associated with the Norse, though a few looked like native British in their arms and attire. The approaching warriors carried flat round shields emblazoned with a variety of patterns, and a few sported long swords, but most had battle axes and spears. Many of the helmets and much of the armor they wore were a mix in the patterns of the Roman legions and their auxiliaries.

"Enemy approaching," he shouted out. "Circle the wagons. Infantry and missile troops, to your positions!"

There was nothing for him to do now but to go to his own assigned position. Arturius ran out to the spot where he wanted the left wing to assemble, stopping in the spot where his people were to join him. He looked around him, assessing the terrain, and though there were more woods a few hundred yards away on the opposite side of the road, everything else was wide open. It might be good calvary country, but there were no other places for footmen to hide. He felt confident he could fully concentrate his forces on the approaching infantry. He felt naked at first as he was all by himself on the left flank, but once he heard his plumbata throwers arrive, a wave of relief swept over him; he was no longer alone.

Brigid had sent out her people to attend to their duties, throwing out metal objects in the grass between them and their attackers, while Petrus herded the noncombatants to the center of the circle of wagons. Then Arturius heard a person run up to his left and stop. He glanced over at the first one to join him, and of course, it was Senna. She returned his glance and gave him a nervous smile. His heart ached. *She depends on me,* he thought. *If we lose this fight today, she will be killed. Or worse.* That could not happen. They must triumph on this day.

Arturius gave her a wink and a grin as he kept the rictus of a confident smile on his face. He tried not to show her and everyone else just how scared he really was. He had nothing to do but watch until all his people joined him, nervously glancing at their approaching foes. The raiders were closing fast. Arturius knew that some of these Saxons had undoubtedly learned their battle skills in Roman auxiliary units, fighting for the empire on the continent. Now they were fighting against the Romano-British who were once part of that empire before Rome had abandoned them. He shook his head at the irony of it; the Roman way of war was being used against those who were trying to keep the legacy of Rome alive.

Their own heavy infantry was fully formed now, ready for the fight to come. A feeling of gratitude filled him. *Well done, Cerdic,* he thought. *Your boys were ready even before my own.* These men in the infantry cadre now stood in the shield wall in front of the caravan like a wall of wood and steel, their shields locked together. They had merged into a hollow oval as the approaching barbarians were clearly more numerous than the defenders. He remembered their first day on the practice fields, how pathetic they appeared. Now they looked like soldiers.

Even though their armor and helmets looked inferior to that of the approaching warband, the shields of their footmen looked more uniform, resembling the legionary shields of old, curved and rectangular in shape. Their shields were taller and wider than the Saxon shields, and they looked too new in fact; it marked these men for what they were. Just like their shields, these men were new to battle, untried and untested. Arturius felt a wave of doubt starting to build up again. The style of combat the boys had been working on was hundreds of years old. Would the old legionary tactics still work?

He fought the feeling of panic gnawing at the pit of his stomach. Seeing the Saxons approach with murder in their eyes triggered his every instinct to run for his life, but his mind knew they had to stay and fight. To flee would be a certain death, as it was when the defensive formations broke down that the killing really began in a battle. *Do not show fear,* he thought. *My people are looking to me for courage.* He glanced left and right and was pleased that all his missile troops were with him now, and Brigid's people had finished their job. They were ready.

"Wait until I give the signal," he shouted. "This is just like we have practiced.

I almost feel sorry for those bastards. Too bad there are not more of them."

He heard some snickering laughter, which helped break the tension he knew they all felt. On came the raiders, less than fifty paces away now as they had formed up into a double battle line. At first the approaching warriors had been silent, but now the Saxons' battle cry could be heard as they came closer, a loud, low- pitched "Arrghh, Arrghh!" Called the Barratus, it was the Germanic war-cry that had assaulted the ears of Roman soldiers since the time of Tacitus, sounding like ocean waves striking the rocky shores of his home, as the Saxon cry was deeply pitched and came in waves.

It was an eerie sound, and if this battle-cry was supposed to instill fear in their opponents, it was working well. Arturius felt the gnawing fear in the pit of his stomach spread into his scrotum, and his bollocks ached now more than ever. Time seemed to slow down; colors were sharper. His senses felt alive, while at the same time, he could feel his mouth go dry and his heart flutter like a captive bird. Arturius tried to ignore the sounds of the Saxon hoard as he waited for the right moment. Finally, he could see the whites of their eyes. *Loose*, he thought. But no one moved. Then he realized that in his state of panic he had failed to give the command.

He croaked out, "Loose!"

Whirrrrrrr, whirrrrrrr, whirrrrrrr.

The sound was pitifully weak, but his people must have heard him as his missile troops sprang into action. A wave of embarrassment swept over him; he thought his voice had sounded like a scared teenager who had just reached puberty. His people had released their first volley of pellets and plumbata, while he could see arrows and plumbata coming from Caradoc's side as well streaking towards the approaching barbarians. *Shite*, he thought, *that volley did not work very well. These fellows know how to use their shields.* Only a couple of the Saxons had been hit, none too seriously. Oddly, his feeling of panic slowly faded away, as he looked at the enemy with a more objective eye as if he was on a practice field like the dozens of times before.

"Loose," he bellowed out, sounding more like a real commander this time.

Whirrrrrrr, whirrrrrrr, whirrrrrrr.

He fired his own pellet in tandem with the rest, and again both sling shots and plumbata arched towards the enemy. The feeling of his muscles working in a well-practiced motion calmed him even further. The hail of plumbata and lead pellets and arrows converged just before the lines hit. A few more of their enemies went down, then seconds later the Saxons plowed into the British line. It was a sound he had never heard before, and he knew it was something he would never forget.

The two shield walls hitting together erupted into a cacophony of crashes, thuds, thumps, and screams. It sounded like multiple pieces of wood being chopped all at once, mixed with the higher pitched clanging of metal on metal. It was the clatter of spears against swords, and the thunk of battle axes striking the defender's wall. It was the din of men grunting and yelling and dying. It was the noise of men screaming in pain followed by a wet thump of a death blow. It was the sound of chaos, the sound of death, and the sound of victory or defeat. For Arturius, it was a sound that could wake him up in the middle of a nightmare for the rest of his life.

Without thinking, Arturius started to yell back, but in a high-pitched "Yahee, Yip, Yip, Yip." He wasn't sure where it had come from, somewhere deep within him. It gave him courage, sounding like something not from this world, but from the ghosts that roamed the desolate moors at night. All around him others joined in the battle cry, and soon every Briton seemed to have joined in. It was a spontaneous outpouring of fear and hate and aggression, like the cry of the banshees their mothers had told them about to scare them when they were small children, and now that sound had come to life.

"Loose," he cried out.

Whirrrrrrr, whirrrrrrr, whirrrrrrr.

A hail of lead pellets, arrows, and weighted darts flew at the flanks of the enemy line. He shook his head in aggravation once more as only a few had been hit. The Saxons in their center ignored the missile troops as they hacked and parried and punched at the British line, but Arturius could tell the missile troops still had an effect. Instead of enveloping the British line, the ends of the Saxon shield wall were bent back to protect themselves. It annoyed him that not many of the enemy warriors were falling, but at least their missiles seemed to be preventing them from overwhelming Cerdic's men. That was the goal, but he knew they had to do better. *Let's see if we can get behind them a little bit more,* he thought.

He bellowed out, "Move forward ten paces!"

As soon as they arrived at the new spot, Arturius yelled out his command again.

"Loose!"

Whirrrrrr, whirrrrrr, whirrrrrr.

A few more of the Saxons were hit and fell to the ground in agony. The deafening sound of battle continued.

"Loose!"

Whirrrrrr, whirrrrrr, whirrrrrr.

More Saxons were hit. Now some of their enemies in their rear line were glancing back at them with worried looks. *That got your attention,* he thought. Arturius looked on with horrid fascination at the infantry melee before him as the British used their shields as weapons by punching them forward while the Saxons did the same. Norse axes and swords slashed and hacked while British gladii thrust in and out. A wave of gratitude swept over him as their men appeared to be holding their own, but if his own missile troops did not do more damage, then the bravery of the men in the line of battle might be for naught. He cupped his hands together like a megaphone so his orders could be heard.

"Plumbata, go with the high and low combination shots. Slingers, go low when they bring their shields up!"

He looked about and saw they were ready. This time he belted it out with gusto.

"Loose!"

Whirrrrrr, whirrrrrr, whirrrrrr.

The volley of plumbata went high, and a few seconds later, he belted out the order for the second volley as the first wave of plumbata started its descent towards the heads of their foes. The Saxons raised their shields in anticipation of the missiles coming down.

"Loose!"

Whirrrrrr, whirrrrrr, whirrrrrr.

Now the plumbata were coming in two waves, as the second volley whirled in to strike their foes below the upraised shields of the Saxon line. Both groups of missiles struck as one, with Saxons falling as their screams of pain melded into the sound of the battle. *Hold on Cerdic,* he thought, *hold on. This is going to work.* Women scurried about as they hauled baskets of more plumbata to allow his people to reload. Again, they launched the high and low combined volley, and more of their opponents fell. He could see there were gaps in the rear line of the enemy now. It was time to pick a target rather than a mass volley.

"Fire at will," he commanded.

For his target, Arturius had focused his attention on a long-haired warrior standing just behind the main shield wall line. He wore an expensive-looking chainmail shirt, and had several silver torcs on his arms, symbols of his prowess as a warrior, perhaps a leader of some kind. His yellow hair was tied into pigtails that trailed on either side of his helm. His beard was forked, with little rings that kept the beard on either side of his breastplate. He had a long, wicked- looking scar that cut diagonally across his cheek on this right side, a souvenir from some previous fight.

Arturius looked at his intended victim with a practiced eye. His fear had completely melted away now, as only the mechanics of being a slinger occupied his mind. *Where should I strike him,* he wondered. Arturius was not sure; he had never considered where to hit an armored warrior from the side. Then the answer came: the head. A smaller target, harder to hit, but it would stun him and perhaps allow one of their own shield wall warriors to strike while his victim was stupefied. He placed the lead projectile in the sling pouch and visualized his target.

Whirrrrrrr.

As the projectile flew the Saxon warlord moved just as the bullet whizzed just behind him. *Missed,* he thought with disappointment. The projectile flew past his target's head and struck another warrior, a man beside him who was tall and thin with stringy black hair. He was young, with just a wisp of a beard, and his armor looked to be of poor quality. He yelped as he dropped his upraised axe, and as he turned towards his injured shoulder, an opening on his shield side appeared and a sword flicked out that penetrated his chest. The lanky Saxon fell back, a shocked look on his face.

The disappointment Arturius felt subsided as he realized that the man who was the unintentional target would be out of the fight now. Old Cato would have no doubt have been annoyed he had missed the chieftain, but at least he hit someone. He smiled for a moment, as the image of the crusty old man popped into his mind. Shaking his head, he focused on the battle once more as the enemy leader shoved a man into the gap created by the warrior who had fallen.

The pig-tailed Saxon shot him a scowling glance, and then he must have decided to do something about Arturius's missile troops that were harassing them. The chieftain gathered a half dozen warriors carrying spears from their back line, and they hefted their shields up as one and started to charge directly at Arturius and his lightly- armed slingers. As he watched the Saxons approach, Arturius felt his gut clinch, as he knew if the Saxons got to them, they could be slaughtered. He quickly loaded another projectile into his sling, and he sent it towards the approaching warriors with lethal promise.

Whirrrrrrr.

Got him, he thought. The streaking projectile struck the leader flush in the face. He stood there, stunned for a moment, then the Saxon chieftain tottered and fell senseless to the ground. At almost the same time, one of the other charging warriors bellowed out in pain, a short, stocky man with a flaming red beard. He had suddenly stopped running, grabbing his foot, impaled by something hidden in the grass. His cry of pain then turned into a gurgle as several plumbata flew into his chest. Now he lay motionless on the ground as two more of the Saxons had also run over something that had impaled their feet.

Once the two enemy warriors fell, the rest stopped their advance, looking towards the ground to see what was hidden in the grass. No longer moving, the hapless warriors had made themselves a stationary target that the plumbata throwers would have little difficulty missing. The Saxons looked panicked as they glanced left and right, and then at each other. Suddenly, the remaining Saxons all turned and fled back to the woods from whence they came, abandoning their comrades in the shield wall behind him.

The plumbata throwers cheered at the sight. The objects that stopped the charging Saxons were called caltrops, concealed spikes that the women and children had sewn in the field just before the battle had started. Each was a constructed like two triangles. Three prongs stabilized it on the ground while one of the four iron spikes was always pointed upward, able to penetrate the foot of a man or horse and incapacitate them. Thrown into the tall grass as the shield wall deployed, these invisible objects had protected the flanks of the missile troops from attack.

That stopped them, Arturius thought with glee, *the caltrops really did work.* He and his plumbata throwers were standing just outside the area where the anti-personnel devices were deployed like a peninsula of safety, extending out from the wagon line into a sea of crippling metal spikes, protecting them while still giving them a clear path back to the wagons. More projectiles flew into Saxons who remained, and it looked to him like their enemies were getting rattled. The tide was turning in their favor. *These bastards are going to break soon,* he thought.

Then he heard one of the plumbata men call out in a panic-stricken tone, "Look! There are some cavalrymen coming towards us!"

He abruptly turned to look back, startled to see mounted troops approaching them from the distant woods from the other side of the road. The riders looked like they were going to pass by the front of the circled wagons, and they were headed straight for them. Up to now, Arturius had been concentrating on the mechanics of slinging, but now the icy grip of fear washed over him again. He thought he might faint. Calvary troops loved to catch missile troops out in the open. *We are about to get overrun,* he thought.

The horsemen were on the trot and moving quickly, and even if they fled now, he did not think they had enough time to get to safety behind the wagons. *Where did they get calvary from?* he thought. *Fortuna, you fickle witch, I have failed.* Arturius glanced at Senna. *I have let her and everyone else down,* he thought. He tried to keep his face impassive, but he knew that he was not hiding his feelings well at this moment.

"Back to the wagons," he bellowed.

Arturius could barely think as he wallowed in sadness and self-recrimination. He was the overall commander, and this debacle was all his fault. He had failed to anticipate the calvary. Perhaps hey should have stayed in the protection of the wagons, encircled by caltrops. Fighting in the open should have allowed them to win decisively, but not now. He glanced to his left, and it was clear Senna was the farthest from the wagons, and she had still not moved yet. *I am so sorry,* he thought. He sprinted towards her to drag her back to the wagons, not thinking of himself; he just wanted to protect her.

We have lost the battle, he thought, *but maybe I can save her.*

CHAPTER
FOURTEEN

Sister Brigid trudged along in the caravan, wondering what in the name of the Christos she was doing there. She was hot and tired, her muscles groaning in places that she did not know she had. *Bloody hell,* she thought, *I am not getting any younger.* She really did not like traveling. Boats made her seasick, horses made her nervous she might fall off, and riding in a wagon gave her migraines from the jostling. Traveling with a bunch of people like this stirred up the dust and made her wheeze. Taking a leisurely stroll about the gentle hills was one of her pleasures, but today's trip was anything but fun.

This trek was putting herself and everyone she loved at risk to be killed. She longed to be in the safety of the Weald, but that was not where they were today, as they had to leave to avoid being overrun by the Saxons. Every moment on the road bore the risk of disaster from brigands and thieves, and Arturius had just put the caravan on the alert. He had seen birds taking flight, and that meant that something had spooked them. The men had put on their armor with anxious eyes as their women and children displayed with worried faces.

She was one of the first to see the brigands emerge from the tree line. *Bugger me,* she thought. *They are coming to kill us all!* Her heart sank into despair as fear gripped her soul. At first her feelings of panic made her stand there motionless in horror, but after a few seconds, she willed herself into action. Brigid had learned the hard way how to control her fears and maintain her ability to think in times like these. From the back of her mind, the voice in her head started its calm refrain. *Breathe,* she thought. *Look around. Pay attention.* This would not be the first time to be in the middle of a crisis, and to survive this, she knew that she needed to act as a leader and not give in to panic.

"Circle the wagons! Circle the wagons!" she cried out.

She directed the people designated to distribute the caltrops as they gathered the baskets that contained the little four-pointed spikes. Fortunately, this was something they had all practiced, and the distribution of those little terrors was going surprisingly well.

She yelled, "Left flank people, go to your positions here! Right flank team, set up over there!"

Within seconds a line was formed on each side. She could tell each team was missing some members, but no matter, she believed they now had enough to do the job.

"Now, ladies, start sowing the caltrops. Left flank, put them here! Right flank, put them there!"

The two lines moved forward. She was pleased. The women were doing their jobs well. Then she looked for the leader of the plumbata throwers of the caravan, and Brigid was disappointed to see her just standing there like a statue, her mouth opening and closing in wordless terror. A wave of disgust filled her. *That silly cow is frozen in fear,* she angrily thought. Brigid ran to the motionless figure and grabbed her shoulder to swing her around.

"Look at me," Brigid said, her face just inches from the woman's nose.

The woman's eyes darted around as if she was unable to see her, and then Brigid slapped her once with her open hand. The woman's eyes opened wide with surprise, but the blow seemed to shake her out of her lethargy as her gaze settled to look back at Brigid's blazing eyes.

"You are the leader of this group, now stop being a feckin' eejit and start acting like one! Gather up your people and move them by the wagon closest to the enemy to wait for further orders. Do you understand?"

The woman stared at her a moment with panic-stricken eyes, but after a few seconds she nodded.

"Answer me with words," Brigid said slowly and deliberately. "Now be so kind as to repeat what I said."

"Yes, S-Sister," she stuttered. I-I Gather my people over there beside the wagons."

Brigid pointed her finger to the spot where she wanted her section leader to go.

"You are going to go right there," she hissed. "Now get control of yourself, dearie."

Then Brigid's features softened as looked searchingly into the woman eyes.

"You can do this. Now bloody well get to it!"

Brigid stomped off to show people carrying the caltrops where to deposit their lethal little presents, and she was gratified the woman she had just slapped was doing her job now. It did not take long to sew the caltrops, and she directed her workers to return to the wagons. Brigid looked at the men forming up between them and the attackers and was pleased to see the infantry and the missile troops were in position. Then she glanced back at the approaching enemy, she felt dismayed; they were a fearsome looking group. *This had better work,* she thought.

Her mind leapt back to the memories of that terrible night when a rival clan attacked her family's home when she was young, and she still had nightmares about it. The pain and humiliation of the physical abuse she had suffered still haunted her. *Those Saxon bastards will never take me alive;* she ruminated. *By the Christos, I will take my own life first.* She fingered the hidden blade she had secreted away in her dress, a small black knife she called by its Hibernian name, a Sgian-Duhb. She swore she would put that blade in the eye of any of those gobshites who dared to touch her.

Brigid looked behind her and saw that Petrus had gathered some of the old and very young to a location away from the fighting to lead them in prayer to the Christos to deliver them from evil. Her husband was such a gentle person, which was why she loved him so. *But right now*, she thought, *we do not need men like Petrus. We need our big, hairy-chested men to kill those mother-swiving buggers.* But she knew what Petrus was doing was also important; she felt both prayers and sharp swords were needed to work their magic on this day. Then her thoughts were interrupted by the woman in charge of distributing the caltrops.

"Sister, some of the baskets of caltrops were packed in the wrong place, and we just now found them. We did not get them all out earlier. Should we try to go back out and___"

I should have checked to make sure they had them all out, she thought. But she knew that she could not do everything herself, that she had to delegate responsibility, and sometimes chaos triumphed. Still, she believed that they had enough put out in the fields to do the job. Sister Brigid shook her head as she touched the woman on the arm.

"No, that is okay. We are out of time. But just in case, keep the caltrops you found nearby, and have your people stay near them."

Brigid pointed to the spot where she wanted them to assemble.

"We need to be ready for anything," she said.

Brigid watched the drama of the battle unfold before her. The lines of shields crashed together. The noise of the chilling Saxon battle cry, the low moaning of the Barratus, grew louder and louder. Then she heard something she had never heard before, a series of high-pitched yips and howls heard over the Barratus, and these keening sounds made her hair stand on end. *Who the bloody hell started that up,* she wondered. It was their own Britons who were bellowing out that banshee cry. It sounded so eerie.

She watched on in fascination as the fight continued, neither side yielding. Minutes seemed like hours as the horror of the carnage before her very eyes continued. She could see that Cerdic and his men were holding, although clearly outnumbered, and the missile troops on either side were still throwing in volley after volley. She was gratified to see Arturius's people had pressured the attackers to make it an even fight, but then she heard a panicked scream behind her.

"Riders are coming!"

She turned her head, and she was dismayed to see a flicker of movement from the tree line on the other side of the road. Moments later she could tell it was a column of cavalrymen that she was seeing in the distance. *Are they enemies or friends,* she thought as her heart raced. *But we have no friends here.* Then she was able to make out the image on the banner the cavalrymen were carrying. It was a raven, a Saxon sigil, so these bastards were not British. *Those are Saxons, and they are headed right for us,* she thought.

"*Sweet Mother, Maria and Joesph,*" she muttered to herself, "*we are arse-buggered for sure.*"

She willed herself to think and not run away in panic. Then she remembered the caltrops they had not used yet. Should the remaining caltrops be put between the circle of wagons and the incoming attackers? She looked at the horsemen more closely. She could not be sure, but they looked like they were heading towards the mass of struggling warriors. That meant they would be passing along the side of them. Brigid hoped their intention was to help their comrades in the infantry fight, and that they would not attack the camp until they had defeated their soldiers first. *That is what I would do if I were leading those horsemen,* she thought. She made her decision without hesitation.

"Caltrops people," she bellowed, "Throw the remaining caltrops to this side of the wagons, between the riders and the battle over there, not in front of us. I will show you where. We want these fecking eejit horsemen to ride over them."

Brigid started shoving women out to the area where she wanted the caltrops to be placed, and then she glanced back. The horsemen were coming at a slow trot, trying not to tire their horses by charging too early. As more caltrops were being sewed, she called back behind her.

"Plumbata throwers, be ready!" she shouted. "The rest of you, take cover!"

Brigid walked up to the woman she had just slapped and muttered in her ear.

"I am sorry I had to hit you earlier, I was acting like a feckin' geebag. Now I want you to command your people to fire when I tell you to. Do you understand?"

The woman gave her a reassuring look.

"Yes sister, I am better now. Thank you for your patience. But be careful about your language there, there are children present."

"That is about the last buggering thing we need to worry about right now, dearie."

She looked behind her and was grateful to see the women and children were finished flinging their caltrops about. The horsemen had picked up their pace, the thunder of hooves audible now as they held the same line of approach. She directed those who were not plumbata throwers to grab spears and stick them out between the gaps of the wagons to make it more of a barrier for a calvary charge. She felt her fear was subsiding, because at least now they were doing something. *We got lucky there,* she thought. It had been nice to have those caltrops handy, and she vowed to keep things in reserve on purpose next time.

She bellowed, "Okay, caltrops people, get your flaming arses back in here now!"

The women and children came flooding back. She felt a wave of relief, the caltrops were out, and her people were all safe in the circle of wagons. With nothing to do now, the thoughts of her capture when she was a little girl flooded back into her mind as she started to tremble in terror, feeling almost paralyzed. *Get control of yourself,* she thought. *If I lose my shite, then so will everyone else.* She closed her eyes for a moment to slow her breathing down, and then she felt calmer. She opened her eyes again. The thundering was louder now; the advancing calvary was almost here.

She muttered a prayer, "Mother Maria, protect us!"

Brigid glanced over to her right and saw the skirmishers from Arturius's group were scrambling back to the wagons. It was a race, and the men on foot were going to be on the losing end if the caltrops did not work. If the horsemen caught those people in the open, it would be a slaughter. She looked back at the riders, and they had picked up their pace even more, almost at a gallop now. Closer and closer they came, the clods of dirt spraying from the flashing hoofs as the calvary passed in front of her.

Suddenly a horse reared up, followed by another, and then another. The charge was stopped. Horses snorted as they milled about, the riders frantically trying to rein in the panic-stricken mounts. Once the entire column had ground to a halt, Wide-eyed beasts were whinnying in pain, their riders unable to control them. Not all the horses were injured, but the remaining riders in the rear pulled up their mounts to a halt their own horses from getting crippled in the field of invisible caltrops. The moving targets for the plumbata throwers were no longer moving.

"Now!" Brigid harshly whispered to the woman she had previously slapped.

"Fire," the leader of the plumbata throwers bellowed.

The weighted darts flew from the line of wagons like a hailstorm towards the floundering riders. Horses screamed and men grunted as the plumbata found their marks.

"Pour it into those scallywags," Brigid shouted out in glee.

Brigid looked on with grateful eyes to see that stopping the riders had allowed Arturius and his people to get to the wagons safely. His men raced through the circle of wagons to join the women and children's barrage as they threw their own projectiles at their foes. Skirmishers continued to swarm around her as they leaped over the barriers to attack the struggling cavalrymen. She wondered what would have happened if that batch of caltrops had not been left behind. *It was an accident that saved us*, she marveled. *Is the margin between victory and defeat really that narrow?*

Then the missile troops arrived. She flinched in horror as the recently arrived Britons started to finish off the outnumbered and dismounted riders. The Britons slowly picked their way through the field, taking care not to be injured by the same spiked gifts they had left for their foes. She grimaced at the horror of seeing throats cut and heads bashed in. The horsemen were being shown no mercy. Horses were snorting in fear as the riders were pulled out of their saddles to be bludgeoned by the crowd of angry Britons. The cavalrymen whose horses were not injured started to flee, but Brigid noticed two riders left behind were wearing particularly fine armor. They looked like they were important people.

She called out to a group of British soldiers, "Hey boys, those two wankers with the fancy helmets, try to capture them alive."

Brigid felt a flood of relief and joy fill her body as she watched the fleeing enemy horsemen recede in the distance, and she leaned against a wagon as she felt the strength from her legs flood away. She started to tremble, not from fear, but from the bloodlust still coursing through her. *What a feeling*, she marveled. She muttered a prayer of thanks to the Christos and to his sainted mother Maria for sparing them from the ravages of the Northmen. *Shouldn't I feel more guilty?* she thought. *I just assisted in the killing of fellow human beings.* But she knew those Saxons were going to kill them or worse; all she felt now was a happy glow.

She remembered the Old Testament was full of blood and gore and the smiting of foes, so she hoped the Christos would forgive her. Though she felt little remorse for the fate of the Saxons, what tugged at her heartstrings was something she had not anticipated. It was the injured horses she pitied now with their heart rendering cries. Some of the poor beasts had been severely wounded by the plumbata and slingstones, and those unfortunate creatures needed to be put out of their misery. Tears filled her eyes. *These are most innocent of God's creatures,* she thought, *just doing their jobs as they were directed to do. No animal deserves to be treated this way.*

Arturius grabbed the shoulder of one of his men and shouting about something as he pointed back to where they had just come from. Then it dawned on her that she could still hear combat going on. In all the excitement she had completely forgotten about Cerdic and the battle he was still fighting. She gazed towards the infantry fight to her right with trepidation. *Oh, Mother Maria,* she thought, *that does not look good over there.* Their men were severely outnumbered, as all she could see were Saxons as their cheering echoed across the field. A chill ran down her spine. *Is that the end of our boys?* she fretted. *If our infantry is gone, we are still in the shite.*

"Brigid, you are a feckin' eejit," she muttered to herself.

What the bloody hell do we do now? she thought.

CHAPTER FIFTEEN

"Yahee, Yip, Yip, Yip!

He was puzzled. *Bugger me,* Cerdic thought. *I've never heard that before.* The new war cry was coming from his boys on the flanks. At first it was just the plumbata men, but now his own men on either side of him had commenced to yell this eerie battle cry, and after a few moments he decided to join them. Up to now, all he had heard was the low-pitched rumble of the Saxons, some twenty paces away and moving fast. Their Saxon eyes were visible, narrowed and angry as they approached at a rapid walk, spears out and shields at the ready. Before it was the barratus, and now that was drowned out as all he could hear was the high-pitched yipping of the British.

Then the enemy line struck the shield wall. He felt like he was the clapper in some giant bell, the noise all around him, a cacophony of crashes, thuds, thumps, and screams filling the air that was added to the war cries of both sides. Their opponents slashed and hacked while he and his men flicked their blades out with sharp thrusts as they ducked behind their shields. Men grunted and cursed and screamed, and the clatter of weapons striking shields provided a sharp contrast to the deeper thumps of shields pounding against other shields. An occasional clang of metal striking metal rang out as unearthly yipping continued to assault his ears.

This was Cerdic's first real battle, and the sounds and the confusion were almost overwhelming. It was chaos, but a chaos that was controlled. Each man in the battleline was involved in their own personal duel with the foe in front of him. As he thrust and shuffled and moved his shield to deflect the blows coming at him, Cerdic was becoming quickly exhausted. The effort required to fight in the shield wall was like chopping wood one-handed while dancing back and forth and moving a heavy shield about with his other arm. It took a lot of energy, and the wood he was cutting was striking back, trying to kill him.

His immediate opponent was a stocky black-haired fellow with a pockmarked face. His appearance was further marred by a misshapen nose and a few missing teeth that were visible as his opponent snarled at him. He wore a leather helmet with an iron rim, and his leather jerkin was protected by metal scales sewn in. He was short and he had a powerful build, and he was wielding a short battle axe and a battered shield. *He does not look to be the crème of the crop to me,* he thought. *I can take that bastard.*

After a few minutes it seemed the contest had been going on forever as neither man could find an advantage, and that seemed to be true up and down the line. His foe was amazingly quick, the tight quarters of the shield wall preventing either man from gaining the upper hand. His disdain for his opponent based on his appearance had evaporated; this warrior clearly knew his business. Cerdic concentrated on keeping his own shield at the proper angle to prevent his attacker's axe from splitting it in two, counter thrusting with his newly minted sword when he had the chance. They exchanged blows back and forth with lethal promise, but no blood had yet been spilled. *By Woden's one eye,* he thought, *this bastard is bloody good.*

What had been an equal fight turned unequal in a hurry. Cerdic's heart almost stopped when the stocky axe man lodged the lower edge of his axe over the top of his shield and pulled it down. It had only taken an instant, but now he was exposed, his shield low enough for his lanky partner behind him to raise his long-handled battle axe high, ready for the killing blow that was about to cleave his head in two. That tall warrior was staring at him in triumph, his axe poised, his crooked yellow teeth visible behind a wispy beard, grinning at him in triumph.

Then, by the grace of the gods, his grimace changed into one of pain as he dropped his axe and whirled to his right. Cerdic thought he saw a slinger's pellet bounce off, and with that unexpected opening, he quickly punched his blade into his enemy's exposed side. He pulled his blade back as the injured warrior fell back from the line of battle. The stocky one was still there, but after he punched his shield forward to knock his opponent back, Cerdic was able to free his shield from the axe with his sword blade. *That was close,* he thought. Cerdic knew he had been lucky. He had almost died in that moment.

His comrade to his right glanced at him with a maniacal grin, and Cerdic nodded. Then he saw a glint of steel in his side vision. From out of nowhere, another long-handled battle axe crashed down on the top of his comrade's shield, splitting it into. The axe head buried itself into his companion's forearm. Splinters flew, followed by a spray of blood. His comrade belted out an ear-splitting howl that was abruptly silenced by a broad-headed spear darting in, impaling his comrade's mouth as the unearthly scream abruptly changed into an unintelligible gurgle, blood bubbling out of his friend's ruined mouth.

The stricken warrior dropped his sword and grabbed the shaft of the spear, but the Saxon wielding it twisted it out, pulled back only a few inches before it was thrust forward into his friend's face again. A hostile wetness suddenly covered the right side of his face as hot blood and gore sprayed out, the contents of his comrade's skull emptying onto him. Cerdic smelled the coppery tang of blood mixed with the odor of shite and piss as the dying man's bowels released. His eye stung and he gagged from the gore that covered his mouth, and his heart ached as now there was a gap in the line. Almost immediately his companion was pulled back as another shield man took his place. There was no time to mourn now; there was still a battle to be won.

I wonder if we have enough reserves left, he thought. Cerdic lost track of time as he pushed and thrust and parried and twisted his shield from side to side to counter the blows coming at him. Finally, he heard a whistle blowing over the din, the signal for the front line to be exchanged with the first, and in a flash one of the reserves took his place. Finally, he was able to wipe the slime from his lips as he was behind the line now, struggling to catch his breath. It seemed only a few moments had passed before it was time for him to go in again. As a section leader, it was his turn to give the signal, so he blew the whistle. Back in the fray he went.

Cerdic fought and pushed and thrust and shoved until he thought he would die of exhaustion as the battle din continued to seem never ending, yet it had only been a few minutes. This time his opponent was a different warrior than before, as the Saxons were alternating their battle lines just as his own men were. Cerdic thrust and parried and deflected more blows, fighting his fatigue until he heard the whistle again. A reserve took his place, his rest period seeming all too brief before he blew his own whistle again, and back to the battleline he went again.

His exhaustion warred with the pride he felt for his men; they were holding fast. He was so proud of them, going toe-to-toe with the best warriors the Saxons possessed and not giving an inch. Then out of the corner of his eye he saw something disturbing; the plumbata men were running away, abandoning them. The Saxons swarmed about to surround the entire formation. With no missile troops to harass them, the Saxons were attacking his men from all sides now. They were surrounded.

Only a handful were left in the center of their formation who were not wounded or dead. They had no other reserves. Cerdic knew there would be no periods of rest now. If even only one man fell, the line could break. They only had minutes left before they would all die unless something changed. *I must do something,* he thought. An idea popped into his head. He gave a mighty shove with his shield to push the Saxon foe he was facing back for just a moment, then he grabbed one of those few remaining warriors in reserve and shoved him into his spot that he had just vacated. He wiped the sweat out of his eyes as he looked around, then he circled around his fighters as he told each man what he wanted them to do.

Then Cerdic called out, "Britons, on my count. One!"

Everyone took a step back, crowded more together now.

"Two!"

They stepped back again, the formation more packed than before.

"Three!"

As his men retreated one more step, a few men he had designated earlier pulled away from the line to act as reserves in the center. The formation was a smaller oval than it was before, and with the men he had called upon having gone into the center, and now the battle line had proper spacing once more. He went around the formation and singled out a few more men to move into the center to expand the pool of reserves and again his voice boomed out, commanding another controlled retreat.

"Again, on my count. One!"

They all shuffled back one step.

"Two!"

Again, they took a step, the line so packed they could barely move.

"Three!"

Several more men dropped back from the line into the ranks of the reserves as the battle line was again properly spaced. His warriors were almost back-to-back now, but there was still a little room for his newly formed reserves to help when he needed. Cerdic was not an experienced military commander, but he knew that a disciplined retreat amid a fight like this was one of the most difficult maneuvers that any soldiers could face. He was bursting with pride. And Cerdic was pissed. *Where are the poxy missile troops?* he thought.

He could not understand why Arturius and Caradoc had left his men high and dry. He could not see much of the circle of wagons through both the enemy and his own fighters that bobbed and weaved between him and the caravan, but he could not see the missile troops anywhere. The fighting continued, and still the line held as he was picking which of his men needed to be relieved now, but he was running low on what reserves he had scraped together, worried about how long they could last.

His men were still holding up under strain, when he heard something different, the new British war cry had started again, this time coming from the direction of the wagons, growing louder by the second. Almost as one, the Saxons backed away from their attacks on the defensive circle that his men had maintained. His enemies were giving each other worried glances as they pointed behind them, muttering in anger. Then the Saxons began to run, melting away from him and his men as their foes scurried back to the woods. Close behind them was a surging horde of angry people. It looked like it was practically everyone from the caravan. *It is about buggering time*, he fumed.

It was Arturius's and Caradoc's men, and joining these warriors were women with staves, old men with clubs, children with knives, and even the dogs were coming to their rescue. Everyone was carrying something potentially lethal, even if it was just a cooking pot, and the one out in front of the mob was none other than a red-faced Sister Brigid carrying a club in one hand and a plumbata in the other. Right beside her was a panting Arturius and a sweaty Caradoc. The mob stopped when they reached the soldiers under Cerdic's command, cheering and yelling, ecstatic with joy. A wave of relief washed over him. *By Thunor's mighty phallus, we beat them*, he thought.

Cerdic was exhausted, and he knew his men had to be as well. The pursuit of the retreating Saxons was not going to be possible, though the slingers and archers felled a couple more of them before the Saxons had completely disappeared into the forest. The crowd of people rushed around Cerdic and his men to congratulate his soldiers, but a few of the women gave out cries of grief upon finding their menfolk injured or even dead. His legs felt weak, and he started to tremble. He dropped to one knee and pulled out the silver hammer of Thunor beneath his tunic, thanking both Woden and Thunor for their victory. When he finally found the strength to stand, he slowly ambled over to Brigid and Arturius and Petrus.

"By Thunor's bollocks, where were you?" he groused. "I thought you left us to die!"

"Not hardly," Arturius snorted. "There was a group of horsemen that came out behind the woods on the other side of the wagons that were trying to catch my men out in the open. We had no choice but to retreat."

"Where are the horsemen now?" Cerdic demanded.

"Dead and gone," Arturius replied. "Mostly dead, in fact."

Arturius gave the diminutive woman a smile as he touched her on the shoulder.

"We all owe Brigid here our lives. Those caltrops stopped their charge and gave us time for our boys to attack them. Then we came back here to you as quick as we could."

"Well," pouted Cerdic, "I suppose that was the best thing to do. But once you left, we almost got overwhelmed. And where did those mother-swiving bastards get horsemen from?"

A weary Brigid looked at him in disgust.

"They were not Saxons, most of them anyway. From their arms and armor, they look to be British, but they were fighting under a Raven banner."

"That is a Norse symbol alright," he muttered. "Those are British traitors. No Briton should be fighting under a Saxon sigil, unless paid handsomely. From what tribe?"

Brigid sighed.

"We do not know yet, but we captured a couple of the noblemen riding with them, so we will find out soon enough."

Cerdic whipped the sweat from his brow as he sighed.

"Well regardless, we won. This was a fight to remember."

"We may have been victorious," Brigid said with a furrowed brow, "but we were also lucky. Next time we might not be. Let's not forget to think of things that we can do better next time."

"Save the celebrations for Caleva," Caradoc added. "We need to get moving. Let's discuss what we can do differently once we're there."

The four of them paused, speechless at the sights before them. The battlefield was silent now except for the groans of the wounded men. The memories of the desperate fight would not leave him. Cerdic's mind kept flashing back to that moment when his shield had been pulled down, when he had almost had his head caved in. He had felt a moment of terror like he had never felt before, not only for himself, but he knew his death in the middle of the shield wall could have meant the collapse of their defensive line. All his comrades could have shared his fate. A tingle of dread spread through his body. *No Valhalla awaits a warrior who lets his companions down like that,* he thought.

He had almost died, and now that he had survived, and the joy of victory had made him never feel more alive, but seeing the wreckage of humanity around him troubled him. During the fight, these men were targets. Once the heat of battle was over, they ceased being targets and became men. Cerdic continued to gaze over the battlefield and the dead Saxons they were leaving behind. The dead did not bother him much, but those who were still alive, that was a different story. The wounded men pulled at his heart strings.

The injured cried out for water, they cried out for relief of their pain, and they cried out for their mothers and wives and daughters and the children they would never see again. They were brothers and sons and fathers, and all of them had a mother who would grieve for them. Their enemies who had been lightly wounded had gotten away, but those the Saxons left behind were the ones with serious injuries, most of them doomed to die. Their suffering was pitiful, but this was the price of defeat. The Saxons were cousins to his Jutes. In a different situation, he may have been friends with these men who now lay dead and injured on the field of battle. It was a bittersweet moment for him.

As for his own men who had suffered, he felt personally responsible for much of it. The bards never sung of this, the sadness he felt of seeing the face of a man he had shared ale with the night before now lying motionless on the ground. He had wandered back to the battle line to find his comrade who had died by his side. Once he found the body, he could see where the skull had split open, the flies still buzzing around the gore. That could have been him instead. Could he have done something different to save him? Cerdic did not know. As he stood there, one of the new men asked if he could be the one to dispatch the seriously wounded, and he nodded in assent, wondering why someone would volunteer for such an odious task.

That night, Cerdic had trouble going to sleep. The faces of two men kept flashing before him. One was of the skinny fellow with the wispy beard and the yellow teeth that was about to cleave his skull in. He was happy the bastard was dead, having found his body on the field of battle, the chest wound proving fatal, but he could not get the image of that man out of his head. His face was frozen in time, and he could see every detail of his enemy's visage as if it were his own looking back at him in a mirror. *Is that man forever in my dreams*? he wondered.

It would be another man who haunted his world even more. His comrade who had died entered his dreams that evening. It was awful. Cerdic visualized a jumbled-up scene where the man's eyes were looking at him just before the spearhead had been thrust in, his face destroyed in a shower of blood and gore as if it had just happened again. As blood bubbled out of the man's ruined face, he could hear his comrade say, "Cerdic, help me." Then another spear shot out to enter his own mouth, and now he could not breathe, choking on blood that was not really there. It was the first time he had experienced a dream like that. It would not be his last.

CHAPTER SIXTEEN

They had just arrived in Caleva; Arturius was hot, tired, and footsore, but he was happy to be alive and unscathed, thrilled they had made it to their destination. His good mood became quickly doused when the caravan was met by the civilian leadership of the community, the most important being a priest named Gildas, recently arrived from Rome as the bishop of the southern diocese of Britannia.

Arturius looked askance at the bejeweled priests presiding over the welcoming party. *Rome sends no soldiers to defend us,* he thought, *but they can still send a religious leader to save our British souls.* Gildas was fat and imperious looking, draped in impressively embroidered robes, his chubby fingers bearing numerous jewel-encrusted rings. Escorting him with an entourage of priestly attendants, flanked by numerous black-clad bodyguards, a white cross over their left breast. The bishop's soldiers numerous and intimidating, with eyes that were wary and expressionless; their hands on the pommels of their swords implied a lethal promise. The aura was less than welcoming.

Arturius had never met Gildas before, but he knew the type, having priests who looked and acted like the bishop back in his home in Tintagel. The contrast between like Brother Petrus and a man like Gildas could not be more extreme. Petrus would give you the shirt off his back, whereas he thought that someone like Gildas would probably take it and everything else you owned saying it was for the good of the church. Petrus tried to serve his people, whereas the Roman priests back home expected you to serve them on bended knee. Petrus was loving and accepting, while the clergy Arturius remembered were quick to judge, not sparing the rod of punishment whether it was deserved or not.

Gildas had coldly welcomed them with a speech and multiple prayers in Latin, which only a few in their party could understand. When introduced to Brother Petrus and Sister Brigid, his eyes suspiciously narrowed in distaste, especially when the obese cleric had offered his pudgy hand to Brother Petrus to kiss his ring, which their leader did not do. Most of the people in the caravan could not understand the Latin that Gildas was speaking, but his look of displeasure spoke volumes. Watching someone like Gildas only magnified his admiration for Petrus and Brigid, leaders who cared for others more than themselves.

After the oddly formal and unfriendly welcome was issued, the bishop went back to his mansion, insisting that later that night Brother Petrus was to stay at the residence of His Holiness as his honored guest. The rest of their party, including Sister Brigid, were to disperse in Caleva to find lodging. Brigid protested with the snub, but Petrus overruled her, saying it would be rude to refuse. Brigid had been livid. Eventually she had swallowed her pride, but she announced they would not stay there any longer, informing everyone she would leave with the scouts in the morning instead of staying in the same town as the odious bishop, but she agreed to hold fast until she and Petrus had finished their group meeting that night.

As Arturius rode through the city streets with his two friends, the feeling he had as he took in his surroundings was disquieting. The town walls were sparsely manned, and the soldiers he saw did not welcome them with enthusiasm. Indifference might be a better description. Caleva Atrebatum seemed like a town of ghosts with few inhabitants, as most of the people

Arturius could observe were soldiers. Those guards at the gates continued to gaze upon them with cold and suspicious eyes, especially the ones loyal to Gildas wearing the black tunics.

The few civilians he encountered gave them no hellos, only blank looks as they scurried away. Matrons who saw them coming closed the doors as they approached. He was disturbed by the sight of emaciated people in threadbare tunics plodding by with listless eyes, no doubt slaves doing errands for their masters. Grass had crept between the cobbles of the street while vines and weeds grew on the walls of the houses and shops, and trash littered the street corners, only attended to by the occasional stray mongrel. The overall feeling was eerie, one of abandonment and neglect.

Arturius and his comrades wound their way to the forum where the largest of the buildings and temples were located, and next to them were the urban villas of the wealthy. Their owners had been the first to leave in the migration to the mainland, and now their dwellings were much too large to maintain for the common folk, so they had been told the entire block was wide open for the taking. These once opulent homes he passed by looked barely habitable, but it was better than camping outside the walls.

Though the paints were faded, and the plaster had fallen off the interiors, there were still roofs overhead and a decent water supply nearby, so these would do for a few days. On the way to the house that he and his friends would be quartered, Arturius had looked back on his role in what they called now *The Battle of the Caravan* with mixed emotions. It had been a victory, but they had made a variety of mistakes, and what had saved them was their ability to improvise. They had been particularly lucky with the caltrops that had saved him and his slingers.

His thoughts concerning the battle were not all bad, of course, and the desultory welcome in Caleva did not detract from the pride he had felt in their accomplishments. Finally, they arrived at the block of houses that would act as their new home. After they had dismounted, they led their newly acquired mounts to a stable near the house they were occupying along with the many of the other refugees. There the boys groomed their horses, chatting away as they did so.

"What do you make of the grand city of Caleva?" Cerdic said in a cheery tone as he continued to brush his mare.

Caradoc looked around himself with a glum look on his face.

"You can tell it was once an impressive city," he muttered morosely. "It looks like a dump now."

Arturius shook his head in amazement.

"When I was a child, I had heard stories about how this was such an important town. I recall tales of how the Atrebetes were considered the most Romanized of the British tribes, how their king was the first to invite the emperor Claudius to send the legions here to conquer Britannia. Mother loved this place. She would often say, 'because of the Atrebetes, this island is civilized.' This town was their capitol, and it does not fit what my mind pictured it to be."

"Boys," Cerdic said, chuckling, "you are right, it is not much to look at now. Where did all the people go?"

"I think most of them moved to Brittany in Gaul," Arturius said.

"Except for the dead ones," Caradoc snorted.

"At least Ambrosius Aurelianus is here now," Arturius said as he sighed. "That might stop this place from falling to the Saxons."

"I do not know about that," Cerdic observed. "These troops look demoralized. And did you notice that most of those fellows are wearing that black tunic with the cross on the left shoulder? I heard they were taken away from Ambrosius, hired by Gildas. It was those bastards in black that escorted our two captives away. I would have preferred we had kept them. I don't trust these black-liveried gobshites."

"I don't, either," Caradoc growled. "And why can't Brother Petrus stay with us?"

Arturius displayed an impatient look as he opened his arms wide.

"We are guests here, remember? Brother Petrus said the bishop wanted to get to know him better, and he made it clear that we should try to get along with the local authorities here. And I heard they have better a place to house prisoners than we do right now."

"Speaking of our prisoners," Caradoc said as he revealed a sly smile, "What did you think of the great war leader of the Saxons, Horsa the Magnificent?"

Arturius shrugged his shoulders.

"He was dressed like a god of war for sure. That chain armor shirt was impressive, and those silver and gold torcs will keep our treasury full for a year. His helmet was something otherworldly. I have never seen the like. Of course, Cerdic, you must also like that sword."

"The one made for me by Senecio is my favorite," Cerdic scoffed. "Even that gaudy weapon cannot compare to mine."

Cerdic then pulled out his own blade. Arturius looked upon it with a tinge of envy. The sunlight glinted off the sharp edge as the three were mesmerized by the beauty of it.

"I say let Caradoc have the captured sword," Cerdic said as he gazed at his own sword with pride.

"So, what did you name it," Caradoc asked.

"Soul Stealer," he said with a glint in his eye. "So, I won't be needing any captured sword myself. So why don't you take Horsa's weapon, Caradoc? I heard it belonged once to some rich Roman general, and the blade even has a name, Caliburnus."

"I think not," he said as he shook his head. "I am an archer. If you don't want it, I say give it to Arturius. And brother, just carry it in a parade. If you tried to use it in an actual fight you would only hurt yourself. We have both seen you use a blade, my boy, and it is not pretty."

As Cerdic sheathed his blade, Arturius's face turned red as the other two laughed.

"That is a nasty bruise Horsa has on his forehead," Cerdic said with a grin. "Arturius, did you give that to him?"

"Yes, I did. Just do not tell the other slingers, as they are still arguing over who should get the glory for knocking him out. Let the other boys have fun bragging about how they felled him. It helps morale."

Cerdic pursed his lips.

"It ruined that beautiful helmet, though, with that is a big dent in the middle. I hope Senecio can fix it. It would be impressive for one of us to wear. How did it happen that you got him?"

"I got lucky, I guess," Arturius said as he shrugged. "As for that other young fellow we captured, the lad looked like a British nobleman by his clothes and armor. Anyway, he fell off his horse and broke his arm, and after that he got hit in the head by a slinger. Horsa had dismounted and was trying to get his unconscious companion on the back of his own mount, when a plumbata struck the beast and it galloped off, leaving those two horsemen without any horses."

"Pity, is it not?" commented Caradoc.

"Anyway," continued Arturius, "that helmet has some gold and silver in it. Cerdic, I say let us strip that off because we can use all the money we can get, so have Senecio modify it for you. It looks too Saxon for me or Caradoc here with those eye guards hanging down off the front brim. Do you agree, Caradoc? "

"I concur," Caradoc answered. "It is way too gaudy for a true Briton, but it is just tacky enough to suit you Saxons and Jutes."

Cerdic chuckled., "It is obvious you two have no sense of style. I'll take it. Of course, any enemy who sees that thing will also want it. It will probably get me killed someday."

All three of them chuckled, and then Arturius looked puzzled as he gazed at Cerdic.

"By the way, were you the one who gagged Horsa?"

"I am happy to say it was me," Cerdic said with a satisfied smile.

"Why?" Caradoc snorted.

"He was being obnoxious. He would not shut up. Apparently, he felt we were not worthy to take him hostage."

"What do you mean?" Arturius said as his eyes narrowed.

Cerdic chuckled, and then he rolled his eyes.

"He was saying how he wanted to speak to a real nobleman, and that he was angry he was not given ale. He called us a bunch of mangey slaves, and claimed our shields were too big, and that our phallus's were too small, and on and on. By Loki's short and curlies, it was never ending."

"Sounds like that was a good decision," snorted Arturius. "We want to get a hefty ransom for him, but I suppose we do not have to listen to him moan and groan like that."

"He was lucky you did not cut his tongue out," Caradoc commented dryly.

"From what little I have heard about him and his brother," Cerdic snorted, "I am pretty sure that is what would happen to us if our roles were reversed."

"So, what is the story about our very young and horse-riding-challenged nobleman from the west?" asked Arturius.

"He is in a bad way," Cerdic answered. "Besides getting smacked in the head by a slingshot, he suffered a nasty compound fracture when he fell, the exposed bone covered in mud. He has not woken up yet, and he may never be right again even if he does. And the healer thinks he will lose the arm. Between that and the head injury, she thinks he may not survive. But Horsa's loose tongue betrayed the boy's lineage. He is Catigern, one of the sons of Vortigern."

The three young men exchanged worried looks with each other.

"That should not surprise anyone," Arturius said. "But having Ordovices this far east is disturbing. And bloody hell, that makes him a relative of mine then."

Caradoc scratched his head as he spoke.

"See there, now you know why my tribe hates those Ordovices. You cannot trust those sneaky arse-wipes."

His friends nodded, then they all resumed caring for their mounts so they could get ready for their evening's activities. Early that evening, the leadership group of the caravan had arranged for an informal get together to establish a plan for the next few days before Petrus was to go to the bishop's house. Flagons of ale were passed around as the group engaged in a low buzz of conversation. The mood was somber. The cold welcome they had received in Caleva was disturbing, except for the warm embrace given to Lucilia and Senna by their beloved Ambrosius.

Arturius knew that this was a Roman town with Roman customs, but it had been jarring even to him to see the poorly dressed slaves scurrying about to serve their masters. He was not alone in that sentiment. Many in the caravan were now freedmen, often by their own hands, and the sight of enslaved people shuffling along with downcast eyes made them uneasy. They had grown used to the egalitarianism they had experienced in the Weald. Finally, the meeting was called as they all sat in the atrium of the largest house they could find.

Sister Brigid was the first to speak when she stood and proclaimed, "I want nothing to do with this place with this obnoxious gobshite of a bishop and its wretched slaves. I am leaving in the morning to go scout for our new home. We can return later and free these poor souls."

With that she sat down with a scowl as she crossed her arms.

Brother Petrus stood up and spoke in a calm and measured voice, "I think every person in this room feels the same, Sister. The reality is that slavery exists in every tribe on this island, not just the Saxons. We must not lose sight that the true enemy here are those barbarian peoples, and we first must unite with the Romano-British tribes to throw them out. Once that happens, then we can convince our co-religionists that slavery is morally wrong."

Brother Petrus grew more impassioned as he spoke, talking about how they needed to form a republic like Rome used to have, but one that was not corrupt. He envisioned their new home would not have a king or an emperor to rule over them, and that it would have a functioning legal system that respected the rule of law, a governmental structure that all of Britannia would envy and adopt someday. Petrus envisioned a place where the common man had a voice, not just the rich nobles.

By Jupiter, that man loves to talk, he thought as he hid his annoyance. Arturius tried to pay attention, but his mind kept wandering. He was certain Cerdic must be going mad from boredom, and that both he and Caradoc were royalists at heart and would be disagreeing with some of what Petrus was saying. Arturius was more egalitarian, but what Petrus was trying to accomplish seemed beyond anything he thought was possible. But try as he might, he could not stop worrying about the next few days.

Something was unsettling about being in Caleva, and he wanted to get on the road now to Camalet or wherever they were going to go. There was danger here. Unfortunately, they needed to rest and refit after the battle they had just fought, especially Cerdic's men, all of whom sported injuries of one kind or another, and they needed the scouts to make sure Camalet was a good place to resettle. He believed in some of the principles that Petrus espoused, but this was taking forever. Finally. Petrus had come to the closing part of his soliloquy, so he started to pay attention once more.

"Think of ourselves like the Rome of a thousand years ago," Petrus said as he opened his arms with a dramatic flourish, "like that small town in the wilds of the peninsula of Italia. We have cast off our kings like the Romans did with Tarquin the Proud, and now it is time to form a republic without kings. We are starting small, but so did Rome once."

Arturius glanced over at Caradoc and Cerdic, wondering what these two would-be-kings were thinking about these efforts at forming a new republic. Then Brigid arose, holding a mug of ale high as she spoke.

"What one man can do, another can do," she insisted. "What one group of people can do, another can do. We must take the best from the past and not repeat their mistakes. We can do this, with the help of the Christos!"

Brother Petrus and Brigid made a sign of the cross and sat down. The council sat in stunned silence. Then Arturius stood and started to clap, and then everyone joined in as they all stood and started to cheer as Brother Petrus turned red from embarrassment.

Senna rose up as she yelled out, "We all should make a toast. To Britannia!"

Arturius revealed a broad smile. *Good for you,* he thought. *We all need a couple of drinks after all of that.*

"To Britannia! Salutem," they all rang out in unison. He thought he saw Cerdic and Caradoc delay in the raising of their cups, and he had his own doubts as an odd mixture of skepticism and hope swirled around in his brain. He suspected his two friends were not the only skeptical ones in the room; Petrus was certainly being ambitious in his vision of the future. The coming day was going to be a busy one, getting the caravan ready to be quickly on the road again. But for tonight at least, most of the people in the room seem of one mind, willing to try and fulfill Brother Petrus's dream. All Arturius wanted to do was to get out of this town before something bad happened.

CHAPTER SEVENTEEN

The *Battle of the Caravan* was over. The high-pitched war cries had stopped, and a strange silence had descended, the stillness only interrupted by the soft moans of the wounded men and the pitiful cries of the injured horses once the din of battle had left. Children stated to move around the field, fending off the crows and picking up the caltrops and discarded plumbata, while the womenfolk assisted the injured and scavenged the Saxon corpses for arms, armor, and hidden valuables.

Ferox wandered around the battlefield, like a crow looking for the eyes of the dead to feast on, grinning as he searched amongst the bodies for any sign of life. He was doing the job he had volunteered for, ordered to kill anyone too badly injured. *And I get to decide who lives and who dies,* he thought. He remembered the sanctimonious words of Petrus when he had loudly announced what to do for the wounded Saxons. Arturius had initially said to let the Christos take care of them, to leave them where they lay. Arturius thought their comrades would come back, and caring for their wounded would slow them down. But Petrus had overruled him, arguing that they should provide medical assistance for those who could be helped, and dispatch the seriously wounded.

"We are Christians," the priest had implored, "we must help the injured, and for those who are dying, it would be a mercy to grant them a quick death rather than let them linger for days in pain." Ferox rolled his eyes as he thought about it. *What a dung-heap of lies,* he thought. The Christians are more ruthless than any pagan, deluding themselves by thinking that they were forgiven. He stopped next to an enemy warrior who was still living, and this one looked to be a Briton, not a Saxon. Ferox knelt beside the man. He had a leg injury and was crying out for water in British. Ferox got on his haunches as he held a water skin with both hands in front of the prostrate figure.

"So young man, let me see what I can do to help you. Tell me your name."

"It is Julius," he weakly croaked out. "Please, sir. Some water. I feel so thirsty."

"Of course, of course. And you were fighting with the Saxons, I see. Why was that?"

"My king sent us to help them. Perhaps that is why I was injured. The Christos may have punished me for fighting for them."

"Oh no, I do not think so," Ferox muttered. "The Christos is a forgiving god. And your wound does not look too serious. You will recover. What tribe are you from?"

"The Ordovices, kind sir. And that is good news that you believe that I will survive. Please, could I have some water now?"

"Of course, Julius. Here is some water for you."

He handed the young man the waterskin, and then Ferox grabbed the wounded man's hair and jerked his head up with one hand while the other sliced his throat with a short-bladed knife he had hidden behind the water container. The young man's look of gratitude melted like wax into one of terrified horror. Ferox chuckled as he stared into the desperate eyes of the dying young man as his blood pulsed out form his severed carotid artery.

"Your leg wound is not bad, but of course, I do not think you will survive that injury to your neck. And Julius, I will tell our priest to curse you to hell for fighting for the pagans. There you can spend eternity with your friends and family, eh?"

He continued to gaze into the dying boy's' eyes until the light went out of them. Then he stood up and resumed his search for more wounded. Ferox glanced around to make sure no one was objecting to his dispatching men who were not really dying. Everyone else he saw wandering around the battlefield looked too busy to care. Ferox was grateful for their negligence, for now he could continue to deal with his victims as he pleased, thrilled that the sanctimonious Petrus had gone back to the wagons.

In Ferox's mind, life itself was a death sentence, so why not derive a little pleasure from their demise. He thought back to the battle, amazed these former slaves had won. Arturius may have been the general today, but he knew that Arturius and his young friends were not the real leaders of these people. *This Brother Petrus is the one with the charisma and gravitas to lead this disorganized rabble*, he ruminated. *What would they be without him*? The rest were boys, former slaves, and one mouthy red-headed nun. Without Petrus, he was certain they would fail. *I need to do something about that man,* he thought.

Petrus was the one who posed the greatest threat to the kingdom that he and Nata were trying to build, and by leaving the Weald these people were moving their community much closer to Durnovaria. Ferox knew of Camalet, and if these people settled there, that location was right on their doorstep, too close to Durnovaria for comfort, only twenty-five miles away as a crow would fly. Nata's kingdom would rise, and this slave republic must burn; their kindness would plant the seed of their destruction as the strong would triumph. They needed to be eliminated as a threat to him and his brother gladiators.

Once he was finished with his grisly task of dispatching the wounded and the caravan was ready to move on, then they entered Caleva, and his initial impression of the place was not a glowing one. The town was bigger than Durnovaria, with larger and more impressive public buildings, but

Durnovaria still maintained thriving trade connections. Nata's kingdom was a vibrant town, while Caleva was practically deserted and was falling apart. The walls were cracked, roofs were sagging, looking like a place suitable only for the shades of the dead.

A delay occurred when the caravan first arrived, held up at the city gates for an interminably long welcoming ceremony performed by an ancient Roman-looking general and a fat bejeweled priest accompanied by a large entourage of black-clad clerics and soldiers. *The priest had the soldiers,* he thought, *so he must be the one really in charge.* The town looked almost vacant, with hardly any shops or food stalls open, but at least the biggest tavern in town was still in business. That night Ferox wasted no time in getting to the watering hole to meet the local soldiery and to get a feel for the place.

After walking through the door, he glanced at the glowing embers from the fire that tried to give the place a cheery atmosphere, but that feeble attempt was overcome by the smells of smoke, wet dogs, stale ale, unwashed bodies, and the hint of vomit. It was just like any other dive bar he had ever seen. The bartender had a purplish bulbous nose and was nearly bald, and it was so gloomy that Ferox could not tell if he was twenty-five or fifty-five. The barmaid flashed a quick smile that revealed a few missing teeth and perhaps the willingness for a dalliance if the price was right. Given her acne and her crossed eyes, Ferox suspected it would not cost much to engage her for a roll in the hay, but those were not the people he wanted to talk to tonight.

Ferox sidled up to the bar, scanning the room with interest. He saw his target immediately, taking care not to be too obvious as he inspected them from afar. Then he requested a mug of ale for himself and ordered a round for the table of four men in the back, dressed in the livery that he had seen many of the guards wearing earlier that day, a black surcoat with a white cross over the left side of the chest, men loyal to the bishop.

Ferox was here to learn about this community's politics so he could work on this knowledge to his advantage, and talking to drunken soldiery was a good way to start. The men at the table raised their tankards in appreciation for his gift, and they motioned him over to come join them. Ferox strode over to their table and sat down. The biggest man of the group, a stocky fellow with a nose that had been broken too many times, spoke up first.

"Well, stranger, thanks for the drinks, the man said as he thumbed the handle of his knife. "But know that ale buys you time, but not our trust. You might have to buy another round of drinks if you want to stay. So, what brings you and your people to our fair city?"

His friends snickered as they looked at him with wary eyes. Ferox raised his brow as he raised his tankard of ale as if he was giving a toast.

"I just want to make some new friends tonight. I am indeed traveling with the caravan that just came in, but they are not my people."

The stocky fellow chuckled., "So who the bloody hell are your people?"

"It is a long story," Ferox said as he shook his head. "I can order that other round for you now, and I can keep it brief. And my name is Ferox."

"Hmm," the man grunted. "My name is Marcus."

They shook hands, then Marcus introduced the other men at the table, and after that, he leaned back and sneered.

"We'll let you talk as long as you keep buying, stranger. Unless you piss us off, of course, in which case we will beat you to a pulp and take your money for our drinks anyway."

Ferox displayed a chilling smile.

"You could try, and you might succeed in that, but I would take one or two of you with me to hell. So let us just share a drink instead. Less bloody this way."

"All right, then," Marcus said. So, what you bloody wankers doing here? Let's start with that."

Ferox warily nodded.

"Sure. The people in the caravan are a bunch of refuges from the forests of the Weald, mainly peasants and escaped slaves that are ordered about by a priest of the Christos and his mouthy deaconess wife. They are wanting to resettle in the west to get away from the Saxons."

"A priest and a nun, you say," Marcus barked out. "We were told that you defeated a large warband of Saxons. Really? How the feckin' hell did that happen?"

"I would not have believed it myself, but I was there," Ferox muttered. "They came up with some ingenious little toys that surprised the rogues, and they were helped by some teenagers who knew enough about fighting to train those peasants. Their shield men stayed in formation long enough to not piss themselves to death from fear while the others shot arrows and threw rocks at their enemy's backs. But not all their foes were Saxons. Many were British, and it was them that lost the battle for them."

Marcus and his three friends sat there in stunned silence.

"We did see men with those antique short swords and odd-looking shields in your group. It does not look like those things would be much good in a fight. Are you telling us this priest and his trollop had built themselves an army that won a fight like that? With those weapons?"

"Well, yes. In my opinion, they got lucky. The priest got them organized and gave them hope somehow. And the wife just tells you what to do like most women do, even when she is full of shite. She does curse like a sailor, though, I will give her that. During the fight itself, the priest just prayed, and the nun and the three teenagers ran the show."

The men at the table looked incredulous. "Three teenagers," Marcus scoffed. "And a nun?"

"Yes. These three boys were nobles once and had played soldier for a little while when they were growing up. That is, when they were not sucking from their momma's teats. So, they taught these other pussies how to fight."

"Nobles, eh?" The old soldier snorted. "So, what are they doing consorting with a bunch of slaves and peasants?"

Ferox took a hearty drought from his mug of ale and then wiped his mouth with his sleeve. He raised his eyebrow and sighed.

"On *The Night of the Long Knives,* Aelle somehow decided not to kill these three, keeping them as thralls instead. The boys escaped to the Weald, and because they are the only ones who know anything about the pointy end of a spear, these children were made the commanders of the rabble."

"Why are they here in Caleva?" Marcus asked. "And what are you doing with these blighters?"

Ferox shook his head in disgust.

"As I said, they say they want to move west to a big old hillfort used before the Romans came. They are here to rest and refit before heading out. They do not intend to stay here."

Marcus gave him an ominous look.

"Well, not staying sounds good to me. I do not want to associate with a bunch of pox-ridden thralls. And you still have not told us about yourself. Is that what you are? Arse-wiping slave?"

"Of course not," Ferox scoffed. "I am a free man. I managed to get out of Durnovaria barely in time when those gladiators took over the place. I did not know where else to go."

Marcus gave him an appraising stare. "So, what did you do there in Durnovaria?"

"I was a soldier in the town watch," Ferox replied, "and I was one of the referees for the gladiator fights. I got away because I was lucky to be working in the arena when they took the town. Most of my friends are no doubt dead now, or they wish they were."

Ferox sensed them warming up to him. *I must make them think I was one of them,* he thought, *a lowly soldier doing the thankless job of guarding the town.* There was a moment of silence, which Ferox broke by offering up a toast.

"To lost comrades."

They all raised their wooden mugs and clinked them together as they loudly proclaimed in unison, "To lost comrades!"

There was a pause as Ferox's gaze met each man's eyes one by one.

"And where did you fine fellows lose friends?"

One of the other men at the table moaned, "Oh bugger me, where have we not lost comrades."

Marcus's eyes teared up a bit.

"Aye, that is the truth. Ambrosius Aurelianus has dragged our hairy arses all over this bloody island for years now, and for what? We got little support from the British kingdoms before *the Night of the Long Knives*, and after that, we did not receive shite. Until we made our oaths to the good bishop, I cannot tell you the last time we have gotten paid. And now we got these pretty little surcoats and some coin in our pockets, don't we boys."

The skinny fellow with the stringy, long hair on his left chimed in.

"Yeah, that is right,", he said in a squeaky voice. "All the British tribes didn't do diddly dick for us. We kept telling our general that we were not fighting for Britannia just to return to the rule of Rome, but that rich snooty toff would not listen. A man of principles, he is, but the old man is too idealistic. We should be fighting for Britannia, not the feckin' empire. And that is just what the bishop says he is going to do. Under him, we will be making Britannia one kingdom."

Ferox arched his brow.

"You are pledged your service to the bishop now? And not Ambrosius?

Marcus gave out a self-satisfying burp, wiped his mouth, and then he nodded.

"That is right, mate. We are not competitors, mind you. Now we are just friendly rivals. So, now me and my mates are serving the bishop to unite Britannia. And what did he call it, boys? 'We are to root out heretics and blasphemers,' as the good bishop likes to say."

Ferox gazed at the man, puzzled.

"But isn't the bishop from Rome himself? We heard he just got here not long ago."

Marcus growled, "Yes, that is true. But the bishop said that it's those arse-licking Goths that control Rome now. The Goths claim to be Christians, but they ain't really. Even their king Theodoric is a heretic he said. What did that bishop name it? I get all these bloody heresies confused. Arianism, I think he called it, or some shite like that. He was sent here by the church in Rome because he was in trouble there, but if he is successful in rooting out our heretics here, then the church might forgive him. And all we must do is to kill heretics, and we just nod and say yes to whatever the priests say. Ain't that right, boys?"

The men at the table all nodded.

Ferox nodded and smiled at them. *This is interesting,* he thought. *I might use the bishop to get at Petrus.* A stringy-haired fellow with a stammer chimed in.

"T-th-th-that's right, he is h-h-h-here to root out heretics. The bishop says that is w-w-w-why he was sent here in the first p-p-p-place."

The shorty, stocky fellow with a bent nose snorted.

"The bishop says Britannia has a certain kind of heretic he is particularly going after. He calls them Pel __Pella __ Aw bollocks, Marcus, what does he call those bastards again?"

"It is named after some British twat of a priest," Marcus chuckled. "And I can't feckin' remember, either."

"Pelagianism, you mean," Ferox asked as his lips curved up into a sly smile. "Is he persecuting people who follow Pelagius?"

"Yeah, that the bloke's name."

Then Marcus looked at Ferox suspiciously.

"You are not one of those gobshites, are you?"

"Oh, by the Christos, no! In fact, that is why I wanted to meet some of you fine men here. I do not want to say anything to get someone in trouble, but I cannot stay with these people. I am a true follower of the Christos, but that two-faced priest and his bitch of a wife were all about following the teachings of Pelagius. Those two are heretics for sure."

Ferox leaned closer to the table and softly asked in a conspiratorial tone.

"Is your bishop accepting more men with experience in using a spear and shield to serve under his banner?"

Marcus blew his cheeks out as he shook his head.

"Brother," he said, "I do not know. But most of Ambrosius' army is now sworn to the bishop. You would have to talk to one of his chief priests about that."

Ferox leaned back as he sighed.

"Well, then, I will need to talk to them. We need to stop these people from the Weald from spreading their poison to the good people of Caleva here. I am sure that your good bishop would be interested in what I have to say."

The men around him nodded in approval, and then they talked of lost comrades killed in pointless campaigns over the years. The men around him were inebriated when he first met them, and now they were stone blind drunk by the time the evening ended. Ferox had learned a lot. He just laughed and drank, but his mind was planning his next move while pretending to listen to their stories. *Ambrosius lost them because money talks*, Ferox thought. *The general is chasing after a rainbow, and his men are tired of it.*

The men he drank with launched into a marching song, and Ferox pretended to know the words as he tried to sing along. It was apparent to him that he needed to meet the bishop personally. *If the bishop is not a stupid arseling and can see past his nose*, Ferox mused, *he might get rid of Petrus and his mouthy wife for us.* It was hard for him to believe that a religious man has more power than the general, but that seemed to be the case here. It was inconceivable to him.

After the song, Ferox told his new friends that he was headed back and get some sleep because he needed to speak to the bishop in the morning. They thanked him for the last round he bought for them as he walked out the door. Once outside, he laughed to himself. *What fecking eejits,* he thought. Both the army in Caleva and the refugees from the Weald were having priests of the Christos lead them. He and Nata honored the gods of war, not some dead Jew who told people to turn the other cheek.

Ferox was glad he left when he did, as he knew the next morning would be crucial, and he did not want to mess it up by being hung over. That morning Ferox was there bright and early, but he had been forced to wait in the bishop's antechamber for hours, cooling his heels for the prelate to bless him with his presence. He had arrived for an unscheduled appointment, and it had taken the vouching of his new drinking buddies to even get him in the door. Now it was early evening, and still no bishop.

Ferox suspected the delay in meeting the bishop was a power move by the priest to put him in his place and make him feel uneasy. *You will have to do better than this,* he smirked. Finally, the rotund bishop entered, decked out in an elaborately embroidered robe and surrounded by his cringing sycophants. Ferox assumed a beatific smile as the bishop's eyes roved up and down, a hungry look, one he had seen all too often before. *This one prefers the boys,* he thought. Looking at the bishop's entourage, he gathered that the prelate liked them young. Ferox seethed but his smile never slipped. *What a pompous arse,* he thought. *I would love to cut this tub of lard's throat and see him blubber as he dies. Christos or no Christos, they all fear death.*

"Your Excellency, I come bearing information you need to hear,"

Ferox continued with a summary of how he had fallen in with the refugee camp as an escapee from Durnovaria, and the fact that he wanted to serve the bishop instead because of the heresies of the priest and deaconess in the Weald. He clearly had the bishop's attention.

When his tale was finished, Gildas asked in a haughty tone, "How do I know that you are not a heretic or a pagan yourself, young man. You should recite the Nicene Creed for me, eh?"

He replied in Greek, the memory of his enslavement by Greek speaking Christians still fresh in his mind. The bishop's eyes opened wide with delight, saying he was honored to meet an educated man like him. Greek speakers were rare in the west. Only a few of the commoners spoke vulgar forms of Latin now, the rest still babbling in their native British. The conversation continued in Greek, suspecting that only he and Gildas could understand each other.

"I am pleased to meet an educated believer, my son. But your mention of the deaconess and the priest concern me. Tell me again, why do you think those two are heretics?"

"I have heard them say many times how much they admired Pelagius. These two conduct their masses in British, not Latin, and they say that one does not need a priest to reach the Christos, and that people can read the Bible for themselves."

The bishops face flushed as his eyes flew open wide.

"Heresy!"

"They also declared that Brigid was her husband's equal in all things, and they talk of tolerance for people of differing religious beliefs, that Jews and pagans should not be persecuted. It goes on and on, your Eminence."

Gildas's jowls trembled as he blustered, "Blasphemers! You are right, my son, to inform me about such matters. What do you know of their plans?"

He kept his smile plastered on, happy to see the bishop was being so easy to manipulate.

"Be assured, your Excellency, that I am not in their circle of leaders, but we had been told that they were to stay in Caleva for just a few days before moving to the west. They were sending a scouting party out today to find a suitable place to settle, and once that is confirmed, they will leave here soon."

"I need to act quickly then, eh," the bishop said, nodding. "I had suspected that priest and his wife of having non-orthodox beliefs, and this re-affirms my opinion in this regard. Thank you again for this information. What are your plans, my son? What can I do for you?"

"Your Excellency, say a prayer for my soul, that is all I ask. But I would like to serve you and the Christos by helping you return this island to the one true faith. Specifically, I would like to act as an ambassador between you and the new king of Durnovaria, the one they call Nata."

"He is a gladiator, a slave and a pagan, is he not?" the bishop sniffed.

"When my fair city fell, I fled for my life in fear. But I have heard rumors of late that some people have returned without consequence. I heard Nata desires a priest to join them."

"Why," snorted the bishop.

"When they were forced to be gladiators, they were under the heel of pagans who hosted those barbarous gladiatorial contests. The Roman pagans are gone now, and they must desire a change, and possibly be confirmed as Christians."

He was lying, of course. *We do want a change*, he thought. *We are the masters now.* He knew the gladiators may have been slaves, but to a man he knew his comrades despised the Christians. Any priest that came would be expected to keep the slaves docile and no more, while he and his comrades would still honor the gods of war. But Gildas did not know that, and this bishop was going to believe what he wanted to believe. Gildas beamed at him.

"I could write you a letter today stating that you were sent by me as an emissary. That should protect you."

"If you would be so kind to do so, my Excellency. And with you as my liege, I believe they would welcome me back home safely."

"Are there any Christian clergy there now?"

"No. the pagans who ruled Durnovaria did not allow it. But as I said, I believe they will welcome one now. As soon as I can confirm it is safe to send a priest, I will send you word, and I will make sure that any apostates will not be welcome in Durnovaria either."

Gildas nodded, silent for a few moments.

"Of course," the bishop said. "But these apostates from the Weald must not know what you are doing. What would you tell those people when you leave for Durnovaria?"

"I will say I heard some of my family still live up by Eboracum, so I would be seen going north and then once out of sight, I will surreptitiously turn around and head south."

The lips of the bishop started to curl into a sly smile.

"You have put much thought into this plan, I see."

"Yes, I have, your Excellency. But I must stress to you again; if you are to interrogate those two blasphemers, it needs to be done with alacrity. I have heard rumors that the wife may be on the scouting expedition, so she may have already departed."

"The priest is already with us now," the bishop said with a smirk. "He is going nowhere. I understand the deaconess has already left with her scouts, but she will be detained when she returns. Never fear, these blasphemers will be dealt with soon. And I must say, young man, it has been such a pleasure to converse with a man as yourself in the tongue of the educated."

Ferox bowed to the bishop, and then he straightened up and looked the bishop in the eye.

"The honor has been all mine, your Excellency."

The bishop put his hand on Ferox's shoulder, and he noticed the hungry look in the bishop's eyes had returned. His gut clenched as the bishops touch ignited old scars, but the smile on Ferox's face never wavered.

"You must be weary from your travels, my son. Come and rest in my palace for a few days before you depart."

The pudgy hand squeezed his shoulder as Ferox maintained a respectful expression. A chill ran down his spine as memories of years of abuse started to flood his thoughts. *Sorry to disappoint you,* he thought, *but I am not spreading my arse cheeks for the likes of you.* Ferox bowed his head as he replied.

"Regretfully, your Excellency, I do think it best if I were to leave quickly. Some of the people in the camp already suspect that my loyalties do not align with theirs. I will send you word once I am safe in Durnovaria."

The hungry look Ferox had just seen in the bishop's eyes went cold again.

"Yes, my son."

The bishop displayed a smirking grin as he dismissed Ferox with a wave of his hand.

"Be off with you then. And may the Christos bless your journey with speed and safety."

Ferox left, his mind aswirl. *That fat pedo was almost too easy,* he thought. He knew the bishop's idea of a conversation with Petrus would involve some good old-fashioned torture, and if things went as he thought they would, Petrus would never leave this place alive. What would happen if Gildas dallied too long, and Brigid did not fall into his net? But as he thought about it, he was not worried. *If only Petrus was eliminated, this would work,* he thought. He could not see Brigid being able to run this group successfully. After all, she was only a woman.

CHAPTER EIGHTEEN

Arturius sat cross-legged on his makeshift mattress, eyes closed, trying to calm his thoughts. He was still in Caleva, his men healing their wounds and replenishing their supplies, and if Brigid and the scouts came back with a favorable report, they were ready to leave. He could not wait to be rid of this place. The heavy hand of the bishop and his soldiers was oppressive, but it was early in the morning, a time that he cherished. These stoic breathing exercises helped calm him; it was just what he needed right now.

His thoughts were also of Senna. During the fight, her safety was all he was worried about, even more so than winning the battle; he had just wanted to get her to a safe place. He would have died to protect her, and that confirmed for him that he loved her. When he had helped her hurry back to the wagons during the battle he felt like the wall of ice was finally melting. Brigid could tell he was in love with her before even he knew it, and she believed Senna felt the same, admonishing him to be patient. He hoped that Sister Brigid was correct.

He and his companions occupied the largest abandoned villa they could find next to the main forum of the town, a comfortable place to stay compared to being on the road. Despite that, he could tell his companions were also uncomfortable being in Caleva, wanting to leave as badly as he did. He had kept reassuring his men that once the scouts returned, they could get back on the road again, all packed up and ready to go as soon as the word was given.

As for the house itself, it had obviously once been the dwelling of wealthy Romanized Britons, but it had been vacant a long time. The roof sagged and leaked in a few places, and the small windows in the semilunar openings of the gables must have been broken now for years. Inside, the once colorful frescos were faded and peeling, with cracks and spots of mold in various places. Past the entrance and anteroom was a small, enclosed courtyard with a shallow pool in the middle called the impluvium. The roof over the courtyard, which once let in light through an oculus, had partially collapsed so the central pond now looked like a wild bog, with weeds and vines everywhere.

The villa's former owners had clearly been pagan, the frescos and mosaics of the house featuring scenes from classical antiquity with portrayals of wood nymphs, satyrs, and other mythological frescoes. Some of the art on the walls had sexual themes, particularly in a small room hidden in the family quarters that was covered floor to ceiling with frankly pornographic motifs. That room had little peepholes incorporated into the room's design, apparently so the watchers could view sexual acts that were being performed within.

The building's air of neglect and decay was disquieting, but the lodgings were large enough, and many women and children were staying here, despite the questionable themes on the walls. Macro had just arrived two days after the caravan had arrived, and his arthritis was reportedly improved. Arturius was happy to yield the mantle of leadership to this old legionary while Brother Petrus was visiting the bishop, and Arturius had come to the unsurprising conclusion that Macro had been fully able to travel, he just had not wanted to oversee the army in a fight.

Arturius wasn't angry about it; he remembered his stepfather telling him that a great general must love his army like his own child, yet to win the battle, he must be willing to destroy that same child he so loved. It took a certain mindset to win a battle. The old warrior loved training them, and he suspected Macro could not stand being responsible when anyone got killed. He knew the feeling.

There were always a few empty chairs after a battle, and he had felt the pain of remembering the dead and injured men he had commanded. *I would love it if someone else could take my role,* he thought, *but who would that be?* No one else was willing or able to assume the mantle of command, a heavy burden indeed, but Arturius was grateful these last few days that he was not responsible for the day-to-day running of the refugees themselves.

Arturius's quiet revery was suddenly interrupted, the sound of shouting in the distance. *Was that Senna's voice,* he wondered. The sound of the commotion grew louder until he heard the front door burst open. He ran in from his side chamber into the atrium to see what the bedlam was all about, with Caradoc and Cerdic right behind him.

The girls were shouting, "We must do something! I knew we should not have come here."

Senna and Lucillia were agitated and weeping, yelling out simultaneously as Arturius and the others rushed in, crowding into the portico surrounding the courtyard.

"Slow it down. One at a time," Macro, demanded, worry lining his face. "What is all this about?"

After a few moments of calming herself, Senna spat out, "That pig-faced bastard of a bishop has arrested Brother Petrus for heresy. He is to be burned at the stake!"

Arturius was stunned as he and the rest stood there in shocked silence.

"How can this be?" sputtered Arturius. "Your father controls the military here. There is no way he could let that happen."

Then a dark realization struck home. If they tried to free Petrus, there could be a civil war between the bishop's men and themselves. What power did Ambrosius actually have?

Senna spoke rapidly in a quavering voice, "Those bloody priests told us to leave immediately when we brought Brother Petrus some honey cakes, and they would not let us see him. They told us what Gildas had planned for him. When I told them my father would stop them, they told us he has no choice in the matter!"

"What on earth did Petrus do to deserve this?" asked Arturius, fear blossoming in his breast.

"We don't know," Senna quailed.

"Petrus was being Petrus," Cerdic muttered. "He has a heart of gold, but he does not know when to shut up."

"No telling what those boy-buggering hypocrites will try to do," Macro exclaimed. "I have heard some unsettling rumors about this Gildas and his cronies."

"We must speak to your father," Arturius said to the girls as he put his hand on Senna's shoulder. "Surely, there is a way out of this! Macro, we need a delegation of us to go to Ambrosius and see what we can do."

They all agreed upon the wisdom of this; the question was who should go. The group bantered back and forth, and eventually the consensus was that Macros and Arturius should be the ones to talk to Ambrosius, and that one of his daughters should go with them. Lucilia was so upset that she could not even speak. Senna seemed the most levelheaded of the two now, and she tearfully said yes. Arturius was glad she had agreed to come. *After all,* he thought, *what man could refuse his daughter."*

When the three arrived at the military compound, the guards in black were their usual sullen and unhelpful selves, but the presence of their commander's daughter eventually led them to be admitted to Ambrosius Aurelianus's quarters. Senna's father looked thin and pale, his face careworn from years of outdoor exposure and the burdens of leadership. In contrast, his eyes were kindly looking, especially when he regarded Senna.

Ambrosius wore a simple white linen tunic with a narrow purple hem at its borders, its only adornment being a military style belt, looking some forty years older than his daughters, a not unusual arrangement in the traditional Roman elites. He grimaced in pain when he stood up from behind his desk to greet them, assuming an erect military posture as he welcomed Macro and Arturius with the quaintly outdated Roman style handshake.

"I believe I know what troubles you and your friends," he said as gave them all a worried look. "Senna, and gentlemen, please tell me your thoughts."

She told her father in a torrent of words of her love for Petrus and Brigid, reminding her father of how they had been surrogate parents for both her and her sister while Arturius and Macro amplified the importance Petrus played in founding their community. After Ambrosius had heard their tale, his brow furrowed in concern.

"I had no idea they played such a role."

Ambrosius stroked his chin, deep in thought as silence filled the room. *How can he say something like that?* Arturius thought. He knew his daughters had lived with them, and he had to know that Brother Petrus and Brigid were the leaders of the community. A cold chill ran down his spine. He thought he knew what was coming next.

Finally, the general spoke in a deep and resonating voice.

"That new bishop is a pompous arse, but he is trying to promote the faith here in Britannia. The empire has withdrawn military and political support, so he is all we have. If we can keep him happy, then perhaps we can stay in the good graces of the Church leaders in Rome."

He started to pace around the room with his hands clasped behind his back as if he was on a parade ground addressing the troops.

"We must become reunited with Rome, and that can only happen if Rome thinks of us as Christians of the true faith. If we cannot get along with this bishop, then we have no chance to rejoin the empire. I have fought all my life to allow Britannia to be able to return to the civilized world. I must work with this man to keep that hope alive."

Senna and the others looked stricken, but no words came. He stopped his pacing and opened his arms in supplication.

"I cannot throw away our best chance at reunification just to save one man. Sometimes, sacrifices must be made, and this is one of those times. The execution of Brother Petrus must proceed."

There was a shocked silence.

Senna blurted out, "Papa, you cannot be serious!"

Arturius's heart went out for her. *Poor Senna,* he thought. His opinion of Ambrosius plummeted, sacrificing Brother Petrus as a casualty of his war in this impossible dream. *The death of Petrus would be pointless*, he thought. *Can't he accept that?* All three objected at once, but Ambrosius shushed them as he bristled.

"These charges of heresy are serious."

"What gives Gildas the right to tell us what to believe," Arturius sputtered.

Macro calmly interjected, "The entire Western Roman empire is falling apart, so the church feels the Christos is displeased in some way, and they need to root out heresy to regain his favor. The question is, what is a heresy and what is not?"

Ambrosius stopped his pacing as he shook his head.

"Indeed," he said, "that is the question. I am an old man now, and a simple soldier. All these theological disputes are very confusing to me, but I do know that Gildas was sent to stamp out the teachings of the British cleric named Pelagius."

Arturius shook his head in disgust.

"Who else does he want to eradicate?"

Ambrosius shrugged his shoulders.

"Gildas also despises Patrick, the bishop in Hibernia. Gildas believes Petrus is his only son, and what better way to punish the father than by killing the son?"

Arturius was stunned. He had no idea that Patrick and Petrus were related. The Hibernian bishop was famous throughout Britannia for going there and performing mass conversions in a place where the Roman Empire never controlled. That made no sense to Arturius to punish a man who promoted their faith so well, but then the Christians often made little sense to him. The tone of Ambrosius grew more somber.

"So, Gildas wants Petrus to burn at the stake, that much is certain, and I cannot stop it."

Arturius was seething, furious at Senna's father to acquiesce to this obvious injustice. Anger and worry roiled together in his heart, but somehow, he managed to keep his mouth shut, his hands clenched so tightly together he could feel his fingernails might be drawing blood, anything to stifle an angry explosion.

Ambrosius shrugged, "Gildas also despises Petrus because he was married, as he does not favor that institution for the priesthood. And not to just any wife, either; Sister Brigid has a forceful personality, I understand. The bishop's homilies in mass have been all about women being temptations of the devil for us men to avoid."

"I cannot believe the churchmen in Rome could be such fools," Senna muttered.

"You have no idea," Ambrosius remarked as he shrugged. "I was told she is red-headed and left-handed, and apparently the Roman's consider both to be evil."

"So Gildas hates women, redheads, and left-handers," scoffed Macro. "What is next? People with freckles?"

"Now," the old general softly muttered, "I heard Brigid is still with a scouting expedition, correct?"

"Yes," replied Macro.

"The best thing you can do is to send out a messenger and keep her away from here," Ambrosius said. "In fact, I would try to get your entire community on the move now. It is too dangerous here for all of you."

Arturius fought the tears that were forming in his eyes. *I cannot believe this,* he thought. His admiration for the old general had disappeared like a wisp of smoke.

"And I am serious about keeping Brigid away," Ambrosius continued. "Gildas has officially asked me to bring her in for questioning. That means she will be tortured and executed. And as for Petrus, my hands are tied. The execution will proceed as planned in the morning."

Try as he might, Arturius could not think of a way out of this horrible situation. Though Arturius realized a civil war within the walls of Caleva would be a disaster, still Ambrosius was doing nothing to help them. *That old man is a cold-hearted bastard,* he thought. *Petrus was more of a real father to his daughters than he ever was.*

"Why in the morning?" Senna blurted out. "That is so quick. Can't we do something?"

She ran up to Ambrosius and hugged him, burying her head in his chest. He looked taken aback, as if startled by the sudden display of public affection, but then his eyes softened.

"My dearest Senna, I can understand why you are so upset, but my troops no longer are mine. And it must be tomorrow, as Petrus was not to die alone. So are the two other prisoners your group captured. Vortigern's son was fighting with the pagans, so his life is forfeited, burned at the stake along with Petrus. He may be dying of his wounds, but Gildas wants him burned while he still lives to feel the flames. That is why the executions need to proceed quickly."

Macro's jaw slackened, then he muttered, "Vortigern will have Gildas's bollocks for that. What in the name of the Christos is that bishop thinking?"

"Believe me, I have tried to reason with him," Ambrosius snorted. "And there is another reason we cannot delay. Petrus specifically requested to be burned tomorrow."

Another shocked silence filled the room. Arturius could not understand why Petrus would make such a request, but then it dawned on him.

"Petrus knows that Brigid is out of Caleva now," he said. "He is trying to save her. If Petrus dies before she returns, she will be warned about Gildas and not allow herself to be taken."

"You may be right," Ambrosius said with a grim nod. "And Gildas is so blinded, he has agreed to that request."

"What about Horsa," sneered Arturius, "Are they burning him for heresy also, though he is not a Christian?"

"No, Gildas has another fate in store for him. The Saxons use fire to send their souls to their gods, so there will be no burning at the stake for him. He is being dispatched in another way they fear, by drowning. Those who die that way cannot ascend to Valhalla."

"This is such a waste. Those bastards would fetch quite a ransom," snorted Macro. "This is madness!"

"This would create a blood feud with Hengist," Arturius muttered. "This bishop is a fool."

Ambrosius held out his hands, distress itched on his face.

"I told Gildas the same, and I got nowhere. He is like a starving dog with a juicy bone; he will not let this go."

Watching the old general, Arturius made a vow to himself. *Generals get used to ordering men to their deaths, so this must seem trifling to him*, he thought. *I swear that I will never allow myself to become this callous as a general.* A depressing gloom filled the room.

"Can we visit with Brother Petrus this evening?" Macro asked, breaking the silence. "Perhaps we can grant some last request he may have."

"Go now," Ambrosius replied in a somber tone.

The old general bent over his desk, his hands trembling as he started to write on a wax tablet.

"I am writing an order to that effect. And I must remind you, if you try to free him, all of you may die, including my daughters. This is what Petrus wants, for you all to leave in peace."

Arturius could not say another word. *I almost feel sorry for him*, he thought.

I don't know if his daughters will ever forgive him. I know I won't. Macro stood at attention and gave Ambrosius a military salute, his closed right fist snapping against his left breast.

"Thank you, general, for hearing us out," Macro said. I understand your position, and we will trouble you no further this evening."

Ambrosius returned the salute but then hugged his daughter in a warm embrace. He held her by her shoulders as he captured her gaze.

"My darling Senna, it has given me such joy to see you and your sister these past few days. To see you both alive and well has been an unexpected gift from the Christos. I failed you in Novomagus; let me not fail you now. You must leave as soon as possible."

Ambrosius looked down in shame, then he glanced up, turning to Macro.

"Centurion, in my absence, I am asking you to be a guardian for my daughters."

Senna gasped, as her eyes continued to well up in tears.

"Father!" she cried out.

Ambrosius gave her a long and tender embrace.

"Senna, I am old. I do not know how much longer I will be on this earth. I must stay here in Caleva for now, but as soon as I can, I will join you, and I swear to the Christos that I will defend you and your sister with my last breath. Until then, Macro, I need your help. So, what say you?"

The crusty old Centurion's eyes misted.

"It will be an honor, sir!"

Ambrosius directed his gaze towards Senna who was still in his arms.

"Stay with me for a while, my daughter, while these two go and visit with your friend."

Ambrosius's eyes welled up with tears, and she nodded. The general called for the guards to escort them to the chambers where Petrus was held. He and Macro left the room, escorted out of the main southern gate to a building formerly used for training gladiators. Now it was the residence for the bishop, and it had been upgraded into a small fortress. The walls had been reinforced with guard towers and platforms with ballistae on the corners of the compound, surrounding by a ditch that bristled with sharpened stakes.

"Arturius, it would be a very bloody affair to try to get past the those walls," Macro said as they walked through the gates.

Arturius eyed the Ballistae with trepidation. He realized an attack with those deadly machines in place would be suicide. *Is it worth trying*? He thought. *What else can we do*? He turned to one of his escorts as he pointed.

"I've never seen ballistae in action before. How good are they?"

"Very," one of the guards crowed. "They can skewer three men at once from two hundred paces or more. In serving with Ambrosius, we have been all over Britannia, and Caleva is the only place that still has them. The legionaries took all their artillery with them when they pulled out. They are hard to build and maintain, but they have served Caleva well so far."

Unlike his comrade, Arturius thought the guard who had just spoken was still loyal to Ambrosius, as he was not wearing the black livery that the bishop's men wore. Still, Arturius knew he had to be wary. The guard spoke up again, this time with a hint of anger in his voice.

"The bishop stripped those machines from our walls to protect himself. Rumors are he may be going north to Viroconium, and if they do, I'm sure they'll take those units with them. It pisses me off, because I ain't going nowhere. I got a wife and kids here, so I ain't so fond of weakening our own defenses to protect the likes of him."

"Can't you make more?" Arturius asked.

"Maybe," the dour guard spat out. "They promised to leave a couple men here that are familiar with them, but it will take some time to construct them and train the crews. It ain't right to do that, but what else can we do?"

The guard in black smirked, "You should come with us, brother. You will get paid for once, and you can always find some other willing doxy wherever we go. And I would be careful about insulting the bishop, my friend. I will keep my mouth shut, but what you just said could be dangerous for you."

"Maybe so, but I ain't finding one who can cook like my Tilla."

"You're being an idiot if you stay," the guard in black smirked, "but it's your life, brother."

The guards fell silent as Macro and Arturius entered the main building of the compound, greeting them once more with suspicious stares. Their escorts showed the officer of the watch Ambrosius's orders, so they were led to a room watched by another pair of surly, black-liveried guards after being thoroughly searched. After the guards let Macro and Arturius inside, the door closed and was bolted behind them. Brother Petrus was engaged in prayer, eyes closed, and at first, he did not seem to realize they had entered the room. After a few moments, he opened his eyes and smiled as he welcomed them.

"It is good to see you both."

His eyes changed from an open welcome to a look of concern.

"They are not arresting you also, are they?"

"No, no, Brother," replied Arturius. "We came to see Ambrosius Aurelianus to see if we could stop this madness. After we spoke with him, we asked to see you."

"You cannot halt the execution, I presume?" asked Petrus.

Both Arturius and Macro nodded as despair clouded his eyes.

"I am sure you heard that I requested that my sentence be carried out tomorrow," Petrus said, "And no matter what, you must keep Brigid away from this place! I can forgive Gildas for his sins, but tell her I said to seek no revenge, as it is evil for one Christian to kill another."

Arturius put his hand on Brother Petrus's shoulder.

"You can tell her yourself if we can break you out of here, Brother."

Petrus pulled the hand away as he stood up in anger.

"No," Petrus barked, "there should be no violence on my account. My fate is sealed, and we can do nothing to change that.

"He is right, Arturius," Macro grunted. "It will be suicide for us to try. I have seen those bloody bolt throwers in action, and it ain't pretty."

There was a solemn silence. Then Arturius finally spoke.

"Brother, what other choice do we have? We cannot let you die here."

"No one must perish on my account," blurted out Petrus. "What will be will be. However, Gildas holds you all in suspicion. Our band must flee this place tomorrow morning at the latest. If you are forced to watch my execution, I feel our people might rise and start a civil war between the garrison and ourselves. Nothing good can come of that."

Arturius replied in an agitated tone, "But Brother___"

Petrus gently took Arturius's hand into his own as he gave him an intense look.

"Arturius, promise me no violence will be used on my behalf. Now say it!"

He gazed into the eyes of Petrus, then he slowly blinked.

"If that is truly your wish, Brother, yes."

Petrus let go of his hand and gently took the grizzled paw of Macro.

"Macro, I want you to promise me the same."

Macro hesitated for a moment, and then he wiped a tear from his eyes with the sleeve of his other hand as he replied in a quavering voice.

"As you wish, brother."

"Good."

A sad silence permeated the room. Then Arturius spoke up, shaking his head as he did so.

"I don't understand why your fellow priests are doing this. Don't you worship the same god?"

"I also find it hard to believe that Gildas and I are reading the same holy scriptures," Petrus muttered, "yet our views seem so different. Nonetheless, he seems firmly convinced of his righteousness. I cannot imagine the Christos approving this, but then again, perhaps my martyrdom may serve my lord's purpose. I must confess I am also struggling with forgiving Gildas for his actions, but my prayers continue."

The mournful quiet returned once more. Arturius was in a state of shock, disbelief, anger, and now resignation. He wanted to bring every man who could wield a weapon here to free their leader, consequences be damned, but what Petrus wanted was clear, and Macro was probably correct that any attempt would be too bloody. *I cannot believe he is praying to forgive that monster,* he thought. Then it dawned on him. Petrus seemed determined to die like a saint.

"You are right, Brother," Macro remarked. "I will order all of us to leave today. I promise to keep Brigid well away from here and safe."

Macro turned to Arturius with a mournful expression.

"Will you help me in this?"

Arturius nodded. Petrus gave them both a searching look,

"I have one other request, one that is irregular to say the least."

Brother Petrus leaned in close to the pair and whispered his plea. As Petrus told them his last request, their eyes opened wide with shock.

"Promise me!" whispered Petrus.

After a period of silence, Macro said, "It shall be done, my brother."

Arturius's eyes welled up with tears.

"As you wish, Brother Petrus."

Arturius knew it was time to go. The pair knocked on the door, signaling to the guards they were ready to depart. They silently walked out with heavy hearts as Petrus closed his eyes and resumed his prayers.

CHAPTER NINETEEN

Caradoc was stiff and sore from the endless wait, aware that the execution of Brother Petrus was slated for two hours post meridiem, and it was well past that now. The schedule had called for a Christian mass in the morning as they condemned Pelagianism and whatever else that fat turd of a priest wanted to drone on about, and now they were late. *Sanctimonious gobshites,* he thought. *Those bloody priests won't shut up.* Still, the extra time would help; the caravan had left at dawn, and he wanted them as far away as possible.

He and his four companions remained hidden in an abandoned dwelling located next to the southeastern section of the town's wall, midway between the southern and eastern gates. From his vantage point, he could see the crowd packed around the two figures tied to stakes about two hundred paces away. Though Caradoc was stiff from staying motionless for so long, he had never taken his eyes off the proceedings. The proper timing of this operation was crucial; it was time now.

Petrus and Catigern were easily visualized, elevated above the crowd on a platform atop a huge pile of wood beneath them. Tied to tall stakes, their arms bound from behind, Petrus stood proud and erect, while the figure of Catigern was slumped over. Caradoc called for his men to come out of hiding when he spied the black-robed priests carrying torches to set the pyre alight. Tendrils of smoke swirled up as the proud form of Petrus remained visible through the haze. The sight of these helpless men being murdered filled him with rage as he tried to keep calm for the task at hand.

"Our first target is the taller one," he barked out. "Ready, aim, loose!"

He and his four archers let fly a fusillade of arrows that sped long and true. Caradoc breathlessly stared at the tall figure still visible through the smoky haze, certain some of the missiles had struck. The body of Petrus had jerked, then his head fell to his chest as if he were unconscious. He felt satisfaction that their arrows had gone where they had been aimed, but he was also overwhelmed by a feeling of sadness. He had done what he had to do, but still the deed filled him with guilt. *But this was what Petrus wanted, and I must be sure he is truly dead,* he thought. He ordered another volley.

"Loose," Caradoc commanded once more.

Another flurry of arrows arched towards the priest. *He will feel no pain now,* he thought. Caradoc and his four archers were the best they had, and they did not miss often. Caradoc blinked away the tears in his eyes as he thought of his own hand being partially responsible for the death of their beloved Petrus.

"Remember, lads, this was the last wish of Brother Petrus, to die quickly instead of by the flames. Do not feel guilty."

He had never experienced a mix of emotions like this before, and he prayed to Dagda and Danu to never present to him a dilemma like this again. He would never know whose arrow had killed him, but he was certain he did not miss. From above him, he heard a crow cry out, and he looked up and saw a black bird with soulless eyes staring at him from a nearby rooftop. *That bird must be the phantom queen, The Morrigan,* he thought. He cursed those three witches of the fates. It must have been them who had made this day happen.

"Okay, boys, Petrus requested us to give the same mercy to Catigern, whether he deserves it or not. So, one more volley, if you please."

He drew back his bow.

"Loose!"

A new fusillade of arrows struck the other motionless figure, then Caradoc cast a concerned glance at the pandemonium as some people in the forum had started to point towards his position. They knew where his men were now, so they had to move quickly. He thought just one volley was enough for Catigern, half dead as he already was.

"Time to go, lads," he barked out to the men beside him.

He and the archers rushed to the ladder they had previously hidden and put it against the town wall, and then they scurried up, pulling the ladder up with them once they reached the walkway. They hoisted themselves over the top of the wall and made their way down to the ground on the other side, and then they ran towards the southeast at a steady, loping pace. Caradoc heard shouts of alarm from the eastern and southern gatehouses, as a few desultory arrows struck the ground well behind them as they ran.

They were several hundred yards away when some footmen emerged from the gates to pursue them, but none were mounted, and once they met their own horsemen, they saddled up and sped away. The group cantered to the southeast, and once out of sight from the town, he and his men turned north after fooling their pursuers as to the direction they were headed. They pulled up at a small, picturesque body of water known as Kiln Pond, where Caradoc was relieved to see the rest of the caravan there.

When he got closer to the rest of their party, Caradoc was surprised to a handful of troops amid the caravan clad in black tunics, accompanied by a portly priest. *Those are the bishop's men*, he thought. *What are they doing here?* He was even more surprised when he spotted the figure of Horsa talking with Macro, Cerdic, Arturius and the priest. The bishop's man looked angry, Horsa appeared furious, the Calevan troops seemed dispirited while his friends all sported bemused expressions on their faces. Caradoc dismounted and strode up to the arguing group of men, when Cerdic greeted him with a scowl.

"Welcome, my friend, to an argument between the two most obnoxious people I have ever met, and neither party speaks the other's language. On this side, we have Amadeus, the bishop's priest, here at this pond to have his pagan captive drowned in dishonor."

Then Cerdic waved towards the scowling Saxon king.

"And on the other side, we have Horsa, with whom you are already familiar. We just happened to stumble upon this cheerful gathering, barely averting the untimely demise of our Saxon guest. Of course, Amadeus wants to drown Horsa, and Horsa wants to eat the priest's liver. I am in a mood to grant both requests, but logic dictates this is probably not the wisest course of action."

Arturius's expression shifted into one more somber.

"Were you and the others successful?"

Caradoc sadly nodded as he tried to fight back the tears. After a few moments of silence, Horsa broke the solemn mood as he started to resume his tirade.

Cerdic cut him off as he bellowed out, "Silence, Horsa, or I will cut out your tongue!"

Then Cerdic turned back towards him and shrugged.

"Killing Horsa when we could ransom him never made sense. Besides gold, that would bring us some goodwill to return Horsa to the Middle Saxons, and then they would be inclined to attack Gildas and Caleva, not us. That is, of course, if they do not find Horsa as annoying as we do. As for Amadeus, I say let him go back and lick the paw of his master. Having Horsa kill him in front of us would upset the Christians among us, even if he deserves it."

Caradoc nodded, then he glanced over at Macro. He had been somewhat surprised to see him join the group in Caleva, and to his eye the centurion did not look crippled by arthritis. *Arturius was right,* he thought. *I think Macro dodged the fight of the caravan on purpose.* Still, Caradoc was not disappointed in him. If Macro did not want to be in command during a battle, there was nothing wrong with that. He and his friends had done well enough, and he was proud of them.

"I assume we all agree to send this bloody barbarian back for ransom, eh?" Macro said as he slapped his centurion's cane in his hand.

All of them nodded.

"Well then," Macro said with a toothy smile, "Horsa claims he is the leader of the West Saxons now in addition to the Middle Saxons, and those are your people, aren't they Cerdic? Could you arrange for this ransom to occur? I understand the West Saxons and the remaining Cantullevauni have a truce now. Do you believe you could go and negotiate a decent price for Horsa's return and not have them remove your head in the process?"

Cerdic's face brightened.

"Yes," he replied, "I think I can. The West Saxons have a strong sense of honor. If they give their word to allow me to negotiate in safety, not even Horsa can break that covenant."

"Then let us make it so," Macro said.

Now that they had a plan Cerdic informed Horsa that he would be returning to his people, and the Saxon chieftain seemed to calm down when Cerdic pointed out he could always return later to feast on the livers of both Amadeus and Gildas. Then Cerdic turned to Amadeus, who became mollified when it was pointed out if he left now, he and his men would not be harmed. Though the priest was nervous about what Gildas would say, he seemed to realize returning empty handed was better than being left to the tender mercies of Horsa.

"Has anyone seen Brigid yet?" Caradoc asked.

"We have scouts out looking for her," Arturius replied. "We'll be able to stop her before she gets very close."

Caradoc was glad that he would not have to be the one to tell her about Petrus. The team of leaders conferred some more, and then Cerdic and a half dozen riders set out northeast with Horsa as the rest of the caravan continued towards Camalet. Amadeus and the Calevan soldiers morosely walked south, shorn of their horses, weapons, and armor. Caradoc gave Cerdic a worried look as he rode away. *I hope that Cerdic knows what he is doing,* he thought. *I am sure he is happy to be going home, but Macro is right, his head just might end up in a basket. May the gods protect you, my friend.*

CHAPTER TWENTY

Cerdic rode horseback along the dusty trail to the village where he hoped one of the key chieftains of the West Saxons could be found. He knew the path well, having traveled this way so many times in his youth, but that had been years ago. He did not know who led the tribe now, or if they were even here, spread out in the countryside as the Saxons typically were. He had also decided to travel alone., hoping one man would not be perceived as a threat. Horsa had been left behind in the safe keeping of the Catuvellauni until Cerdic would call for him after the ransom had been arranged.

He tried to control his nervousness, hoping his head would not adorn a pike in front of the village by tonight. He had no idea if anyone would recognize him, or if they would receive him as a friend. One of his father's old companions was the chieftain of the village he was headed to, a man who he hoped was still influential with the tribal council the Saxons called the Witan, but if someone else was in charge, they might attempt send him back to Aelle. *And if they try,* he thought, *then I will not go down without a fight.* His thoughts flitted back over the last few days as he rode along.

Cerdic had entered the Catuvellauni capital of Verulamium without incident and had received welcoming comments from the guards who recognized his name and respected his father's legacy. He had left the city as a boy, and he returned as a man. No one recognized him until he introduced himself, but once he had, he was greeted by the people and the city council with the enthusiasm of having seen a person alive whom they had feared was already dead.

His father had ruled as a king, but after his murder on *The Night of the Long Knives,* the tribe had been controlled by a committee of its most prominent citizens, with the leader of the group changing on a yearly basis. The Catuvellauni had not fared well under this system. More than half their lands, the south and east, were now dominated by the Middle Saxons. The West Saxons, not surprisingly, had stayed in the west and were nominally loyal, but as for the Catuvellauni themselves, they were now primarily holed up in the walled city. Most of the people tribe were concentrated in the town itself, forced off the land by the current turmoil.

The population of the city itself had been depleted by war and immigration as trade and commerce had ground to a halt. Verulamium was not as abandoned looking as Caleva had been, but even with the influx of people from the countryside, the total population of the tribe was a pittance compared to what it was years ago. Cerdic's father, Cynric, had been elected as dictator for life by the ruling council, but his demise had prompted infighting among the various nobles of the tribe. The rotating system of leadership satisfied no one and had been less than effective in dealing with the Middle Saxon threat.

When Cynric ruled, the tribe's Saxon and Jute auxiliaries, combined with the native tribal levies, had formed an effective fighting force against their enemies. After the passing of Cynric, the bonds of trust had started to break down between the native British and their allies. Horsa had arrived via the Middle Saxons to fill the void of leadership of West Saxons, and Cedric had been told that relations between the Catuvellauni and the West Saxons had been in a downward spiral ever since.

War had been barely averted, in large part because Horsa's ambitions in the west had taken him away for the last year. It had taken Cerdic several days to convince the council that ransoming Horsa was in their best interest, but agreeing to share a portion of the ransom helped sway their opinion to allow him to continue to the Saxons' camp. Despite the risk, he was happy to go, as he longed to see his family once again, hoping the West Saxons knew where his mother and siblings had gone. They were probably living with Jutes allied with the West Saxons further to the east, and he vowed to find them when his business here was done.

Cerdic' sense of foreboding rose to a higher pitch with each passing mile as he moved from the tilled fields of the British into lands smelling of livestock so favored by the Norse; he was now in West Saxon lands. Unlike him, his horse seemed unconcerned as it plodded along until he spotted the Saxon village. Cerdic felt the butterflies in his belly that he always experienced before a fight, his chest thumping like a drum. Once he was outside the main entrance, his heart seemed to skip a beat when the massive gates opened, and a gaggle of warriors streamed out. He held his chin up and hoisted the white banner higher, painfully aware the white flag of truce was a Roman symbol. *I hope these bastards remember that*, he thought.

Cerdic's helmet hung by his saddle and his weapons were sheathed. He tried to keep his face looking calm while hiding his roiling apprehension. Even if he were recognized, Cerdic knew he could well be killed as a traitor, coming alone and representing the British. He hoped that he could make it past these guards to speak to the chieftain, hoping the approaching men would allow him to keep his head still on his shoulders. *And if the chieftain does not welcome me,* he mused, *I do not want to think about that.*

Several furiously barking dogs had accompanied the footmen, and Cerdic was happy to see that his nag seemed unconcerned by the mongrels. He was not the greatest of horsemen, and if the beast had gotten spooked by the hounds, he could end up with his arse in the dust. The approaching warriors gazed upon him with suspicious eyes as they spread out to surround him, their spears at the ready. He stopped the horse and raised the flag even higher. *If they attack now, I am done for*, he thought. There was a menacing silence for a few moments as he stared down upon the warriors who looked ready to skewer him.

"I come in peace to talk to your chieftain," Cerdic loudly called out.

Another long and uncomfortable pause ensued. Finally, a tall and muscular looking warrior spoke up.

"Cerdic," the guard said in a questioning voice, "is that you?"

Cerdic gazed at the imposing spearman closely. A wave of relief flooded over him.

"Ord, I see several of your canine wives greeted me when I arrived, but what did you do with those pigs you used to shag?"

The group burst into laughter as Ord flushed beet red.

"You are confused again, young Cerdic," Ord retorted. "I had to eat the pigs you were swiving, so you must settle for buggering some old, toothless thrall instead!"

"Those weren't thralls," Cerdic chuckled. "You must have them confused with your randy sisters."

With that he dismounted, and the childhood friends greeted each other with a bear-like hug as the laughter continued.

"Cerdic, what are you doing here?" Ord gushed. "By Thunor's hammer, it is good to see you! I heard you were dead."

"I can't die yet," Cerdic snorted, "Not until I have my way with that sister of yours, the only pretty one in your family. What was her name again? Hildur, I think."

Ord shook his head as he chuckled., "That is not going to happen. She has three children now and is bigger than your horse. She also happens to be married to Sibley over there."

The entire group descended into laughter once more, then Cerdic touched his friend's shoulder.

"In all seriousness, I am here to speak to your chieftain. I have come to talk about returning your leader Horsa to you."

"Horsa?" Ord scowled. "By the Gods, you can keep that randy gobshite. He was perpetually drunk, always trying to bed someone's wife, sister, and mother, and maybe even your goat.

"In that order?" Cerdic said with a grin.

Ord laughed, then his countenance darkened again.

"Horsa is an obnoxious oath breaker. That svein hund can go back to his brother Hengist, or he can go to Hel for all I care."

The group of men with Ord growled in agreement. At first Cerdic was taken aback, then he broke into a grin.

"He was bloody annoying when he was a prisoner with us, but I had no idea he was so unpopular here."

"How did you capture him, Cerdic?" Ord snorted. "Did he get drunk and fall off his horse?"

"No, it is a long story, and I will tell it to your chieftain tonight. You'll hear the details then."

Ord grabbed him by him by both shoulders and said, "Stay with me as my guest, Cerdic, my wife Gytha and I welcome you!"

"Of course."

Cerdic wondered about what happened to Ord's other sisters, but he did not want to broach that topic. *I do not want to piss off any other husbands right now*, he thought. He spent the day reconnecting with old friends and that evening Cerdic headed to their chieftain's longhouse with trepidation, relieved he had gotten past the riskiest part of the journey, but he knew that his behavior tonight would make or break their offer for ransom. He was still nervous, but he had felt reassured when he stumbled upon his old childhood friends, and most of those old companions would be there tonight.

Growing up, he had split time between his father's household and that of his mother. His parents wanted him well versed in both cultures, but in his heart, he heard the call of his Norse ancestors. He had made many friends growing up here, and that had saved him today. He also felt comfortable in the world of the Britons, but the continual emphasis on worshiping the nailed White Christ had never resonated with him. *Turn the other cheek,* he thought, *love thy neighbor, sex only in a never-ending marriage with only one woman. That is not a warrior's way*!

It felt odd to be representing the interests of the Britons in negotiating with his mother's people, but among his mother's clan, a man's oath was considered sacred. Arturius, Caradoc, and he had made an oath of fealty to each other when they were slaves of the South Saxons. They had sworn loyalty to each other, and to punish Vortigern and Aelle for what they had done. It was the kind of vow that would earn a perpetual curse by the gods if you broke it. Jutes took their blood oaths seriously and that had priority over clan and sometimes even family. Cerdic knew it was an odd trio to be so devoted to each other, with Caradoc honoring the old gods of Britannia and Arturius being a part of the Roman world, but despite this they were firmly bonded together as brothers.

He was giddy in anticipation, feeling the glow of welcoming as he approached the great hall, a large rectangular building with a steep roof, adorned with intricately carved Norse imagery on the gables that encircled the entryway. Once inside, his senses were assaulted by the cloying smell of stale beer, wet dogs, perfumed and unperfumed bodies, and a barely detectable whiff of vomit. The stench contrasted with the pleasant smell of smoke from the fire and the delicious aroma of cooking food. He thought this was what Valhalla must be like: he had come home.

Although the sun was setting, it was still achingly bright outside compared to the smokey dimness of the long hall, but the gloom was contrasted by the cheerfully crackling firepits in the center of the room. Loud laughter and muted talk dominated the interior as men and women sat around the long tables that were nestled against the walls. The buzz of conversation was punctuated by the occasional growl of dogs fighting over a bone or the yelp of a serving maid being pinched by a drunken warrior.

His gaze was directed to a corpulent man who sat in the chair of honor at the end of the room. Cerdic was glad to see the chieftain was someone he remembered, his father's friend. Wulfgar was his name, and he sported a long yellow beard, well flecked with food stains, while his bald head contrasted with a fringe of yellowish-white hair about his ears. The beard was forked, well strewn with gold and silver clasps that kept the beard in its proper orientation.

The chieftain had numerous silver torcs on his arms, attesting to his prowess on the field of battle. The bald areas on his head were covered in blue tattoos, the whorls of Nordic knots and a wolf's head visible above each ear. He was not pretty to look at as his left ear was missing, his nose enormously bulbous and pitted, crisscrossed with multiple dilated blood vessels.

Cerdic made sure he kept his face in a friendly smile instead of laughing out loud. *A model of male beauty Wulfgar is not,* he thought, *but he is a leader of renown, and he respected my father.* Wulfgar had to be in his fifties at least, looking older than Cerdic remembered from his youth, but he saw intelligence in the chieftain's eyes as he shrewdly appraised the world around him. Cerdic sat to his right as a guest of honor, closest to Wulfgar's only functioning ear.

Serving wenches kept filling his drinking horn with ale, but to keep his wits about him Cerdic drank as sparingly as he could under the circumstances. He would surreptitiously spill some ale under the table, or he would go out to urinate while holding a full horn of ale, and he would then come back with an empty bladder and drinking horn. He liked the feeling of alcohol, but he preferred to avoid the sloppy drunk so favored by the Saxons. He had a tale to tell, and he needed to keep his mind sharp to do it.

When it came time to tell the story of his adventures to the group, he glossed over the degradations of being a slave and highlighted the battle against Horsa. At the end, he told of the rescue of Horsa from Gildas's troops, and what a tale it was. The crowd listened with rapt attention, but when it came to the rescue of Horsa from drowning, the hall grew strangely silent. It was apparent to him that the ill feelings towards Horsa were shared by many.

"Well, Cerdic," declared Wulfgar, "that was quite a rousing story for one so young, and you told the story well. I will call for a meeting with the Witan to decide what to do next. As for the ransom, that should be the responsibility of Hengist. Horsa being captured by you fighting for some British king showed he is unworthy to be our leader. I believe it is Hengist's problem to deal with, but it is the Witan that must decide."

With that, an audible sigh of relief filled the room, and the drinking continued again in earnest. Now that he had finished his performance, Cerdic felt he could relax and drink ale without fear of making a fool of himself. After a few more tankards he wandered outside, accompanied by Ord, searching for the latrine. They both laughed and staggered at the same time as they found a willing bush to accept the contents of their bladders.

"By Woden's missing eye, it is good to see you again, Ord! How are your parents doing? It sounds like your sisters are all doing well, but you have not told me about your mother and father."

"Mother is fine, living with Sibley and Hildur and helping with their children. Father died a warrior's death a year back, I am happy to say. He did not want to die like a Nithing, in bed as an old man. He was leading a war band that caught some Angles raiding our territory up north, and he died with his sword in his hand, taking two of those smelly, lice-ridden Angles with him. I hope the Valkyries took him to Valhalla. He deserved it, I think."

Ord paused for a moment as his cheery mood seemed to darken.

"Cerdic, I was sorry to hear about your mother and your brothers."

A cold feeling swept over him. He felt chills run up his spine as the hair on his back stood up.

"What do you mean, Ord?" Cerdic asked warily.

"You mean you don't know?" Ord asked.

"About what," Cerdic mumbled, trying to stave off his sense of panic.

Ord's eyes slowly blinked, then he put his hand to his forehead as he looked down at the ground. He then gazed straight into his eyes as he told him the news. Cerdic blanched in shock. The merriment of the evening was over.

CHAPTER TWENTY-ONE

Cerdic stood outside the large ring of stones, nervously opening and closing the hand holding his shield as he waited for his opponent to show up, and the svein hund was running late. He was furious. *Where is that bloody arsehole,* he thought. *I cannot believe that Nithing is making everyone wait like this.* Cerdic was forced to just stand there and stew while his mind kept replaying the events that had led to today's duel-to-the-death. He was about to fight in an Artwig, the ancient trial by combat that rival tribes of northern Germania used to settle disputes without an outright war. Much was at stake today. The winner would become the recognized leader of both the West Saxons and the Catuvellauni tribe. The loser would be feeding the worms.

Ord leaned forward to Cerdic's ear.

"The gods should be with you, Cerdic. That bastard murdered your mother and sold your siblings into slavery. Everyone in our village despises him, and we are not alone. All the West Saxon warbands want you to prevail."

Mentally preparing for the fight to come, he didn't acknowledge Ord's words. His face was a hard mask, but his insides roiled with nervousness, a witch's brew of anxiety, fear, anger, and excitement, but he also felt confidence in his own ability and skill to prevail. Most of all he was fueled by his desire for revenge. He noticed his hand gripping *Soul Stealer* was a little slick, so he bent down and grabbed a handful of dirt, and as the dust dried it improved his grip. The handle felt good, an extension of his arm and mind.

Fighting in an Artwig meant the two parties were asking for justice, the winner to be recognized by the gods as the righteous party. His opponent: Horsa. A large crowd had assembled to watch the event, the ring of combat surrounded by small hills that created a natural amphitheater for the crowd of Saxons and Catuvellauni to watch this thrilling event. Grey clouds scudded overhead in the moisture laden breeze, the hair of the spectators waving like banners in the wind. Rain was coming, but it was not here yet, and neither was his opponent.

For the West Saxons, what Horsa had done to Cerdic's family had been the final straw. Although his drinking buddies had given Horsa an alibi the night his mother was killed, everyone knew they had lied and that Horsa was really the guilty party. The whispers were that she had fought back when he had attempted to violate her, and her courage had been repaid at the cost of her life. Hers was not the only death in Cerdic's family. Horsa had often complained that Cerdic's siblings were potential rivals, and soon after her death, they had disappeared, sold into slavery, supposedly to pay his family's debts. Later he learned that the ship carrying them to the slave markets had gone down in a storm. Cerdic's immediate family were now all gone.

Arturius was here because he had accompanied Cerdic to the Witan to meet the leaders of the West Saxons and to plead for peaceful relations once the ransom was paid. Once Horsa became a free man, he exercised his freedom the day the ransom was paid by declaring his intention to kill the man who had humiliated him. Horsa had blamed Cerdic for his capture and had issued the challenge for the Artwig. Cerdic had consented to the challenge, and the Catuvellauni and West Saxons had both agreed that this trial by combat would determine their own future, decided upon by the will of the gods. *All the stars had to align in Valhalla for this*, he marveled, *and even that blaggard Hengist agreed.*

The East Saxon king had forced Horsa upon them by his brother, and to keep the peace, the governing council of the West Saxons had agreed to allow Horsa to return after Hengist paid the ransom, but if Horsa died in the Artwig, then it would not be the fault of the Witan. Instead, it would be the will of the gods. Hengist might be furious if his brother died but he could not blame anyone else. Everyone seemed willing to take the risk of allowing a boy like himself to become their ruler just to get rid of the drunken Horsa.

Cerdic figured that Hengist had agreed to the Artwig, thinking that Horsa would kill him. His brother was renowned as a fearsome warrior, drunk or not, as the rumors were he became a berserker in combat. What Hengist and Horsa did not know was that both the Catuvellauni and West Saxons had practiced swordplay with Cerdic, and both parties had been impressed with what they had seen. *But if Horsa wins, the Catuvellauni are buggered,* he thought. They would have to flee west, but Cerdic was confidant it would not come to that.

Once victorious, he planned to unify the West Saxons and Cantullevauni again to help each other against their rivals. Cerdic was still surprised Hengist had not ordered him killed outright, but his brother wanted to do it himself. Horsa wanted revenge as badly as he did, and the spectacle of an Artwig suited Horsa's purpose nicely. Kings needed the people to believe their leader was lucky, or people would not follow them. Having been captured by mere boys and former slaves had been unlucky indeed. Horsa had been humiliated and needed revenge. *He is not the only one needing revenge,* he thought. *I crave it more than he does.*

As he thought of his mother, tears welled up for a moment. Everyone said he looked like her, all blonde haired, blue eyed, and big boned. He had also inherited her sense of humor. When he was a child, she had helped him dodge his dreaded tutor to go fishing or riding, and she was even pretty good with a sword. Cerdic had respected his father, but he loved his mother. His heart ached, but he was told she had died with a knife in her hand. If a woman was ever in Valhalla, it would be her. His younger brothers had been all piss and vinegar, but now they were forever in a cold and watery Hel with the goddess Ran. It made his blood boil to think about it.

Then the crowd started to murmur as heads swiveled to look at three men who had just made their appearance. Cerdic heard them before he saw them. One of the figures in the trio made howling noises like a wolf baying at the moon. Cerdic knew it was not a wolf, but it was not fully human, either. Horsa had become a changeling, having taken the spirit of wolf as his own. Finally, Cerdic watched Horsa and his two seconds enter the fighting ring from the opposite side of him, but his assistants had called on others to carry their shields for them, as they had their hands full trying to keep the wolfman from charging.

Cerdic would have felt better if he had armor on, but the rules of an Artwig did not allow it. He felt almost naked without his normal protection, and Horsa really was naked. He only wore a wolf's pelt, the upper jaw and head perched atop his head as the rest of the pelt hung down, tied around his waist. Otherwise, he was dressed as he was the day he was born. Cerdic was surprised to see Horsa had an erection as well. *Bugger me,* he thought. *I cannot say I have had to deal with that problem in a fight.* Cerdic glanced at his friends as they grinned.

"Cerdic," Ord said, chuckling, "that does looks like a phallus, only it's smaller. Surely, you won't let a man with his manhood the size of a worm beat you in combat now, will you?"

Cerdic cracked a smile, but then he looked back at his opponent with a glint in his eye.

"Thank you for your words, Ord. Horsa is not a wolf changeling. That is a mere mortal, a drunk with a phallus smaller than mine when I was five years old. I can take him down for sure."

He gazed with steely resolve as he watched his foe halt his struggling long enough to grab a tankard of ale from his friends. His howling had stopped, and now Horsa seemed a bit more in control of himself as he swayed back and forth, guzzling down even more ale as he readied for the upcoming fight. Cerdic knew that drinking alcohol before going into battle was not rare in the Saxon world, but he could not understand someone downing that much before a battle.

He supposed that it was Horsa just being Horsa. When he was first captured by the Britons, Cerdic had noticed the man had been groggy and confused. After a few days, Horsa had descended into a trembling madness, claiming to see visions of monsters and ghosts. Their medicus had a Latin word for it, calling it the delirium tremens, the derangement that occurs when a heavy drinker suddenly stops drinking. After a few more days, he recovered, and became his morose, foul-mouthed, and insulting self.

Once back with his fellow Saxons, he had heard that Horsa had made up for lost time. He woke up drinking ale, spent the entire day drinking ale, then started his serious drinking that night until he collapsed into a drunken stupor, and then in the morning would wake up and start all over again. Cerdic was pleased to see he was looking to face a drunk opponent, but berserkers typically went into battle, addled from ingesting henbane seeds and the gods alone knew what else, and mixing that with alcohol made them lose all reason.

The buzz of conversation from the spectators stilled as the crowd parted like a ship plowing through the waves as a giant of a man strolled through the throng; it was Hengist, here to oversee the Artwig, accompanied by a Norse priest. The Godi walking behind him led a horse, and the two were followed by a gaggle of women carrying large, empty pans. Approaching the two combatants, the group stopped outside the ring equidistant from the two warriors.

Hengist was in full battle array, looking like a Norse god of war. His magnificently decorated helmet resembled the one Horsa had worn when captured, though this one was unblemished and was polished to reflect the sun like a mirror. His beard was braided and adorned with the sparkle of multiple silver rings. His byrnie, the Saxon name for a coat of chainmail, flashed in the sunlight. His blood-red cloak was thrown over his shoulder, closed by a magnificent golden clasp. He looked like Thunor brought to life. The East Saxon King raised his hands as a blessing to the gods while Horsa continued to be restrained by his friends.

Hengist's incantations were interrupted when Horsa threw his tankard of ale into the ring as he bellowed out, "Let us feckin' well get on with it, brother!"

People in the crowd wore expressions of shock as Hengist shot his sibling a look that could kill. Hengist shook his head, and he walked up to the head of the horse as Horsa started to howl like a wolf once more. Hengist's Godi held the horse's bridle, trying to calm the animal. The priest was short and advanced in years, and his gait and mannerisms had a feminine quality to it. Cerdic knew that this was a man who in his heart felt like a woman, as the gods had made him a blend of both sexes. For those like him, men not destined for battle, the role for such people was to serve their community as a Godi.

The priest was clad in what appeared to be women's clothing, and his head was shaved and dyed black, as were his ears and eyelids. His neck and face were covered with runic tattoos, and he wore an array of sparkling necklaces and an earring on one side. The priest pulled back the horse's head, and quick as a flash, the king flicked his seax across the neck of the horse and blood began to spurt out. The women gathered the dripping blood beneath, catching as much of it as possible into the pans. The drugged horse slowly dropped to its knees before eventually collapsing to the ground before them.

The Godi and the king dipped small tree branches into the pans of blood, and then went around the circle, flicking the branches to spray the crowd with the blood. They turned to the two combatants and spattered more blood on them, muttering incantations the whole time. Once enough blood had been distributed, the women dragged the sacrificial horse back to the village to be prepared for the feast to follow. Hengist's servants had brought him a chair to sit upon to watch the upcoming battle as Horsa resumed his howling.

Hengist sat down and called out, "Fighters, assume your positions!"

Finally, he thought, *it is time to kill this scoundrel.* The crowd erupted into a ragged cheer as Cerdic cautiously stepped into the ring, his shield in his left hand as he assumed a classic neutral stance, left foot forward with the edge of the shield just below his eyes, his sword nestled beside the right edge of the shield. Cerdic felt a strange calmness, confident in the knowledge that he had prepared for this his entire life, but he was also troubled. He was trained in combat, but never with a maniac like this.

Horsa was being anything but cautious. After he had thrown the tankard into the ring, he had resumed working himself into the fury of a berserker, howling and foaming at the mouth like a mad dog as his brother had tried to conduct his blessings. His two attendants had required some additional men to hold him from prematurely entering the ring, as Horsa was struggling like a wild animal. The blue tattoos covering his body writhed like living creatures as he struggled to be released.

The frenzy of Horsa was a terror to behold, his red-rimmed eyes darting about as he looked to be oblivious to anything else. One of his attendants tried to slip on a shield to his left arm, but Horsa began to bite at the shield's rim as he impatiently cast the shield down in fury. The berserker pulled a second sword from the scabbard of one of his seconds, the foam of his mouth was now tinged with red. He continued to twist and writhe to get into the ring as his men struggled to hold him back. The crowd looked on in silent awe.

Hengist called out once more, "Begin!"

The men holding the berserker let go of the snarling animal that Horsa had become, and he leapt into the ring like a released hound. Most men never had the fortune to own one sword; Horsa now had two. His seconds scattered away when they had let him go to prevent them from being the accidental targets of Horsa's battle frenzy. Horsa sprinted to the waiting

Cerdic, eyes wildly blazing, snarling like a wolf as he approached. Cerdic was unsure as to what to do as he had seldom practiced against a man wielding two swords at once, and this was not the time to make a mistake.

Horsa ran at full speed straight at him, and jumped into the air, thrusting both feet forward in a rabbit kick at Cerdic's shield, striking the wood like two sledgehammers. Cerdic had thrust his shield forward at the same time, but the power of Horsa's kick caught him by surprise. The shock of the blow shot waves of pain down his arm as he was propelled backwards. He fell to the ground hard, his head snapping back to hit the dirt with a loud thump. Pain flooded into his skull as he noticed the salty taste of blood in his mouth, and stars swirled around his peripheral vision as he lay there, stunned.

Move, he thought, his brain still in a fog. He had been disoriented for only a second, but it had seemed like an eternity, and he was amazed that he had not been killed in his moment of weakness. Somehow, he had maintained his grip on both the sword and shield, even though he could barely feel his arm now. *"Why aren't I dead,"* he thought as he looked for his opponent. Then he knew why. He saw a puddle of vomitus in front of his foe, and Horsa was still scrambling to pick up one of his swords. The wild eyes darted up to him as Horsa wiped his mouth with his arm.

Cerdic had flung his shield forward at the same time Horsa hit him, and the blow must have knocked him down just as it had Cerdic. Horsa had landed on his back, and the impact must have been just as tremendous as what Cerdic had felt, but with his recently downed tankard of ale, he must have thrown up the contents of his stomach. That had given Cerdic a precious few seconds, as in all the mayhem, Horsa had also dropped one of his swords, which he was now scrambling to retrieve. Cerdic felt in his bones that waiting for Horsa to launch again would be a recipe for defeat. He needed to change the dynamic of the fight and establish the initiative.

Attack, he thought. He sprinted right at his opponent just as Horsa stood up to rush at him, slashing at Cerdic with both swords simultaneously.

Cerdic was able to block the right-hand blow with his shield as he continued to move forward to rob Horsa of the full power of his swing. Saxon sword play was typically slashing and sweeping type blows, but Cerdic was fighting like a legionary, something his opponent had not encountered before. He thrust his sword up, adjusting his grip so that the pommel rested in the middle of his hand to lengthen the reach of his sword.

Soul Stealer flicked up just as the hand of Horsa was sweeping down. The tip of the sword met the hand at the wrist, and the wickedly sharp blade cut like a hot knife through butter as Horsa's hand was completely severed, dropping the sword in a harmless clatter. Blood spurted out in a pulsating flow as Horsa paused for a second, looking with widened eyes at his ruined hand twitching on the ground. Cerdic did not pause to even blink as he thrust his forehead forward into a vicious headbutt against Horsa's face.

Crunch!

A spray of blood erupted from the stunned Horsa as Cerdic saw stars once more, but for only a moment, as the stunned Horsa continued to sway in confusion. Quick as a lightning bolt from Woden, he viciously thrust *Soul Stealer* into the chieftain's throat, just above the breastbone. Horsa's mouth opened wide as Cerdic felt the blade scrape along the top of the bone, plunging deep until he felt the tip scrape against the spine of the back of the neck. Horsa fell like a sack of stones as his opponent's remaining sword clattered onto the ground.

Cerdic's sword was stuck, so he put his foot on the fallen man's chest, and after a moment he was able to pull *Soul Stealer* out, accompanied by a sucking sound and a great gout of blood. Horsa lay twitching and bleeding in the dirt, his head and neck a mass of bloody gore. The stench of fresh blood and ripened urine mixed with shite filled the air from Horsa's dying body as Cerdic stood there, the circling stars fading as the fog in his brain receded.

Horsa's eyes looked at him in desperation. *I wonder what he wants,* he thought. *Aha, I know now.* Cerdic released *Soul Stealer* and grabbed the blade that Horsa had dropped, and Cerdic saw Horsa's eyes follow him as he squeezed the sword's grip into his remaining hand. Blood continued to bubble and froth out of that ruined face and throat, and as he continued to stare into Horsa's eyes, Cerdic saw the anxious look fade away as Horsa realized Cerdic's attempt to let him die a warrior's death could allow him to be worthy of entry to Valhalla.

He despised the man, but even this wretch deserved that chance of afterlife. The dying man's eyes became peaceful, and then they glazed over as *Soul Stealer* had lived up to her name. Cerdic dropped down to one knee, trembling in exhaustion, even though this was the quickest fight he had ever been in. Now that he had won, Cerdic worried if the onlookers might feel that the fight was over far too quickly. *Did they actually want me to win,* he thought, *or did they favor one of their own?*

The crowd around him uttered a collective murmur. A wave of disappointment swept over him. He had been victorious, but this was no contest for the bards to sing about. He was sure the onlookers expected a combat like they had heard of in these songs and poems, a contest where each man hacked at each other for hours until both were near death. This fight had only lasted a minute, and he had not even received a scratch. And what did they think of him giving Horsa a chance to go to Valhalla?

The murmurs grew to cries of joy and applause, growing louder by the second as more cheers filled the air. People stood and clapped and called out his name. A wave of relief flooded him. Ord and his friends must have been right; the Saxons really did want him to win, and the people were not angry at him placing the sword in Horsa's hand as even a man such as he deserved the option of a judgement by the Valkyries. He had not thought about it, he had just reacted, but the buzz from the crowd reassured him that he had done the right thing.

Murmurs of the king's name wafted across the killing field, and then he glanced up. It was Hengist. His heart stopped for a moment. *What does he want,* he thought. Cerdic knew the outcome was clearly not the one Hengist expected, but his face showed no emotion as the mighty king strode into the ring of combat. Once Hengist reached his side, Cerdic felt his happiness sweep away as a wave of fear came back over him. *Is he drawing his sword to kill me?* he thought. His fear melted away as Hengist took a thickly braided silver torque off and then knelt and placed it on his own arm. The crowd continued to roar with approval.

"Behold the victorious Cerdic," Hengist called out. "He is now your king. May you serve him well!"

Without a change in countenance, he then leaned closer to Cerdic and whispered, "This is not the end of this, you impudent whore's son! Someday, I will put your head on a stake in front of my hall, boy!"

Cerdic heard him, but he did not say a word. He met the glare of Hengist without a flinch, but he felt drained and weak as a kitten, his battle fury slowly subsiding away. Then Cerdic closed his eyes for a moment as he fingered the amulet of Thunor's hammer under his tunic. He thanked the All-Father for guiding his sword, then he reopened his eyes under the icy gaze of Horsa's brother. Cerdic grinned as he returned that glare with one of his own, wondering whom the gods would favor when their blades finally did cross. Only the Norn's knew, and they were not saying. *But it will be your head on a stake, old man,* he thought, *not mine!*

CHAPTER TWENTY-TWO

People were calling it *the Great Trek.* Over a year and a half had passed since the now famous Artwig when Cerdic had assumed the mantle of king for his tribal alliance, and the leadership of both the Catuvellauni and West Saxons had agreed with Cerdic's pronouncement to leave their current settlements in favor of relocating to the abandoned lands in the west. The pressure from their various Saxon and Angle rivals was just too much to tolerate in the long term, and both the Catuvellauni and West Saxons had agreed to migrate together. Because of Cerdic, the old alliance had been restored, and they had spent the winter preparing for their march, and right now they were on the move towards a new life together.

The wagon train had been assisted by the new settlers living at the great hillfort of Camalet. This was the start of a new confederation between Cerdic's realm and Camalet and Caleva; they were calling it Novum Brittania, the New British alliance. Camalet was a natural ally, and the departure of Gilas and his men had left Caleva relatively defenseless, so they had also joined the confederation. With the help of their new allies, a great caravan had been assembled, and these last few days the people of his new kingdom were on the move.

I understand how Arturius felt, he thought. *Now it is my turn to worry.*

Today the sun was just peaking over the eastern hills as the ponderous line of wagons filed out of the gates of Londinium on the way to the Thamesis River crossing. They had started their trek from Verulamium and had stopped along Londinium along the way to pick up more migrants there, resting a couple of days before moving on. Now they were back on the road for the most dangerous part of the journey. Once they had crossed the Thamesis River, he knew they should be relatively safe, and that the perilous crossing point of that river was coming up soon.

Usually, Cerdic itched for a fight, but not on this trip. Everything he had won could be wiped out, and being on the move made them vulnerable. Cerdic had been pleasantly surprised as the trip had been uneventful so far, but then he spied two scouts thundering at him, and he knew the situation was about to change. The two riders pulled up their well-lathered mounts and gave him the Roman salute, their closed right hand thumping against their chest over their hearts.

"Sir! There is a blocking force at the Pontes, just as you said there would be."

His mouth went dry. *I hate it when I am right*, he thought. They had been so close to making it without a problem, but now he knew there was going to be a fight. The presence of the enemy at the river crossing was not a surprise, as that was what he would have done if he were Hengist. The East Saxon king had sworn revenge, and that river crossing was where the caravan was most vulnerable. Cerdic was not personally scared of combat, but now that he was responsible for all these people, he was sick with worry.

"Very well," replied Cerdic. "See to your mounts, and we will make the preparations as we had discussed."

Cerdic turned to his companions riding beside him.

"I knew this was too good to be true," he quietly said. "Hengist is not going to let us go in peace. I am only glad we have not been attacked until now."

"If we are going to be ambushed," one of his friends replied, "at least this is where we thought it would occur. We are ready, sire. Your plan is a good one."

They were stopping just in front of The Pontes, the Latin word for the bridges, a place where two Roman-built stone bridges spanned the Thamesis River. The eastern span crossed to a small isle called Church Island, then the second longer bridge continued from the island to cross the western half of the river on the way to Caleva. Though he was hoping they could cross the river today, Cerdic had anticipated an enemy blocking force could prevent it, so he had a marching camp secretly constructed for just this eventuality. Tonight, they would prepare for battle; tomorrow they were going to cross those bridges or die trying.

The stop at Londinium had been stressful enough; a handful of Britons still lived within that city's walls, and those people had requested to join their exodus. Caleva, nearly deserted as it was, seemed more defensible than Londinium, as the city's walls were just too extensive to defend it. This had been a bittersweet moment. The new migrants were welcome, but Londinium, once the largest city of Britannia, would now be completely abandoned. It was a poignant reminder of how much the world had changed for the worse in the last hundred years.

Once they reach Caleva, the plan was for the travelers to go off in different directions. Some Britons were to stay in that town, while others would join the ever-growing settlement at Camalet. His own people were planning to settle farther south, in the deserted areas around Venta Belgarum, but for all that to happen, they all had to get across the Thamesis in one piece. The next twenty-four hours would determine their fate. As the scouts led their horses away, Cerdic glanced behind him to see Arturius galloping up from the rear of the column with several of his companions. When he arrived, the two groups of horsemen exchanged another Roman salute.

"Greetings, brothers," Arturius called out as he dismounted.

The two groups of horsemen shared the news of their respective scouting parties. Once Cerdic and Arturius conferred, it was apparent that besides the large force ahead of them blocking the entrance of the Church Island bridge, an even larger body of warriors was coming up hot behind them They were seriously outnumbered. It had to be Hengist and the combined armies of the East and Middle Saxons, and there may have been some Angles with him, all lusting for booty and new thralls.

"Well, then," Cerdic said, "our task is to get across the river before we are crushed like a bug between those two forces."

"According to these reports," Arturius said, grimly nodding, "the Saxon army behind us is still forming, so if get into the camp tonight, we can attack the enemy at the bridges early in the morning. If we break through, then we can get behind the walls of Caleva before they can muster their full forces against us. I will take a few scouts up ahead to the marching camp and get a look at those warriors blocking the bridge. You are going to be in the advance column meeting us there, correct?"

"Yes," Cerdic replied with a grin. "And I expect a full report when I get there. Make it so."

Arturius put his hands on his hips as he laughed.

"That is what I am supposed to say, Cerdic."

"I stole that phrase fair and square from Macro and Petrus," Cerdic said with a smile. "I am a king now, remember? Hah! Need I remind you that I am the overall commander of the expedition here, so only I get to say that!"

"Well, well, aren't we getting the big head," Arturius said as he shook his head in mirth. "And I get to oversee the *entire* army when it comes to the fight, don't forget. Then the only thing you must worry about is your infantry and your own fat arse."

Cerdic crossed his arms as he shook his head in mirth.

"It will me and my men who will bear the brunt of the fighting," Cerdic said. "The infantry does the real work, you know, not like your slingers who are hiding behind their shields."

"You were the one to volunteer for that duty to be a ground pounder," Arturius scoffed. "And it was Macro, you and Caradoc that selected me for this job. Somebody had to think of the big picture and make sure everyone does what they are supposed to do."

"Oh yes," Cerdic said in a sarcastic tone. "That means you sit on a horse in the rear and tell us what to do while we are all doing the real fighting. Well, that sounds dangerous. Don't break a fingernail doing that job."

"Now, now, now, Cerdic, my boy, you will do a wonderful job in the shield wall. Fighting and not thinking is what you do best."

The men with them guffawed at the exchange. Once they settled down, Arturius galloped on ahead. Cerdic joined the head of the column, and as he rode along, he looked up at the sky anxiously. They had needed another rain-free day for the trek to success, and so far, Thunor had cooperated, an unusual gift for Britannia. He muttered a prayer of thanks to Thunor for his largesse, and hopefully the favor of rain-free skies would continue for tomorrow.

He glanced behind him; the plodding wagon train behind him was quite a sight. The older men and young boys drove the wagons, while the women and older children trudged along to keep up, pushing small hand carts loaded with personal possessions. The wagons themselves carried the group's supplies with the old and very young all crammed inside. He knew the advance column could get to their stopping point in front of the bridges by midday, and he expected the ponderous second column to arrive at dusk. *This might just work,* he thought.

His view of the civilian column disappeared from his view as he along with the advance column crossed a ridge, then he directed his attention to the warriors marching beside him. They were *his* warriors now, toughened by drills and endless marches over the past year to get ready for this great migration. By relentless training, he had molded the West Saxons and the Catuvellauni into one functional unit. It had been a herculean task, and he could not have done it without the help of his friends and supporters.

The men trudging beside him had the look of Roman legionaries. Leather covered shields were slung over their left shoulder and their helmets were slung around their necks as they hoisted baggage poles that were placed over their right shoulders. From the pole was suspended a potpourri of items, their baggage, spears and several stake palisades were all strapped to the pole. He was so proud of all of them. Over the winter they had become one, and now his job was to keep them all from getting killed.

By midafternoon the advance column crossed the last ridge, and Cerdic could see the camp they were to occupy that evening. He breathed a sigh of relief, seeing it was still empty, not touched by the Saxons camping at the foot of the bridge. Located about a mile from the river crossing, the hilltop that they were about to occupy had already been flattened and cleared. Weeks before, work parties from Camalet and Caleva had labored to prepare the site for the marching camp. Cerdic ordered the pace of the march to be quickened; his troops should be visible to the enemy at the bridge, and they had to get there quickly to set up their defenses.

They arrived without incident; thankful the Saxons had chosen to stay put. The spinning of the threads by the Norns were holding true; the plan was working for now but tomorrow could be a disaster if those three witches weaved it so. Once they arrived at the campsite, a portion of his warriors arrayed themselves in a protective array while he directed the rest to enhance the earthen defenses of the camp. His men enlarged the surrounding ditches while adding to the turf walls behind the defensive moat, and the sharpened poles they had carried were placed to create a hedgehog of spikes that surrounded them.

Prior to the arrival of the troops, the marching camp was not obviously a fortification, but after a few hours, it had become a very defensible position, surrounded by ditches and earthen walls that were supplemented with wooden spikes. It would be a tough nut to crack now, so they would be safe for the night. He was sure that when the enemy first arrived at the bridges a few days ago, this place had been just a square of dirt with some shallow ditches around it, not a threat. They must have seen these preparations but had ignored them. *They were probably afraid of getting dirty,* he thought. Now it was too late, confronted now with a well-manned fort right on their doorstep.

The main body of the caravan arrived in the evening as the setting sun reflected its dying rays into the faces of the exhausted arrivals. Campfires had already been lit, and the earlier arrivals helped the migrants with finding the correct spots to camp. He was sure the troops that had prepared the camp were feeling tired, but the noncombatants filing in looked worse. The young men had trained for this, while the civilians had not.

Senna and others from Camalet had hidden in the nearby woods from the approaching Saxons awaiting the caravan's arrival, emerging only when the first contingent of troops arrived. Cerdic looked upon these helpers from Camalet with gratitude as they aided the new refugees to get settled into camp. *The people of the Weald are the ones who really made this happen*, he marveled. *I will never forget this.*

Cerdic went to bed that night feeling good about their progress but tomorrow would be the day of reckoning. The Saxon's fortifications blocking the crossing point of the Thamesis were not very high or deep; his people should be able to breach their enemy's defenses if things went according to plan, but as Caradoc would often say, "If" was a big word. The marching camp fortifications his own people had made were impressive. He kicked at a clod of dirt; *the legionaries had conquered the world with their shovels,* he thought, *why can't we? And tomorrow our enemies will taste our iron.*

Unlike many of his men, he went to bed early that night. Before a battle, the West Saxons would typically drink ale and sing bawdy songs and recite martial poems and brag and sharpen their blades, and now even the Catuvellauni did the same. But he and Arturius shared the same command tent, and they talked quietly about their hopes and dreams for the future as well as their tactics for the morning. Before retiring for the evening, he had visited with both his West Saxons and the Catuvellauni campfires to chat with his men. He knew most of them by name now, and he tried to portray an aura of confidence to his men.

Being a king was a lonely business, and only Arturius knew what he was experiencing that night. This past year, he had endured the burdens of command. Though he was confident they had done all they could to be ready, he worried about everything that could go wrong, and how he and Arturius would be blamed for any defeat. Cerdic had a hard time drifting off to sleep. What if they could not break through the barriers at the foot of the bridge, or were attacked simultaneously from both his front and rear? Would the Catuvellauni and West Saxons fight well together? On and on, the worries continued, until he drifted into a fitful sleep.

Then another nightmare happened again. He was in a line of battle when the Saxons charged. In his dream, a spearhead flashed in entering the neck of a friend beside him, beheading him. The head tumbled to the ground as it continued to stare at him, releasing an anguished scream, "help me, Cerdic." The headless torso continued to stand next to him, blood and gore spurting out until he was entirely covered in the stuff. Then Cerdic realized he had not been paying any attention to his enemy in front of him, violating the first rule of combat.

He felt paralyzed, unable to move. His opponent in front of him was no longer faceless, and it was a thin and tall youth with a wispy beard and rotten, blackened teeth that were revealed behind his wicked grimace. His eyes were bright with a look of joy and triumph. The youth slowly raised a massive two-handed battle axe high. Cerdic looked on with fascination at the blade of the axe hovered above him for what seemed to be eternity, sparkling in the sun. All he could do was watch, somehow paralyzed, unable to move.

He felt his panic grow as the blade descended, slowly at first, then faster and faster, and within moments, he was armless and legless, dismembered by the bloody axe, though his mind was still alive. He lay there motionless, unable to move, as he looked on in horror as enemy soldiers poured into the gap that his fallen body had created. The line of his comrades collapsed like a house of cards, his enemies slaughtering his fellow warriors with ease. His heart filled with shame. He had let his men down. It was his gap in the line that had led to the death of his friends; it was all his fault.

A different man appeared before him, laughing as he pressed on his chest down with his elegantly made boot, the pressure on his chest suffocating him. It was Aelle. Cerdic felt a wave of fear overwhelm him. The South Saxon king lowered his breaches and pulled out his phallus to piss on him, as the rest of his enemies pointed at him and laughed. And then he woke up, thrashing and dripping wet from his own sweat, his heart racing. *These bloody dreams,* he thought. *When will they stop?*

CHAPTER TWENTY-THREE

The smell of breakfast being prepared filled the air just as the sky in the east began to lighten. The people in the marching camp were awake despite the early hour, happy to know the Saxons behind them had not attacked yet, but everyone knew what would happen if their warriors could not break through the blocking force at the bridge. The civilians looked pensive as the troops were fed first, and then the soldiers marched purposefully out towards the Pontes as the sunlight behind them continued to brighten the horizon. *Today is the day,* he thought.

From atop his horse Arturius watched the army tramp through the western gate of the camp, the infantry in the lead, followed by three oddly shaped carts drawn by oxen as he and his mounted warriors followed the carts. He muttered a prayer to Jupiter to not embarrass himself by falling off his horse as the column slowly rumbled on towards the bridge. About two hundred paces from the enemy position the carts stopped, still out of bowshot from the Saxon's archers. *That took forever,* he ruminated, *but at least the sun is still in their eyes.*

His stomach fluttered at the jeering of their enemies off in the distance as the men attending the carts assembled their machines. The units resembled a large metal-framed crossbow, a smaller and more portable version of the ballista that protected Caleva, machines of war unique to the Roman military. Once the Roman legions had pulled out, the knowledge of how to build and maintain artillery had become a lost art in Britannia, except for in Caleva. It seemed to him half the morning had been frittered away as the artillerymen assembled their machines, but finally they were ready. Arturius signaled, and the cornu player by his side called out for the attack to begin.

Ta Dah! Ta-Ta Dah!

The infantry spread out from a column into a line of attack and started to move forward, the cavalry close behind them as they marched past the artillery. The West Saxons held the center of the line, their brightly painted round shields displaying an array of patterns. On the right flanks were the men of the Weald, their larger oval-shaped shields all painted in a uniform color. On the left were the men of Cantullevauni; their shields flat and rounded like that of the Saxons, all painted in the same pattern of the legionary troops that were once stationed in Verulamium. Located on each flank of the infantry were the missile troops, a mix of plumbata men and slingers.

Arturius glanced over at Cerdic, standing on the far left of the Saxon's portion of the line, bearing a shield in the Saxon style that was painted green with a red cross. He worried about his friend being in harm's way on the front line of battle; to his mind, it was an unnecessary risk, but Cerdic's own Saxons expected nothing less. It was one reason why he was in command of the fight today, as Cerdic felt he needed to be with the men of his newly formed kingdom in the place of greatest danger, and not watching from afar as a Roman-trained general would.

The handful of mounted warriors with Arturius were positioned twenty paces from the back from the line of infantry to function as a mobile reserve. His fingers nervously drummed on the handle of his sword as he watched his infantrymen advance. He was no horseman, and he knew it, but this was the job he had assigned himself. *What was I thinking?* he thought. *I won't be able to use my sling atop this bloody beast*! If the need arose, he could always dismount, and his sling remained tucked in his tunic just in case; he felt naked without it, but he hoped he never had to use it.

He had trained his missile troops to be able to skirmish without him because he needed to view the entire battle rather than be in the middle of the fight itself, one of the things he had learned from *The Battle of the Caravan.* He was nervous about how they would do, but it was out of his control now. He had made sure that Senna was safe in the camp instead of being with the plumbata throwers this day, giving him one less thing to worry about.

He rested the long calvary spatha on his saddle, thankful that its tip was rounded so he could not stab himself in the foot. Arturius would not last a minute if he had to use his gaudy sword, preferring his sling, but Cerdic and the others insisted that he carried it anyway as a symbol of authority. The bloody thing even had a name, *Caliburnus*, a blade once owned by some pompous Roman general before Horsa had acquired it. It was his now. They only had a handful of these longer swords, and Arturius felt guilty carrying it as he felt like it was wasted on him.

Ahead of them stood the enemy Saxon fortifications, just daring the Britons to come and attack them. The scouts had discovered the troops opposing them were the Middle Saxons, and their numbers looked daunting, more men than Arturius had in his entire warband. A chill ran down his spine as he experienced a moment of doubt. Attackers were supposed to outnumber the defenders, and that did not look like the case to him. Even worse, the enemies before him were ruthless, products of a culture that valued death in battle as the noblest of virtues.

The two bridges ahead were a strong defensive position for his enemies. The Saxons could hold the entrance to the first bridge, then retreat to the exit to make a new stand if pressed. After that they could retreat again to the entrance to the second bridge, and then the second exit could once again act as another bottleneck. On paper, Arturius knew they should not win today, but battles were not fought in a book; he had some surprises waiting for his enemies that he hoped would make up the difference.

The Middle Saxons stood at the foot of the bridge, shield to shield, gathered in a wall of wood, iron, and courage, as they were whipping themselves into a battle frenzy. The Saxons put their mouths just below the edge of their shields and started to bellow out the barratus, low and terrifying, slowly rising and descending in a crescendo of noise that sounded like the waves of a stormy sea crashing against a rocky shore. Another chill ran down his spine as he thought the great battles of the past. This sound must have been the last thing the legionaries at the massacre of the Teutoburg forest had heard when centuries before, three entire legions had been wiped out. Would history repeat itself today?

Initially, Cerdic's men in the line of infantry stood there, transfixed and silent.

Then he overhead the young cornu player beside him nervously mutter to a nearby warrior, "I heard that Hengist feeds his prisoners to his war dogs."

He wanted to say something, but then the comrade beside him scoffed, "Shut your pie hole, boy. We are going to break through those scum on the bridge long before Hengist can even finish taking his morning shite."

The two of them laughed as Arturius breathed a sigh of relief that someone else had stopped the spread of false rumors. Suddenly the silence in his ranks was broken by the warriors from the Weald.

"Yip, Yip, Yahee!"

It was the unearthly scream he had heard before, growing louder as it pierced through above the din; the men of Camalet were repeating the war cry that they first thundered out in *The Battle of the Caravan.* The high-pitched call of the banshees echoed back to counter the low rumble coming from the Saxons at the bridge. Then along the entire British and West Saxon line, some of the others started to join the men of the Weald in their war cry.

Arturius saw the grizzled warrior turn to the cornu player.

"Bloody hell," the veteran chuckled. "That sounds louder than your sister after I had my way with her last night!"

The embarrassed cavalryman gave his friend a withering look, and then they both joined in to the call of battle. For most of the men here, this British war cry was a new thing, but now they were all starting to use it. The artillery men flashed the signal to Arturius that they were ready to begin the barrage. Arturius turned to the cornu player.

"Sound the call for the ballistae. Now we'll show those people what Roman artillery can do."

Above their heads, Arturius detected a new sound above the din, a peculiar noise he had heard before, but still it made his spine tingle.

Whoosh, whoosh, whoosh.

Bolts from the ballistae flew over his head in a high arc, paused, and then sped downward to crash into the barbarian fortifications.

Crash!

A section of the crude palisade wall splintered into jagged pieces as the mighty bolts tore through the Saxon defenses. Each time a bolt struck home his men cheered. *Saxon warriors are fighters, not workers,* he thought. *They do not like to dig ditches and walls. That will cost them today.* But watching men die before him also sickened him. These were men with mothers and brothers and sons and daughters. What he was witnessing felt like murder. But he also knew those Middle Saxons would not hesitate to kill his own people without mercy.

Whoosh, whoosh, whoosh.

Cries of pain could be heard coming from the bridge.

Whoosh, whoosh, whoosh.

Whoosh, whoosh, whoosh.

Arturius shook his head in amazement, unable to understand how these men could stand there and take it. Then, barely discernible above the din, the keening of marching music could be heard. *That is the bagpipes I am hearing*, he thought. *Caradoc and the men from Caleva are here*! Off in the distance and across the river, Arturius saw men rushing out of the woods to block the exit point of the far bridge. Their own snare was complete; now it was the Middle Saxons who were trapped between two armies.

Arturius saw Caradoc's archers and infantrymen rushing up to form a shield wall on the far western side of the Pontes as his own soldiers chanted "Caradoc, Caradoc," as they celebrated the arrival of their allies. Caradoc's archers lined up, and the group of bowmen fired as one. A manmade cloud of arrows flew into the sky, delivering death and destruction upon their enemies. Arturius almost felt sorry for the Middle Saxons, assaulted on two fronts now and unable to fight back. A few arrows were fired back towards Caradoc's men, but those had fallen short into the river as the Silures could shoot farther than the Saxon bowmen. Volley after volley of arrows flew from Caradoc's men as the ballistae continued to pound their fortifications with deadly accuracy.

Whoosh, whoosh, whoosh.

Finally, the Middle Saxons, bellowing in anger, started pouring out of their collapsing defenses to charge against his infantry line, enraged by the senseless slaughter of their comrades. *This is it*, he thought. They were no longer behind barricades now; it would now be a fight out in the open. This was what they had trained for, but were they truly ready to take these experienced warriors on in a face-to-face battle? He would know soon enough.

The pagan horde broke into clusters of men moving towards them at a deliberate pace, visibly reduced in numbers, but despite their earlier losses, the remaining numbers of warriors before him still made an imposing sight. Arturius felt the familiar aching in his bollocks as his mouth went dry. Could they hold the line? Would his British melt away when the two forces crashed together? He was pleased to see the Saxons coming in disarray. They had not yet coalesced into an organized battle line as the enemy warriors continued to rush into a battle line piecemeal.

"Now," Arturius called to the cornu player by his side.

Once more the horn blew, and this time it was the skirmishers who responded, already in their assigned positions in front of Cerdic's men. Plumbata and slingers stones flew into the air as more Saxons fell. His missile troops stopped to reload, then they fired and retreated again until they formed up on the flanks of the line of the waiting infantry. More enemy warriors littered the ground now, but still they kept charging. The allied infantry stood their ground as the attacking Middle Saxons drew nearer. About thirty paces away, the enemy charge stopped as they struggled to form up their own battle line as a smattering of javelins were thrown towards them.

His people hunkered down behind their shields when the light spears hit, and most bounced off harmlessly, though a couple of his men cried out in pain. The waiting British infantry reached behind their shields and pulled out their own plumbata. They had successfully endured the Saxon's spears, and now it was time to respond. The Middle Saxons could only carry one or two javelins, while each of his own men had five plumbata, and behind them were several women carrying baskets to resupply the infantry if they needed it.

"Two volleys, high and low," he called out. "Loose!"

His infantrymen let fly a deadly volley with an underhand motion as the enemy battle line was still forming, and the Saxons that were ready thrust their shields high to deflect the plunging missiles headed towards them. He waited until the right moment.

"Loose!"

Now the overhand missiles were thrown, timed to hit the enemy line just when the high volley was to plow into the forming line. Plumbata thumped in from two different directions, and the results were chilling. Men fell like bowling pins as they were struck by the projectiles as cries of pain rang out across the field. The Middle Saxons could not begin their charge as they tried to protect themselves from the continuing onslaught. The skirmishers and infantrymen continued these high and low attacks for several rounds until Arturius thought they were ready for the next phase of the fight.

"Signal ready for the charge," he called out.

His men got their shields ready as their swords and spears bristled. Arturius turned to the cornu player again.

"Now," he said.

The new clarion call for the attack rang out, and the British line moved forward as their call of the banshees filled the air. The enemy line looked ragged from the Saxons who had fallen, and many of those who were still standing had their shields adorned with multiple plumbata sticking out of them, rendering them almost useless. The battered Middle Saxons tried to shuffle in closer to tighten their formation, and Arturius was gratified to see they were slow about it. He was glad it was not him in that wavering line right now.

Then the charge of the British army crashed into the disorganized Saxon line. Screams and yells and grunts and groans were offset by the high-pitched yipping of his men. Wood crashed against wood, and Arturius heard the sharp ringing of iron striking iron as a spear tip met the metal boss of a shield, or a sword would meet another blade in midair. It was the sound of death that he had heard too many times now, and the melee looked to be evenly matched as both sides fought there, toe to toe for several minutes with neither side budging.

The ends of the British line bent backwards to form a semicircle so as not to be flanked, and those flanks were protected by the plumbata throwers who stayed some thirty paces away from the struggling infantry to pelt any Saxons from trying to curl around. Here and there men fell on both sides, but Arturius could tell the British were giving as good as they got. He was impressed with the West Saxon's bravery; they had been disorganized at first, but these were true warriors who knew their business. He continued to watch the struggle in horrid fascination, barely able to breathe from his excitement. *Our boys are doing well*, he thought.

Then he heard it. It was the bagpipes, sounding closer than before. The keening sound of the pipes brought tears to his eyes. He thought of the times that he had cringed when he heard Caradoc playing the bloody things, but now it was the sweetest sound he had ever heard. It was hard to see it now from the struggling mass of men in front of him, but he thought he could see the Silures must have taken both bridges now, and he saw some men were coming up from behind the enemy line. *They are trapped between our two forces now,* he thought with joy, the final surprise coming to fruition. Closer and closer the pipes sounded, and now he could hear the cries of Caradoc's men as they approached their enemy from their rear.

Arturius knew if he could hear this, so could the Saxons. Heads swiveled. Men shouted with looks of alarm. Caradoc's forces were not numerous, but being attacked on two fronts was too much. One man bolted to the north. Two more joined him. Then the entire left side of the Saxon line melted away. Faced with the loss of their left, Arturius saw the center and right of the enemy line dissolve. The battle line on both sides had disintegrated now as the British infantry chased after fleeing Saxons, scampering away in panic. It was time for the coup de gras.

"Calvary, charge!"

His horsemen let out whoops of joy as they galloped off to run down their fleeing enemies. The rout was on, and now the slaughter could begin in earnest. Once their line broke, the Saxons were doomed, and they knew it. The sound of cheering receded as his men continued to give chase, and he basked in the warm glow of victory as he sat there alone on his horse surveying the scene. *By Mars Ultor, we've won,* he thought.

What was that sound? It was somehow different. Then something made him look behind him. His heart stopped. In the distance, Arturius saw hundreds of people boiling out of the entrance of the marching camp as they headed right towards him, looking like an ant hill that had been kicked open. The sounds of their terrified shouts must have been masked by the sounds of battle, but now he could hear them, the screaming of mothers and the crying of children. His mood of elation flitted away as tears came to his eyes.

The only explanation: Hengist and his wolves were at the camp! *Can we get back in time?* he wondered in desperation. He looked around in despair. He was a mile away, and his soldiers were scattered to hell and gone, chasing the fleeing Middle Saxons. He started to yell with urgency at anyone within earshot to form up and get back to the undefended civilians behind him. His heart thumped like a hammer on an anvil as a sick feeling continued to flood through him. *We may have won this battle,* he thought, *but we are about to lose the war. And Senna is there!*

CHAPTER TWENTY-FOUR

Senna stood frozen on the ramparts of the marching camp, paralyzed with fear, her breathing ragged as the enemies' axes bit into the gate below. The splintering of wood and the Saxon war cries sounded like the crack of doom, as she knew what would happen once they got in. She did not think it would take long for them to break that gate down. The black abyss of fear was smothering her, leaving her unable to move. All she wanted to do was to run and hide somewhere. *No,* she thought. *I cannot do that. These people need me!*

Senna glanced behind her. The camp was a seething mass of bedlam, panicked civilians with no soldiers to protect them. What defenders they had, the few older warriors manning the gates, had already left. Only one remained, a grey bearded West Saxon with a look of resignation on his face. There was no one else to protect them. Their own army was in the midst of a battle a mile or more away; they were on their own. A group of refugees had gathered below her, and they gazed up at her with naked fear written on their faces. They needed someone to tell them what to do. She knew she had to take charge.

"We have time," she called out to the crowd, "but go to the western gate now. Leave your things behind. The Saxons will be inside any minute now!"

The people below scattered like chaffs of wheat in the wind. Once the barbarians broke through the front gate, she knew they would be looking for loot and plunder. Searching for that should slow them down, and that had given her an idea. She decided to get some ale and leave it for the Saxons to find it once they entered the camp, thinking alcohol would be better at stopping their advance than a hundred men right now. Senna prayed that the people would have the sense to do as she told them and get their families out immediately. She closed her eyes. *Oh Isis,* she prayed, *please spare us this day. And forgive me for lying to them about having enough time.*

The pounding on the gates continued as she hopped down from the wall, and quickly she found a container of ale. She and one of her scribes had just finished rolling the barrel close to the entrance when the front gate suddenly crashed in. Enemy warriors spilled into the fortified camp as their deep-throated cheers of triumph sent chills down her spine. If that had happened a few minutes later, then she could have been heading towards the western gate, but right now, she was on the opposite side of the camp from where she needed to be.

She hitched up her skirt and sprinted westward, trying to get lost in the maze of tents and lean-to's left behind by the fleeing people. Her scribe ran beside her, but then she heard a thud and a yelp of pain. Her friend had tripped and fallen. Senna continued a few more paces before she stopped, unsure of what to do. Paralyzed, she glanced back and saw the desperation in her friend's eyes as two Saxon warriors pounced on her like hawks striking a bird on the ground. There was nothing she could do.

She reluctantly pulled her gaze away and resumed her run to safety, but the haunted look on her colleague's face would be forever in her mind. She ran to a lean-to and crouched behind it for a moment, catching her breath, her heart racing like a captured bird. Senna glanced about and then she continued to slip away towards the western gate, a quick burst of running to find hiding spots among the temporary dwellings left behind by the fleeing people. Her fallen friend had indirectly saved her life, the Saxons attacking her friend instead of chasing her. She would feel guilty later, but for now, those feelings would have to wait. First, she had to survive.

Senna continued to dart from shelter to shelter, slowly moving to the other end of the camp, trying to shield herself from view as she heard Saxon warriors, both mounted and on foot, thundering down the main thoroughfare of the encampment. She was surrounded and was concentrating on being stealthy to avoid being seen, having witnessed several women who had tried to run in the open get caught. Many of the people who had left promptly had already made it through the gates, but not all had been quick enough. The ones who had dallied to gather their things were now the ones in trouble.

She heard screams of terror, the pitiful sounds of children crying, and the whooping of delighted warriors as they tore through the marching camp looking for booty, women, and ale. Senna had never been so scared in her life. She had been lucky to escape from the sack of Novomagus Reginorum as a girl, and she shuddered at the thought of how her mother and sister must have suffered. Was it her turn to experience the same fate? Her anxiousness ratcheted even more as she helplessly watched one hapless mother being held down as her clothes were being ripped off, while next to her a small child lay motionless in the dirt. *Better death than that,* she thought.

She slipped out of sight once more as she continued to make her way through the abandoned tents. She could do nothing to help that poor woman or anyone else: all she could do now was to save herself. Once again, she scanned the ground in front of her, looking for the next place to run to and hide. She was closer to the exit now. *There*, she thought as she saw another abandoned tent ahead of her. Again, she was safe for the moment, unable to see anyone near her right now. The noises she heard terrified her, but she screwed up her courage, and she continued to run from one hiding place to another as she prayed to Isis for no one to see her.

So far so good, she thought. No one had spotted her yet despite her hearing the marauders all around her. Her panting slowed as she looked for the next place for her to move to. She had never felt terror like this before, and she prayed to Isis to never feel this way again. It took every ounce of emotional strength to keep moving rather than to just hunker down somewhere, but the logical side of her knew she had to keep moving despite the risk, or she would become captured or dead.

She was almost there now. Senna was perhaps fifty paces away from the exit when she was finally able to get a good look at the opening of the western gate. The flame of hope grew brighter. Standing there at the exit was a knot of British soldiers, some of them carrying shields that identified them as being from Camalet, there to prevent their attackers from pushing on out of the encampment. She could see the British soldiers were beckoning fleeing refugees to come on through.

If I can make it to that gate, she thought, *I will be safe!* As she remained hidden, Senna noticed that one of the soldiers at the entrance was someone she recognized. Her heart lurched; it was Arturius, alive, and mounted on a horse. She cautiously stood up and waved, and his eyes lit up with delight as he saw her. He signaled to her to come to him. She nodded as she waved back, then she ducked down again, breathless in anticipation. She was so close now, just a short distance from freedom.

She was hidden behind a low-lying tent, the entrance closed by a blanket over the front. Sounds of chaos were all around her, but still, she could not see any enemy warriors nearby. Senna crouched low, scanning left and right as her heart felt like it was beating out of her chest. She tried to slow her breathing down to control the feelings of panic that threatened to overwhelm her. She was almost free now, but a pitiful sight had stopped her from making her final run to freedom.

She had spied an elderly British woman lying on the ground, a dribble of blood coming from the poor woman's nostrils. Senna thought she was probably dead as her unblinking eyes stared vacantly into the uncaring sky, but beside her was a fair-headed girl who looked to be about five years old. The terrified child was pulling on the matron's hand and bawling tearfully, looking around for someone to help her. Their eyes met. The tableau tugged at her heartstrings. *I must help that poor little girl,* she thought.

Her eyes darted around furtively as she heard an unusual sound, the nickering of two mounts all alone in the corner of the compound, but no riders were visible. The gods alone knew where the horsemen were as she glanced around in desperation, but there was no sign of them. Senna had to get moving, and she decided to take the chance. She sprinted towards the girl, picked her up, and then she started to run to the waiting gate. The girl cried out in pain as the hand of the matron's corpse was tied to the girl's hand, dragging the dead woman along with them as they attempted to flee. *Why is that?* she wondered. Suddenly, the flaps of the tent that Senna had hidden behind burst open, and two laughing Saxon warriors stepped out.

The taller one smirked, "Our blonde-haired bait worked."

The one who had just spoken grabbed her, and he put his face right in front of her as he looked her up and down with hungry eyes. His feral grin was terrifying. Two of his front teeth were completely missing, while several others were just yellow stubs. She gagged as she smelled his fetid breath while he twisted her wrist, forcing her to release the little girl from her grasp.

He reached over and grabbed her other wrist, and then he jerked her hands together behind her back. The plaintive screams of the little girl reverberated in her brain as the shorter man struck Senna in the stomach, knocking her breath out. Stars swirled in her peripheral vision as she felt herself being dragged into the tent and roughly thrown to the ground. The taller one pinned her arms down, then he put his head next to her, muttering into her ear.

"You may not feel the phallus of your husband much," he said in his guttural Saxon tongue, "but when I am done with you, you will know what a real man feels like, you British whore!"

Senna felt her dress being pulled up, still pinned to the ground by the shorter man. She struggled and squirmed, but they were too strong for her, still weakened from trying to catch her breath after the blow to her stomach. She felt her undergarments being ripped away, and then her legs were forced apart. Tears of rage and fear filled her eyes as she tried to scream, but she did not have the breath to do so. Senna felt the horror of it all, of being shamed and helpless, burn into her brain. Her eyes were clamped shut in fear and fury as she felt him start to clamber on her when she felt some warm fluid spill onto her belly. *Is that his seed?* she thought in horror.

She felt more fluid splash onto her legs, but then the pressure on her limbs eased. She looked up at her attacker, and all she could see was a surprised expression on his face. Then the coppery tang of blood permeated the tent. A moment later, she saw the edge of a foot appear above her attacker's shoulder, and then she heard a sucking sound as the Saxon slid to the ground to his left. She watched in amazement as a blade emerge from behind the man, blood dripping down its glittering edge, and holding the handle of the blade was Arturius. She would never forget the emotions she saw flickering over his face: anger, fear, and steely resolve. But most of all, his expression held no mercy.

The gap-toothed man holding her arms tossed her into a heap against the side of the tent, and she curled herself into a ball as he went to grab his spear in the corner. She looked down and saw that her lower legs were covered in blood, fortunately not her own. She drew her legs up to her chest to make herself as small and inconspicuous as possible as the Saxon scrambled out to face Arturius, clearly focused on him, not paying attention to her at all. Senna wanted to just lie there and close her eyes.

Her mind was numb, but a voice came creeping into her consciousness. *You have got to do something,* she thought. She glanced around her as an idea formed. Senna crawled over to the now prostrate man that Arturius had killed and spied the handle of a short sword, a seax, on his right hip. Senna could see the legs of the barbarian as he stood just outside the tent entrance as the ring of a sword meeting another sword rang out. She reached over and grabbed the handle of the knife, slickened with its owner's blood. Senna viciously hacked at one of the Saxon's feet and she felt the blade bite deep into his bones and tendons. Blood spurted back into her face, stinging her eyes with the salty liquid as his howl filled the air.

Her eyes felt like they were scalded, the hot, sticky goo forcing her to keep them closed. While she was still blind, she heard a wet smack, followed by the thud of a body collapsing onto the ground like a sack of grain. She fought to open her eyes, the pain in them still overwhelming her. *I have got to help Arturius,* she thought in a panic, *he is no swordsman.* As a slinger Arturius could take a man's head off at fifty paces, but she knew he was otherwise helpless with both sword and spear. She scrambled to her feet, knife in her hand, ready to throw herself at the raider, but still she was unable to see. Finally, she was able to wipe her eyes well enough to visualize something despite the watering and stinging.

Through the hazy blur, she saw a body on the ground, and her heart stopped. *Arturius is dead*, she thought, *and it is all my fault.* Senna wiped her eyes, her vision clearing even more, and she breathed a sigh of relief as she realized it was the Saxon on the ground and not Arturius. An intense wave of gratitude flooded over her as she realized he was still alive. She pondered the revelation that she would have died to protect him. She was not thinking of herself, just him. *I must love him*; she thought in surprise.

She gazed upon the back of the fallen Saxon's head with a mixture of gratitude and horror as the blood pulsed out of the horrible gash in his neck that Arturius had just delivered. The precious red fluid pumped up and down like a fountain, but the rhythmic spurting weakened over the next few seconds. The flow slowed to a trickle as it pooled and covered the ground. She started to gag as the stench of fresh blood was now supplemented by the smell of urine and shite. It was the smell of death, and that memory would be with her forever.

Senna was stunned, unable to move or speak. Then she retched, and only a thick yellow bile came out. She retched again, feeling exhausted and as weak as a newborn baby. The flap of the tent flew open and there stood Arturius, concern etched on his face. She shivered as the flood of adrenaline faded, her muscles aching. They both stared at each other as if in a stupor, but after a few moments, she seemed to wake up, and he did as well. He grabbed her hand to pull her up and out of the tent, and they both stumbled away from the pool of sticky wetness covering the ground. Her legs could barely move, but she willed them to keep going, knowing that to stay there was to die.

She could barely walk at first, but the seriousness of their situation kicked in, and she looked about to see if any new threats were approaching them. After a few moments her wits returned, as did her strength, and now she was able to move. Senna felt Arturius's rough hands gently put her onto the back of his horse, then with a tender look, he cut the bonds of the little girl away from the dead woman and placed the blubbering child onto the horse to sit behind her.

Arturius stood there for a moment as he looked around, and then holding the reins, he began to trot beside them as he led the horse to the western gate and to safety. No one seemed to notice or bother them as they reached the gate to the cheers of their comrades. A huge wave of relief filled her body. They had made it. She was alive! Once there, the men clapped Arturius on the back with congratulations. He picked the stunned little girl up and hoisted her behind another horseman and gave him orders to bring the orphan to safety across the river. Then Senna heard Arturius speak to the men at the gate.

"We need some volunteers to stay here and delay these bastards from leaving the compound for as long as we can. We must get the people and their wagons across the river. Once we're past the first bridge, our rearguard can hold them off, but until then, we are vulnerable."

She then heard her father's voice. *I did not know he was even here,* she thought.

"I will organize the defenses here," Ambrosius said in a firm tone. "I will stay with the grey beards of the West Saxon's and British, and we will delay them."

She looked up and saw the kindness and concern in her father's eyes, as he pulled her and Arturius together.

Ambrosius leaned closer to her and whispered, "Senna, are you alright? Are you injured?"

"I am fine, Father," she said. "This blood covering me is not my own. But how did you get here?"

His eyes had a haunted look as he gazed at them both.

"I was with Caradoc and his men at the battle down by the river, and when I saw the camp was being attacked, I came here."

"I-I am so happy to see you," she stuttered.

"We have no time left," he said with a steely gaze. "I am going to stay here and hold the bastards back until all these people are safe. Do not mourn me, dearest daughter. Today is a good day to die."

Then her father turned to Arturius and gave him a pleading look.

"You must swear an oath to me. Macro is dead. Once I am gone there will be no one to look after Senna. I leave you in charge of protecting my daughter. Can you do this for me?"

A wave of despair flooded over her.

"Macro died?" she blurted out. "What happened to him?"

Her father turned to her with a look of tenderness on his face.

"He collapsed on the road while coming here. I think his heart just gave out. It was quick, and I don't think he suffered very much. It is all an old man can wish for, eh?"

She was saddened by the news, but not surprised, as the old centurion had been complaining of pains in his chest and a lack of energy recently. Her mind was aswirl as her father spoke up again.

"Now, Arturius, answer the question. Will you look after my daughter."

A few seconds passed as Arturius looked searchingly into her eyes, and then he gazed back at her father, a look of earnestness etched on his face.

"I swear it. By Jupiter Maximus Optimus, I swear it!"

"Make it so," Ambrosius replied, tears glistening in his eyes. "Be off with you both then, and godspeed."

Ambrosius gave a slap on the rump of their steed and off they went westward. Senna looked back, the figure of her father slowly receding, her eyes misting with tears as she knew she would never see him alive again. Her fingers dug into Arturius' tunic as if he alone was keeping her anchored in the world. The news of Macro saddened her, but seeing her father for the last time chilled her like an ice-laden Norse wind, but then the warmth Arturius' body helped stop her shivering. *Arturius should have died*, she thought. *He saved me, and I saved him. I think I must love him after all.*

She clung to him even tighter as they rode towards the bridge that crossed over the River Thamesis and safety. Once she heard the horses' hooves strike the planks of the bridge, she glanced back at the burning camp behind her, hoping to catch a glimpse of her father, but all she could see now was smoke and the debris of battle that was strewn along the empty road. She closed her eyes as she thought of her father and the lessons of stoicism. She would grieve for her father forever, but she would not let that grief consume her. Death was a part of life, and she needed to channel her energy into the cause she and Arturius so cherished, the preservation of civilization from the barbarian hordes.

CHAPTER TWENTY-FIVE

Ambrosius stood there for a moment as he watched his daughter ride away, awash with a mix of emotions: relief that his daughter was safe for now, happy that he and their forces had achieved victory, and fear that they were about to fight the invading Saxons. He thought that he would be more scared, but oddly enough, he felt a sense of relief. He did not know Arturius well, but he had seen enough; Ambrosius had seen the way he had looked at his daughter, and he knew Arturius would take an arrow for her. And the boy had charisma: Ambrosius thought he could be a great general someday, provided he lived long enough.

By his oath, Arturius had revealed himself to be a pagan, but Ambrosius wasn't bothered by that. Many of the patrician class had never fully embraced Christianity. *This boy must have the soul of a true Roman,* he thought. Ambrosius felt fear, not of dying, but he wanted a clean death in combat, not a lingering illness. He knew the pagans might have a good point about a glorious demise in battle, as he hoped his passing would be a noble one. The Saxons feared the death of an old man in bed, and he shared that sentiment.

Back in Caleva, the medicus told him he had the disease of the crab, what he called cancer, and it was causing his liver to enlarge and get lumpy when he palpated his abdomen. He had stayed alive longer than the medicus had thought, but now his health had worsened considerably in the last couple of weeks. His skin was starting to turn yellow, and he was itchy all the time as his abdomen kept getting larger while the rest of him seemed to be shrinking. And Ambrosius felt completely knackered, oh so tired.

His sleep had been fitful for weeks now, as he had to urinate increasingly frequently with an ever-smaller stream. He feared waking up again in the middle of the night and not being able to urinate at all, crying in agony as his bladder burst; that was not the way he wanted to go. He thought it was a miracle that he had gotten even this far. He was dying and he knew it, but he felt strangely at peace. *It is better this way,* he thought. *To die in battle, protecting your friends and loved ones, now that would be a noble death.*

Riding here had been a struggle almost beyond belief, as every movement of his mount shot pain deep into his groin. Now that the hour of his own death was upon him, he had a fear of the unknown. How would the Christos view his desire to kill as many Saxons as he could with his dying breath? And how many men had died because of his orders to put them in harm's way? He was not sure how the Christos would forgive such things. His greatest desire was that he prayed he would meet his wife again in heaven. He also hoped his other daughter, Ria, the one taken during the sack of the city, would be there. He did not want her to be still alive as a slave to these heathens.

A Saxon war horn broke him out of his revery. He turned to his comrades and barked out his orders. The grey beards of the West Saxons lined up, a wall of wooden shields and iron spears to block the gate. With them stood some of the older men of the Cantullevauni, as these were the men left behind to guard the compound when the main battle was taking place by the bridges. Time had passed them by; they were no longer elite warriors. Despite this, they had proven their worth today. His eyes misted in tears of pride at the thought.

They had delayed the East Saxons from entering the compound, and most importantly, they had allowed them in at the right time, so the barbarians would be preoccupied with pillaging and plundering while the bulk of their people escaped west. Ambrosius respected the fighting prowess of the Germanic invaders, but he thought of these Saxons as an armed rabble, not a disciplined fighting force. If it were his army attacking, he would have bypassed the compound, coming back later once victory was assured to collect the spoils of war. He muttered a prayer of thanks to the Christos that their foes were not disciplined like a true Roman army.

These older men, both British and West Saxon, had performed admirably. They had stayed and obeyed orders and had volunteered to guard the exit of the western gate, acting as the cork in the bottle to hold the Saxons in check as their friends and loved ones evacuated to live and fight again. These greybeards knew they were never coming home as they lined up for the last time, eyeing each other with respect for what they were about to do.

"Alright, men," he said as gripped his shield even tighter. "This is for our families to see tomorrow, and for the lads who died for us at the bridge."

The shield wall did not waver as he watched the Saxon leaders try to get their men under control to continue their assault. It would be a while yet, but every minute gained would save more lives, and it filled his heart with joy to know that they were not going to die in vain. Their dreams may have differed; Valhalla waited for some, the heaven of Christos for others. All of them were his brothers today. *And this day, we will all die together as men,* he thought.

CHAPTER TWENTY-SIX

Arturius saw her leave the entrance of the northwestern entrance of Camalet, book in hand, heading down the trail towards the tree-lined river and the wooden bridge that crossed it. The span had just been built a few days ago to make that road usable for bringing in supplies. He wondered where she was going, and he was a little nervous she was by herself. *The Battle of the Caravan* happened only a few weeks ago, and the memories of her being assaulted were still fresh in his mind. On impulse he followed her, ignoring the duties he had assigned himself. *It is good to be the commander,* he thought. *I won't get in trouble if I ignore my own orders.*

Senna continued to walk on with a purpose, and she had no idea he was behind her. She crossed the bridge to walk south along the stream, away from Camalet and the gaggle of women who were doing laundry in the river north of the bridge. *She is looking for solitude*, he thought. She still had not seen him. The attack she had endured had no doubt affected her, and he respected her desire for privacy. Camalet was still new to them all, and they had been incredibly busy building their new home, but still he worried about her, and he wanted to stay close to her just in case.

She walked along the edge of the trees for a few hundred paces when she stopped and looked in the direction of the stream for a moment. Then she walked into the trees towards the water. *She must have found what she wanted,* he thought. The whole time he had skirted along the trees as well, trying to stay out of sight. He could not explain why he remained hidden from her, and now that she had disappeared into the tree line, he regretted doing that. Now if he snuck in there, he might scare her, and that was the last thing he wanted. He crept up close to the spot where he last saw her and then called out.

"Hello, Senna, it is Arturius! I am coming in right behind you."

He walked in the same direction as she had gone, and this section of the woods seemed to feature some very old trees, mainly willows, birches, and alder. The dappled sunlight streaming down from above was both pleasing and warm. The chirping of birds and the sound of the leaves rustling in the gentle breeze filled his heart with a feeling of peace. Then he saw her sitting in a small glade right next to the water. She gave him a smile as she waved. He walked over to her where she was sitting next to a fallen tree in the glade. She had laid a blanket next to the trunk, and a book lay on the ground in front of her.

"Sorry, I did not mean to scare you," he said.

"You did for a moment. But I am glad you are here."

He stammered, "If-If you want me to go, I can__"

"No, please stay," she said as she reached out to him. "Here, come sit beside me. You can read with me.

"I am sorry. I did not bring a book."

"Of course not," she said as she rolled her eyes. "That was silly of me. Here. You can read what I am reading."

He glanced at the book as he sat down beside her.

"What is it?" he murmured.

"De Vita et Morribus Iulii Agricolae," she shyly said.

"That was written by Tacitus, wasn't it?"

"Yes," she said, nodding. "It is about the Roman conquest of Britannia by his father-in-law, governor Agricola. It is interesting to read about the ancient tribes of our lands and what the Romans thought of those people."

Arturius was impressed. He knew Tacitus was not a light read.

"I haven't tackled that book yet, so I'd be happy to join you."

She glanced at him as he slid down to sit beside her.

"Once we get more established here," she said, "we will need to meet with some of these same tribes someday. They are still here, with the same rivalries as they had even back then. The alliance we have formed will need to grow if we are going to resist the barbarians."

"Senna," he asked with a worried look, "I would prefer you not to just set out alone like this. We haven't been here for very long, and we do not know who else might be wandering around. You need someone to come with you."

"I am fine," she said with a pout. "And now you are here."

He crossed his arms as he looked at her.

"I am the commander of the garrison, you know. It is not safe for you to go wandering around by yourself like this. I am going to assign you some guards to accompany you the next time you want to go out. Promise me you'll do that in the future, will you?"

"I like being by myself sometimes, you know, to get away from people, and to bask in the beauty of nature, and to read. I love doing that."

"I'll make sure the guards will stay at a respectful distance away from you. You know better than to do something like this, don't you?"

She shrugged her shoulders as she looked at him.

"I know. But the memories of the *Battle of the Pontes* kept me up at night. I still have nightmares about it. It's just not fair."

"What is not fair?"

"Being a woman, worrying about going out alone by yourself."

"Well," he scoffed, "who said life was fair? And in a strange country like this, men must be careful, too."

She paused for a moment, then looked out in the distance.

"I am just trying to conquer my fears, I think."

"You are a courageous one, that is for sure. I almost lost you once, and I am not going to let that happen again."

She touched his arm as she started to speak. It sent a shiver down him. He just wanted to grab her in his arms and kiss her like they had done in the glade in the Weald so many months ago, but he was scared she would reject him. He could not bear the thought of that.

"No, Arturius, you are the brave one. You came to save me with only a sword in your hand against two Saxon warriors. What you did was stupid; you barely know how to use one. You should have been killed."

She pulled her arm away as he felt a hot flush come over his face.

"You saved my life, too," he said softly. "When you hacked that seax on to that warrior's foot, that distracted him enough that I got my blow in first. He would have killed me quick otherwise."

She paused for a moment, and then she gave him a searching look.

"Why did you come for me?"

His thoughts started to swirl around his head as he decided what he should say. *Do I tell her the truth?* he wondered. He was dying of embarrassment. His mouth went dry, and he felt his heart thudding in his chest, but the only thing he could think of saying was what he was really feeling. And wasn't that what Stoic's were supposed to do, to act with honor. He sighed, closed his eyes for a moment, and then he opened them again. It was time for the truth, consequences be damned.

"Because I love you more than life itself. I would rather die than see anything bad happen to you."

Her eyes opened wide as she stared at him for a moment, her cheeks turning red. Then she looked away.

He felt his heart stop. He closed his eyes again. *By Venus,* he thought, *I have just made a fool of myself,* as he felt another wave of embarrassment flood over him. Then he felt her hand gently touch his cheek, and he opened his eyes again in fear. She leaned over and kissed him on the mouth. It was tentative at first, as he did not know what to do. But she slid in closer to him, and he felt her other hand gently cup his head on the other side. Her lips pressed against him more firmly, and then he felt her mouth open. Her body pressed against his as her tongue flicked out to play ever so gently against his lips.

He almost started crying in relief. He put his hand behind her head, and he began to kiss her back in earnest. He did not want this moment to ever end. Before he had never been so scared in his life, having spent night after night dreaming of this, and now it was happening, and the reality was exceeding his wildest dreams. A lifetime seemed to pass. Then she pulled her body back as her eyes gave him a searching look.

"That is all I am ready for right now. I hope you understand. I need a little time after that attack."

"Of course," he muttered, thinking he sounded like a simpleton.

He had not even thought of doing anything more. What had just happened was a bloody miracle as it was.

"I think I love you, too," she sniffed. "Now keep your hands to yourself, and let us read together for a bit, shall we?"

The sense of relief he felt was indescribable. *Did she just tell me she loved me?* he wondered. He felt as if a great weight had been lifted, the air tasting like honey as he felt like he could breathe freely at last. He wanted to sing, to shout, and to jump up and down in joy, but he just sat there, stupefied. He did not know what to say or what to do. Slowly his wits returned.

"Promise me," he said, "that you will always have someone with you when you go wandering off like this. Preferably a couple of big men with swords in fact. Now say it."

She heaved a big sigh, and then she giggled.

"Okay, I promise. And you must promise me the same. You need bodyguards, too. You are a general now. And if you die, that will break my heart, too."

He nodded in silence, his mind flying about like a flock of starlings, shapeshifting in the summer breeze.

"Say it," she said in a firm tone as she crossed her arms with a mock frown.

"Okay, I'll be more careful. too," he muttered, embarrassed.

She gave him a smile, and then she looked back at her book and started to read again. He felt like he had the concentration of a three-month-old puppy, but he stoically sat there, because he was, after all, a Stoic. But he slowly crept his hand closer to her, and then they held hands as he started to read along with her. Later, he would remember this day as one of the best in his life. Minutes and then hours went by, and he continued to read and hold her hand, but then he heard the cawing of ravens in the distance. Would the call of the wolves be next? Why couldn't the world be truly at peace?

CHAPTER TWENTY-SEVEN

Every morning was the same; Brigid would reach over, the disappointment palpable as her hand would find the bed beside her empty once again. *By the Christos, the mornings are the worst,* she thought. *But they are also the best. It is my time to be with Petrus.* When Petrus was alive, this was their special time where they snuggled together, bonding in the warmth of their nakedness under their covers. Now it was the time that she used to remember the spirit of Petrus. She worried that the memory of his face would fade. It seemed harder now to remember what he looked like, even though it had been only a little more than two years since he had died, and she wanted to never forget him.

Once again, the tears started to well up. *I want him in my heart forever,* she thought. *But when will these feelings of sadness and abandonment leave? Will my life always be like this?* But in the mornings, oh the mornings, that was when she missed him the most. Her mind snapped back to her present reality. During the days now, she kept busy enough, and the feeling of loss could be shoved to the back of her mind. Brigid was scheduled to conduct a meeting that day, where she and the leaders of the community would start their week with a progress report of how things were going.

She hurriedly got dressed and tumbled out the door of her hut in a rush to get to the meeting in time, the memory of Petrus tucked into the back of her mind, always there to give her courage to face the day. The breeze was from the west, as clean and fresh as laundry that had dried in the wind. Every morning the view would take her breath away when she saw the world from atop of the hillfort at Camalet. When it was clear, she could see for miles, able to visualize hawks circling below her as if their home was with the birds. Even the peak of Avalon was visible today, some twelve miles away to the northeast.

Camalet was a massive limestone rock that protruded up from the rolling hills some five hundred feet in the air. Many mornings she would wake and find a fog obscuring the land below, giving her the sensation that she was flying above the clouds. It felt magical. Other days, they would be shrouded in a fog themselves. But not today, as the sun was shining, and the breeze was gentle. Days like this were the best anyone could hope for. *I pray that heaven is like this every day*, she thought.

The top of the hill was a beehive of activity, covering some eighteen acres. They were only living in a corner of the place for now, but they were busy building housing and defensive walls and re-occupying the abandoned Roman villas and farmlands in the countryside. When the Romans controlled the lands around them, the primary crops were grains, such as barley, from massive plantations that used dozens of slaves for labor. Now these estates were being broken into small tracts for smaller groups that emphasized the raising of livestock.

Someday in the future, they might only need to meet once a month or so, but in the founding days of their new sanctuary, they were meeting once a week to iron out the problems they faced. They were hacking out a new settlement on top of this windswept hill that had only contained sheep when they first had arrived. It had been a fortress before the Romans had come, but there had been no one living on this hilltop for hundreds of years. Now that *the Battle of the Pontes* had been won, she prayed that they would have peace for a while to make Camalet an island of safety that no one could threaten.

When she entered the library, she was greeted by the warmth of a cheery fire that revealed the various leaders who had just arrived a few moments ahead of her. As Brigid looked around, she was struck by the shine of the tiny little drops of water on each of the participants when she walked in. Red and yellow light sparkled on everyone's clothing and faces, reflected from the glow of the fireplace. The flickering firelight was also bouncing off the honeycomb of slots for books and scrolls, making it look like a magical hive of bees. She was a queen here, and it felt like home.

For now, Brigid was always the moderator. She had started the community in the Weald, and she was the one person in Camalet with enough gravitas to run these sessions. She had founded the refugee camp in the Weald, and now she was considered the leader of this new community, and with Petrus and Macro gone, everyone looked towards her for answers.

Once their legal code and governmental legal structures were in place, she would love to retreat into other duties, but for now, they needed her in an active presence. Someday in the future she wanted to organize the healthcare of the community into a model that all of Britannia would envy, and she wanted to be with the army doctors and nurses when they were on campaign. The horrors of the battlefield made for good training for those whose mission was to save lives, but for now, those dreams were on hold. A middle-aged matron abruptly started complaining to her as soon as Brigid entered the library.

"Sister Brigid, these women are being stupid! Some of these ninnies seem to think that their laundry is just not clean enough! I cannot___"

Brigid calmly interrupted her.

"Now, Velvinna, you will get a chance to discuss your problem in just a bit, but we need to hear the reports from the other departments first."

Brigid and the impatient Velvinna waited until the rest of the department heads wandered in. Once they started the meeting, Brigid saw that poor Velvinna could barely contain herself as the construction crew complained they were short of nails, and how the sewage ditch to the creek needed to be enlarged, plus they needed more wagons to haul rocks. On it went, until finally, it was Velvinna's opportunity to talk.

"As I was saying before, you know how important it is to have fresh urine to clean things properly, and these people are not saving enough of their own piss, and what they do send us is of poor quality because it has gotten stale, and___"

Velvinna prattled on and on as Brigid kept quiet, a bemused expression on her face. *She just needs to vent,* she thought. Brigid knew she needed to listen to her and give her sympathy and understanding, although if the laundress did not shut up soon, she might just smack her. Brigid looked at the faces of the people on the committee and noticed that the newly arrived Brother Mattius was getting ready to jump into the conversation. A flicker of a smile flitted across her face as she looked upon her fellow priest. *And now Mattius is going to think like a man and offer a solution, and Velvinna is going to just lose it*, she thought in amusement. Sure enough, Mattias spoke up.

"Now, Velvinna, calm down! What if we assign one of the older children to___"

"Don't you tell me to calm down, Brother Mattius!" sputtered Velvinna.

Brigid smothered her groan. The worst thing a man could tell a woman was to calm down.

"As I was saying, those ungrateful hags just do not understand___"

It was all Brigid could do not to laugh aloud. It was all so predictable. Women wanted to share their feelings while men wanted fix things. And it was not just a male or female issue; different personalities made decisions in a variety of ways, but the basic patterns kept repeating themselves. Brigid knew she lacked many things in life, but she could read people well, and she could often get them to cooperate despite themselves. She thought this ability was her best strength.

As for her weaknesses, the chief among them was that she could not imagine anyone considering her to be pretty. She had flaming red hair and skin that freckled in the sun to make her look like a hyena. Her teeth were somewhat crooked, but then again who didn't have that? At least she still had hers. Men nowadays liked their women to be voluptuous, and she was skinny as a rail. Most men would not give her a second look, and she knew it, but at least she would not leave their wives jealous if she talked to their husbands.

The Christos must have made me this way for a reason, Brigid thought. *Thank you, Christos, for not making me both dumb and redheaded. That would have been a bad combination.* But when Petrus looked at her, she had felt different. He only had eyes for her; he told her all the time that he thought she was beautiful, although she knew that was not true. What her husband must have valued was her mind, her wit, and her sense of humor, but Petrus had made her feel special. She had been his best friend, just as Petrus had been just that for her. *By the Christos, I miss him,* she thought.

Bringing her attention back to the debate raging before her. The tension in her shoulders relaxed as she looked at him, grateful that he had come to help with the burden of managing the Christian community, but with the verbal tirade he was receiving, he was probably regretting his decision to join them just now. She regarded him with a mix of hope and pity. Mattius was a nice man, but he was hopelessly naïve, having just arrived from Brittany with his wife in tow. When the word of Camalet had reached his ears, Mattius had set out to join this place that was devoted to Pelagianism, and his help had been invaluable.

Brother Mattius was short and stout, with a bulbous nose and a face well pitted from a childhood bout with smallpox. He seemed such a gentle soul, just very gullible, always believing in the goodness of others. He was kind but clueless, but people liked him. His wife, on the other hand, was a different kettle of fish. She was a beautiful woman, to be sure, but something seemed off about her. Canna's eyes were like a frozen lake in winter; cold and lifeless, possessing no soul. Her predatory countenance seemed particularly chilling when she gazed at women she must have regarded as competition, pretty girls like Lucilia and Senna. It was disturbing.

Watching Mattius and Canna together was painful, as he groveled to please her while she regarded him with the compassion of a snake devouring a mouse. He was always apologizing to her, prattling on about how he was sorry about this and that. They were the oddest-looking couple; she was a stunning beauty, while he was anything but. Still, she felt sorry for the man. Fortunately, the wife had chosen to live in an elegant villa near Camalet with a large entourage of her servants. The less Brigid saw of the woman the better, so she was glad Canna was not in Camalet itself.

Finally, the venting of Velvinna had wound down. Mattius looked like a whipped dog. Maybe he had learned his lesson, and she decided it was time to save him. She would coach him in how to handle such interactions in the future, though whatever he had heard from Velvinna was probably child's play to what he heard at home. As usual, the meeting took forever, but finally it ended and so she scurried off to something far more enjoyable than a bloody meeting.

She headed to the library, where she found Senna and Arturius together, tucked in a corner playing a game of Latrones, the Roman strategy board game. Brigid silently walked up to them, neither one aware of her presence as they were both too engrossed in the contest to notice anything. She studied the board for a moment, and it looked like Senna had the upper hand, while Arturius's pieces looked almost cornered.

"So Arturius, do you ever win any of these games against her?" Brigid asked in a sweet tone.

Senna giggled as he glanced up at her with a startled look on his face.

"I win sometimes," he said.

He smiled as he directed his gaze towards Senna, her knee brushing against his, a secret touch amid the scrolls.

"Don't I, darling? I won two games ago, didn't I?"

"You win almost half the time," she said coquettishly as she gave Brigid a surreptitious wink.

"No, I win maybe one in four," he growled as he shook his head. "But I am getting better, aren't I?"

"Yes, dear."

Brigid could not help but smile. After their return from *The Battle of the Pontes*, Senna and Arturius became lovers. Seeing them together like this reminded her of her times with Petrus, and these two seemed to have a relationship like she remembered she had with her own husband, being friends as well as lovers. It was heartwarming to watch. They both had almost died, and that trauma had brought them together.

Brigid approved, thinking they were perfect for each other, and that they should get married someday. Brigid was pleased neither had parents trying to arrange a match for them. Arturius was estranged from his mother, and the rest of their parents had passed on. Marriage for them would be a choice, not an obligation, but neither one seemed to be in a hurry about it. Brigid sighed to herself. *I need to be patient,* she thought, *not my strongest suit.* The library was Brigid's pet project, and Senna oversaw its development of it. And when Arturius was not out playing soldier, he spent every waking moment by her side in the library.

The couple had many things in common. They both loved to read, discussing literature and poetry when they weren't trying to destroy each other's army on the gameboard. Senna and Arturius helped to supervise the scribes, but Arturius helped when he had time, which was not often. She knew Arturius would prefer to be in the library every day, but right now, these two were alone when they should have been working. She just prayed that Senna was doing what was needed to do to avoid pregnancy.

"So, where are all the scribes right now?" Brigid asked.

"My scouts found a cache of scrolls in an abandoned villa," Arturius muttered, "and the scribes are going out to fetch them. They will be back soon."

"Good," she said as she arched her brow. "You two cannot just fritter the entire day away playing games, you know."

"Yes, Sister," they replied together in unison as they refocused on the game before them.

The world had its share of turmoil and grief, but seeing those two together never failed to bring a smile to her face. On the day went as she bustled about making decisions and helping to build a living community out of a hilltop untrammeled by man for centuries. Keeping herself occupied kept her sane. Even then the most trivial of things would remind her of Petrus throughout the day, but she would not dwell on her memories until the sun had set.

At night, she would say her prayers to the Christos and his mother, Maria. Then came her other favorite part of the day; it was the time for her to think of her beloved. It was in these quiet times that she would talk to Petrus about her hopes and her fears, her aches and her pains, and she kept him up to date on the events and people around her.

She sighed*; There are times I wish I had died with him that day,* she thought. *But this mortal shell I inhabit will wear out and die before I know it, and then Petrus and I will be together forever. I look forward to that.* Her talks with Petrus were the highlight, but trying to sleep the night away was a gift from Christos that she had taken for granted *before the Battle of the Caravan.* Now a new reality had set in. Though her prayers and talks with Petrus would calm her mind, the nightmares would come unbidden.

The images from *the Battle of the Caravan* continued to haunt her. In her dreams, she would order people into battle, and they would look at her in horror as they died, sounding like the wounded horses that had pulled on her heartstrings. She did not want to be responsible for the deaths of anyone, even her enemies. Their cries of horses still echoed in her brain. In the future, she wanted to help the injured to heal, to save lives, not to encourage death. Life was short enough as it was.

For now, she was devoting her energies to establishing an equitable governmental structure in Camalet so she could go back to caring for her bees, building her library, and acting as a mother to Senna and Lucilia. Her most recent interest, to become a healer, was her long-term goal. She did not have time to do all these things, and so she was thrilled to have Mattius here to take the primary duty of caring for the Christian community. Then she thought of Canna, and a frown crossed her face. *If only he was married to someone different*, she thought. *That woman needs watching.*

CHAPTER TWENTY-EIGHT

Canna had lived near the burgeoning settlement of Camalet for over a year now, annoyed that the good Bishop Gildas, had moved north to Viroconium. The fat bastard had worn out his welcome in Caleva and had chosen to leave for greener pastures, and she was not happy about it. Gildas had been a protégé of her own family in Brittany and had been a natural ally. Her oblivious husband didn't know her parents supported Gildas both politically and financially, and she was not about to enlighten him. She was an active spy for the bishop, and she had to send her messengers so much further now to pass on these juicy tidbits of intel about Camalet.

The new British alliance was still getting organized, and the community council had called for a meeting to discuss their future. They wanted their new priest to attend, and she had come along to play the wifely role to learn what their plans were. Rumors were that the council wanted to send out emissaries to their neighboring kingdoms to expand the alliance. How would that confederation be structured? Who would be invited in as members, and who would not? And what people would be sent? She sighed. Many questions made for a long meeting, but knowledge was power. She would do what she had to do to endure it.

These people are nothing more than upstart peasants, Canna thought. *I cannot believe I am here.* She sat beside Mattius, looking regal and interested in the proceedings, knowing she looked stunning tonight, but there was nothing new about that. She was uncommonly beautiful, and she knew it. In a place like Camalet, she felt she was a crystal goblet in a room full of wooden bowls. Her blonde hair was piled up in the latest Roman fashion, and her gown was stunning. Her high cheekbones, full lips, striking green eyes, and well-proportioned figure gave her a truly remarkable appearance, and she relished it, as she enjoyed seeing men stumble into blushing and mumbling idiots while their wives shot at her dagger-eyes of jealousy.

She had put in her usual effort to make herself alluring this evening. Her handmaiden, an Egyptian named Sekhmet, was skilled in many things, including the tasteful and subtle application of makeup. Canna did not want to look like a powdered whore, but a little enhancement here and there was welcome. She forced her face into what she called her party smile, taught to her by her mother to use as few facial muscles as possible to prevent wrinkling. The surreptitiously hungry glances the men in the room gave made her smile. Every man there wanted her, and every woman envied her; the power of it was intoxicating.

Canna's husband now had the floor, droning on about Pelagianism and Christianity. Boredom filled her despite her efforts to look engaged. *Oops,* she thought, *I almost rolled my eyes during these discussions again. That will never do.* Her mind wandered into more pleasant thoughts as she continued to ignore the endless prattle her husband spewed out. Her nickname for him was *The Insipid Fool.* He was no prize to look at, yet here he was, with a stunningly beautiful wife by his side. *Mattius must be so grateful to have me,* she thought.

He adored her; how could he not? Mattius should thank the Christos every day that she had graced his life. The pathetic man was like a lovestruck puppy dog as he begged for scraps of her attention. *It could be so tiresome*, she thought. Canna serviced her husband as rarely as possible as he was repulsive to her, but fortunately, her control over Sekhmet was complete, so Canna had forced her to have an occasional tryst with him. Having her exotic and sexually adventurous handmaiden seduce her husband had taken the pressure off her, and it gave her some ammunition if she ever had to divorce him.

Fortunately for her, he was often gone on the road to minister to his parishioners, as was expected of a man in his position, so the frequent absences gave her freedom. In some ways, she thought of him as the perfect husband, hopelessly naïve and easily manipulated, oblivious to her private life. It was child's play for her to do whatever she wanted to do, and his frequent and prolonged absences provided her with welcome interludes that enabled her to fulfill her ambitions.

Then she felt an uncharacteristic pang of jealousy. This was not the first time she'd seen a man's eyes sliding past her to linger on the lithe form of Senna, this time it was her own scribe, here to take notes on the meeting who looked smitten. The scribe's fearful glance towards her meant he knew she had seen him paying undue attention to another woman, and that sent a thrill through her. Tomorrow, she would make him pay for his insolence when she used her riding crop on him. Her smile grew wider. *Calm down,* she thought, *relax your face, we do not want wrinkles to form.*

She also needed to sexually indulge her bodyguard tomorrow. Brutus was a huge, blond German type, endowed like an ox, but dumb as one as well. Brutus's loyalty had been bought with sweat and feigned groans, a small price to pay for a man who would casually slit someone's throat upon request. She needed him and his thugs to run her blackmail and protection rackets, as well as to manage the stable of fallen angels in the brothel Canna controlled. If the little tarts became rebellious, a beating might be required, something Brutus and his boys were able to provide with enthusiasm.

She was pleased with her own ingenuity, as the various nefarious enterprises she had established in Camalet continued to thrive. Her primary source of profits came from the labors of her servant women, sating the beastly desires of the wayward men for a price. Prudes and priests would consider her a manager of whores: she preferred to think of herself as an enabler of sexual fantasies. Besides the direct reimbursement for her trollup's services, the information they derived was valuable, juicy secrets shared with Camalet's enemies, for a price of course.

Canna had expensive tastes, and her charmingly oblivious husband had no idea how much money she needed to maintain her lovely façade. She liked being in control, out from under the domineering thumb of her own mother. She passionately hated her Carissima Mater, or dearest mother, the name she had been forced to call her when she was growing up. Being able to flee Brittany was one of the reasons she was willing to emigrate to an abandoned province like Britannia.

But Brittany was not too far away, as she could still call on her father, the Pater Familia, to help her, a man of wealth and power who would do anything for his daughter. Roman law gave the head of the family life or death control over his slaves. The scribe's dear mother was a servant there, which ensured his loyalty. So was Sekhmet's son. The handmaiden had no choice but to prostitute herself to keep the brat alive. Family ties like these were so very useful.

Sekhmet was her best spy, providing sex to men of power to pass on to Canna what was murmured during pillow talk. The Egyptian knew amazing techniques on how to drive a man wild, though if a man Canna wished to exploit was noble and handsome enough, sometimes she had taken matters into her own hands. Canna thought back to the education she had received from her own mother, how to exercise her full skillset of female powers once she came of age. She would make sure Sekhmet taught her young daughter those same skills as she grew older.

Men made the laws, fought the wars, and ran the show in this cruel and uncaring world. What was a girl with ambition to do? Well, one must do as her mother had taught her; find a pliable man of means and exploit him to the hilt. In fact, she had already had a wonderful match in mind for her own little princess. Marriages among the rich and powerful were business transactions, not a love match, and the royal family of the Ordovices had caught her attention.

Vortigern's naked grab of power during *the Night of the Long Knives* had been a beautiful thing to behold, but he was antiquated. Soon one of his two sons would be inheriting his throne, then if her daughter married one, then her little princess could help engineer the demise of the other sibling to ensure that Canna's family line would reign supreme. She would have to decide which lucky bastard would put the ring on her finger, but Canna had more time yet before she had to decide which son would be the easiest to manipulate.

To curry favor, she planned on telling Vortigern and Gildas about all the proceedings tonight with the expectation of generous compensation. She would prepare the messages tomorrow and send one of Brutus's minions with an innocent letter that would have hidden in its recesses coded information that the king and the bishop might find useful. Then someday, perhaps her little princess could become a queen of the Ordovices.

The Ordovices clearly had the best shot to win the throne in Britannia. If her daughter married into that brood, then could she become queen over the whole island? *Perhaps so,* she thought with a smile. *That would ensure I can live in luxury.* Her own husband had disappointed Canna in that regard. Mattius was set to become one of the richest men in Brittany through inheritance, but *the Insipid Fool* found that he loved the Christos more than gold, and had refused his family's money, dragging her to this godforsaken place. Being away from her mother was good, but why not somewhere more civilized, such as Constantinople?

She gave a slight shake of her head as she thought about it. But she was proud that she could make the best of any bad situation. She always did. Her wandering mind refocused on the proceedings. She did not want to miss anything important. Canna reworked her party smile back into focus.

She needed to help Gildas and Vortigern so they would be beholden to her. Perhaps she could find a way to rid the alliance of this pesky boy general.

The lad seemed amazingly resistant to her own sexual charms and the virtues of Sekhmet, a fact she found perturbing. He had recently married that skinny librarian of his, and he only had eyes for her. Even before then, he had resisted her stable of prostitutes, as stoics were not the kind of men to visit brothels. Apparently, he had a strong sense of morals, and a man who couldn't be blackmailed was dangerous for her business.

A round of applause and cheering broke her reverie. She was even more annoyed now; that cheer she had just heard was so obnoxiously enthusiastic. *It is for that boy, Arthur. What a joke,* she thought. She had to address him by his real name in today's meeting, but in her mind, he was just a glorified peasant. The common people had started calling the young upstart Arthur, as Arturius sounded too Roman and she called him the same. She liked giving a peasant's name to a man not born into true nobility. Her own family was an honored lineage, and his was not.

As the meeting had droned on, the ruling committee decided that Arthur, this glorified plebian, was to become their general in charge of their army. She shook her head in disgust. *One should keep to one's station in life,* she thought, *that was the plan of the Christos.* Certainly, Gildas and his masters in Rome thought so. In the meeting tonight, the council had just confirmed that the upstart was the permanent commander. That was intolerable. *Something needs to be done,* she thought.

Camalet's town council was gushing about how he was such a skilled warrior and a natural leader, but Arthur was not the only thorn in her paw: there was also Senna. Her recent wedding to Arthur had been a well-attended affair, and Canna had done her best to outshine any other woman there as she always did, but for the first time in her life, she had failed. Senna had been a fresh and radiant beauty, and all eyes had been on her. Even worse, the little bitch's family lineage was even more exalted than her own, being related to patricians who were some of the most ancient in Rome.

This was the first time she had ever been jealous of another woman, and Canna did not like the feeling. What with Senna's noble lineage and being married to a successful general, the brats those two spawned could even outshine her own. That would never do. Canna prayed to the Christos for Arthur to be killed in some meaningless battle somewhere while Senna died while giving birth to a stillborn baby. Her eyes narrowed as she kept her smile plastered on her face. *It would be better to crush Arthur now before he grows too powerful*, she thought. *This boy could be king someday, and that would never do.*

Then a happy thought popped into her head. Her bodyguard Brutus was one of those smelly Angles to the north and his friends and relatives up there had helped with a discrete murder or two on occasions. Perhaps Arthur could meet with an unfortunate accident in his upcoming travels. Brigands were all over these days, and sometimes travelers would just disappear. With her sources of information, it would be easy to learn about any future travel itinerary. Her smile became more pronounced again. A creative imagination could make even a dull evening like this enjoyable. *Life is like that sometimes,* she thought.

CHAPTER TWENTY-NINE

Arturius wordlessly stood there, Caradoc by his side, transfixed by the view as they gazed out from the grove of primordial oak trees that topped the crest of the hill. The sun had started to set, casting a reddish glow off the reflection of the River Sabrina like a shimmering red ribbon winding its way to the sea. A few clouds could be seen silhouetted in the sky, gradually changing from white to pink to deeper red as the sun descended. The full moon had risen as well, so once the sun had completely departed from the sky, it promised to be a well-lit night. He missed Senna, and the beauty of the place made him wistful, wishing that she was here to see it with him.

Arturius gazed with awe upon the skimming swallows as they darted about the river, and an occasional bat could be seen flitting overhead as the flying creatures feasted on the insects in the coming twilight. In the distance across the river were the imposing walls of Glevum, once established as a Colonia, a community developed for the retirement of the Roman Legionaries. Its strong military culture had remained, so Glevum had been spared some of the deprivations that had afflicted communities farther to the east. He gazed upon the tableau in wonder; certain he was in a special place.

Caradoc and Arturius were here on a mission to visit Glevum to acquaint the various realms of Britannia with the new alliance they had just formed. The two of them had been chosen by the council to represent Novum Britannia, now composed of Camalet, Caleva, and Cerdic's new realm in Venta Belgae. After their stop in Glevum, they were now on the way to visit Caradoc's people at Venta Silurum. It would be the first time that Caradoc had been home, and Arturius was pleased to note his friend was capable of smiling.

They had been treated with cautious respect during this visit to Glevum as a potential alliance had been discussed. The goodwill visit that might pay dividends in the future, and now the Glevans had some faces to go with the names they had heard about. Caradoc was bursting with excitement this evening, having dragged Arturius to one of his favorite spots. Arturius smiled even more broadly. *I cannot remember ever seeing Caradoc act so happy,* he thought.

The hill they had just climbed featured a circle of stones at the top, lichen covered and marked with carvings of whirling patterns that had been created by an unknown people who lived in Britannia hundreds of years before, perhaps as old as time itself. The stones were taller that a man and twice as wide, flat and shaped like a funerary tombstone. Arturius wondered if ancient skeletons were buried underneath. Arturius thought the patterns of whorls and three-sided trefoils were perhaps a form of writing long forgotten by the world.

"I couldn't wait to show you this," Caradoc said in wonder.

Even Arturius had heard of this sacred grove of trees, with its ancient stone circle atop the hill. The Romans had cleared the land down to the river, but to the west, the land had been left as the gods intended, a forest untrammeled by man. Caradoc had wanted to show him this place held to be sacred by the Druids, and Arturius was duly impressed. The hilltop certainly had a spiritual feeling about it.

"This is indeed a magical place," Arturius quietly murmured.

He gazed back over to the river. All he could think of was that Senna would have loved to have been here. Still newlyweds, and his heart ached so much that she could not come with him on this trip, but she was busy getting the library organized, and travel in Britannia was still a hazardous enterprise. Still, he made himself a promise that he would take her here someday to see the setting summer sun, just as it was that very evening.

"This trip to Glevum has worked out well, thank the gods," Arturius said. "It was a good thing that Gildas tried to stay here first before settling in Viroconium. I think their city council found the bishop to be just as annoying as we found him. They may join the alliance not so much as they liked the idea, but more because they hated Gildas as much as we did."

Caradoc smiled along with him.

"I heard the feeling were mutual," Caradoc grumbled. "He supposedly left in quite a pout. So why did he go up to Viroconium?"

"They want the prestige of a real Roman bishop" Arturius said, "and they promised to build him a church."

"The folks in Venta Silurum would not build that fat gobshite an outhouse," Caradoc scoffed.

"I think that victory at *the Battle of the Pontes* intrigued the Glevan city council. I know nothing has been agreed to yet, but they sounded interested in joining the alliance."

Caradoc grumbled, "Maybe, but I believe it's because of the bloody Ordovices. Glevum hates them as much as my own tribe does."

"Your Silures make them nervous," snorted Arturius, "but they seemed to hate the Ordovices more. I think the idea that alliance members cannot attack each other caught their attention. If both your tribe and Glevum are in the same alliance, they don't have to worry about you anymore. They seem interested in working together if we continue to produce victories."

"If."

"You sound like a Spartan. You should be one, as little as you talk sometimes."

Caradoc just grunted.

"If we can just keep the Ordovices neutral, that would be good, but finding Vortimer's brother with Horsa on the road to Caleva was a bad sign."

Caradoc shook his head.

"Hope they stay put. The only thing they understand is the point of a sword."

"Speaking of the Ordovices," Arturius muttered, "I wonder if Vortigern is still alive. He is an ancient relic. He should be dead by now!"

"Hmph."

Arturius chuckled as he gave Caracoc's shoulder a playful tap.

"I bet they paid some Egyptian to mummify him to make people think he is still alive. Half dead or not, the Ordovices will not be pleased if we form an alliance with Glevum. And didn't your father send you a message saying he thought you have a solid chance to become the ruler of the Silures?"

Caradoc pursed his lips and hesitated before he spoke.

"Maybe."

"Wouldn't that be something! Cerdic is a king now, and if you and your father could make this happen, we three would all have armies at our backs, and we could help each other."

Caradoc rolled his eyes.

"If."

They both chuckled for a moment.

"There you go, sounding like a Spartan again. Do you know the story of that? The word if?"

Caradoc shrugged as the face of Arturius brightened. He loved talking about history.

"When Alexander the Great's father, Philip of Macedonia, sent a long message to Sparta that basically said If I invade your country, you will be destroyed, never to rise again, and Sparta sent back "if" as their one-word reply."

Caradoc shrugged again.

"Caradoc, you are hopeless pessimist. If we can form a functional alliance with some of the other kingdoms, we could stop the chaos in Britannia and bring back peace and prosperity once more like we had a hundred years ago, but this time independent of Rome."

"If," he grunted. "It has not happened yet. There are many things that can go wrong."

"This idea seemed like a fantasy when were captives of the South Saxons," Arturius said as he clasped his hands together in excitement. "But really, this is coming together."

A dark thought entered his mind. *Do not get too excited,* he thought. *It is times like these the gods like to mess with you, just when things are going well.* He shook it off as unnecessarily negative thinking. Both fell silent as Arturius continued to revel the aura of the place, but the sound of raucous laughter broke his reverie. He looked down to where their escorts, a half dozen horsemen from Caleva, were waiting for them, dismounted and sharing a flagon of wine at the foot of the hill. They were clearly having too good of a time.

Arturius muttered, "Those bodyguards are the least soldierly out of anyone at Caleva."

"Yes," grumbled Caradoc, shaking his head in disgust.

Arturius muttered, "I suspect the garrison commander wanted to stop them from drinking Caleva dry, so they gave them to us. I suppose they look enough like soldiers to keep the bandits away, just so long as they do not fall off their nags."

Caradoc shook his head.

"How was it that we ended up with these fellows as our escorts anyway?"

"That was my fault," Arturius said as he raised his arms in frustration. "The few soldiers remaining at Caleva were cavalrymen without horses, and we have a few now, but no real cavalrymen. So, I agreed to let them be our escorts. They looked so pitiful, begging me to get back on a calvary mount once more. I felt sorry for them."

Caradoc rolled his eyes as Arturius chuckled, "If they go arse over tits on this trip, we are dead. Remember that next time, Arturius."

The two of them were alone atop the hill, their bodyguards claiming they didn't want to see the faery ring because they were Christians, and Arturius knew that was a crock of shite. *They were just too lazy to climb up the hill,* he thought, shaking his head in disgust. Finally, the men below them quieted down, and once again silence and peace reigned as the dying rays of sunlight continued to take his breath away. Arturius thought of Cato and wondered if the emotions he now felt mirrored his stepfather's stories about mystical places like this.

The crusty old slinger would get a misty look in his eyes as he had described some of the special locations in the world where he said he could feel the presence of the gods, places such as the Oracle at Delphi. His stepfather remembered feeling the spirits of the gods there, and Arturius felt he was experiencing the same now. Then suddenly, the sound of galloping horses on the Roman roadway below drew his attention back to the present.

"Hercules's bollocks," Arturius said with a sudden intake of his breath.

A dozen armed riders had burst out of the trees by the road ahead of their party. Their escorts were lolling beside the roadway, still sharing their skins of wine, while their horses were munching nearby on grass, and they had been clearly taken by surprise. Their horses had gotten spooked, and none of their men were able to control their mounts before the beasts fled. The attacking riders swept in and made short work of their hapless comrades, slashing at the dismounted Calevan's with their flashing spears. It was over in a minute. Caradoc and Arturius looked on, stunned by the ferocious attack.

Now the two young men were trapped on the hill without any weapons, other than the knives at their sides and the sling Arturius always kept in his pocket. Arturius felt that familiar ache in his bollocks as fear fluttered into the pit of his stomach. He noticed the killers were ignoring the saddlebags of the men they had just killed. *They are looking for us,* he thought, *not loot.*

Arturius whispered, "Who are those bastards. Are they Ordovician?"

"No. Saxon maybe?"

"Perhaps," Arturius whispered. "Whoever they are, they mean trouble for us. These are not just bandits, someone betrayed us. Maybe the Glevans were not so happy to meet us after all?"

"Did they see us?"

"We will know soon enough," he replied.

The two of them stayed motionless as the horsemen below gazed up the hill in their direction. They dismounted and spread out and started to trudge up the hill as the familiar ache in his pelvis increased. *They really are looking for us,* he thought. Now he was thankful that Senna was not with them. She had wanted to come on this trip, but Sister Brigid talked some sense to her, and so she stayed home. A wave of sadness swept over him. They had planned a lifetime together, but that might not happen now. Today could be his last. Their last parting had been all too brief, and he wished he'd told her how much he loved her, but at least she was safe at home and not getting murdered upon this hill.

Ice continued to run down his spine as Arturius softly muttered, "They are definitely coming for us. They mean to kill us."

Neither spoke for a few moments, then Caradoc whispered, "Let us disappoint them then. We need to move deeper into the forest and lose them in the woods."

"Okay," he muttered back.

Caradoc took the lead as they moved down the western slope, trying not to leave an easy trail to follow. Arturius pulled out his sling, grabbing a few stones from the top of the hill, but they were not river-smoothed like he was used to, and a knife would be of little use against spears and swords. Arturius continued to follow Caradoc as they slowly picked their way down the slope, trying not to make any noise.

By the sound of it, Arturius could tell their foes were spreading out along the tree line to catch their quarry. Onwards the two moved, stealthily dancing through the gloom of the forest as their pursuers crashed through the trees behind them, loudly calling out to each other in their search. He and Caradoc had to be quiet, but there was no such compunction by his enemies to do the same.

His mind was awash with emotions: fear of dying, anger at the thought of betrayal, disgust at the gods for dealing them such a hand. The sounds of their pursuit grew closer as he touched the amulet that Senna had given him to ward off the evil eye. He had promised her he would return, but it looked like their blood might be feeding the oaks instead. The gloom of the forest made it hard to see and even more difficult to run, but still he prayed for the blackness to quicken so they could slip away. Suddenly, Arturius cried out as he tumbled to the ground, twisting his ankle on a hidden root.

He grimaced in pain as he hissed, "Save yourself, Caradoc! Go!"

A wave of despair filled him. He did not want his own stupidity to kill his friend.

Caradoc softly growled, "We live or die together, brother."

Caradoc helped pull Arturius with him as they staggered along. Before, he thought they had been staying ahead of their pursuers, but now that he had to be half carried, they were clumsy and slow. Still, he was proud of his friend, as Caradoc refused to abandon him to the wolves. Tears filled his eyes. *Caradoc is going to get killed because of my clumsiness*, he thought.

"I see the bastards! There they are! Go get them!" loudly rang out from their pursuers.

The words were not in British or Saxon, the accent unmistakable. *Why are Angles chasing us,* he wondered. *Did someone in Glevum betray us?* Arturius did not understand what was happening, but he did know someone wanted them eliminated. Arturius wondered if his musings about his two friends becoming kings had angered the gods with his hubris. *Just when things were going so well,* he thought.

Arturius muttered, "What in Hades are these Angles doing this far west?"

"I do not think they will bother to tell us before they kill us," deadpanned Caradoc.

As he again touched the amulet around his neck, his fear started to recede. An icy feeling of resolve filled his soul. *If I die,* he thought, *then it will be with the honor of a true Roman.* He would make Senna proud, taking as many of them with him as he could. He fruitlessly glanced around him to find better stones to use, but the floor of the forest littered with leaves, so he had to make do with the ones he had. Their foes were on both sides of them now, fleeting images just visible through the trees. They were trapped.

Arturius stopped and loaded a missile into his sling, and then he whipped it at the only Germanic warrior visible to him, missing by inches. His target ducked down, looking for where the attack had come from, he then reloaded and fired again, and this time the warrior disappeared with a yelp of pain, buying them a little time. He and Caradoc were stuck at the edge of a small clearing, and he was uncertain where to go.

Caradoc softly hissed," Should we try to cross to the other side?"

"They will see us easily if we do," Arturius whispered back. "If they don't come all at once, we can jump one of them and get one of their spears, and then___"

"Shh!"

He could see glimpses of a couple of Angle warriors armed with spears starting to converge on them, creeping ever closer to their location. Suddenly, new noise intruded.

Whirrrrrrr, *Thwack!*

An arrow suddenly sprouted into the chest of one of the Angles to the right. The enemy warrior grunted and slowly slumped to the ground. Off to the left, he heard another yelp of pain. An unexpected feeling of hope returned, as did his fear and anger. *What is happening right now?* he thought as he pulled out his knife and ducked down, ready to fight to the death.

Then a stocky blonde warrior in pigtails, wearing a leather jerkin covered in armored scales, burst through the brush and charged, his broad-headed spear pointed towards him. Arturius was clearly the target, so he rose up and jumped off his good right foot towards his left as he held out his pugio. He rolled and resumed his crouch, still brandishing his blade. The spearman thrust at him, and he turned to his side to avoid the spear, his free hand flashing down to knock the spearpoint away. Arturius stepped forward and raised his knife, ready to strike.

Whirrrrrrr, Thwack!

Arturius felt a sudden punch knock his breath out. Moments later he heard another arrow hit, and glancing over he saw it quivering in the neck of the barbarian. His enemy's bearded mouth opened, and blood started to bubble out as his hands clutched his throat, his spear now dropped and forgotten. Arturius closed his eyes for a moment, and then he opened them again, not focused on the plight of the Angle warrior. Instead, he was staring at a different arrow, the one protruding from his own left arm.

He felt a searing pain in his chest as he dropped to one knee. It hurt to breathe, but strangely, his arm felt numb. He heard a buzzing noise inside his head, and he could not think clearly. *Are the gods trying to kill us all?* he slowly thought, as the world started to spin. He heard Caradoc shout out in some language he did not seem to know as he fell to the ground, with cries of alarm and the sound of more arrows filling the air. The last thing he saw was the faint outline of the rising moon through an opening in the clearing before a deep darkness enveloped him.

CHAPTER THIRTY

Arturius woke up, his mouth dry as sand. His arm was numb, immobilized by a tight binding pressed in against his chest. Each breath felt like agony. He lay on his right side, and he could see the foliage of trees pass by overhead. It was daylight. *Isn't it supposed to be nighttime right now?* he wondered. He turned his head and looked up ahead of him and realized he was being carried, surrounded by men dressed in forest green. He did not recognize them. He looked towards his own feet to gaze at the man carrying the litter from its rear. This one looked familiar. He fruitlessly searched in his memories, his mind all a fog, unable to place the name. *It is someone I know,* he thought, the name finally coming to him. *Ahh, it is Caradoc!*

Arturius croaked out, "Water."

No one heard him. His mouth felt so dry. He tried it again.

"Water!"

He saw Caradoc glance up at him.

Caradoc grunted out as he carried the litter, "Welcome back to the world of the living. We have been dragging your fat arse all night long while you slept like a baby, lazy bones."

Arturius's left ankle felt swollen, and it was throbbing, but the worst pains were shooting through his chest as the litter bounced along the forest trail.

"Water," he tried one more, a little louder this time.

They stopped, lowering the litter to the ground with gentleness, and then they gingerly sat him up, holding his left arm in place as they did so. Arturius glanced around him. There were four of them besides Caradoc, all dressed in forest-green, with leaves adorning their jerkins and hats. He thought they looked like wood fairies, but they were not: they had to be Silures. He dropped his head back in exhaustion, grateful to still be in the world of the living. *I am not in the Elysian fields,* he thought. *If I were dead, it would not hurt this much.*

He wondered what gods had tried to kill him and which ones had favored him, but he knew that in the land of the Silures the old gods of Britannia were still revered, and so he would ask for Caradoc to give them a sacrifice if he survived this journey. One of them lifted a waterskin to his lips and he drank greedily; it was warm and tasted of old leather and forest soil, but it was brilliantly refreshing all the same. The man who held it was young, stocky, and his head was just as dark and curly as Caradoc's was. All of them, in fact, had that same dark curly hair and light-colored eyes. *How odd*, he thought.

"I am called Lucius," the young man said, "and I am honored to meet you, but I do regret that I almost killed you. You should have stayed still instead of jumping around like a hare."

Caradoc retorted, "No, you should only be rescued by a Silurian who can shoot an arrow at where he is aiming, not this lump of clay."

Caradoc started to chuckle.

"It would be funny, except it probably hurts for you to laugh right now."

Arturius asked in a hoarse whisper, "Where are you taking me?"

"One who is favored by the gods who can help you," replied Lucius. "I hope you can forgive me. We do think you will survive this, unless that arrow went into your lungs, of course, but then you would be coughing up blood by now, and___"

"Lucius," interrupted Caradoc, "give it a rest. You sound like a gossipy old woman right now. Arturius, you are going to be fine. Have another drink and rest. We have a way to go."

He drank a little more, then the litter was hoisted back up again, and on they went. The journey seemed to go on forever. The numbness in his arm was wearing off, the aching exacerbated by a sharp stabbing pain in his chest whenever the litter bounced. Finally, they entered a forest clearing where a series of small round huts were located surrounded by a ditch and a staked palisade wall. He was brought into a hut where a wizened middle-aged man was sitting in a corner, his legs crossed, and his eyes closed.

The man's erect posture suggested he was tall and thin, but somehow, he displayed a dignified appearance. He was dressed in a simple black robe and appeared to be in a trance. His hair was predominantly white with a few black streaks, hanging long and straight and unbound about his shoulders. Despite his care-worn face, his salt-and-pepper-streaked beard was short and well-trimmed. After placing the litter down, Lucius approached the man and gently touched him on the shoulder. The man opened his eyes as if coming out of a deep sleep, his expression startled as he glanced around the room.

The older man spoke, his voice a deep rumble, "Well, young Lucius, what have we here?"

Lucius told him the story. The man got up and approached the litter.

"Hello there, young man. You are the unlucky recipient of one of our arrows, it seems. Lucius here called it an accident, and that you are a friend of Caradoc. But whether intended or not, it will hurt the same regardless. I am the Myrddin of the Silures. In Latin, you might call me the Merlinus. That means I have many roles for my people here, but one of those hats I wear is that of a medicus in your world. I am going to see what I can do to help you."

"What in hades is a Merlinus?" Arturius croaked, unsure if he wanted the man to help him.

The man replied in a patient tone, "It is a title given to a leader of the wise ones, we who carry the knowledge of the ancients for the people of this tribe. You Romans would call us Druids, and to us, being a Druid can mean many things. But fear not, we will not burn you alive in a wicker-man basket as that liar Julius Caesar claimed. I am a healer. have studied the writings of your famous physician Galen, and the methods used by surgeons in the Roman Legions. I have even traveled to Alexandria to study there, though we Druids already had considerable lore about healing."

The Merlinus smiled at Arturius.

"Let me have a look here. Let us bring in a few more torches. Lucius, you get to hold this mirror to improve the lighting. You young men did well in not trying to remove the arrow yourselves."

The Merlinus opened a small and elaborately carved box lined in cloth and took out a strange- looking device, a thin wooden frame that fit on top of one's nose. The instrument had two pieces of convex glass attached to it that settled in front of each of his eyes, and the reflected image made his eyes look as large as a cow. The foresters gasping in amazement.

Lucius asked, "What is that thing you put on your face called?"

"In Latin, they are called specula," replied the Merlinus. "But I would call them eyeglasses. They help to magnify so I can see fine details up close. I heard about them in Alexandria, and I had a pair made while I was there by a skilled Egyptian glassmaker."

Arturius had seen hand-held magnifiers before, but nothing like this. *What a clever idea,* he thought. *I shall have to remember this.* The men holding the torches looked on in awe as sounds of "Ooh," and "What magic," flitted about the room.

The Merlinus gently unwrapped the bandage and inspected the arm and chest closely.

"A lucky shot," he muttered. "The arrow went through the back of your upper arm before hitting chest," observed the Merlinus. "That slowed it down. A finger breath differently and it would have pierced your heart. A fascinating injury to be sure, but the arrowhead did not go into your lung. Now, Arturius, I need to give you some juice of the poppy mixed with henbane to get you relaxed, but as you can guess, what I am about to do will be painful. Your new friends here will need to hold you down when the time comes."

Arturius glanced up at Caradoc who gave him a nervous smile and a wink. Then he closed his eyes and tried to relax.

"While we wait," the Merlinus said, "I am going to pour a little vinegar on your wound, and that will sting a bit. I must prepare my instruments by boiling them in vinegar, then I must wash my hands much as the Jews do before a meal. I'll be back in a few minutes."

Arturius took the drink he was offered, and it burned like fire going down, and he closed his eyes once more. Images of the fight in the trees kept flashing in his mind as he tried to rest. He closed his eyes as he thought of the events of the day. He was so excited to see Caradoc get home and help him become a king. Then he had fallen into despair thinking he was going to die while on the brink of success. He had lost hope, ready for the end. And then a miracle, and now they were saved. But he was wounded and still he might die.

He had told Senna that he would be home in a week, but he suspected it might be months before he could travel, and winter was coming. *And if this gets infected, then I will never come home,* he thought. He closed his eyes to visualize her face as he clutched the amulet again, desperate to see her once more. He started to feel dizzy as the medicine kicked in, his mind getting foggier by the second.

He heard the Merlinus mutter some prayers invoking the name of the Goddess Danu as he hung a wreath of mistletoe above the bed. Arturius was in a strange dream world now, vaguely aware the prayers were over and that Caradoc and the Merlinus were talking about him. Snippets of conversation filtered in. He listened to the Merlinus as he said he had sacrificed a rabbit to aid in his recovery, but there was something unusual about it, some vision about the future, that the gods had spoken.

He vaguely heard the Merlinus said, "Your sister's hands must heal what you have broken," then Arturius heard a name: Gwenhwyfar. *What an odd name*, he thought. He drifted off as the biggest fight of his life was about to begin.

CHAPTER THIRTY-ONE

Caradoc could tell the drugs were working, as Arturius was in a stuporous delirium. He was ready, and so were the three burly men who were to help him to hold his friend down when the cutting was to begin. He looked up expectantly at the Merlinus entering the open pavilion operating room wearing a snow-white robe, fastened by a golden cord at the waist. The Druid said another blessing over the mistletoe wreath, then he sat down and put on his eye magnifiers. He glanced up and asked one of his attendants to hold a mirror to direct the sunlight to the site of the operation, while another assistant waved a fan to keep the insects away.

"It is time," the Merlinus said.

He and his companions firmly pinned Arturius down. *Danu, heal my friend*, he prayed. *He is the hope of all Britannia. We need him.* He vowed to find a nice rabbit for Arturius as a sacrifice for him when they were done. The Merlinus used a small saw to cut off the shaft of the arrow on the inner aspect of the arm. The entry wound was as small slit, while the exit wound was larger, surrounded by a substantial bruise. The Merlinus quickly pulled the shaft out and applied some pressure, then he grasped a wooden-handled wire that had been heated to red-hot in the nearby brazier. Flesh sizzled as he used the hot iron to stanch the bleeding.

Smoke curled up as a burnt odor wafted through the air, making his stomach churn, but nonetheless Caradoc was mesmerized. He had never seen surgery done before, and it held a terrible fascination. The smell was similar to that of cooked pork, reminding him that he was hungry, a nauseating thought right now. Arturius tried to squirm away, but the four of them had him well immobilized. It was clearly painful for his friend, but he was in such delirium he was sure that Arturius would not remember it.

The Merlinus said Arturius had been lucky. The humerus bone had not been broken, nor were any large blood vessels cut. He poured a mixture of honey, and a powdered rock made from a holy place across the sea in Hibernia, a place called Fermanagh, into the wound. Then the Druid wrapped a linen dressing soaked in vinegar and honey around the injured arm. The Merlinus muttered some more prayers, then he clucked his tongue as he looked up.

"This chest wound might be more problematic, Caradoc. But I will do what I can."

The Merlinus enlarged the chest wound with a long, thin knife, then a stream of blood started to rhythmically pump out, but the Merlinus was able to stop it when he tied a ligature over the vessel that had spurted out the blood, then he used his heated needle once again. Once the bleeding had fully stopped, the bright red muscle was visibly exposed, looking like a hog had been butchered. Insects started to buzz around the wound, and the Merlinus directed the assistants to wave some fans to keep the flies away as the Druid continued to work.

After the bleeding had been stabilized, the Merlinus took out an instrument, something the Romans had developed he called *the Spoons of Diocles,* that looked like two large spoons put together. He introduced the device around the stubby shaft as Arturius squirmed and groaned in pain, but when the Merlinus tried to pull the arrowhead out, it seemed to be stuck.

The old man continued to pull harder until suddenly Caradoc heard a pop. The arrowhead jumped off the rib as Merlinus fell on his backside from the effort. Caradoc rolled his eyes in relief, trying hard not to laugh at the image of the dignified priest landing in an undignified heap upon the ground. The priest then stood up and offered up a prayer to Danu with all the men holding his friend down joining in.

Now the wait would begin. *Will Arturius heal, or will the gods take him?* Caradoc thought. That night he fulfilled his promise as he sacrificed a fat rabbit to speed up his recovery. Early the next morning, Caradoc came into the hut and looked upon a sleeping Arturius with concern, lying there unresponsive and swaddled with dressings. Before today he had never really paid much attention to what the healers did, but that was a different story now. He turned to the Merlinus and asked him what to expect.

"His healing will come in two phases," replied the Merlinus. "First, we must see whether the arm develops the weeping black sickness, what the Roman doctors would call gangrene. If that develops, we will have to do an emergency amputation, and even with that, he will not likely survive."

"How long it before something like that occurs?"

"It will show up in the next two or three days, perhaps up to a week. Gangrene is the most feared result from a wound like this. It is a painful and terrible way to die."

Caradoc wrinkled his nose.

"What do we look for?"

"We will look at the pus coming out, and what we will want to see is the good kind, which is thick, white, and odorless. The pus of gangrene is different, watery and muddy brown, and it has an awful sickly sweet kind of stench that once you smell it, you will never forget it."

"So, what are the odds of him getting gangrene?"

"Perhaps one in five with this kind of wound. We will continue to apply honey and vinegar-soaked linen dressings to the area, changing several times a day at first. And of course, we will need prayer and sacrifices. This is in the hands of the gods, really, we don't have much control."

Caradoc blew out his cheeks in a slow exhale.

"By Jupiter, what else do we have to worry about?"

The Merlinus continued, "A more likely issue would be the drowning cough, what the Romans would call pneumonia. With a chest injury like this, it is very possible. That rib is undoubtedly cracked, and the underlying lung must be injured. Once the risk of gangrene has faded, the possibility of getting pneumonia increases."

Caradoc shook his head. *There are so many ways to die,* he thought.

"By Hercules bollocks, so when does that occur?"

"It will show up around a week from now if it indeed comes. That will be the most critical time. He needs to walk about and take deep breaths, to exercise the lungs, but it will be difficult because it will hurt every time he breathes. And young Caradoc, I fear you have spent too much time away from home. It is unseemly for the king of the Silures to curse like a Roman, so be a bit more circumspect in what you say in the future. But also know that I am on your side. I support your father's ambitions for your future."

Caradoc grunted sheepishly.

"Sorry about that. And thank you for your understanding and your support. Blame my friend here for teaching me Roman curses, but you are right, I need to watch my mouth. What else can I do to help him?"

"The most important thing we can do is to pray to the gods. I will keep the sacred mistletoe above his head, and I will also make the sacrifice of a white ram to the Goddess Danu tonight in the sacred grove. I will have one of my acolytes stay with him constantly. It should be a virgin who is favored by our Gods, but I need to ask her permission for this holy task. And for this, Caradoc, I will need your permission as well."

"Why do you need my permission?" he replied with a puzzled look.

"You remember what told you earlier? Before I had done this surgery, I had performed a ritual to help foresee the future and to determine what we can do to help in his recovery. I disemboweled a white rabbit and read the signs of the gods when I examined the pattern of its entrails. It was most peculiar. You remember when I mentioned to you that your sister is becoming a skilled healer? Well, I know now that the gods want your younger sister to have a special role to play in helping Arturius heal."

"You mean Gwenhwyfar," he blurted out in a surprised tone.

There was a pause as the surprise of it took Caradoc aback, but then he consented. *Who am I to question the prophesies of the gods?* he thought.

CHAPTER THIRTY-TWO

Gwenhwyfar sat on the side of the bed, holding Arturius's right hand as she daubed his forehead with a damp cloth. He was burning up with fever, but the Merlinus had stressed the importance of keeping his body warm. Cooling his face was something that seemed to soothe him, and the Merlinus felt that it was a good thing to do provided the rest of him was well covered. She had been assigned the job to keep this young man alive, and she would do anything in her power to accomplish that.

Unlike her brother Caradoc, she did not possess dark hair like most of the Silures; instead, her hers was wavy blonde and worn in a short bob. In her tribe, married women wore their hair up, and single women wore their hair long, bound with ribbons and ties. Hers was different, as she was an acolyte as a Druidess in training, and her hair style reflected that status. If she became a full-fledged Druidess, she would never cut her hair again, but it would be years before she could be fully ordained into the order.

She was of a medium build and was lean and well-muscled, but her breasts were already starting to develop, and it suggested that when her body would reach its full maturity, she could become a woman who could keep her children fed and her man well satisfied. She knew others considered her pretty, with blazing green eyes, but the most striking thing people complimented her about was her smile, which displayed startling white teeth adorned by a prominent dimple on each side. The smile reflected that she had generally a happy disposition and possessed patience and a nurturing spirit, and that disposition was being tested with the task she had been given.

Most of the maidens training to become a Druidess never finished because of this, requiring years of uncompromising commitment, and she had doubts about herself. Part of her wanted children someday, and that was not the way of the fully fledged priestesses of the order. The lower levels of Druids could marry, but not the leaders. Mothers nurtured their families while priestesses nurtured the entire community instead of children or a husband. What sounded like a good idea when she was nine had become uncertain to her as she got older, but Druidesses were also renowned for their knowledge and wisdom, and that had appealed to her.

What she really wanted was to have it all: a man she could love, children she could raise, a community she could help, and a life of constant learning so that she could be respected for her wisdom. In her world, she was unaware of any women who had all those things, but as she had gotten older, she realized that the world was more than her village near the Silurian capital. Perhaps she could live someplace where she could really have it all. As the daughter of one of the most prominent men of the Silures tribe, she might have options that others might never have, and now her body was changing, boys seemed a little less dull than before. She did not know what to think about her future.

But that was a problem for another day; for now, her priority was to save a life. She and the other acolytes had been assigned to work in shifts to help prevent their young patient from dying. They were to say their prayers, give him medicines, make their sacrifices, change his dressings, and keep their guest warm. She was a nurturer, and if ever a man needed nurturing, it was now. Arturius was often in a delirium, and although he was lucid at times, he spent much of his time in a fitful sleep.

He would talk to himself sometimes, often unintelligibly, but sometimes his words she recognizes as being in different languages. The Saxon phrases he uttered were primarily curse words, and when he spoke in the Latin tongue, she could tell he was asking for help from Jupiter or from Marcus somebody, maybe Aurelius or Aurelianus. In British he would call out for Cato, or her brother's name, or a person called Cerdic. Sometimes, he would be incredibly quiet and ask for someone named Petrus.

But most of his jabbering was concerned a person named Senna. Caradoc had told her that she was his wife, and Gwenhwyfar could tell that Arturius missed her terribly. Caradoc said they were deeply in love, and she could tell that he truly cared for his wife just from the tone and the look on his face when he spoke. Gwenhwyfar found herself getting a little envious of this woman she had never met. If she ever got married herself, she would want her husband to love her as much as Arturius seemed to love Senna.

When he was awake, he would gaze at her with grateful eyes. He would ask her to tell him stories about herself and her people, and about the Druids and her traditional Celtic beliefs. She was eager to teach him, as he truly listened and asked thoughtful questions, but then he would become exhausted and would fall back asleep and enter his dream world. She could tell he was a kind soul. He was charming in fact. She imagined herself marrying someone like him, but her desire to be a Druidess conflicted with matrimony, so she buried those thoughts for now.

She was thirteen and was just coming into womanhood. Even if she were not a budding druidess, in her tribe, a marriage decision would be her choice and would also be an eternity from now, at eighteen or even older. It would not be with this young man, as he was already married and he looked like he would be dying any day, but as each morning started, he seemed to keep hanging on. The worst was his coughing. He would expectorate a yellow green sputum, and with each violent hack, he would wince in pain.

Gwenhwyfar, along with the others, spent much of her time spooning with him under the covers to keep him warm. Other female acolytes oversaw the heating of stones in a fire that the two maintained outside, shuttling back and forth to bring in hot stones and then carry out the ones that had cooled. These stones kept the hut warm without the choking smoke of a fire, something the Merlinus felt could affect his pneumonia, so the heated stones and body warmth kept Arturius warm without hurting his lungs.

As the days wore on, she could tell the arm was healing nicely; the main problem now was with his breathing. At times, it sounded like he was drowning. Arturius's life thread hung on the edge of entering another world for more than two weeks, but then there came an evening that changed her life forever. Gwenhwyfar had gone to his bed as was her duty, but in the depth of the night, she was startled into wakefulness.

She was not sure what had awakened her. At first all she could perceive in the darkness was the sighing of the wind in the trees. Still, she had an ominous feeling. Something unusual was happening, and she could not determine what it was. She lay there unmoving, listening intently. It was silent at first, but then she heard a rustling sound outside their hut. *What is that?* she thought. Her fellow acolyte was fast asleep in the corner, and Arturius was still in a motionless slumber. Something was moving about out there.

A chill shivered down her spine. The healing hut they occupied was near the main settlement but outside the palisades, nestled solitarily in a grove of majestic oaks, so their hut was alone, isolated, and vulnerable. She continued to lay still, listening intently, trying to hear what it was that made the noises outside. Was it a fairy? A wolf? Could this be a Hibernian raider wanting to steal her into slavery? Or was it a war band of Saxons or Angles here to kill them all?

She held her breath and continued to listen. Silence. Once again, the noise could be heard. A rustling. A step. Her feelings of fear increased. *That does not sound human*, she thought. *Is it a Banshee? Is it a good Faery, or an evil one?* She crept slowly to the doorway and gently, ever so carefully, she pushed the door flap to the side while keeping herself hidden. She peered out to the flickering light of the dying fire. There! What was that?

She saw a creature, and it was definitely not a person, as it stood on four legs. The apparition looked off into the distance. Then its head turned, and the beast looked right at her, ears twitching. It seemed to her the creature's impassive brown eyes looked right through her soul. It was a hind, a female red deer, her coat golden in the firelight. She was magnificent. The creature stared at her for the longest time, then the hind bounded away through the woods to the east and was out of sight within moments.

The female red deer was an animal considered sacred by the Druids. It was said that sometimes a hind was in fact a faery woman who had shape-shifted into one of these graceful creatures. Some called these deer Faery Cattle, as it was reported one could see the faeries milking them on the mountaintops. But how could the hind be asking her to make a choice like that? The bards said that seeing one was a good omen, as it meant your life was about to change in a positive way.

She felt a shudder as she drank in the animal's spirit, feeling the tingle of goose bumps all over her body. This had been a spiritual moment, that the gods had given her a sign. Or was it a warning? For an instant, she felt a premonition that she was going to have to make a choice someday, the dilemma of Achilles: was the hind asking her to choose a quiet life of personal happiness, with family and children, or instead she would prefer eternal fame, but dying young, leaving no children behind. Her name could be sung by the bards for ages, but a life of turmoil and an early death would be the price if she wished to receive such accolades.

Then her heart sang a song of joy. There could be no premonition, how silly was that? This could only mean one thing: *Arturius is going to live,* she thought. She crawled back into bed with certainty that Arturius would survive. She lay there for the longest time in wonder and excitement, but eventually, she drifted off to sleep until the twittering of the birds awakened her. She went to the door of the hut to open it, and it revealed a brilliantly sunny morning. She was groggy at first, but then she remembered her vision. She turned to the young man beside her and felt his forehead. His fever was gone. He was pale but no longer hot and flushed.

Arturius woke up and he gave her a smile. He said he was hungry. This was the first time he had asked for food since she had been with him. He was weak as a kitten, and he complained that his chest hurt, but he was alive. She hurriedly put on her cloak and called for her fellow acolyte to come in and watch over him while she ran to get the Merlinus to give him the good news. She could not wait to tell Merlinus about seeing the deer.

What did it mean? she wondered. *Was that a dream? Or was it a real Golden Hind?* She burst through the door of the hut of the Merlinus like a hawk pouncing on a mouse. The Merlinus was sitting there, eyes closed in meditation, but then his eyes opened wide with alarm upon her abrupt entry. Her story bubbled out in excitement as he gently grabbed her shoulders and asked her to slow it down and tell him what happened. Once her story was complete, he nodded appreciatively.

"Aha," he said in amazement, "a Golden Hind!"

He confirmed for her this was clearly a sign from the gods. He said his divination at the sacrifice of the hare had told him as much, that Gwenhwyfar and Arturius would be destined for something, but together or separately, he could not say. The Merlinus was not sure what the meaning of the hind was, but clearly Danu had spoken, and he stressed that auguries like this were difficult to interpret.

"Gwenhwyfar, I need to get dressed. Next time, it might be more considerate to knock before bursting in, but fortunately I was not in a complete state of nakedness, so no harm was done."

"I appreciate your understanding and forgiveness," she said as she blushed in embarrassment.

Gwenhwyfar bowed and scuttled out of the hut, and then she waited not so patiently for him to exit and accompany her to the healing hut and witness the miracle of the recovery of Arturius. She resisted the temptation of bounding ahead of the Merlinus like a puppy, but he did walk in such a manner that she could barely contain herself from grabbing his hand and dragging him along.

When they arrived, the Merlinus and Gwenhwyfar ducked inside the hut and found that all was indeed as she had described. After he questioned and examined Arturius, he pronounced him to be on the road to recovery. However, he cautioned the young man that the healing journey had just begun. The old Druid said it would be weeks before his journey to good health would be enough for him to travel.

Gwenhwyfar puffed up with pride as the Merlinus informed Arturius that she was still in charge of his rehabilitation. She would deal with his day-to-day needs, his companion and instructor in building him back to full health. It was not often a thirteen-year-old girl could have a grown man at her beck and call, even among the Silures, but they were in Druid-controlled Britannia, and she had heard her people gave their women more rights and responsibilities than the Romanized Britons did. She was thrilled, though she suspected that Arturius might be less enthralled with the idea, but she also knew he had little choice in the matter.

The days passed, the weather grew colder, and Arturius grew stronger. She and Arturius became friends, and she could tell that the bond between her brother and Arturius was growing stronger as well. The people in the community said they were thrilled to have her brother back and they were also pleased to see Arturius in their midst. She sensed that despite their relative youth, news of their victories had given Arturius and Caradoc an aura of gravitas.

And so had her own status had grown. Her parents, and even the adults in the community treated her differently now. The Merlinus had been effusive in his praise, and the news of her experience with the Golden Hind had convinced most of the adults in the Silures tribe that the gods had indeed singled her out for something special. Her talks with Arturius had been eye-opening for her as she learned about life in other parts of Britannia, the culture of the Saxons, and of the magic of books that revealed the glories of the Greco-Roman world.

She was now thinking that perhaps she could have it all. Women often served the role of the medicus in Britannia now as both midwifes and healers. Arturius said that was not the norm on the mainland, but it was true here. They were respected. And they could be married and have their own families. And based on her conversations with Arturius, she had decided that she was going to learn how to read. She had not totally abandoned the idea of becoming a Druidess, but now her feelings were even more muddy than they were before.

She was still leery about the more Romanized Britons who were so unlike the still wild Silures, and Gwenhwyfar was alarmed to hear of the fear and loathing that some of the followers of the Christos had for the people of the Oak and the Mistletoe. He said the followers of Pelagius were not of much concern, but for the other Christian sects on the island, the Druids were despised. It sounded to her that someone like the bishop Gildas was truly evil. Up until now she had not heard of the various schisms in Christianity. *What a strange religion*, she thought.

Now that he was feeling better, Arturius had been invited that night to meet her parents. Gwenhwyfar's father, Mordred, had severe rheumatism and was now house bound, although he was still a powerful and respected man in the entire tribe. Tonight, they were going to discuss the future of his only remaining son, Caradoc. Her oldest brother had fallen in combat Hibernian raiders, while the middle brother had died a mysterious death. He had awoken one morning with a fever and belly pain and within a few days, he died. It was as if the black sickness often seen with battle wounds had taken him, but the illness seemed to have come from within.

She remembered how depressed her father was after *the Night of the Long Knives* when they thought Caradoc, his only remaining son, had also been lost. He thought his line had been cursed, but then Caradoc appeared miraculously out of his captivity. The Merlinus said that people followed a leader who was lucky, and even Gwenhwyfar felt that her brother's rise from the ashes of death to fame in battle meant that perhaps the gods had marked him as the chosen one to become their tribal leader.

Her entire family was now devoted to making that happen, and that would be the main topic this evening. When the three of them entered her parents' dwelling, she looked upon Mordred with sadness. *Poor Father*, she thought. *He had wanted to be king himself once, but the gods had denied him that.* He had been a vigorous man in his youth, but now he had been plagued by rheumatism of his joints, especially in his hands. his fingers splayed out to the side like a fan. He could no longer grip anything, and he could barely walk, but his good humor and indomitable will still shone through. Mordred started the proceedings with a welcoming smile.

"Greetings, Arthur, a most hearty welcome! I am honored to meet you for the first time. I cannot get out much now, so I appreciate you coming to my home to share nature's bounty with my family. And we have many things to discuss."

Arturius looked puzzled.

"I've noticed that everyone here calls me Arthur, even when I introduce myself as Arturius. Why is that?"

"Why, you are a true Briton, young man," Mordred said, chuckling. "We are not overly fond of Latin names, so we are converting Roman words into those that flow more easily to our native tongue. Venta Silurum for instance, translates to Gwent in our language; hence, we are all now calling it that. And we all call you Arthur now."

Arturius rolled his eyes and chuckled, "That would be news to my mother, but as long as you call me for dinner, it matters not."

"We will call you whatever you prefer. For tonight, it will be Arturius then.

I know your heart is British no matter what you banner says. And I have heard of all your recent adventures, of course. Who hasn't? But I would love to hear you enlighten us a little about your life."

"Of course, but first, I must congratulate Gwenhwyfar for her dedication in caring for me during my illness. I lost two weeks of my life where I barely remember a thing. I would not be alive today if it was not for her. And I enjoyed getting to know her. She is a remarkable young lady."

Gwenhwyfar blushed as her father nodded.

"We are very proud of her. I hope she had not been too bossy over you while she had overseen your care."

Arturius smiled., "As long as I did what I was told, I was just fine."

"Then she is just like her mother. I do the same."

Laughter echoed around the table. Then Mordred looked upon Arturius with interest.

"Regrettably, neither Caradoc nor Gwenhwyfar have told me directly much about your life up to now. Tell us more about yourself and what your plans are."

So, Arthur gave them a rundown of his life to date: his childhood, his experiences as a guest of the Saxons both before and after enthrallment, his life in the Weald, and now.

After their guest's tale had finished, the patriarch smiled at Arturius and asked, "So what is your ultimate ambition? To become king of the Britons?"

Arturius was taken aback.

"No sir, not at all! My goal is to preserve our culture against the onslaught of the barbarians. The alliance of Britannia Novus can only unite us if our leader does not favor any one tribe or kingdom over another. I have taken an oath to honor that commitment. It is the only way for this new alliance to work."

The old man looked at him appraisingly.

"To be united, now *that* is an important concept. We also need to unite the Silures to contribute in any meaningful way to your proposed alliance. I have a plan to make your friend, Caradoc, the leader of our people, and I would appreciate your support in this endeavor. There are three ways kingdoms can thrive and grow: through military conquests, through political alliances, or best of all, to get into bed with the right woman. And my wife and I feel that to unite the Silures, we need to make love, not war."

Gwenhwyfar started to giggle, but she stopped herself just in time. Mordred guffawed uproariously, while the rest of them smiled, all except Caradoc, who flashed a look of concern at his father.

"What are you talking about?" Caradoc said with a shocked expression. "And more importantly, who are you talking about?"

Once Mordred stopped his laughing, he looked at Caradoc with serious eyes.

"In the City of Gwent, the city council provides the leadership. The mayor of that council has a daughter who is beautiful, charming, and available. I have met her, and I believe you will be pleased. Arwen is her name."

Gwenhwyfar nodded. *Ah yes, Arwen,* she thought. *She seems a levelheaded girl, and pretty. A good match.* She knew Arwen was a Christian though, and if she was a devout one, that could be trouble, but Gwenhwyfar was not overly worried. She did not know her well, but she knew that if her parents had recommended this girl, they would have picked someone they would be proud to call a daughter. But Caradoc had never met her, so he had to be nervous.

Gwenhwyfar giggled, "You mean cross-eyed Arwen with the wooden leg? Isn't she one who is so ugly that her mother had to tie a piece of sausage around her neck for the dog to play with her?"

Caradoc turned white while Mordred scowled at his daughter, but then she stopped giggling and assumed a more serious expression.

"I jest. She is a lovely girl, and I like her."

Mordred looked at her and shook his head, and muttered, "There are times, Gwenhwyfar, when I swear I will __ well __ let us get back to the topic at hand, please."

Mordred looked at Caradoc.

"If you two wed, it will merge the two major factions of our tribe, the Christians and the followers of our traditional gods, into a unified whole. But here's the problem: the council at Gwent insists that any children of your union be raised in the Christian faith. And you, my son, must be baptized, as they call it. They give you a nice white robe and gifts, and then they dunk your head under water Following that the priest will mutter some Latin words, and then you are done. I do not understand why the Christians take great stock in this, but they do."

"In my heart, you must know that I could never be a Christian," Caradoc said, panic written on his face. "I will always honor the old gods."

Her mother leaned forward.

"Of course, they will never change your heart, my son. You would only put on a public face occasionally. For instance, they want you to go to a ceremony that they call a mass, but nothing bad happens if you do not. I go sometimes, but you know in my heart that I am still a child of the Oak and Mistletoe."

Mordred nodded.

"She is right, my son. After this ceremony, nothing else changes. You can live your life as you normally would. I too have been baptized, and some of our warriors have been three or four times. The Christian do not keep good records, so they go from church to church to different priests, omitting to tell them they have already done it so they can get even more gifts."

Her mother raised her brow.

"Here is the beauty of this, my boy. If you agree to the baptism and the raising of your children in their faith, the priest will then later perform a ceremony in which this Christos himself ordains you as king. The half of our tribe that follows the Nailed White Christ would be bound by their faith to follow you as their monarch. It adds legitimacy, and to oppose you would be a sin. Even if you become crippled later, you would still be king, and you can still pass on the throne to your heirs.

"My brother, our British gods, they are not jealous like the Christos."

Gwenhwyfar said. "You can still sacrifice and pray to them as you normally would. You can still tell your children about the gods of our people, and they can choose their own path as they come of age."

Gwenhwyfar smiled to herself. In her family, the privilege of talking at the dinner table was a rite of passage into adulthood, and she had contributed to the conversation, and no one thought less of her. Her mother looked at Gwenhwyfar appreciatively,

"Your sister is correct.", she said as she smiled at her. "I have negotiated with the priest. He promises that our tribe would be allowed the freedom to practice any faith they choose. No one would be forced to follow Christos."

"My warriors will follow any leader who is lucky in battle," Mordred sighed, "and they care not what faith they proclaim, but for us to unite, we need these city dwellers. And they will only follow one who had been baptized."

Caradoc was momentarily silent.

"It is much to contemplate, Father. Let me think it over. As far as becoming a Christian, I will always honor Danu and Dagda, but sometimes in politics one must compromise. This sounds like one of those times. I had not anticipated getting married yet, but I understand the point you are making. I would like to meet this woman, under supervision of course."

"Caradoc," her mother said, "your father and I love each other deeply, but we did not have a love match, our marriage was arranged to serve the best interests of our families. However, we met before we married, and I decided your father was a man I could grow to love. Now I cannot imagine life without him. You should meet Arwen and if you do not think she is suitable, we will respect your wishes and pursue this no further. But know this, if you wed, you may become king. This is no small opportunity that the gods have given you."

Caradoc gazed at his father and then his mother. "I will meet her," he said solemnly.

Arturius gave him a gentle punch on the shoulder.

"I will support any decision you make, my friend."

Then Arturius winked at Gwenhwyfar.

"And remember this. Ugly, cross-eyed, and one-legged women need love, too!"

They all laughed, as Caradoc turned red as a beet.

CHAPTER
THIRTY-THREE

If a British wedding was to be held on the day of the spring equinox, then one thing was certain: it was going to rain. Though the mist that night was light, it was still wet. Brigid wound her cloak tightly around her as she scurried down the main road through this unfamiliar town cursing the weather, but grateful for the paved roadways. These Roman towns still amazed her, their closely fitted stone and orderly bricks so different than the plastered daub and wattle of her childhood. She would have preferred to be in a native village, so warm and inviting compared to these cold stones the Romans so loved, but at least her feet were wet instead of muddy.

She could barely see. Once she and her companions had entered the forum, she could just make out the huge structure that dominated the square. The Christian church of Gwent was just at the edge of the forum, and she hoped the house of the priest was nearby so she would not have to slog through more rain puddles. She had to concentrate on seeing her companions as she followed them. They at least knew where they were going. She had no clue. She was cold. She was wet. And she was angry. *I cannot believe that fat gobshite Gildas is here,* she thought.

They stopped at a house which was situated next to the church, one of the largest she had ever seen. *I'll wager This priest misses few meals*, she thought. *He might be bigger than Gildas.* But she had been told he was a reasonable man who loved his congregation, and he was a married clergyman, something not favored by the Rome-loving followers of Gildas. She hoped they were right, or she was getting wet for nothing. They stopped in front of the main door, her face bearing a smile lacking warmth; her Petrus would never have lived in opulence like this.

"Caradoc, are you sure you just cannot send some men over there and kill that fat pig tonight and get this over with?"

Caradoc shook his head as he raised his brow.

"Sister, you know we cannot. Much as I would like to do that, we must honor the fact that he was accepted as a guest here by our priest."

Brigid had not planned on visiting the Christian priest of the Silures this evening, but the news of the arrival Gildas had changed all of that. If they were not successful this evening, Caradoc and his bride-to-be would be together, but the wedding could be politically pointless. No one was told Gildas was coming, but the local priest had sent messages out to the surrounding communities that all clergy would be welcomed. Caradoc had just been told that Gildas wanted to not just attend, but to officiate at the wedding, and that the local priest was giving in to his demands. Her eyes narrowed. *This local priest has not yet consulted with Mordred*, she thought in anger. *Or the bride and groom. Or me!* She saw the arrival of the bishop for what it was, a play for power.

As soon as she heard of the surprise arrival of the bishop, she had organized this expedition, so here she was, wet and angry in front of the priest's house, and huddled around her now was Brother Mattius, Arturius, and Caradoc. She tapped her fist sharply against the door, the noise echoing down the street. There was silence in the house. Once again, she knocked on the door, even harder this time. Now there were sounds of movement inside the dwelling. The door opened just as Sister Bridget was starting another knock, causing her to miss the door.

The local priest called out in a startled tone, "Is there an emergency? What is happening?"

"Let me manage this, boys," she said as she held up her hand. "So, Brother, Um, Brother Philippus, it is?"

The man nodded.

"My good Brother Philippus, we need to talk. Now!"

With that, she barged in as the befuddled priest gazed in bewilderment. The three men accompanying her hesitated and gave each other quizzical looks, but soon they followed her.

Philippus sputtered, "But it is late, and ___"

Brigid shushed him.

"Turn around my good brother," she said, "I must see your back."

The priest frowned but he did as she asked. She gave him some hearty pats on his back, starting between his shoulder blades. Caradoc's face displayed a wispy smile as the other two men looked on with puzzled expressions.

"Well, this is good news," she declared. "It appears you do have a spine. Now we are about to see if it is made of bones, or of soft jelly. Now turn back to face me."

The befuddled priest turned around, his mouth agape.

"It also appears that you may be a man. Must I confirm that by inspecting you for the presence of testicles?"

Philippus placed his hands in front of his crotch.

"No," Philippus snorted, "I've three children, Sister. Ask my wife if you must."

Arturius covered his mouth to stifle a laugh, Caradoc's smile grew less wispy, and Mattius just looked shocked. She twisted her face into a picture of sweetness.

"That is good, because we must talk. Brother Mattius and I are the religious leaders at Camalet, and we are both here tonight with an urgent matter we need to discuss. It concerns the arrival of that creature, the one who calls himself a bishop. He has created a crisis. I understand Gildas had insisted that he should preside over the wedding ceremony tomorrow afternoon. Is this true?"

He stammered, "Well, yes, but ___"

"You did not agree to this, did you?" she asked in a honeyed voice.

He paused for a moment.

"Well, I told him I would need to discuss this with the bride and groom tomorrow, but it seemed to me an excellent idea. It would be such an honor to ___"

"An honor? Really? From that pig faced ___ Well, I must calm down. He was responsible for the execution of my husband, so I must confess that consequently I do not hold Gildas in high esteem."

She took a deep a deep breath and slowly exhaled. The man's vapid grin had made her even angrier. *This man must be denser than a rock,* she thought. She kept her smile plastered on.

"But regardless of my feelings about the man, you do realize what he is doing, don't you?"

The priest looked even more confused. Mattius also looked befuddled, but Caradoc's smile disappeared as his eyes narrowed. Off to the side, Arturius was gently shaking his head as he rolled his eyes. She knew he must be trying hard not to tell the priest what he thought of him, but she didn't care.

"Whatever do you mean, Sister?" he replied, a puzzled look on his face.

"You are like Brother Mattius and I here. We are people of faith. We tend to our flock and try to see the goodness in people, and sometimes, the evil that people do can escape us. This is especially true if it is from another man of the cloth. Gildas may tell you he is trying to honor this ceremony with the blessing of Rome, but it is more than just that. What he is really doing is trying to set a precedent."

Brigid kept the smile on her face as she seethed. She put her hand on his shoulder as she spoke.

"You have already agreed to follow up this wedding in a few weeks with the coronation of young Caradoc here as king, correct? I understand that this was agreed to by you and your city council, which will unite Gwent with the outlying communities of your tribe, forging the Silures into one strong kingdom. Do I understand this accurately?"

"Well, yes, but ___"

She pulled her hand back as she crossed her arms.

"What Gildas is really doing is trying to establish his authority over you. Some of his entourage and escorts have been disturbed by some of the antics going on in Viroconium, and they have been talking to us, very discreetly of course. We know his plans. Gildas has a bit of a surprise in store for you if he is allowed to officiate tomorrow."

"Whatever do you mean, Sister?"

Brigid tried to keep patience in her voice as she relaxed her hands so she would not clench them into fists. Martius's eyes opened wide in understanding. Arturius looked inscrutable while Caradoc maintained his disciplined stare.

"He plans to announce in front of the entire congregation that Rome has granted him the authority over you to conduct the marriage, because he would announce that this church is under his bishopric. Therefore, it would be Gildas' prerogative to that any upcoming coronation would have to meet with Rome's approval. He will claim to have ecclesiastical power over you, including the decision who your king will be."

The eyes of the speechless Brother Philippus grew wide. *Aha*, she thought, *the light is beginning to dawn in the empty windows.*

"He does not have the authority to do that, does he?

Her hands slid to her hips.

"Only if you give it to him, dearie. And Rome would probably agree with him. The more power Rome can claim for themselves, the better for them. You see, Gildas wants to make it clear that the clergy here in Gwent do not have the power to crown their own king. He wants to make the people think he has spiritual authority over you and Gwent."

The jaw of Phillipus tightened as he muttered, "Rome didn't build this church. Our people did, stone by stone, after Rome stole our legions."

Arturius sighed as he joined in the conversation.

"So, the question is this, Brother Philippus. Do the religious leaders of Gwent have the final say as to who is to be their king? If you agree to this, then Gwent loses the ability to decide its own affairs."

"But could Rome excommunicate us?" Philippus asked as he wrung his hands.

"The church council in Nicaea did not say we must lick Rome's boot in selecting our clergy," she said. "But having that bishop in front of the congregation, he could claim otherwise."

Caradoc joined in the conversation with a scowl.

Brother Philippus," he said, "She is correct. It was not Rome that made you the priest here."

Brigid's smile stayed on while her mind kept spinning. *This priest may a pleasant enough fellow,* she thought, *but he is a dunderhead. I pity his congregation.* Then she joined back into the conversation.

"The Ordovices have the bishop in their pocket. Gildas could select someone loyal to him to enable the demise of Gwent, either by direct betrayal, or by choosing someone incompetent to allow the Ordovices to triumph over you. Do you finally understand what is at stake here?"

A concerned look clouded the countenance of Philippus.

"Are you sure about this?"

"Yes, Brother," Caradoc said as he nodded. "My father's informants in Viroconium say so."

Shock was reflected in Brother Philippus face, then his countenance shifted, looking more determined as he glanced at the diminutive nun with a furrowed brow.

"Yes, Sister," he said, "I do have a spine, and I also have bollocks. This will not happen on my watch. We may not be able to stop Gildas from attending, but the ceremony will be mine."

Brigid flashed a worried glance towards Caradoc as she spoke.

"How many soldiers did they bring with them? He has a private army now, doesn't he?"

"He does not have enough men to worry me," Caradoc said.

"They disarm everyone going through the city gates," Arturius said as he nodded. "Caradoc has every Silurian now armed and on alert, and the have been guards doubled."

"Good," she said with a satisfied smile. "Then let him attend at the back of the church. And I will sit next to him. I cannot wait to see his face."

"I will arrange for Gildas and his people to leave immediately after the ceremony," Caradoc said as he chuckled.

Brigid's eyes narrowed as she scoffed, "Speaking of which, this could be a good opportunity to arrange an unfortunate accident."

Philippus looked askance.

"Oh no, Sister Brigid, we cannot have violence against a man of the cloth while he is under our protection."

She raised her brow and scowled as she wagged her finger.

"Then you best hustle him out as quick as you can. I am serious."

"She is right," Arturius said. "We have many people here from the Weald for the wedding. They also hate Gildas for what he did to Brigid's husband. Confine him to his quarters until the ceremony, then get him out of here immediately afterward if you want no violence."

Brother Philippus sighed.

"It was late when you all came, but I am glad you did. We should control our affairs here in Gwent, not Rome. I have also heard other disturbing rumors coming out of Viroconium. This wedding will be the joyous affair that it was intended to be, and it will be I who officiates the coronation of our new King Caradoc."

Philippus turned to the diminutive nun with a smile.

"And Sister Brigid, it would be inappropriate for me to inspect you as you did with me, but I suspect you may have a pair of stones yourself."

The group laughed together, and then they talked some more about the plans for tomorrow. The crisis was averted. Now the fun would begin, but for Brigid, the next few days would be bittersweet. *I wish that Petrus was here to see this wedding, she* thought. *And Gildas is so close, yet there is nothing I can do. But if there is a next time, well ___.*

CHAPTER THIRTY-FOUR

The next day began with a grey sky, but by that morning the rainstorm finally ended, and as the day wore on, the gloom transitioned into sunshine and fluffy white clouds. It did not matter if it was raining or not. Weddings could be held anywhere, and usually no closer to the church than its steps, but for this royal marriage, this would mark the first time in Gwent that a ceremony would happen within the church itself. Still, every time Caradoc set foot inside the place, he was appalled. *It is so strange to have a celebration of the gods inside a building,* he thought. *This is such a Roman thing.*

Caradoc knew the Romans were mainly city dwellers, while the British celebrated nature to honor their gods. He shook his head in annoyance. *It is under the trees where the gods really live,* he ruminated, *not under a roof.* But he was pleased that his baptism last week was outside in a river, so that was not so bad, a good excuse for a bath. Caradoc gazed at the interior of the building with a veiled look of distaste. *This place symbolizes man's desire to control Danu, the mother of nature,* he thought.

The fluted columns reached up to the tallest ceiling he had ever seen. Flaming torches were set in iron brackets in the walls, and the smoke curled up to the ceiling in lazy tendrils. The room smelled of unwashed bodies, wet wool, smoke, and the cloying sweetness of incense coming from little pots scattered around the altar. The sweating priests wore heavily brocaded vestments on top of strange looking robes and were conducting the ceremony in the musical drone of a language that few in the church understood.

The walls and the curved ceiling were covered with peeling white plasterwork that had scenes painted on them, some still visible. He could not tell what they were exactly, but he could make out pictures of men in odd robes with golden circles around their heads. The shadows of flying sparrows that bounced around the ceiling in the flickering light made him think ghosts were living there, their souls trapped within a stoney cage.

Now he was ignoring his surroundings when his bride-to-be made her entrance, looking upon Arwen with a lump in his heart, more nervous now than he had ever been in a fight. He had never seen her look so lovely, her virginal blue veil shimmering in the candlelight. The bouquet she carried were sheaths of wheat and flowers that symbolized fertility, a touch of the druids in this alien setting. He glanced back at each of their mothers, holding the ribbons to be used for the handfasting part of the ceremony. His pocket held the ring made for their nuptials that had been broken and had been hung around their necks until this day. Earlier this day the rings had been rejoined together by the smithy to be exchanged as part of their vows.

Then the ceremony started, Caradoc had to admit the pomp and circumstance of the Roman Mass was an impressive display. For many in attendance, it was their first time in the church. The Christians familiar with the Latin ceremony would stand and bow on command, and at times would join in the strange chants the priests made while the pagans remained seated and silent. *I feel like a stranger in a strange land here,* he thought.

He had been told the ceremony was the same, whether in Rome or Constantinople or here, but he really did not believe it. Caradoc knew that the church was riven by many differences, and some were even visible here today. The priest of the Silures and Brother Mattius had the front of their heads shaved, while Gildas and his people had the crown of the head left shiny, not the front. They both called their hairstyle a tonsure. *They are the same, but they are different,* he thought, *even sending those with those different haircuts to death throes amongst the flames.*

Then it happened. Brother Philippus had just started his homily when a handful of priests sporting Roman tonsures suddenly stood up and stomped out the church with Gildas in the lead as they muttered "blasphemy" and "heresy. "As they departed, they were accompanied by scowling guards as Brigid flashed dagger eyes at them, and once they were halfway out, she and the priests with the Celtic tonsures stood and applauded, accompanied by the laughs and giggles of the congregation. The universal smiles in the crowd showed that Phillipus and the Celtic priests had won the hearts and minds of the people of Gwent, not the dour Romans.

Caradoc kept his face impassive as the ruckus died down, trying to keep his mind focused on Arwen as the proceedings resumed. The two of them had bonded together before the wedding itself. She was a happy person, always smiling and could talk about anything, but she was also observant and clever. He felt that she was becoming a friend of his, much as his own parents were with each other. She was a person that he could grow to love. *That is what I am really looking forward to,* he thought, *is the thought of being with her.*

He endured the ceremony as best he could. His mind wandered, but he paid enough attention to act appropriately for the exchange of the newly welded rings and the binding of their wrists with the traditional handfasting ceremony. He sighed. *These Christians stole this idea from us Druids,* he thought. The priest made the sign of the cross again as he muttered the words he was coached to say. And then it was time to kiss the bride. She gazed up at him with softness in her eyes.

"Thank you for enduring this ceremony for my faith," Arwen softly murmured, "but make this a chaste kiss. Let us save the real one for your gods, husband."

His smile and that of his bride knew no bounds, and everyone in attendance followed their lead. According to his colleagues, a more joyful and enthusiastic mass was never seen before. The couple was pelted with bread and grains of wheat and barley when they exited the church, again to symbolize fertility. He chuckled to himself; he knew that would not be the only time that day this would happen. Honey-mead flowed, and small wedding cakes were devoured after the ceremony with gusto. Caradoc continued to smile, as he knew that would be a mere warm-up for the Druid ceremony to follow.

Once he left the church and headed to the woods, Caradoc was pleased that the cloying scent of the Roman incense had dissipated, replaced by the sweet smells of the woodlands. It was time for the true ceremony to begin. Caradoc had made no secret of the druidic wedding to Sister Brigid and Brother Mattius. They knew what would follow, and were not pleased, but they had no choice. The Christian clergy, minus Gildas and his cronies, went to the home of Bother Philippus to have refreshments and conversation, knowing that the pagans were going to have their say now as they drank wine and prayed for everyone's souls.

Once the sun had set, a crescent moon became visible. They all met at a large sacred circle of woven hazel branches located in a spot well known by all to be a sacred grove to the Druids. The Merlinus presided, standing at a wooden altar with an overhanging arch in the center of the circle. He was attired in a snow-white robe tied with a golden cord, the gown itself decorated with the images of crescent moons and running hares. From the top of the altar hung a sprig of mistletoe, the symbol of eternal life. The bride and groom stood in front of him.

The Merlinus announced, "We are gathered here in peace for the sacred occasion, the rite of marriage between Caradoc and Arwen. As this circle has been woven and consecrated, this moment in time and place has become blessed. Let each soul truly be here, that the spirits of those gathered may be blended in one sacred space, with one purpose and one voice."

With that, the tinkling of dozens of bells could be heard as each of the guests rang the tiny bells they had been given for the ceremony.

"Let us call to the gods of the four quarters of our world, that this rite be blessed by the gods of our ancestors and of all Creation."

"Spirit of our God Cernunnos, who hath powers over Winter, guardian of Earth and Stone and the strength of the Stag, I ask that you honor this, our circle, as we honor thee. Witness and bless this rite. Hail and welcome!"

The tinkling of bells again filled the air.

The ceremony went on as the Merlinus next paid homage to the gods of spring, fall, and summer. The honoring of each corner of the world was accompanied by tinkling bells and laughter and happiness, and none were happier than Caradoc. *We are outside in the glory of nature where the spirits around us really live,* he thought. *I could never truly honor the gods with a roof over my head.* The Merlinus then blessed the mistletoe hanging above the altar, as it was forever green in winter and symbolized the perpetual love this couple was to embrace.

"In the name of our gods in the center of our circle, our Goddess Danu, and our God the Dagda, you who are chief among all the Gods on the high throne of Tuatha De Danann, I ask that you honor this, our circle, as we honor thee. Hail and welcome!"

Caradoc and Adwen then placed the offerings of mead and bread on the altar.

"Do you both come to this place of your own free will?"

The couple replied with a simultaneous, "I do."

The three then walked to the four quarters of the circle as he announced blessings to the east, west, north, and south and the gods and goddesses in each realm. The couple then grasped each other's wrists as the Merlinus tied them together with an embroidered cloth that the bride had made. This was Caradoc's favorite part of a Druid wedding. *This is the real handfasting,* he thought. Then he saw Arwen give him a sly wink as she adjusted the cloth to allow the cross she had woven into the fabric to be exposed as the Druid continued his chants.

"At sacred times and places, our ancestors clasped hands when they would wed, and such hand fasting witnessed by the gods and the community were lawful, true, and binding, as love binds one heart to another. Are you ready to declare your vows to each other, vows that will bind you together, joining the bloodlines of your ancestors, as witnessed by those who are gathered here this day?"

"I am," they replied.

"All things in nature are circular. Night becomes day, day becomes night, which again gives way to the day. Moon waxes and wanes and then waxes again. There is Spring, Summer, Autumn, and Winter, then Spring returns. These are the flowing rhythms of the cycle of existence, yet in the center of the circle is the stillness of the source, eternal and brilliant. Did you bring with you this day your symbols of these mysteries of life?"

"We did," they answered, and then Arturius and Cerdic brought the repaired wedding rings to the Merlinus.

Further blessings were made, and the rings were exchanged with still even more thanks given to the gods. These were the same rings that had been used earlier that day, and he was sure the Dagda would not mind, and the Christos was supposed to be forgiving. After the ring ceremony, the Merlinus then took the wedding stone from the hands of Caradoc's father and placed it on the altar.

"This sacred Earth is our home. It offers us the power of life, nourishing us, body, and soul, and holding us from birth until we go once more into the worlds of spirit. Each rock and stone, and each pebble and gem contain within them the stories of all time. You have chosen this stone together as a foundation stone of your marriage from this point on. Do you now swear upon it, as a symbol of this sacred land and our holy Mother Earth, the goddess Danu, to keep your vows?"

The couple replied, "We swear."

The Merlinus continued his prayers as Mordred grasped his shoulder and whispered, "the next moon, this same circle will see you crowned king, my son."

After more blessings to the gods accompanied by the tinkling of bells, the ceremony came to its conclusion."

"Then let all the gods of this Earth, the Dagda, and the Goddess Danu witness that Arwen and Caradoc are joined in love and freedom. So, let it be. Let your vows be sealed with a kiss!"

Arwen looked up at him again, her kiss this time more passionate than he thought possible.

"See," she said coquettishly, "The Dagda's blessings are sweeter than Latin."

The couple embraced and then they were showered by the guests with flower petals and seeds of grain, as the bells rang once more. The newlyweds exited the sacred circle to cheers and applause and the ringing of bells. The Merlinus beamed with joy, and the real celebrations began, but the honeymoon would prove to be short, as they had to plan out the future of both Novum Britannia and Gwent. Making a marriage work takes planning and effort. The making of a new nation even more so. They celebrated as they discussed the next moves for their nascent alliance and Caradoc's coming coronation.

CHAPTER THIRTY-FIVE

Arturius was mesmerized. The building complex before him, the bathing complex of Aqua Sulis, was famous throughout Britannia, and now he knew why. It was the largest enclosed structure he had ever seen, but like the empire itself, the building was in a sad state of disrepair. The paint was peeling, plaster was cracked, and the aura of neglect and abandonment was unmistakable. He was with a group of people in the courtyard in front of the massive structure, the roofless and ruined temple of Minerva Sulis on their right next to the small enclosed sacred spring. The main structure itself sprawled west and east off the back of the springhouse, the size of four basilicas put together, and despite the lack of maintenance, it was still impressive.

A grand council of Britannia had been called by the newly formed British alliance, a gathering of all the Romano-British leaders who were interested in a common defense. It had been more than a year since the wedding, and the people at Camalet had been busy, settling refugees, reoccupied villas, refurbishing hillforts, and planning out the details of a proposed alliance. He and his friends had not seen each other since the wedding.

The alliance decided on a location that was conveniently situated with good road access. The meeting was being hosted by the ruling council at Glevum, which controlled the area around Aqua Sulis, and they had arranged for a tour of the baths. They had all met that morning at the grand entrance with Senna by his side, along with a retinue from Camalet that included Lucilia, Brother Mattius, and Sister Brigid. Caradoc, the Merlinus and Gwenhwyfar had also traveled to this ancient site, along with Cerdic and a few other key leaders of his new kingdom.

It was not just familiar faces with them today. The men from the north had also arrived, chief among them was the corpulent and jewel-encrusted leader of the provincial center of Eboracum. He called himself "Einion the Great" and spoke of himself in the third person. The king was accompanied by other leaders near Hadrian's Wall, seemingly blood-related to them all. It had been Einion's loins that were truly great, as his horde of daughters had married into almost every important community in the North.

There were two exceptions to this phenomenon, and Arturius was curious to meet the leaders from both of those communities. One was the magistrate from the Colonia at Lindum, a garrison located ninety miles south of Eboracum, but he was not due in town for another day. The other region that was not within Einion's sphere of influence was represented by the dashing young Owain Rheged of Luguvalium. His community was perched along the great wall at its most northwestern end, and Arturius met him for the first time last night.

Arturius was amused to see the faces of the ladies light up when they saw him approach. The cavalryman was blonde, square jawed, and remarkably handsome. His hair was long, wavy, and shining, and his smile was infectious. Owain's brilliant blue tunic matched his eyes, an elegantly embroidered costume capped off by a red cloak, pinned at the right shoulder with a golden fibula cunningly fashioned to resemble a horse, a symbol of the Roman equestrian class. His pants were golden yellow and tight fitting, and they showed off his muscular legs well.

He almost laughed out loud when he saw Lucilia's jaw drop when she first saw him. Senna giggled, nudging her sister for her to maintain a shred of dignity. *Cupid must be in fine form today*, he thought. Lucilia wore a fashionable stola that just happened to match the blue in Owain's attire, so much so that they both laughed when they were introduced. It was the first time they had laid eyes on each other, but it looked like it would not be the last. Lucilia and Owain talked and flirted and grinned at each other like love-struck fools. Arturius rolled his eyes. *This is hard to watch,* he thought. *It looks like love at first sight. Well, lust anyway.*

Arturius glanced at the Merlinus, and he noticed the Druid looked away from the baths over to the ruined temple Sulis of the Druids with a scowl on his face. Though silent, he saw the Druid's eyes flash with a mixture of anger and disappointment. The site had been vandalized. That was a new word, named after the Germanic Vandals tribe who had sacked Rome so brutally a generation ago, but it had not been Vandals that had destroyed this temple. Instead, it had been Christians, and the Merlinus was clearly seething over the desecration. As he stood next to them, Arturius overheard the Merlinus's gloomy whispers.

"This natural hot spring was once a holy site for the Druids," the Merlinus muttered to Gwenhwyfar. "When the Romans conquered us, they built this monstrosity of a commercial enterprise, merging our god Sulis with the Roman one named Minerva to make the people worship a Roman deity for a hefty fee. I am happy to see this place is falling apart now, as Mother Nature is taking it back. Good for Danu!"

With that, the Merlinus and Gwenhwyfar walked back to their quarters. Arturius shook his head sadly; for those two, it was obvious the tour was done, having had enough of a reminder of the heavy hand of Rome. The tour guide ignored the fuss as he continued telling the story of the baths from their inception, built by the legionaries in the time of Nero. In mind numbing detail, he droned on about the history of the place over the last three hundred years with pride. Though only some of the baths were still in operation, today's visitors would be allowed to partake in the waters. *I cannot wait to try them,* he thought. Then Brigid pulled him away from the group as the guide was still droning on.

"I am sure you will enjoy the baths, dearie, but don't forget that is not the point of being here. After you get naked and relaxed, then you big, hairy men will have a chance to talk without the women about. This is when alliances are discussed, deals are made, and kingdoms are forged. Be wary. Commit to nothing. And after you confer, then we all need to get together to discuss what has been proposed. We womenfolk may give you some valuable insights, and Senna and I should be involved in the decision-making, don't you agree?"

Arturius felt a bit sheepish.

"Of course, Sister."

Brigid and Arturius rejoined the group as they followed their guide into the section of the complex where the Great Pool could be found. He gasped as he entered the great hall; he had never seen anything like it. The size of the manmade lake was colossal, perhaps twenty paces wide and more than fifty paces long. Faint wisps of steam curled up from the blue water, the inch-thick lead lining visible beneath. The water was perhaps four feet deep and was surrounded by a low limestone wall and a semicircle of steps used to enter the pool.

The rectangular body of water was enclosed by an impossibly high vaulted ceiling that towered several stories above them. Dust particles danced about in the rays of light that flickered in from the high windows above, revealing the grandeur of the tall Corinthian columns that lined the pool. Various alcoves jutted out from the walkway that surrounded the pool, each big enough to seat a half dozen people. The walls had once been painted red on the lower section, while the upper walls and the columns themselves had been painted to resemble marble. Though impressive, Arturius felt sadness at the signs of decay.

The colors of the walls were faded, full of cracks and holes where the plaster had fallen away revealing the limestone and bricks beneath. Water dripped from the open windows, and the squawking of birds echoed though the vast chamber as the feathered creatures flew about. Bird dung was randomly scattered on various surfaces throughout the building. The avian interlopers had gained access as the wooden louvers over the windows had rotted out long ago. Despite the general feeling of neglect, the Great Pool still had the power to fill him with awe.

"Could use a new coat of paint," sniffed Caradoc.

"And new plaster as well," chuckled Cerdic as he kicked at a recently fallen section of the wall that lay neglected beside the path.

"I wish I could have seen this in its heyday," Arturius marveled. "It must have been so grand. It is a shame that the place is so run down. Can you imagine the expertise it took to build it?"

Finally, the tour concluded, and the men stayed to bask in the warmth of the various baths on the eastern side of the complex, to be followed later by the women. Tomorrow there would be a series of official meetings but now was when the real decisions were to be made. Arturius found his friends sitting with a couple of the other delegates in one of the recesses on the side of the pool. Owain was with them, along with Quintus, the magistrate who represented Glevum and the former Roman Colonia at Deva and Lindum. Arturius turned to Owain.

"How goes it in the north? You are about the only fellow we have met so far who is not related to Einion by blood or marriage. How did you manage that?"

"It is but for the grace of the gods," Owain chuckled. "Einion has only one eligible daughter left, and he has made it known he would like to add me to his extended clan, which I must say does not thrill me. The people of Luguvalium would like to keep their independence, and so would I. You have met some of his daughters, have you not?"

The other men grinned, all except Quintus, who looked slightly annoyed. Cerdic could not suppress his mirth.

"By Frea's wet cunny," Cerdic said, chortled, "those lasses were a sorry looking lot. Fat, flatulent, and full of moles, the lot of them!"

Once he stopped chuckling, Owain grew serious again.

"You can see why I am looking for a politically advantageous union with women who had not sprung from the loins of Einion. But let us talk about more pleasant topics. That Lucilia, for instance; what a charming young lady. I understand she is the daughter of Ambrosius Aurelianus, an old and respected Roman lineage. She is your sister-in-law, Arturius, is she not?"

"She is indeed," Arturius said as he nodded.

"So, you must be acting as her paterfamilias, the head of her family, yes? You have control over her legal affairs, such as where she lives or who she marries."

"Yes. Along with Sister Brigid, we have that legal obligation. But she is a strong-willed woman, and she will choose her own path. We support her wishes in most matters."

Quintus's eyes darted about as he glanced at Owain with a worried expression.

"She is not the only fair maiden in Britannia eligible for matrimony," Quintus said in a conspiratorial tone. "Glevum views Einion as a potential ally, and by extension that makes his daughters also influential. I need not point out, my dear Owain, that a marriage arranged for political purposes can still work well, even if the initial physical attraction could be tepid. An alliance with Einion could be beneficial for both parties."

"I am afraid Cerdic here has the gist of the situation," Owain said with a wry smile. "The reputation of the females in that brood is considered, shall we say, mercurial and unappealing. The rumors are that being the recipient of unremitting nagging, complaining, and tears is the fate of the nobles who have married into that family, or so I have heard, a fate I wish to avoid."

Everyone chuckled once more except for Quintus, who looked even more distressed.

"You are the king's son," Quintus said. "We patricians do not get to pick our brides for their looks. That is how we select our concubines, my boy. The only important thing in a noble marriage should be how it helps you politically."

Arturius knew that Sister Brigid and Senna were trying to facilitate a union between Owain and Lucilia to bind Rheged to Camalet tighter than Einion's purse strings, but it looked like the representative from Glevum had different ideas. *We need to be careful with this fellow,* he thought as he glanced at Quintus.

"Now Quintus," Cerdic chortled, "doesn't he have the choice to find a woman with big tits?"

Laughter filled the alcove, but once that settled down, Owain grew more serious.

"Having Einion's extended family rule other kingdoms of the North has helped them stay unified, but by the Christos, an alliance to a southern realm may be more advantageous. Having influential friends who are not your immediate neighbors is not a bad thing."

Owain's face shifted from a furrowed brow to a more pleasing smile.

"But on a more pleasant note, Arturius, I certainly hope you and Sister Brigid would be amenable to allowing Lucilia and I the opportunity to know each other better."

"I think Lucilia shares that sentiment," Arturis said with a grin. "I will see what I can do. She is not only lovely, but she is a kind and good-hearted person. You would be lucky to woo her."

Caradoc seemed a bit annoyed by the direction of the conversation.

"Owain," he said, "enough of this prattle. Tell us more about how things with the barbarians are going up there in Luguvalium?"

The conversation turned back to political matters, and as the afternoon progressed, they spoke of the various alliances and rivalries of the lands in the north. Arturius continued to regard the man with caution. *He could sell snowballs to a Pict,* he thought. After Owain had discussed some of the problems in the north, Arturius decided to probe Quintus further.

"Quintus, I want to talk to you about the concerns other British communities may have. We need to be honest with each other, agreed?"

Quintus nodded, and then he leaned in towards him.

"This alliance is an intriguing concept," Quintus said. "So, Camalet has a democratic republic, something never attempted in Britannia before. You are proposing each kingdom is to control their own affairs, but the alliance would have a unified military, with laws that all the kingdoms must follow. But we are free from the yoke of Rome now. The question is, why would we want to subjugate ourselves to anyone, including this alliance?"

Arturius glanced about with an expectant gaze, and no one spoke. It was up to him now.

"If we do not act together," he said, "the barbarians enslave us all. Previous attempts for unity failed because the tribes looked to their own interests, not the common good."

"Those are all fine sentiments, my boy," Quintus scoffed. "But you are asking us to give up some of our independence to become a full member of the alliance. That is a big ask."

"But look at what you will gain," Arturius said in an impassioned tone. "It is not just a common defense we are proposing. We are asking for laws that protect the common man.

Quintus shook his head with a wry smile.

"It is true that we need some sort of legal system. Everyone hated lawyers until we did not have any, and now everyone wants law and order to return. But something concerns us, and frankly it is you, my boy. Armies are controlled by their generals, and generals become kings. We fear we would be helping you to become king over us all."

Caradoc scoffed. "Our generals pledge loyalty to the republic, not themselves. And so will the soldiers."

Quintus turned to him and put his arm on his shoulder.

"Of course I trust you, my dear boy! But there are many in Glevum, Deva, and

Lindinis who have some concern. Troops develop loyalty to their commanding generals. By sending our men to your alliance, we might be sowing the seeds of our own destruction. How many times did that happen in the Roman Empire? You know the answer."

As steam curled around them, sweat rolled down Quintus' face as he talked, and Arturius wondered what lay beneath the mask of his smile. Then his eyes narrowed. Quintus was being vaguely disrespectful as he kept calling him *boy*, and it was getting on his nerves. He tried to keep his voice calm.

"How can I convince you that I am not like that? Look at the governance of the military force we have built. As Cerdic said, our soldiers swore allegiance to the alliance, not me. We have built safeguards into our command structure and governance to prevent such an occurrence."

Cerdic threw his hands up into the air.

"By Woden's one eye, I have my own kingdom now, and I trust Arturius to do as he says."

"As do I," Caradoc said as he nodded. "I am also a king, and I trust him with my life."

Quintus opened his arms wide in a gesture of conciliation.

"I am sure of that, my fine fellows. But the town councils that I represent are just being prudent. Look at Ambrosius Aurelianus; we wanted him to fight for Britannia, yet he tried to bind us back to Rome. And that did not end well, eh?"

Quintus paused for a moment to take a quaff of wine. He wiped his mouth and then sighed as he shifted his gaze back to Arturius.

"I am on your side in this debate, my boy. Countless generations of my family were trained as an advocatus, and the return of the rule of law is something that I would love to see happen. This alliance you propose may be a fine sentiment, and I stand in favor of it, but details do matter. So, I will be looking those documents over some more, and we will talk further."

Quintus adopted a beatific smile as he glanced around at the people surrounding him. Arturius noticed that when he mentioned he was in favor of joining the alliance, that his eyes had glanced upward and to the left, the tenor of his voice had subtly changed, and he had squirmed a bit. *He is lying,* he thought.

"While we are contemplating your kind offer for us to join you, what is your grand alliance going to do first? What is your top priority?"

"Our first move will be to neutralize the expansion of Aelle," Arturius decisively said. "That may take time, but we need secure borders in the south before we can help the north."

"And just how are you going to control these Saxon raiders?"

"We are going to build defensive berms to hem them in, an earthen version of Hadrian's wall, constructed along the borderlands between us and the Angles and Saxons in the east."

Quintus looked taken aback as he sat there in silence for a few moments.

"So, my boy, so you all intend to dig ditches up and down all of Britannia? Really?"

He is calling me boy again, he fumed. *I might smack him if this keeps up.*

"Not just ditches, but earthen fortifications, and they do not need be continuous, as they only need to cover the routes of travel, starting first with Aelle."

Quintus slowly displayed a sly smile.

"That certainly sounds ambitious. Good luck with that. We will be watching with interest."

Arturius grinned back. Quintus was not going to help, but he had to maintain the façade.

"And thank you Quintus again for your generous donation of men to help us in our southern campaign. It was very gracious of you, and it will not be forgotten."

Generous my arse, he ruminated. *Ten heavy cavalrymen from Deva, and a handful of light horsemen from Glevum.* On they talked, and so it went for two days. Offers were made, alliances were discussed, and concerns were aired. Everyone was feeling each other out, trying to build bonds that had been ignored for a generation. The attempts to unite the province in the past had all started with the best of intentions, but those had all collapsed in a heap of broken promises and shattered dreams, and everyone there in Aqua Sulis knew it. But still, there was hope, and this conference seemed to Arturius to be a good start. And at least they were talking.

CHAPTER THIRTY-SIX

Sister Brigid and the other leaders of the alliance were staying in a once elegant villa located just outside of the city walls of Aqua Sulis. Abandoned for years, the outbuildings down to the foundations, now invisible with brambles and briars that had grown over to cover the remains. The main house itself still had a clay tile roof that was largely functional, and the well had water, but everything else was a shadow of its former self. There was no furniture, and the internal plasterwork had faded into barely discernable shadows.

The atrium had seen hard use. The once elegant mosaic floor had been desecrated, the dancing dolphins and beautiful geometric patterns violated by a charred black hole in the center of the room. It was just a firepit now, the ceiling above it coated in soot. Sister Brigid looked forlorn, saddened by seeing the mansion in such a condition, but at least it was big enough to hold them all. *I am embarrassed,* she thought. *We may call the Saxons barbarians, but are the Britons any better?* She reached for the battered cross around her neck, something she touched whenever she thought of Petrus. *How I wish you were here to help us, my love.*

The leadership cadre all sat on blankets covering the cold tile floor with a cheerful fire casting shadows on the walls. It looked as if the ghosts of the former occupants were flitting about in disapproval of the interlopers squatting in their home as Brigid and the others discussed the future of their alliance. The meeting with the other kingdoms of Britannia had just concluded, and everyone was going home tomorrow Now was the time that decisions would have to be made for Novum Britannia's future.

Sister Brigid had asked all their representatives to give their impressions of the just concluded meetings, everyone sharing what information they had gleaned. Questions and answers flew back and forth, commentary was made, and discussion abounded. Their goal tonight was to formulate the long-term strategy of the alliance, and it seemed that everyone that they had talked to whom they wanted to join the alliance had the same concerns. Arturius opened his arms in frustration as he summed it up.

"Everyone seemed worried about me. They think I will place a crown on my head, and they question the safeguards we have put into place."

Brigid scrunched her face in annoyance.

"We are establishing the rule of law, not a kingdom run by a despot. Arturius, they do not know you. They see what they fear, a sword in your hand, not the pen of a scholar."

Caradoc shook his head in frustration as he clasped his hands together.

"That sneaky bastard Quintus should have figured out that you were no war monger, but I thought even he was skeptical. He went home with Einion, no doubt to negotiate a better deal for himself and his kingdom. I can't say I trust that fellow."

There was silence for a moment, then she turned her attention to Bellicus, the grizzled commander of the garrison at Calcva who had also accompanied them to the conference.

"General Bellicus, the main person we need to convince to join forces with us in the alliance is King Einion. You have met him before, haven't you? You know him better than anyone."

"That is correct, sister. When I was second in command under Ambrosius Aurelianus, we campaigned up in the north several times. We are well acquainted."

"What did you find out when you met with him?"

"Precious little, I am afraid," he grumbled. "Einion is a slippery one, but it is clear that he wants us up north to assist them before they will consider joining the alliance."

"What does he want us to do up there?" Arturius asked.

"We are to take the big fortress north of Hadrian's wall, the Dun Guaire," Bellicus growled. "They want us to prove that we are a competent military force before they will help us."

"Oh yes," Brigid said as she shook her head and sighed. "We heard that from the womenfolk as well. And the kicker is that even if we are successful in taking Dun Guaire, we are not to garrison it, ceding control of that place back to Einion and his followers."

Caradoc and Arturius, both blurted out at the same time, "What?"

A stunned quiet in the room.

"No way," Cerdic said as he shook his head. "We all have heard that place is impregnable."

"Bollocks," Bellicus snorted. "Even if we could win that battle, returning it to them is bloody ridiculous."

Silence continued to reign as the group processed this revelation. It was obvious to Brigid that these men in the north were only looking to their own interests, not the big picture of what was best for all of Britannia.

"Fight and die for Einion?" fumed Brigid. "And we are to get nothing for our sacrifice except an empty promise and a pat on the back. That is like teats on a bull, not much good."

"Like it or not, we need these other kingdoms," Arturius said with a sigh, "and they will not ever join us unless we help them first. But say that if the Roman legions could take the Dun, then so can we. Giving it back to Einion means nothing to us. What else would we do with it?"

"Why does Einion want this place so badly?" asked Brigid.

"Whoever holds the Dun Guaire controls the northeast coast," Arturius said. "It defends Eboracum from Norse raiders coming from the sea."

Caradoc scoffed, "I can tell you, taking the place will not be easy, and we are not the legions."

Arturius narrowed his eyes., "What one man can do, another can do."

"Arturius," Cerdic said, chuckling, "you say that all the time. So, what philosopher ever said that?"

"I just made it up one day."

Senna giggled, "I am pretty sure somebody else said that, but I don't remember who. But Arturius is right, I also think we could take that fortress. We know how to build mobile Ballistae now, and artillery could make all the difference."

"We have started construction on some of those units now in Caleva, Bellicus said. "We are the only place in Britannia with those machines."

"So why do we need these northern gobshites as allies anyway," Brigid groused.

Arturius stroked his chin as he sighed.

"I think we can stabilize the south on our own, but if we are going to ever defeat the barbarians north of us, we are going to need help. They grow larger in numbers every year. But the first thing we need to do is to protect ourselves, to build fortifications, keeping the Middle Saxons contained. If it works there, then we do the same with Aelle and the South Saxons. Once our homelands are protected, then we can go up and help the northern kingdoms.

"When the Middle Saxons have been defanged, they cannot stop us from fortifying their border," Cerdic said with a shrug. "But not so with the South Saxons; they would bring an army to stop us."

"I think that is a battle we can win," Arturius said with enthusiasm.

"I disagree," Bellicus said as he shook his head. "We need more infantrymen to take them on, but what Cataphractarii Deva is sending us will be very helpful when we do need them."

Brigid rolled her eyes as she threw up her hands in frustration.

"Why? We have light horsemen now, and Owain is sending us cavalry men as well, isn't he?"

"True" Bellicus said," but with the cataphractarii, the heavy calvary riders and horses are armored head to toe, and they can be very intimidating when they charge. They can actually break an infantry shield wall."

Bellicus tuned to Brigid and placed his hand on her shoulder.

"And Sister, a combined arms force is necessary to defeat the Norse. We need light horsemen as scouts, missile troops to soften our enemies up, and infantry to exploit the breakthrough once the cataphractarii have charged through them. Then once the bastards are on the run, we need some medium cavalry to run them down. A combined force will win this, but if all the pieces are not there, we won't."

"I doubt that," scoffed Cerdic. "Horsemen cannot break or disrupt a shield wall."

"I don't know about that. I have read of these cataphractarii," Senna said, "and from what I read, they should be able break through."

Cerdic arched his brow as he snorted.

"That may be true in your books, Senna, but books do not fight. No horse ever made by the gods will charge into a well-ordered shield wall with spears. They will shy away."

"Bah," Bellicus growled. "I have seen cataphractarii in action before, when I served in the Illyrian legions. If you see a line of massive steeds ridden by men encased in iron thundering towards you with a twelve-foot spear pointed towards your face, even trained infantrymen will piss in their pants and run. These Saxons we will be facing would have never seen the like."

"Whether we have the cataphractarii or not," Cerdic groused, "we also need more infantry."

"I agree," said Bellicus. "We can always train more plumbata throwers, but with infantry, those wankers do not grow in trees. The Saxons have trained all their lives, and I don't think our peasants and newly freed men can match up with them any time soon."

"Cerdic, that is where you come in," Arturius announced. "I want you to tell everyone about the Jutish settlement you just found."

The room descended into silence once more. Cerdic visibly brightened as he spoke up.

"There may be a way to get more infantry who know their business. Just before we left for Aqua Sulis, my scouts discovered a Jutish settlement on the island off our southern coast headed by a man named Wight. He is relative of mine, and in Jute's Land, family is everything. He is returning to the fatherland soon, and I could accompany him to recruit more people."

Brigid tried to keep her face emotionless. *That is all we need, more Germanic barbarians, she* thought. *But at least they would be our barbarians.* But what would happen years from now when Cerdic was out of the picture? Would these new West Saxons stay loyal to Britannia? Caradoc glared as he crossed his arms.

"Bring more Germanic settlers here? Do we want more foxes in the hen house."

Everyone seemed speechless at first as Brigid closed her eyes for a moment to gather her thoughts. What other choices did they have. Then she spoke up.

"The Norse fight among themselves just we Britons do, and I am certain Cerdic can find settlers who hate the tribes that Aelle and Hengist control. We must solve today's problems today and let the future take care of itself, and I trust Cerdic to find the right kind of people."

"Thank you, sister," Cerdic said. "Does anybody else have a better idea? We will never have enough competent infantry unless we do this."

Silence reigned once more, everyone looking around the room at each other. It was obvious no one else had a better plan. Then Arturius grinned.

"Cerdic is right," he said. "We have no other choices, and I trust him also. You should go, Cerdic. Bring us some warriors. Now, as for the long-term strategy for our alliance, I have been talking with Senna and Bellicus, and this is what we think we should do."

The three of them shared their ideas with the group. The plan was bold and audacious, and some were skeptical at first, but eventually they came together and agreed. First, they would stabilize the borders by building defensive earthworks to pin the Saxons in, starting with the Middle Saxons who had already been declawed. Once they had perfected the technique of building and defending the berms, they could do the same with the South Saxons.

Against them they would have a fight on their hands, but by that time the army would be ready. Once their homeland borders were secured, then they could help the Britons to the north, which meant they had to take the Dun Guaire. If victorious there, their fellow northerners could join them in confronting their biggest threat, the Angles to the north. A consensus was reached and allowing Cerdic to go to Jute's land became part of the plan.

I wonder if he knows what he is in for, Brigid thought as she went into her room for the night. *He might lose his head to those feckin' eejit barbarians up there.* Once Brigid was left alone with her thoughts, she laid down on her pallet in the dark to talk to the man she loved the most. She grasped the cross around her neck, worn down by her hands over the years as she would hold it whenever she thought of him. *Oh Petrus,* she thought, *you would be so proud of the young women and men I was with this evening. I so wish that you were here*. She pulled the cross around her neck and pressed it to her lips. *And watch over Cerdic, my love. I do not want any more of the people I love to die.*

CHAPTER THIRTY-SEVEN

Arturius looked upon the blackened ruins of the villa with anger. No doubt it had been grand once, a prosperous farm, productive for over a hundred years, but now it was much like Britannia itself, the victim of Saxons raids and long abandoned. This was why he was here today, to put a stop to these endless incursions and restore a bit of civilization back into this chaotic world. If things went as he hoped, then perhaps this place, like so many deserted farms he had passed on the road today, could come back to life. Ahead of him loomed the earthworks that were his destination, a welcome sign of civilization in the borderlands between his native Britons and the Saxon invaders.

He was astride a trotting horse, his hand tightly gripping the reins, nervous that he might fall off at any second. He had been raised on the coast of the southeast peninsula of Britannia where the land was mountainous, and the seas were rough. He did not like boats, and he liked horses even less. The rough country of his childhood was not suitable for riding, so he had never learned how to handle these beasts when he was young, but he had no choice today. Despite his misgivings, he was still excited to see firsthand if these defensive earthworks would work.

Accompanying one of their newly formed quick response teams of the British army, he had been impatiently waiting at the cavalry headquarters for days now, but finally they had received word of a raiding party crossing the border, and so he and his fellow horsemen were on a mission to catch the bandits. He thanked the gods that not much was expected of him today. Though he was the commander of the entire army, today he was just here to observe.

He gazed upon the calvary leader with envy; Owain was a natural horseman, full of charisma and confidence, riding his steed like he was born for it. After their marriage, Lucilia's husband had moved south with a small contingent of men from Luguvalium. Today, he was acting as the decurion in charge of these twenty horsemen that were with him on this mission. Arturius felt like an imposter, taking a perfectly good horse away from someone else who would have been a better rider. He was terrified he might embarrass himself or get some of his men hurt because of his incompetence.

And they were in a hurry. Workers had labored for months to construct these earthen walls to keep the Saxons out, and once completed, the berms were impressive. If bandits did manage to get over them, then calvary units like this one were to intercept the interlopers before they were able to slip back. Units like this were to be established all up and down the frontier someday, and he was here today to see how well this defensive scheme was going to work.

He was uncomfortable, the price of being atop a horse. The saddle's pommel horn continued to gouge against his leg, but he was grateful for it, as at least it gave him something to hang on to. His thighs were burning with the effort of keeping his knees pinned against the side of his mount, and Cerdic's borrowed calvary shield, slung off one of the rear saddle horns, kept banging against his back. Arturius was miserable, but at least the shield reminded him of his friend who was already headed to Jute's Land. *Mithras, please watch over him,* he thought.

North of here, the River Thamesis functioned as an effective barrier between

Caleva and the Saxons. The bridges were well guarded where the river flowed north to south, forming a natural line of defense. Below Caleva, the river flowed directly east into the Saxons lands, making for easy travel in both directions before butting up against the high Weald and its impenetrable forest. The southern aspect of the valley was marshy, but the higher ground north of the river was a natural entry point, and hundreds of workers had labored for months to construct the dike that loomed up before him to keep those bloody Saxons on their side of the border.

The calvary unit was almost there, cantering up to the gate of the village that abutted the massive earthen barrier. Once there, he and the others dismounted, greeted by a welcoming party that included the village chieftain. Arturius wiped the sweat off his brow, grateful to be off the beast, his body aching in places he did not know existed. Owain thumped his chest with a Roman salute as Arturius surreptitiously stretched his aching limbs. He was exhausted, thoroughly annoyed that the other riders still looked fresh as daisies.

"Greetings," the headman called out, his face beaming with a smile. "We welcome you to our little outpost on the frontier!"

Arturius looked up in awe at the walls that towered above him, running several miles north to the forest at the end of the valley. It was twelve feet tall with a deep ditch in front, and the side facing east had a slope around forty-five degrees. Atop the defensive wall there ran a path wide enough for a column of men to move both north and south. The western side of the defensive structure had a more gentile incline, a difficult climb for horses but not bad otherwise, but the eastern side was much steeper, well-nigh impossible for calvary or stolen livestock to cross over. It was an impressive sight. Arturius flashed what he hoped was a confident smile.

"These are formidable-looking earthworks that you have built here," he said. "This is my first time seeing it. You all have done well!"

"It is thanks to your people from Camalet," the village headman answered with an enthusiastic smile. "They came in the hundreds. It was a miracle to watch. This will certainly curtail any Saxon swine from bedeviling us. I must know, general Arturius, how did you come up with this idea?"

Arturius's lips curved into a sly smile. *He may not like the answer*, he thought.

"Really, it was my wife's idea. She found a book that described the details of how to build fortifications like these while reading about the battle of Alesia won by Julius Caesar some five hundred years ago."

"What is old is new again, eh? And you say a woman thought this up?"

Arturius kept his mouth shut as he suppressed his annoyance. Senna was both intelligent and beautiful, yet many were not acquainted with educated Roman women. Among the British, most females were illiterate, but the people of Camalet were trying to change that with reading and writing skills being imparted universally now. Change would take time, but they needed peace to do it, and that was why these borderland towns were being built, to keep civilization alive.

"I must confess that she is the brains in my marriage. I am just here to shake hands and to look handsome."

His fellow riders chuckled as the headman gave him a bemused glance.

"I'm sure those raiders had to struggle to get over this," Arturius said, "and they bloody well won't be able to bring any stolen livestock back."

"Yes sir, that is the idea," the village chieftain said as he nodded.

Then the head villager looked along the wall and pointed to the north.

"The signal came from our farthest tower," remarked the chieftain. "The raiding party crossed over the berm less than a day ago, and now you are already here. I am impressed."

"Berms alone won't stop wolves," Owain snorted. "That is why you need warriors like us."

Arturius gripped his reins tighter as his horse snorted, the nag seemingly impatient, as if the smelly beast wanted him to remount and get back on the road. The rest of the men and horses also seemed restless, itching to get on with the mission. Arturius shook his head as he regarded the chieftain's fawning smile. *I have done nothing to impress anyone,* he thought. *It's the cavalrymen and the villagers living here who are putting their lives on the line.*

"Your people did well," Arturius said. "The signal towers worked, and the courier you sent allowed us to quickly depart. These bandits might be able to plunder a farm or two, but when they try to cross back, we will be waiting for them."

"Well," the chieftain grudgingly said, "give my congratulations to your wife for producing this defensive scheme."

They were silent for a moment when Owain broke in with a concerned look on his face.

"We need to be leaving now," the decurion grumbled.

"Certainly, my good sir," the chieftain said. "We have a few men who want to march along the top of the wall to help you keep these scoundrels from escaping. May they do so?"

"Of course," Owain responded.

"So," Arturius said, shrugging, "we must be off now if we are going to teach these rascals a lesson. Again, well done. We hope to be back soon with a few Saxon heads!"

He could not believe he had just said that. The idea of beheading someone was disgusting to him, but Arturius supposed he had to sound like a fearless warrior when he was talking to his soldiers. *They might be appalled if they knew the real me,* he thought. *I need to make them think I am tough.* Owain shouted out his orders, and they all remounted and started north. Owain ordered their two light horsemen to gallop ahead to find the location of the intruders while he and the rest of the more heavily armed cavalrymen went along the base of the wall to trap the invaders.

Arturius was lost in thought as he trotted along. *My arse is sore,* he thought, *my knees are raw, and I do not think I will be able to walk again for a week.* He was chastising himself for what he had just said. The thought taking the heads of their enemies as trophies was barbaric, and now he could hear the men riding beside him casually discussing it like it was an everyday occurrence. *Surely, our soldiers do not keep the heads of their foes,* he thought in horror, but he kept his mouth shut as he tried to keep up.

The calvary detachment went on for a couple miles before they could see one of their scouts was retuning; apparently the raiders had been spotted. Arturius glanced behind him, and he could see some movement of the militia from the town along the top of the berm. They were not traveling as fast as the horses, still half a mile behind them, but by the time his cavalrymen engaged the interlopers, he thought the infantry would be in position. Ahead was a dark greasy plume that was more than just a cooking fire. Somebody's homestead was going up in flames.

"Stay here, boys," Owain ordered. "The general and I are going to talk to the scout."

Arturius and Owain went forward and met the light horseman out of earshot of the soldiers behind him. Once the sighting of their enemies was confirmed, Owain sent the scout back to continue to observe their enemies' movements, then the cavalry leader smiled.

"Arturius, sir! I know you are just here to observe, but I need your leadership. I would like you to lead a squadron on the far side of this clearing and try to keep our boys from charging in too quickly. Dismount and hide in the woods over there until you hear my signal to mount up. They are to attack in line formation when they leave the woods, and they should do so in a controlled trot, not a wild gallop. These young ones have the patience of a three-month-old puppy, so having you there can help steady them."

"Of course, commander," Arturius said as he nodded. "But Owain, take care of yourself. Lucilia will have my bollocks for breakfast if you get injured."

"There isn't a Saxon mongrel alive who can match me when I am astride a horse. And you be careful yourself. Your bloody job is just to not fall off, eh?"

They both chuckled for a moment before the two leaders trotted back to the column to pull up beside the rest of the men.

"All right, you bastards," Owain shouted out. "I need half of you over there at the edge of the forest along the tree line, so company Alpha, you go there. General Arturius will oversee you. The rest of you swinging dicks are going to follow me. This little thicket of bushes and trees here should hide us well. It looks like those sons-of-whores Saxons will be coming up here between our two groups. Company Alpha, I will blow the horn when we should charge. Is that clear?"

"Yes, sir," the men answered as one.

"We want our attacking lines to meet up at the same time, so depending on where the Saxons are, one company will need to charge first. That means you bastards with me in company Beta, ignore the horn, and I'll tell you myself when we charge so we all hit them at the same time. Got It?"

"Yes, sir!" they shouted out again.

"Hail Britannia," one man shouted out, and then the rest joined in the cheer.

"Okay boys," Owain grumbled, "that's enough. We don't want those Saxon pigdogs to hear us. Company Beta, follow me.

Owain flashed Arturius with a wicked grin, then he gave him the Roman salute again, his right fist thumping over his heart. With a whoop, he and his troopers headed to their hiding place. The cavalrymen of company Alpha looked upon him expectantly.

By Mithras, he thought, *don't bollocks this up!* Then he glanced at the men beside him.

"Forward," he barked out.

The squad took off, cantering over to the far side of the clearing to hide in the trees as ordered. Arturius' bollocks ached even more while he thought about his predicament, a sweaty death grip on the reins as he tried to keep his balance. Normally he used his left hand to hold on to one of his saddle horns while steering the horse with his right, but the charge was different. Now he would be expected to hold his spear in his right hand while still grasping the reins and shield in his left.

He was worried; he had not thought to practice this seemingly simple task. Could he guide the horse lefthanded? *Jupiter,* he prayed, *please do not let me fall off this bleeding horse when we charge.* Arturius decided that he would not fight as a cavalryman. These men might not respect slingers much, but he decided to dismount and use his weapon of choice when the combat started. If he tried to fight with a sword or lance, he wouldn't last long.

Arturius had the squadron dismount and settle into the tree line, and there he waited, impatiently fidgeting with the sling in his pocket as he and his men held the bridles of their mounts, waiting for the enemy to appear. The passing hours were glacially slow as he nervously scanned the open ground ahead of him. He heard them before he saw them, the lowing of a cow and the tramp of marching men faintly wafting over the hill. Then he saw movement over the gentle rise, the heads of men bobbing up and down as they approached.

Slowly, the Saxon raiders came, his own men remaining eerily silent. Arturius counted a dozen of them as they wordlessly plodded towards them. As they came closer, he could see the raiders leading a handful of captured cattle and two horses loaded with loot. Arturius peered at them through the leaves of the bushes with his horse's bridle in his hand. He turned his head to whisper to the others next to him.

"I wonder how they were planning get those captured animals over the dikes?"

One of the men softly replied, "Maybe they brought some shovels with them to fill in the ditch or something. That takes time, though. General, we may not get here in time to stop a raid, but we sure as hell can kill 'em on the way back. It kind of discourages those cheeky blighters from raiding in the future if their menfolk never return home, don't you think?"

"I hope they did bring shovels with them," one of the others quipped. "That would mean less work to bury their bloody corpses."

The first man whispered back, "Bugger that! Keep the shovels and let the dead stay where they lay for the pigs. We like those wild hogs well fed so they taste better, don't we boys?"

Arturius heard some soft chuckles behind him as he silently shuddered. *I might never eat wild boar again,* he thought. Silence descended once more as he continued to watch the Saxons approach. The enemies were over the crest of the hill now. Then Arturius heard the horn in the distance calling out their unit's signal. It was time for the company to attack.

"All right men, mount up," Arturius commanded.

Once he settled into the four horned Roman saddle, his feet dangling down with nothing to hold them, Arturius glanced left and right. The men grinned back at him. They were leaning forward in their saddles, ready to charge. Then the horn blew.

"Let's go," he called."

His horse stayed in line with the rest as they trotted towards their foes. He saw the Saxons look up in dismay as the attacking line approached. His men were spread out and moving fast as their enemies franticly tried to coalesce into a shield wall. Suddenly, Owain and his riders from the other side burst out from the bushes that concealed them, and the Saxons looked panicked as they glanced in both directions, outnumbered and trapped between the two groups of horsemen. Arturius bounced along unsteadily, somehow still managing to cling to his saddle.

Twenty paces away from the enemy's shield wall, Arturius dismounted, throwing his spear at the forming shield wall. The projectile bounced harmlessly off one of the shields, but by now, he had loaded his sling with a walnut-sized lead pellet. The rest of his men had already spread out and were riding around the circle of shields, the enemy spears at the ready to skewer the riders if they got too close. He noticed the horses would not charge into the unbroken line of shields. *Maybe I can help after all,* he thought. Arturius whirled his sling in a circle over his head, ready to fire when he saw an opening. *There!*

Whirrrrrrr, *smack!*

One of the Saxons gave out a yelp as the pellet struck him in the shinbone, shattering it. The man fell to his knee as he dropped his spear. The pellet Arturius had selected was small, and he was sure the Saxons never saw it coming. He reloaded and sent another shot whizzing towards the enemy warriors, this one striking the ankle of one of the men on the other side of the circle of shields, the victim also screaming in agony as he fell. His stomach churned, the thought of injuring someone repellant, but this was war, something he had trained for his entire life. And it was not the shot he had wanted, missing the man he had been aiming at, but at least it had hit someone. *Mithras has favored me with luck today*, he thought. *May it always be so.*

This second breach of the shield wall he had just created opened further as the decurion's riders joined the melee as they thrust their lances into the enemy host as the defensive shield wall, ragged to begin with, was starting to fall apart. Spear tips flashed in the sun as the riders galloped by, tearing into the sides of the men who had been exposed by the open spaces in the line. Arturius could tell the discipline of the enemy shield wall had been broken, and now the real killing would begin. *Poor bastards,* he thought.

More Saxons cried out in pain and anger as the horsemen continued to circle, their longer lances thrusting in to find flesh and bone. The defensive circle had completely disintegrated now; it was every man for himself. Several Saxons broke out of the circle and tried to escape to the woods but were ridden down and speared from behind, impaled from several directions at once.

Arturius watched in horrible fascination at a lone Saxon who had managed to make it to the sloping earthworks before the riders could run him down, but he had to drop his shield and spear to climb up the berm. The militia men on top of the dike were waiting for him, and the Britons thrust their spears down, the marauder uttering a garbled cry of pain as the sharp iron tore into his face. The Saxon tumbled back down, forever still as his blood drenched the ground beside him.

It was over in minutes, and Arturius breathed a sigh of relief. He was sickened by the killing, but still he was happy with the outcome. *I stayed on my horse, and it was my sling that broke down the shield wall,* he thought. His legs felt weak, as a wave of gratitude flooded in. He never felt more alive after surviving in a battle like this, but it was tragic to watch those men in their moments of desperation once their line collapsed. Arturius had almost hoped that the last man would have gotten away, but he knew what would have happened if the roles were reversed. The Saxons would have shown no mercy, either.

A chilling silence descended as his fellow cavalrymen dismounted to search the bodies for valuables, laughing as they cut the throats of any Saxons who still lived. Looking upon the dead was bad enough, but with the wounded, it was worse. It seemed so cruel to just kill them like that, cutting the throats of the helpless ones. *We call the Saxons barbarians,* he thought, *but are we less cruel?* But this was war in all its ugliness, and he thanked the gods that none of his men were seriously hurt. Arturius walked over to find the pellets he had cast at his foes. Owain was also dismounted, and he led his own horse over to Arturius.

"General, congratulations! These berms look like they are going to work well, but I need to point out that you also lost your nag. Your commanding officer, and that is me of course, is not terribly pleased about that. I may need to put you on latrine duty for negligence.

Owain broke into a huge grin as he pointed back toward the woods.

"Your beast is over yonder, eating the grass. I'll send one of the men to fetch it."

"Thank you," Arturius said with an embarrassed grin.

Arturius overheard a nearby cavalrymen complain to one of his comrades, "The general fought like a footslogger, didn't he lads. Not much of an Equestrian, eh?"

Arturius was not the only one to have heard him.

"Trooper," Owain angrily yelled out, "It was his sling that broke down that shield wall, you blathering fool! We would have taken them down eventually, but we might have had a casualty or two along the way, maybe even you. I might have slingers and archers join us long term, eh? Now go fetch the general's mount and be quick about it. And when we get back to base, you and I are going to have a little chat."

The man sheepishly left, and Arturius put his hand on the rump of Owain's steed.

"Your men did well," Arturius said with a grin. "How many of them are from Luguvalium?"

"Six. Your Britons are being mentored by my men. And your boys with us today all did well."

"Well, I am pleased to hear that your training is progressing nicely."

"It's the best of the volunteers that gravitate to the cavalry, you know."

Arturius was thrilled that the concept of defensive berms seemed to be working, but it would take a huge number of workers to build these berms all over Britannia. This construction project might keep them busy for years, but if it worked here, he hoped it would work everywhere. Then Owain glanced back at him.

"We can train enough calvary to make this work cause we don't need many," Owain grumbled. "But we will need settlers who can fight and be willing to live beneath the berms like this to give us enough warning before we try to build these at the South Saxon border."

"I know. Aelle will counterattack us for sure when we try to build earthworks along his border."

"Well, your idea to send Cerdic back to Jute's land will help. Those Jutes are good fighters, and they don't mind living dangerously. Just being in Jute's land would be a lot riskier than a settlement beneath the earthworks."

"You're right," Arturis said as he shook his head and sighed. "We can't seem to get any refugees in Camalet to do this. They all want to be as far away from the Saxons as possible."

"I can't say I blame them for that," Owain said, chuckling. "I just hope Cerdic can dredge up enough folks to do this. He can be charming even when he is not drunk. This should work, provided those poxy bastards don't kill him up there."

"Oh, he'll be fine," he said, trying to show confidence he did not feel.

I bloody well hope he'll be fine, he thought. Arturius could not talk about his fears, worrying about his friend in his quest. And was bringing even more Germanic settlers to Britannia a good idea? But if the immigrants stayed loyal to their friend, it should work, but would they truly honor their promises? Certainly, they needed men, and this was the only option he could see. The Jutes had trained all their lives to fight, unlike the farmers and freedmen of Camalet.

Most refugees living in Camalet were only suitable as workers, not warriors, and as Owain had said, the best had joined the cavalry. The rest were mostly militia and missile troops, not demanding skills, because they all wanted to work to support their families rather than become warriors; it was hard to do both. Perhaps a permanent warrior class would be better, provided they could be controlled, but for now the Jutes would be warlike enough. Arturius could see the smiling face of his friend in his mind. *This is such a risky thing he is doing;* he ruminated. *But if anyone could pull this off, it would be Cerdic.*

CHAPTER THIRTY-EIGHT

Cerdic felt like he wanted to die. He retched again, bringing up a yellowish bile and not much else. His stomach had been emptied long ago. His mouth was dry, and his cracked lips still retained the faint smell of vomit. The stricken young man kept his head over the side of the rolling ship and into the freshening wind as the smell of manure from the open cargo hold was overpowering to him. This was one of the most miserable times in his life, but it was also one of the most exciting. He was going to his ancestral home, Jute's land, the place his mother had spoken of so many times. The ship continued to plow through the waves at a leisurely pace, the spray flying up from the bow as droplets of seawater landed on his face while he clung to the ship's rail in abject misery.

He glanced up at his second cousin, the commander of the ship, a man named Stuf. The Jutish captain stood with one leg propped up on the bow, enjoying the sunshine and the rise and fall of their ship as the vessel plowed through the waves. Cerdic was full of envy at his skill of riding the seas like a stallion. Stuf was short and built like a bulldog, with a large chest and well-muscled arms. His blonde hair and reddish-tinged beard whipped about like a flag in the breeze, He was wearing the baggy pants so typical of the Northman, and a bright yellow tunic that blended in with his hair. Stuf glanced down at him and grinned,

"How are you enjoying your trip so far, Cerdic? Wait until we get into really rough seas. You'll be feeding the fish with your guts all the way from here to Jute's land at this rate."

Cerdic was embarrassed beyond words. He wanted to ride the Whale Road like this man from the north, but his body was not cooperating. *This sickness should soon pass,* he thought. Cerdic looked over at his traveling companion on the other side of the bow. His friend was also draped over the side, and he too was heaving his guts out. He felt bad for him, but it gave Cerdic some comfort that he was not the only one feeling ill. Lucanus was a friend from the Weald who thirsted for adventure and had volunteered to accompany him on his quest.

His companion had been raised a Christian, but he had come to honor the gods of the north, and he longed to see the lands where his new gods held sway. Though he had not been born a Northman, he had the heart of one, the hammer of Thunor hanging from his neck instead of a cross. Lucanus was as tall and thin with bright blue eyes that contrasted with his dark, curly hair. He was clean shaven in the Roman fashion, with prominent dimples and chiseled features that caused young maidens to blush, but he wasn't so handsome now, his face streaked with the contents of his stomach.

"Ahoy, Lucanus,", Stuf called to his friend on the other side of the bow. "Now I am really surprised at you. You look worse than Cerdic."

Lucanus groaned in misery as Stuf laughed in the wind.

"You were raised in Novomagus there on the coast, yes? Didn't you ever get in a boat?"

Lucanus moaned again while the Jutish captain guffawed. They had left the white cliffs of Britannia behind them as they headed across the Mare Brittanicum towards the Mare Germanicum, heading north of the western tip of Gaul that was closest to the British shore. Their caravan of cargo vessels was accompanied by several Saxon warships, sleek clinker-built long ships that rowed along beside them with thirty or more rowers, escorts to defend them from the pirates and raiders that plagued these seas.

The wind that sprang from the southwest filled the small sails of the ship as they were slowly pushed towards the north shore of Germania. The groans of the ship and the sound of the timbers creaking and the sails flapping was music to his ears despite the nausea that was still welling up. The cargo ship looked ungainly compared to the rowed warships, carrying cargo back to Jute's land with thralls, livestock, and booty, all to be sold for a profit. Fore and aft was a deck that protruded about a fourth of the way to the center mast, and the crew would sleep under the cover of the planking with their sea chests and other trading valuables, while the thralls and livestock were exposed in the open.

The bleating of the sheep and the groans of the British thralls in the hold filled him with pity, and he could have done without the smell of the barnyard and unwashed slaves. He felt a little guilty, being complicit in bringing these poor people north into slavery, but this was the weavings of the three fates that they had been enthralled, and he was not going to question the will of the gods. Lucanus had once felt the lash of a wealthy merchant in Novomagus until Woden had blessed him with luck and allowed him to escape to the Weald, and now he was courageously risking his life to see the land of the Jutes, the wellspring of the gods he now honored.

It seemed like a lifetime to him before the ship finally stopped at an old Roman port controlled by the Frankish invaders that they now called Boulogne. They anchored in a large bay, and waiting for them were a group of massive vessels that were to accompany them to Jute's land. Recovering from his motion sickness in the calm waters of the bay, he gazed in wonder upon the ships before him, absolute behemoths that made his own ship look like a child's toy. The captain stood beside him, and Cerdic turned to him.

"What are those things?" Cerdic asked in wonder.

"Those are Roman cargo ships from the Eastern Roman Empire," Stuf said. "Now we Jutes have hired them out to help move our people from the Father's Land to Britannia."

"How many people can they hold?" Lucanus asked in wonder.

"Up to four hundred."

Cerdic whistled in amazement. He continued to marvel at the great ships as Stuf pointed out the various features of the vessels, some one hundred and fifty feet long and forty feet wide.

"How do they row that bloody thing?" Cerdic mumbled.

"They don't," snorted Stuf. "There is no place for rowers on these beasts. They use those massive sails woven tighter than a Frisian's purse to move those vessels. Our own sails are as loose as a whore's cunny compared to theirs."

"Imagine that," Lucanus proclaimed, "a ship that does not need someone to row it."

"They are hard to maneuver and need deep water," Stuf marveled, "so as we move north, they will stay anchored offshore, and boats like ours will bring cargo and people back and forth. We cannot go very far or fast, so we must hop up the coast to stop at every little port we pass to trade with the locals and take on freshwater and supplies."

Lucanus's eyes widened.

"You mean we will be stopping at places controlled by Friesians and Angles? Aren't they your enemies?"

Stuf chuckled for a moment.

"Yes," he said with a raised brow. "Some will never be our friends, but they will not be our enemies, either. Trade is trade, and gold is gold. We just need to be careful."

"So," Lucanus said as he raised his brow, "what will happen when we get to Jute's land?"

Stuf threw his head back in laughter as he patted Lucanus on the back.

"With your unshaven Roman face, why your corpse could be feeding the fish. But don't you worry. As one of Cerdic's hirdmen, you will be welcome, even though you look like an unshaven boy. We will meet Cerdic's uncle there, a jarl of southwestern Jute's land, a chieftain among chieftains. He is gathering the willing immigrants wanting to come to Britannia."

Stuf gave Lucanus an inquiring look.

"What brings a Briton like you to the Father's Land? I thought you Christians were fearful of us wolves of the north."

"I was raised a Christian," Lucanus said, shrugging as he unconsciously fingered the amulet hanging from his neck, "but now I honor the Aesir just as Cerdic does. We became friends when he and I were refugees in the Weald. Woden has blessed him with luck, and so now I am oath sworn to him. I will follow him to the ends of the earth with my spear by my side."

"Huh," Stuf said with a chuckle. "So, you are a warrior now, are you? I must say, you don't look it."

"Cousin," Cerdic said as he patted Lucanus on the back, "he is one of the best I have ever sparred with. He has the heart of a true Norseman. And you will be growing a real beard soon enough, won't you Lucanus?"

Lucanus nodded, and then they resumed gazing silently at the ships around them. Cerdic harbored some guilt that he was carrying fellow Britons into a life of slavery, but it had been their choice to follow the Christos, and so the Norns had woven these people a different fate. To Cerdic, the world was divided between the lucky and the unlucky, between winners and losers. He was going to win if the Norns wished it, and if he remained successful, others would follow a leader like him. *As long as I remain lucky in war and friendships*, he thought, *then I do not mind getting seasick. I cannot have good fortune at everything.*

Once the convoy left the port, they meandered up the coast along the lands of the Franks, past the Friesians, and along the northern coast of Germania until they anchored off the Saxon shore. From there he knew it was a short hop up to the great peninsula that was Jute's land. At each stop, the routine was the same: a jarl would welcome them to their hall, while in return, the local lord kept their bellies full and their tankards overflowing with frothy ale.

Then came the day when his life would change forever. Today the harbor and town looked like all the others they had visited, a cluster of wooden huts surrounding a great hall, swarming with eager children, smiling traders, and coquettish girls accompanied by their scowling mothers. Cerdic stepped onto the jetty, his legs stiff and sore, his gait still rolling with the swells of the sea despite being on dry land. He had been told the chieftain of this berg was friendly with Aelle and his South Saxons, so had had been warned he had to be cordial, cautious, and calculating. This jarl was a rival, not a friend. Still, Stuf had brought gifts for the nobleman, principally an amphora of wine from the impossibly distant Mediterranean. All Northman drank, but this fellow was known to be a drinker of immense quantities, hence the nature of their gift.

As usual, the luminaries of the convoy were invited to the jarl's great hall, which included himself, Stuf and Lucanus. The chieftain's hall was also like all the rest, a large and ornately carved wooden structure with a high-pitched roof and firepits in the center of the floor. Trestles lined the back walls, and the rear of the room had an elevated platform where the king and his honored guests sat. When he was introduced, Cerdic tried to ignore the jagged scar on the jarl's face that deformed his left eyelid, so that when he blinked, the blind eye remained open.

That white and unseeing eye turned out to stare at nothingness, while his watery blue one was staring directly at him when they were introduced. The damaged globe appeared as red as a fresh burn, angry looking and weeping a crusty discharge, a wound that could never heal. While he spoke with the jarl, Cerdic tried to concentrate on the pale blue eye that was regarding him, trying to ignore the horror that was the rest of his face. The ruined eye looked painful, and a man in chronic pain could be testy and short tempered. Stuf had already warned him that he was reputed to be both.

The jarl's son was then presented to him, his eyes boastful and proud, and to the jarl's left sat his wife, a creature as corpulent and crusty as he was. What remained of her fading beauty was enhanced by expertly applied makeup, but her age and history of heavy drinking combined with a florid complexion made the most expertly applied cosmetics insufficient to completely camouflage her. Even more remarkable was her hair, which had been styled in the elaborate curls and patterns he had seen before in Roman statues. Neither in Britannia, nor in his travels in the north, had he ever seen anything quite like this.

This Roman hairdo was beyond description. It boasted a tightly curled anterior frame complimented by a perfect whorl at each temple, an elevated semicircular arc of perfectly arrayed waves that created a halo effect in front, while the back was plaited and coiled into an elaborate bun. Cerdic knew that a trained hairdresser and cosmetics artist, a slave called an Ornatrix, would have had to spend hours to put that hirsute monstrosity together, so it was clear the Jarl's wife had one. He wondered where they had found someone with those skills this far north.

The evening's activities went as they always did with music, dancers, toasts, and lots of ale. To Cerdic, this just was another routine feast, but he enjoyed looking at a wide-eyed Lucanus as he participated in the festivities. He could tell his friend was thrilled to be an honored guest instead of being a servant, with happiness written all over his face. Then he felt someone staring at him and he glanced over at the jarl's son and noticed that one of his piggish little eyes was narrowed and looking right at him. Not so the other eye, as it was pointing away the boy's nose while his left maintained its steady gaze. *What is that all about,* he wondered. Then during a pause of the musicians, it was the jarl's turn to affix his watery blue eye upon Cerdic as he pointed towards his equally portly son.

"Well, young man, you look like a stalwart young fellow. Your companions were bragging about your ability to wrestle like a true Saxon instead of the mangy Jute that you are. You call yourself a king I hear, so I would like to see how you would fare against my son here, a true Saxon. I propose a wager."

The chieftain pulled a thin silver torc from his left arm and held it up.

"I offer you this bauble if you win. What do you wager in return?"

They both continued to stare at Cerdic expectantly, the Jarl's left eye crossing outward, while the young prince's right eye turned towards the other wall. The sight of these two one-eyed men staring at him, each with one eye going off in different directions, struck Cerdic as hilarious. He bit his lip as he tried not to laugh, but he could not hold it back as he started to snicker, which caused the only eye of the jarl to narrow even further. *Bugger me,* he fretted, *I should not have done that.* Now he had no choice but to accept the jarl's offer. Cerdic gave Lucanus a wink as he turned back towards the jarl and his son with a grin.

Cerdic removed a gold ring from his hand and held high in the air as he loudly replied, "I accept! And in return, I offer this."

The Jarl's son roared out with approval as he thrust his arms into the air. The drinking horn in his hand struck the edge of the table as his arm went up, sending the cup spiraling toward his mother's head, the ale flying into her face. Her elaborate hairstyle was knocked askew, her makeup ruined and streaking down her face like a melted candle. The jarl roared in laughter as his son recoiled in horror, the wife displayed a look of pure venom towards them both.

"You stupid oafs," she bellowed out, "my hair is ruined. I need my Ornatrix. Ria! Where is Ria?"

A servant scurried into a side room off the great hall and hauled out a petite girl in a plain tunic and threw her at the jarl's wife. The thrall looked upon her charge in horror, and then the pair hurried into the room from which she had just exited. The Ornatrix looked familiar to him somehow; in fact, she looked too familiar. *Ria,* he thought. *Isn't that the name of Senna and Lucilia's sister? Surely not.* Cerdic glanced at his friend, and Lucanus had visibly paled as he looked upon her in open-mouthed surprise. *Maybe that is her,* he thought. Ria was alive, and she was here. But what was he going to do about this?

CHAPTER THIRTY-NINE

Lucanus had never been so scared in his life. When Cerdic had laughed at the sight of the jarl and his son standing together, a wave of dread had filled his chest. In his heart, he felt like he was still an outsider. He was a formerly enslaved person that was now sitting at the table like he was an honored nobleman. Deep down, he had doubts that he did not belong. Lucanus had a fear that someday the charade would end, and he would be thrown back into servitude. Stuf had warned them that this jarl was no friend of theirs; although the chieftain had officially welcomed them, and if he took offense to something, then things could go sour in a hurry.

When the handmaiden to the jarl's wife appeared, he felt his heart stop as the bitter taste of bile arose in the back of his throat. His eyes opened wide with surprise as a wave of anxiety flooded through him. The Ornatrix was no ordinary slave; it was Ria, the daughter of Ambrosius Aurelianus. In the days before Novomagus had been sacked, he had known her as a member of the nobility. In his earlier life as a slave, he had been tasked with serving guests at the various banquets his master had held, and Lucanus had waited on Ria more than once.

He doubted that she recognized him, but she definitely stood out in his memories; it had been years ago, but he was certain it was her. He had assumed she had been killed when Novomagus had fallen, but here she was, a thrall now. He and Cerdic were now good friends with both of her sisters, and Lucanus knew he had to tell Cerdic of what he had just seen, but then what? What would Cerdic do when he told him who the Ornatrix was?

His mouth was dry as sand as his stomach turned, done with eating and drinking for now. He paid little attention to the wrestling match, lost in thought. He had always liked Ria, as she had been uncommonly kind to the serving staff during those times when she had been a guest of his master. He longed to find a way to free her from her current situation, but how could they? *Cerdic will think of something,* he thought, *but will it get us all killed?* He fidgeted as he sat there, wondering what would happen next.

"Look at Cerdic," muttered Stuf, "he is just toying with him.

Lucanus's attention snapped back to the ongoing match as he saw Cerdic had allowed the lad to yank him into a hold, winching in faux pain for the crowd, then he winked again at him and Stuf just before he wriggled out like an eel to face his panting opponent again as the crowd roared.

"You are right, captain. But we must get out of here as soon as this is done. We need to talk."

The contest seemed to go on forever as Cerdic hammed it up for the crowd. Cerdic was famous for his wrestling skills, and the lad was not a worthy opponent; Cerdic was just putting on a show to fool the crowd and give the fellow the illusion it was a close match. Lucanus fidgeted nervously as he waited for Cerdic to put an end to the charade, and he breathed a sigh of relief when the match ended abruptly. The jarl's son had vomited while Cedric had him in a headlock, and getting drenched in vomitus was no doubt enough for him. Cerdic quickly pinned the jarl's son down into submission. Despite his victory, instead of just accepting the prize, Cerdic swapped his gold ring for the silver torc in honor of the spirited fight the jarls' son had given him. His generosity brought a roar of approval from the crowd.

Cerdic, Lucanus, and Stuf excused themselves from the great hall as they went outside to help their king clean up, accompanied by a serving girl sent to help them. As luck would have it, the thrall that accompanied them was also a Briton, a captive from a conquered British tribe in the east. They went to a nearby hut, and the girl and Cerdic went inside to clean up while Stuf and Lucanus waited outside. Once Cerdic had returned to them, Lucanus asked the girl to wait by the door as he hustled his two companions out of earshot. When Cerdic heard the news, he seemed to sober up completely.

"I thought that might have been her," Cerdic said as he stroked his beard. "We must do something. We can't just leave her here."

There was a long pause as his king contemplated the situation. Then Cerdic told him to go back to the thrall and ask her some more questions while he and Stuf conferred. Lucanus did as he was asked, peppering her with questions concerning Ria and her duties there, information such as where she slept and the like. As he questioned the girl, Lucanus frequently glanced back at Cerdic and Stuf as they continued to whisper to each other. *I know that look*, he thought. *Cerdic is planning something risky.* Cerdic and Stuf seemed quite animated as they conferred with each other.

He heard Stuf raise his voice, "Are you mad? Do not be a fool!"

"Yes, we can," he heard Cerdic say. "We have to!"

He saw Cerdic put his hands on Stuf's shoulder. The two men continued their muted conversation, and then Lucanus detected a look of resignation cross over Stuf's face. The ship's captain nodded his head as Cerdic beamed, and then the two of them shook hands. It was clear that a decision had been made. Cerdic motioned Lucanus over to them as he told the young British thrall to stay beside the door.

"Lucanus, I have an idea. I am sure you are aware that neither of us could look Senna or Lucilia in the eye again if we did nothing. Do you agree?"

Lucanus paused for a moment, panic stricken, but then he overcame his fear and nodded despite the chill running down his spine. He thought back to when he had agreed to his parents' request for himself to be sold into slavery so that his younger brothers and sisters could be fed. Being enslaved had been a nightmare, and so he wanted to rescue Ria from that life. But now Cerdic was asking him to risk his own life and freedom to save someone he barely knew. He was terrified, but it was Cerdic the Lucky who was asking him. Lucanus was scared, but the Norse had taught him to be brave. He would be loyal to his king, and if Cerdic said he should risk his life, then he would do so, having sworn an unbreakable oath of fealty to his friend.

"Yes," he said, and Cerdic grinned once more. Then the three of them walked over and stood by the trembling girl before them.

"What is your name?" Cerdic tenderly asked the girl. "Not your thrall's name, but your real one."

She glanced up at him and then looked down to the ground like a whipped dog.

"Minura," she muttered.

Cerdic gently put his hand under her downcast chin and lifted her face up to his. He was making her do something that thralls could not ever do, to look a nobleman in the eye."

"Listen to me, Minura, and listen well. We will take you from here and set you free if you help us. I will give you my word on the one eye of Woden for the gods to strike me dead if I lie. Do you understand me?"

She nodded, but still she gazed at him like a scared rabbit.

"The thrall that they called the Ornatrix, Ria, do you know her?"

"Of course," she mumbled.

"I would like to buy her. Do you think that could be arranged?"

Her eyes found the ground again and paused for a moment. Then she looked Cerdic in the eye.

"I think not. The Domina places great value on her hair and makeup, and there is no one like Ria who can do what my Domina needs. She cannot be replaced. I do not think she would be for sale for any price."

Cerdic thought for a minute, his brow furrowed, and then he touched the girl on the shoulder.

"Could I buy you?" he asked.

"I have no great value to anyone here," she softly replied as she averted her gaze. "So, that may be possible."

"Minura," Cerdic said with a nod, "know that I will speak to your master, the jarl here, and I will buy you. When we return to Britannia, I will let you live with us, or with the settlement in Camalet, or anywhere else for that matter. You would no longer be a thrall. But there is a price for this; we must take the Ornatrix with us. Do you understand?"

Minura's eyes teared up as she nodded. He put his hand on her shoulder.

"Minura, you need to help us in my plan to make this happen. If we can free her, then you, too, would be free. There will be some risk to us all if we do this, but I have a plan. Do you agree to help us in exchange for your freedom?"

She paused for a moment. Then she looked back up at him, her eyes meeting him with a look of resolve.

"Yes. But I must ask you to do something to show your sincerity. Give me you knife."

Cerdic grinned, then he reached to the scabbard by his side and presented to her his pugio. She stared at him for a moment, then she sliced the palm of her hand. She held it out, the blood slowly dripping into the dust.

"Swear me a blood oath to your gods as I will do to mine, and I will help."

Cerdic's eyes opened wide in surprise at first and then he started to laugh.

"By Loki's short and curlies, I must say you have a pair of stones yourself, young lady. I have never heard of a warrior oath swearing with a woman before, but by the gods, I so swear."

Cerdic took the blade from her and did the same to himself, and they shook hands while they both uttered fealty to each other. Lucanus was awestruck at the bravery of this thrall. Cerdic shot a mirthful glance at him and Stuf.

"Well, my fine fellows, you must do the same, eh? Don't make me oath swear all by myself."

Stuf's eyes opened wide, speechless at first. Then the hint of a smile curved over his lips, and he chuckled for a moment, his eyes twinkling in the moonlight.

"Never heard of a blood oath with a woman before either," he muttered with a shrug. "But why not? This ought to make the gods sit up and take notice, eh? What else can a man ask for."

Stuf took the knife, and another oath was sworn. Then Lucanus grasped the blade with a trembling hand and followed them all in the blood swearing. He shivered, but it was not from the cold or the pain in his hand. They were all committed now.

"All right then, Cerdic muttered, "this is what we must do."

CHAPTER FORTY

As the rest of the fleet remained anchored offshore, Cerdic stood near the prow of his ship as it entered the bay, gazing at the wharf and the village ahead of them. They were returning to the place where the one-eyed jarl and his crusty wife ruled to complete the bargain he had made when they had left weeks before. He had been in numerous battles and fights so far in his life; skilled warriors had tried to kill him, and friends had died before his eyes, but he had never felt as anxious about anything as he did right now. *What in the name of Woden was I thinking?* he mulled to himself.

He was committed, but he had no regrets. This was Senna and Lucilia's long-lost sister he was trying to liberate. In a sword fight, he felt confident. It was something he had practiced all his life. What he was about to do was something he had never done before. True, he and his companions had rehearsed their roles multiple times with the plan he had concocted to liberate Ria, but so many things could go wrong with this caper. They could be killed, or worse, enthralled. He would die before he would let that happen again.

He tried to keep a smile plastered on his face as they neared the dock. The sun warmed him as squawking sea gulls circled and wheeled about in the brilliant blue sky on this bright and cloudless day, and as they glided to the shore, a group of people congregated around the dock waiting for them. In front were the jarl and his wife, and as a twinge of panic struck again, he was able to control it by using the breathing techniques that Arturius had taught him years ago. He put on his best smile and waved. The wife's hair was even more elaborate than before, a beehive of bouncing curls and trembling tresses, no doubt requiring hours of work to put supporting pins and woolen inserts into the monstrosity perched upon her head.

Cerdic tried to wipe his face clean of expression. *Ria had been busy,* he thought. He hoped this was the last time that poor girl would labor over that woman's vanity. He felt a bump as the ship nudged up against the dock. He gazed at his friends and tried to give them a confident smile. They looked back at him and grinned; they did not appear nervous, but he knew they all had to feel it like he did, and no one was hiding their anxiety better than the girl. Minura held her chin high and looked as calm as a millpond. Her courage amazed him, as she had the most to lose in this gambit. *That girl must have cast iron stones,* he thought. She was going back into the lion's den, yet she looked so cool and collected. He was impressed.

Cerdic kept the plastered smile in fine form as he and the rest of his party left the heavy leather casing on the ship that was to be their gift, and he marched down the gangway like he owned the place. Cerdic greeted the one-eyed jarl and his overly quaffed wife, and they responded with the appearance of warmth and good cheer. Cerdic's heart hammered in his chest like a woodpecker working away on a dead tree as he tried to make small talk and not look nervous.

His welcoming smile remained intact as he prayed to Woden that he and his friends would not be caught. *I am risking everything on this,* he thought, *my kingdom and my life. But this is for my honor, and for my friends. And when we pull this off, this story will be on the lips of the bards forever. I will become either Cerdic the Lucky, or Cerdic the Dumb and Dead. But do this I must.* He was sure that Stuf was correct, that the gods in Asgard must be watching this drama with interest. How could they not?

Rotting seaweed on the rocky shore smelled like sweet perfume compared to the wet dog odor that the jarl brought with him as he gave Cerdic a hearty bearhug as a welcome. The cross-eyed son scowled. The sheen of makeup covering the wife's face almost cracked as she broadly smiled. The jarl had made a barter deal with Cerdic, one that they had rubbed their hands together with glee when they had discussed it on their last visit. Their mood seemed even more excited now, their greed so nakedly displayed in their faces. They were practically pissing over themselves in excitement to complete their trade before Cerdic changed his mind. *They must still think I am being played for a fool,* he thought with relief.

When he was here last, Cerdic and the jarl had already concluded a portion of the transaction buying the British serving-wench for a paltry sum, but the wall hangings, now that was a different story. The tapestry of the hunting scene that Cerdic had seen during their last feast together must have been unremarkable in their eyes, but Cerdic had claimed that he loved it and wanted it for his own hall back in Britannia. It was somewhat grimy from smoke stains and spilled ale, but it was impressive, nonetheless. Cerdic said he coveted it, and the jarl's wife had feigned an abiding love for that piece of art. Cerdic had offered a trade, but in exchange for what?

In their ship they carried a variety of trade goods to the north, and one of them was a looted Roman tapestry, a renowned pagan work of art, or so Cerdic had claimed, rumored to have been hidden in a bishop's personal residence, and when the monastery was sacked, the sinful piece of art had returned to pagan hands. It was purported to be a hundred years old or more, but it was in a remarkable state of preservation, depicting various scenes of the Roman celebration of bacchanalia in an amazing vibrant riot of colors. This woven artwork had it all: naked women, drunken satyrs, flowing wine, and not so discreet scenes of furtive copulation. It was unique, to be sure. He was sure the Saxons had seen nothing like it.

Cerdic could tell the hunting scene weaving looked rather worn and unremarkable compared to the tapestry of the bacchanalia. The artwork that the jarl was receiving was in pristine condition, and compared side to side, it certainly looked like he and his wife would be getting the better deal of it. The pair looked nervous as they asked him if the exchange was still on, and Cerdic declared that it was. The visage of greed the jarl and his wife displayed grew larger at the news.

After the transaction was declared to still be in play, Cerdic marched back to the ship with Lucanus and Stuf, the two men wordlessly exchanging nervous glances with him as they made their way back up the gangway to their ship to retrieve the case that held the tapestry. *This is such a crazy thing to do*, he thought. Lucanus knew Ria, though, so he was willing to do this, and he was also oath sworn to him. At heart Stuf was a risk taker, and he had an old grudge with this jarl, and Cerdic knew the sea captain thought this would settle the score. And was there a better way to die, with the gods in rapt attention?

They pulled out the leather carrying case from its niche in the forward hold of the ship and marched up the pier and into the jarl's longhouse accompanied by two of the ship's carpenters. The crewmen called for a ladder that was quickly produced, and the carpenters purposefully strode to the back of the hall and climbed up the ladder to pull the hunting tapestry off the wall. Cerdic looked a bit askance at the soiled artwork, and his hosts looked at him anxiously, but he declared that a deal was still a deal.

Then, the magic moment. The carpenters pulled the new artwork out of its case and unrolled the tapestry up against the wall to size it and see how they were going to hang it. The assembled throng gazed upon the magnificent artwork in awe, but not all eyes were so fixated. Cerdic and his friends were shooting furtive glances in another direction. They stood to the side against the wall and held the old tapestry up to keep it off the floor as they readied the process to roll the heavy woven cloth into the leather carrying case for transport back to the ship.

As they held the old tapestry up high, it was able to cover a door from the view of the crowd. That door led to a side chamber; the same entrance used in their previous feast by the jarl's wife when she fled after being doused by her son's ale. The door quickly opened, paused for a moment, and Minura disappeared, hidden from the crowd. Then two figures silently reentered the great hall, and the door creaked shut. It was loud, sounding like a bolt of lightning in his mind. Cerdic nervously glanced around the room, but no one seemed to notice as the crowd was still abuzz in conversation about the vibrant work of art being displayed to them for the first time.

He breathed a sigh of relief. The sound had been masked by the chatter and applause as the crowd in the great hall looked upon the mysteries of bacchanalia. Cerdic was grateful to see that no one seemed interested in what they were doing. Minura moved beside him, and he glanced back at the open door to see a furtive figure lay down beside the tapestry case, still shielded from view by the weaving they held aloft. He felt the tapestry move, as the attention of the crowd continued to be focused elsewhere, Cerdic, Stuf, and Lucanus proceeded to roll up their woven treasure.

They placed the weaving within the leather casing they had brought. The fit for the case was tight, but they had practiced this maneuver numerous times on the ship with Minura acting as Ria. They knew it would fit, and it did. Ria was in it now, but when they tried to lift the case. Cerdic bent over to lend a hand, grunting in exertion. *By the gods, this thing is heavy*, he thought. He wiped the cold sweat from his brow, but now with just one sweaty hand on the case, it slipped out of his grip and hit the ground with a loud thump. He heard a sharp whimper of pain. His own heart stopped. *We are going to be gutted,* he thought in a panic. Minura's eyes flashed as she glanced at him, and then she abruptly put her hand up to her cheek. He looked at her, confused. Tears welled up in her eyes as she recoiled away from him,

"I am sorry, Dominus," she whimpered. "That was my fault. I will not cry out in pain the next time you hit me. I promise."

Cerdic paused for a moment, confused at first. Then it dawned on him.

"Silence, thrall!" Cerdic growled. "You are not allowed to make a sound when I beat you. That was nothing. We will see if you can hold your tongue when I whip you again on the ship. If you cannot take your punishments in silence, I may have to cut out your tongue. Is that clear?"

She cowered as if she was in abject fear as his friends got a firmer grip on the heavy case. He backed away, letting Stuf and Lucanus take the load as they had practiced on the ship. Why he tried to help them a minute ago, he could not explain it. It must have been his nervousness, and his mind swirled with anger at himself for his stupid move that had almost cost them everything. Some of the crowd had looked back at him during the exchange between him and Minura, and they smirked with knowing glances. They must have thought his newly acquired thrall had been cursed with a harsher master than the one she had just left.

Once the tapestry was secured in the case, his stomach still churned in anxiety as he strode up to the jarl and effusively thanked him for his generosity. The Saxon chieftain beamed, with pleasure, saying his new tapestry looked magnificent. *That was close,* he thought. *Thank you Minura for your quick thinking.* He would make an offering to Frea for her when they were back on board the ship and safely away from here. He was angry and disappointed in himself, and he itched to get out of there as his nerves were shot.

His two friends hoisted up the case and started to carry it out of the hall as Minura walked behind them, looking like a whipped dog, the crowd still buzzing with the beauty of the newly acquired piece of art that now graced the noble hall. No one seemed to notice that the rolled tapestry hidden in the leather case seemed thicker than the one that had originally entered the room. Fortunately, Stuf and Lucanus were strong, and the two men made the heavy load appear to the casual onlookers as much lighter than it really was.

They had almost gotten the tapestry out the front door when Cerdic was grabbed by the ebullient jarl who was insisting on sharing a toast and thanking him for his gift. Cerdic motioned to his friends to go ahead and get out of there, and he would be along as soon as he could, but as his friends went out the door, Cerdic looked on with horror upon the jarl's wife's face. She had teared up in joy, and that had disturbed the Egyptian makeup that graced her eyes. She daubed at the tears, and the dripping streaks of Kohl that had nestled themselves into the cracks of her skin were upon her hands now. Her face contorted as she realized her artifice of beauty had been marred.

"Get the Ornatrix,", she hissed as she glared at the serving thrall beside her.

The slave scurried into the side room that had been so recently covered by the rolling of the old tapestry. *By Loki's bollocks,* he thought, *I knew our luck could not last!* Cerdic tried to pull away, but the jarl had his hand on his shoulder and had proposed another toast. He had just sent a servant for some special honey mead that had yet to arrive. Cerdic was stuck there. His heart pounded so loudly that he thought it impossible that the jarl couldn't hear it as the previously taciturn man had suddenly turned loquacious. Meanwhile, as the thrall sent to find the Ornatrix had slunk back again with a puzzled look on her face. As he was being toasted, he strained to hear the conversation going on beside him.

The thrall had just told the wife that she was not sure where the Ornatrix was, and her mistress gave her a scowl of disapproval and a hissed, "Well, go find her, you silly goose!

The quarrelsome matron turned to face the front door.

"Guards! Search the grounds for the Ornatrix, and make sure she is not trying to sneak aboard one of ships in the harbor. A bag of silver for the man who finds the little bitch."

The jarl seemed oblivious to the wife's predicament as he continued to prattle on. The guards scurried out on their quest as Cerdic prayed to Woden to get the jarl to shut up so he could get out of there. Only a minute or two passed, and the seemingly endless toast was nearing its end as the thrall had returned once more and whispered into the ear of her mistress.

Cerdic kept his smile plastered on while his heart sank; he could see the jarl's wife grow beyond furious. The Ornatrix could not be found. When the crestfallen serving-wench had returned without her task being successful, the jarl's wife spilled her rage onto the distressed thrall, and she started to beat the hapless girl without mercy. Her husband shot him an embarrassed glance as Cerdic thanked him for the last time.

The toast was finally done, and moments later Cerdic was out the door, the screams of the beaten thrall slowly receding behind him, another life ruined by a Domina's malice. He hurried to the dock, all the while trying to look like he was not in a hurry. *Bugger me, that was close,* he thought as he felt a surge of relief when he boarded the small boat to row him back to his ship. He had just set his foot inside the small craft when suddenly Cerdic faintly heard the shout, "stop that boat," emanating from the great hall. He looked behind him and saw a group of people had run out the door and were waving at him.

"By Woden's beard, row fast," he ordered, and the boat shot away from the shore.

The distant shouts grew louder as they sped along. He gave a furtive glance back to the shore, and none of their boats were leaving the dock yet, but he wanted to cover his tracks, and what better way to do that than to have an excuse as to why they did not hear anything.

"All right, boys, do not look back, row hard as you can, and start singing! Now join me in this sea shanty."

The men in the boat grinned as they rowed, drowning out any other noises as their ribald song echoed across the waves. As soon as the small watercraft touched the cargo ship, they leaped on board. Cerdic yelled for them to get underway immediately. He wanted to get as much water between them and the jarl as soon as they could. He glanced back at the shore and saw a gaggle of people, including an angry-looking jarl, standing at the dock waving at them, but there were still no boats in the water, so there was no catching them now. He breathed a sigh of relief as the thrill of success washed over him.

Loki, he thought, *you were an arsehole with the way your toyed with us in there. But I will give you an offering tonight.* He felt pity for the thrall left behind. He was sure this was not the first time that poor servant had been the recipient of the fury of her mistress, and it would not be her last, but now it would no longer be the fate of Ria or Minura to be a victim of that woman's anger. But once he was back on the main deck, he turned to Stuf and Lucanus and clapped them both on the shoulder.

"We did it boys!"

Then his eye caught Minura's, then he glanced at his two comrades.

"And a bow for this lady, lads. It is well deserved."

They bowed; she returned the favor with an ear-splitting grin. Then he was surprised to see that although the tapestry was out of the case, it had not yet been unrolled.

"Why is she still in there?" he asked with a frown.

Stuf chortled as he slapped him on the back with glee. "I told them to wait until you were back on board. She isn't going anywhere, you know, and I thought it would be fun for you to see her emerge. It was your idea to do this, you know."

Cerdic knitted his eyebrows together as he shook his head in disgust at first, but then his facial expression lightened, and he chuckled.

"By Frea's tears, get her out of there, would you!"

Stuf and Lucanus both laughed as they lifted the edge of the tapestry and Ria rolled out. She lay there for a moment, her tear-filled eyes blinking into the sky. Slowly, she stood up, covering her eyes in the bright sun as she glanced around. She looked stunned at first as silence reigned on the deck, but then she smiled as her eyes locked onto him, and they stared at each other for a few moments. She ran over to him and embraced him, clinging to him like a drowning woman, her fingers imbedded into his back like she would never let go.

Cerdic was startled, not knowing what to do, but after a moment, he put his arms around her and hugged her back. He had never experienced anything like this before; he felt like her soul was merging into his as she trembled in his arms. He felt moisture where her tears of happiness were soaking through the fabric of his shirt. Cerdic had many lovers in his life, but he felt some emotions stirring in him that were new. Ria wanted nothing from him except to show her gratitude for changing her life forever, risking his own life and those of his friends to help her. It touched his heart.

Now that he was considered a powerful man, his relationships with the opposite sex were complicated. As king, he knew that he was an object of attention to the fairer sex, and he could never really tell if someone was interested in him or if they just wanted to bask in the glow of his money or power. Women now wore a façade to please him, and he could not tell if someone wanted to be with him because they loved him or if they only loved the idea of being his queen. He loved the ladies, but now he was forced to be wary of them as well. Whom could he find who loved him for being him?

He did not want just any woman; he wanted a love match, not a political union. Though his parents had a politically motivated marriage, they truly cared for each other, and he desired the same kind of relationship for himself, a wife who would accept him as is with all his flaws. He despaired of ever finding a match like that once he became king, but with this embrace, he felt something different. She had touched his heart. Somehow, he knew that she would watch his back and not plot and scheme, as happened so often in many arranged marriages.

Cerdic smiled, thinking of the story of when Cleopatra of Egypt had snuck into her palace in a rolled-up rug. She had been exiled by her brother, as the two of them had competed for the throne, and she had come upon an idea to meet a visiting Roman general who could help her. So, when the floor covering unrolled, the beautiful girl popped out at the feet of a startled

Julius Caesar. Cleopatra's brother had ordered her to be executed, so she had to sneak into the great man's quarters to plead her case to Caesar. Not only did Caesar make her Pharoh instead, but the Roman general fell for her in a love story that people still talked about. His smile grew broader. *Who knows,* he thought, *maybe history will repeat itself.*

The caravan of ships wound its way down the coast of northern Germania and back to Gaul without further incident, crossing the channel to anchor near the Isle of Wight as the coastal craft moved their immigrants to their respective destinations. The Roman Oneraria then returned to the same deep-water port off the coast of Gaul to meet some Angles who were on the same quest that Cerdic had just completed, to add more of their own to their great migration into Britannia. Some of the Jutes he had collected on their journey stayed on the Isle of Wight, but most of them moved up the coast into the territory now controlled by Cerdic.

Ria and Minura became fast friends. Cerdic was indeed smitten: not with the tapestry, but with Ria. Lucanus was also smitten, but it was not with the tapestry, either, as Minura had apparently caught his eye. Years later, visitors to Cerdic's royal hall would wonder why that dirty old thing hanging behind the thrones of the king and queen held such a place of place of honor. The other works of art that graced the hall were much more impressive, but none could compare to the meaning that the old moth-eaten and worn hunting scene held for the royal couple. To them, it was the most beautiful thing in the world.

THE HISTORICITY OF THIS STORY

Did King Arthur ever exist? Only two eyewitness accounts survived over this darkest part of the dark ages, a three-hundred-year period or more, and neither mentions him. Many historians believe he was a mythological invention and was not a real person. Accounts of him were written only centuries later, full of fantasies, magic and thrilling adventures. Though he is mentioned in numerous poems and oral legends from Wales and Cumbria that were recorded centuries later, the first written account of him was in the ninth century by a Welsh monk named Nennius in his work *Historia Brittonum*, not a historical treatise in the modern sense, but a glorification of a warrior for Christ.

Parsing out the facts from fiction is well-nigh impossible, and much of Nennius's so-called history was not credible, such as Arthur singlehandedly and without assistance killing 960 men in the battle of Mount Badon. In his history, Arthur was mentioned as a general, not a king, so that factoid was kept in this series, but much of the rest of the accounts by Ninnius was left out of the book.

The stories of the Arthurian legend that people are familiar with, such as the Round Table and the Holy Grail and Lancelot and the like, were all written more than seven hundred years later, amid the Middle Ages. Many of these features of these classic stories were purposely left out. The reality of this historical period was there were no knights in plate armor, and no shining cities, miracles, or magic. A few nuggets of Arthuriana were included, such as the sword Caliburnus, the Latin name for Excalibur.

Instead, this story showed what Britannia may have been like at the time of Arthur, and not the origin of his legends. In this time period, society had collapsed. People were starving, towns were abandoned, and chaos reigned. There were no money or merchants, and bandits ruled the road. Walls and roads and houses were falling apart, and no one knew how to fix them. The arms and armor were spears and boiled leather and scraps of old Roman gear.

If Arthur was a genuine historical personage, one would think he was a big guy who was good with a sword and spear in addition to being a strong leader, a true warrior king. He would have had to have been a good fighter to be considered a leader in desperate times like those. There is absolutely no evidence he was a short skinny guy, skilled at being a slinger: that was chosen just to make things entertaining, more of a David than a Goliath to be Arthur.

The Anglo-Saxon invasion was real enough, though the amount of violence involved, as well as the actual number of migrants, is still a matter of debate. Archeological evidence showed there were findings that corresponded to the initial Anglo-Saxon advance into Britain in the mid fifth century for a generation or two, followed by a reoccupation of some territory by native Britons. The interlopers were pushed back. The excavation of burial practices and grave goods showed the native Britons holding on to parts of England for another generation or two, following which the Anglo-Saxons resurged to occupy the entirety of today's England. Only Scotland and Wales were spared.

Numerous sources mentioned the high point of the resistance of the Anglo-Saxon invasion by the Britons occurred at the Battle of Mount Badon (Mons Badonicus), a British victory by all accounts, but we do not know when, where, or who fought there. It would have occurred around 500 A.D., give or take a decade or two. Whether one of the men responsible for that victory was named Arthur or not does not really matter; there was certainly an Arthur-like figure, but who that was and what they did remains a mystery.

The two sources we do possess that were written contemporaneously to the age of Arthur were written by two Britons who were Christian priests, the first being St Patrick of Ireland, and the second treatise was penned by Saint Gildas, who wrote a sermon concerning events at the time entitled *On the Ruin and Conquest of Britain*. Patrick's writings tell us little, so the sermon by Gildas was the best source of material we have of that period. As a document of history, it was deeply flawed as this was intended as a sermon. Facts and dates were unimportant; it was the message that mattered.

Gildas claimed he was born in the same year in the great battle as Mount Badon. He noted that the British won a decisive victory over the Germanic invaders, but he does not mention who fought in it, as presumably he thought his audience would already know that detail. He never mentions Arthur, but he does describe in glowing terms a Christian general named Ambrosius Aurelianus, "the last of the true Romans." His sermon was primarily intended to castigate various contemporary kings and clergy as being bereft of true faith, for which God was punishing them by allowing the pagans to triumph.

So, was King Arthur a real person? In my opinion, there must have been some leader with the name of Arthur in Britannia, based on the number of legends and stories. What accounts that survived were meant to entertain or preach a message and were not truly historical accounts. Why did Gildas not mention him? It is not clear, but my theory is that Arthur may not have been a Christian, hence someone like Gildas would have deemed him unworthy of mention.

Based on archaeology and other sources, Brittania at the time hosted a diversity of cultures, a multireligious mosaic, with native Celtic gods, Norse deities, and even old Roman pagan beliefs coexisting with native Christians. There was diversity within the Christian world itself, with some local Celtic beliefs deviating from the Roman church on issues such as what a tonsure looked like and when Easter was to be celebrated. So, although we will never know for sure, the character portrayed in this story was of an Arthur that was pagan Roman in his thinking, and a philosopher who admired Stoicism, a belief system common in the ruling classes of the empire.

As for the other characters, Cerdic was indeed the name of the first king of Wessex according to the history of that kingdom, the Anglo-Saxon Chronicle, written around 800 A.D. as authorized by Alfred the Great. Other than his name, we do not know his origins, the identity of his wife, or who exactly succeeded him. He had an Anglicized version of a Celtic name, yet he was in command of a Germanic kingdom. Nothing else was known about him, but he would have been contemporaneous to Arthur.

Similarly, the name of Caradoc was common in medieval Wales, and the first king of the Welsh kingdom of Gwent, a Christion by all accounts who bore that name. Caradoc was also the name of a knight of the round table in the medieval accounts written over seven hundred years later. Someone of that name was mentioned in the Welsh triads, in Geoffry of Monmouth's *Historia Regum Britanniae*, and in various French romances. It was a common name.

Brigid was also frequently used in Ireland at the time, the name of a traditional Celtic goddess, and of Saint Brigid of Kildare, the female patron saint of Ireland. but there was no mention of a Brigid in the Arthurian literature. The later books in this trilogy will discuss the historicity of the legends of the Saint Brigid with the feisty Hibernian in this story.

Hengist and Horsa, whom some scholars believe were legendary figures and not actual people, were both mentioned by Gildas and numerous other accounts as early Germanic invaders. If real, they probably were present in England a generation or two earlier than the battle of Mount Badon, but because there were no surviving records, we do not know what was going on at that time. Though they may have been from an earlier generation, their names and stories were just too entertaining to pass up.

Other characters, such as Senna, Lucillia, and Lucanus, were not in the historical record, but their names are contemporaneous, based on the archaeological discoveries documented on a website of the University of Cambridge that features the Celtic personal names of Roman Britain. Similarly, Anglo-Saxon names of the minor characters used in the story were contemporaneous to the period.

Pelagius was indeed reviled by Rome as a British heretic during the fifth century, though little is known of him or his teachings other than he emphasized human free will and that one's actions could determine fate rather than by predetermination. Pelagianism emphasized the ability to choose good over evil, rejecting the doctrine of original sin and the necessity of God's grace for salvation. There was nothing to suggest he talked of notions of social justice or equality, and we know of no association with the Isle of Mann. That island served as a fictional link to the earliest inhabitants of the British Isles to give a rationale as how Pelagius developed his rather modern beliefs as portrayed in the story.

The Weald was as described, and was used as a refuge during this period, and much of it still exists. Camalet was an early way to pronounce Camelot. The ancient iron-age hillfort that is now known as Cadbury Castle had been proposed as a possible location for Arthur's Camelot for centuries. It was actively occupied during this period when so many other Roman towns had been abandoned, so it was a possible location, if in fact the Camelot of Arthurian legends existed.

No *Battle of the Caravan* was mentioned, though one source mentioned Vortigern's son Catigern and Horsa both falling in the same unnamed battle. Vortigern himself was documented in a variety of histories. He was castigated in the sermon written by Gildas, though it is uncertain whether that was his name or a title, and when and where he reigned is still an open question. He was also a figure in Arthurian legends, but in all accounts, poems and legends he wrote were widely reviled, except in the royal house of the early Welsh kingdom of Powys, a region partially occupied by the Ordovices. There he was feted as a hero.

His son Vortimer was mentioned in Christian sources as a fierce opponent to his father's Saxon allies and was considered a Christian saint. Was Vortimer a bad guy? It is unknown, and the priests were the only ones writing things down when he died in battle against the heathens. One man's sinner is another man's saint.

The Night of the Long Knives was described by Gildas and other sources as an event when a cadre of British leaders were slaughtered, and indeed the legends were that Vortimer was given Hengist's daughter Rowena as a reward for betraying his fellow British.

Aelle was a king of the South Saxons who sacked Novomagus, and although he would have been contemporary to Arthur, he was not mentioned in Arthurian legends. Hengist ruled the East Saxons and modern Kent, and Horsa, his brother, was not associated with the Middle Saxons, though the names of kings from that tribe are unknown. Some reports claim that Horsa and Catigern were both killed in the same battle.

Britannia at this time was a collection of tiny kingdoms, and some of the place names of those realms persist to this day. The South Saxons were in Sussex, the East Saxons in Essex, the West Saxons in Wessex, and the Middle Saxons were in Middlesex. Norfolk and Suffolk were the locations the North Folk and the South Folk of the Angles that had settled in East Anglia. There were dozens of other kingdoms throughout the island, but it would be the West Saxons who would eventually win the Game of Thrones in England. Today's royal family traces their lineage to Alfred the Great and his forebears, which included Cerdic.

The arms and tactics of the period were a bit mysterious. For instance, no one knows exactly what a shield wall looked like, though numerous accounts told of fighting that could last for hours with few casualties until a line broke, and it was then that the killing would begin. The legionary tactics were better documented, but no record of a cache of legionary weapons being found in a bog was ever recorded.

Plumbata's were found in Britain and were used in the late Roman army, though this projectile would have been more difficult to make than a spear. Even if deployed in Britannia, the widescale use of plumbata as mentioned in this story almost certainly did not happen. How plumbata would have been employed, such as the volley tactics described in the book, were unknown, but would have been simple to use, so they were featured in the book because even a freed slave could quickly master using them. I personally used a modern version of that weapon, a 1970's lawn game long banned for reasons of safety called "Jarts." The high and low approach of missile attacks work, I can assure you.

Slingers were an important element of the legions, and the most renowned of those types of soldiers hailed from the Balearic Islands and slingers were clearly present with the legions in Britannia as numerous lead pellets were found throughout the island. However, they were not very accurate compared to bowmen, and they were probably uncommon in fifth century Britain. The odds of King Arthur being an accomplished slinger were about as good as discovering that Elvis still lives.

The reluctance of the Romans to use formerly enslaved people in their armies was well known, and the diaspora of Britons to inhabit Brittany was a historically documented event. The Breton language, a derivative of ancient British, is still spoken today. Archeology has discovered that many of the Roman towns and cities in Britain were abandoned during this time, including London, but continuous occupation did occur in some places, especially in the west.

In the Roman colonial period, Britain had a peak population of perhaps 3.6 million of mostly rural inhabitants. The size of the population in the Dark Ages that followed was unknown, but a demographic collapse was certain. In 1000 A.D., the population of Britain was 1.25 million. It is unknown how many people occupied Britain during the timeline of this story, but towards the end of the sixth century, after the Late Antique Ice Age and the Justinian

Plague, it was probably less than a million.

The use of elaborate earthen fortifications was historically accurate. Southern Britain is still crisscrossed with the remnants of World War One style trenches and walls, locally known as dikes. In the nineteenth century people thought these were built to hold water, but it is now known these structures mostly dated to the fifth and sixth centuries and represented fortifications that both the British and the Anglo-Saxons used for defense. Exactly how they would have been used is somewhat speculative, but the descriptions used in this story were likely realistic.

The was no documented *Battle of the Pontes*, but Roman bridges made of stone did exist in that location as described in the story, and the Roman name for the crossing of the Thames River at Church Island was indeed called the Pontes. The road linking Caleva to Londinium was called the devil's highway because of the prevalence of bandits and thieves that plagued travelers along that stretch of road, but the roads that the legionaries had built remained in use for centuries, allowing rapid travel across the entirety of England.

Ballistae were a staple of the Roman Legions and were highly accurate. Though mainly used in siege warfare and in defending towns, portable versions were built and mounted in wagons to carry them into open field battle. They were sophisticated and difficult to manufacture, and knowledge of how to build and maintain those instruments of war did not last long once the legions left. When deployed, they could pick off single soldiers up to three hundred yards away, and the largest of them could hurl sixty-pound weights over five hundred yards.

The technology of shipping used by the Saxons was controversial. The Celtic world was known to have used ships with sails prior to the Roman invasion. The only known Saxon-era warship was discovered at the Sutton Hoo site, and the funerary vessel resembled the long ships of the Viking era, except it had no sails. It was a glorified rowboat. So how did all of these people get to Britannia?

Exactly how many Angles and Saxons and Jutes migrated into Britannia, and what kind of ships they used remains controversial. There is no documentation of the use of Roman vessels to aid in this great migration, but these massive cargo ships were well described. Poetic license was used to make this means of transport responsible for this mass movement of peoples from Germania to Britannia.

Gwenhwyfar was the Welsh spelling of Guenevere, and the Merlinus could have been a title, not a name. The Silures tribe was greatly feared by the Romans, and the tribesmen were described as ethnically unique, olive skinned with curly dark hair. The English longbow was a Welsh invention, but the art of archery in this period was purely speculative. Wales was the British hotbed of archery where the famous Medieval longbow was perfected, and an intact longbow was found in a Somerset bog dated from 2700 B.C.

The Druids were ruthlessly persecuted by the Romans, though the religious artifacts of traditional Celtic Gods could still be found after the Legions had left. What did the Druids believe? They were famous for writing nothing down. What knowledge was lost is speculative, but the art of bee keeping as described in this story was not actually invented until the nineteenth century.

The gladiatorial arena of Durnovaria was the largest in Britain and could have held up to 10,000 people. Emperor Honorius was responsible for outlawing the gladiatorial games, and he also was the emperor who told the Britons in 410 A.D. that Rome would no longer be supplying troops after the legions had departed. Once Britannia was on its own, no doubt Honorius was not a popular man among the locals.

Did the outlawed games just move outside the empire once Honorius banned them? This was speculation, but the games were fascinating, so they were thrown into the story. The description of the styles of the combatants and their weapons and armor seems reasonably accurate, but the details of these fights, such as what the referees did, how often the fighters died, did they take breaks during a fight, etc., were unknown.

Britannia did attempt to organize itself into a functioning political entity during this period, and for a generation or two they were able to stem the barbarian invasion. In this story, they tried to form a modified Roman style republic with modern sounding ideas, which was unlikely, but the writing of Cicero and other Romans did strongly influence the founding fathers of the United States. The government of Sub-Roman Britannia was a failed state, so we know nothing about it, though the iron age tribes originally conquered by the Romans probably still had relevance in this period.

Some scholars debate just how violent the Anglo-Saxon migration was, but the sermon from Gildas and other sources were explicit that it was a bloody affair. Still, the native British culturally merged with the Germanic kingdoms to create a uniquely Anglo-Saxon England. The migrants came from the north shores of Germany and modern Denmark, and we know little of their society or religious practices, but they must have been culturally similar the Viking invaders arriving some three hundred years later. Old English and Old Norse were enough alike that the Vikings and the Anglo-Saxons of 800 A.D. could probably have understood each other.

Though the two languages were similar, modern English speakers cannot understand hardly anything in Old English, though some vestiges of our mother tongue persist. Our days of the week still have pagan Old English roots. Woden's day was Wednesday, Thunor's day was Thursday, Frea's day was Friday. Sunday was for the sun worshipers, Monday was for the moon worshipers, and Tues was their god of war. Only the Roman Saturn's day (Saturday) survived the apocalypse of the Anglo-Saxon overthrow of Roman Britannia.

One could assume that the language of the warriors of the time was laced with various salty epithets and curses, and I removed modern words like the f-bomb word for more archaic sounding Anglo-Irish expressions so that modern readers might be less offended by the language. Some expressions like "Woden's one eye" and "Svien hund" were indeed used by the Norse, and "by Jupiter" by the Romans, but otherwise we have no idea what curses they actually used.

Once the conquest of England was complete, the pagans had wiped out almost all Roman cultural influences, including Christianity. When monks from Ireland and Wales finally converted the Anglo-Saxons over a hundred years later, there was no Latin or British words in their language, and no Christians left. The previous civilization had completely collapsed, and a new identity emerged into what is today England when the Anglo-Saxons embraced Christianity and joined the rest of the mainland in that faith. It was the monks of Ireland and Wales that were largely responsible for the rekindling of the faith in western Europe, including England.

Today, people invoke the vision of a zombie apocalypse as a metaphor for the end of civilization, but there is no need to invoke the living dead or dragons or aliens: the collapse of the western Roman empire was a disaster of epic proportions. In 400 A.D., the city of Rome had more than a million people. It was first sacked by the Visigoths in 410 A.D., a benign affair compared to the Vandals a few generations later, and by 500 A.D it was down to 100,000.

Three hundred years later, when Charlemagne was declared the Holy Roman Emperor, Rome only contained 20,000. In 79 A.D., when the empire was at its peak and Pompei was destroyed, that settlement had a population of some 20,000 people. It was an average city at the time, nothing special. When Charlemagne took the throne in 800 A.D., the largest city in western Europe was Paris, with 5,000 souls.

The Late Antique World in the west clearly suffered a demographic collapse. The Dark Ages of the former Roman empire were just that; truly dark. Reading and writing disappeared except among the clergy, and continual wars, famines, and plagues devastated the countryside. If one wants to learn what it is like to be in an apocalypse, just pick up a good history book covering this period. But stories need audiences to read them, and the horror of what the world was probably like then was not accurately represented in this tale: it would be too depressing. But it happened. And regrettably for the characters in this story, things are about to get worse.

GLOSSARY

Achilles: A famous warrior from the Iliad written by the Greek author Homer.

Adonis: A figure in Greek mythology who was a very handsome young man.

Advocatus: A Roman lawyer.

Aesir: The main group of gods of Norse mythology, such as Thor, Odin, etc.

Aine: Celtic goddess of love.

All-father: Another name for Woden.

Alt Cult: The primary fortress of the Scottish Kingdom of Strathclyde, currently know a Clyde Rock.

Amorica: The region in France between the Loire and Seine Rivers that includes the Brittany peninsula inhabited by the Bretons.

Amphora: A clay vessel typical in the Mediterranean world that was used to carry liquids.

Amulet: An ornament or piece of jewelry thought to give protection against evil, danger, or disease. In this tale, Thunor's hammer, Mjolnir, is used by Cerdic and other Norse pagans as one of these.

Apostonik: A head covering worn by Christian nuns.

Aqua Sulis: Modern town of Bath, famous for its natural hot springs, a religious site for the combination of two goddesses, the Celtic Goddess Sulis and Minerva of the Romans.

Archery practice butts: Targets used for archery practice, often made of straw.

Arianism: A Chistian doctrine considered a heresy by the Roman church, with rejects the notion of the holy trinity, believing that Jesus was a creation of God and therefore distinct from God.

Aristophanes: A famous Greek playwright from the classical period of Athens.

Aristotle: A famous Greek philosopher and intellect.

Armorican peninsula: Brittany in France, where the natives speak Breton, a Celtic language derived from the British migration during this time.

Arse over tits: British slang for something that goes upside down, a disaster. It could also mean that someone fell down in a dramatic way.

Artwig: A judicial dueling tradition, ceremony, one on one combat to settle a dispute like the Norse Holmgang.

Asgard: In Norse religion, one of the nine worlds, the fortified home of some of the gods and the Aesir tribe that is somewhat analogous of the Christian heaven or Greco-Roman Mount Olympus.

Atrebetes: Tribe in southern Britannia.

Augustine of Hippo: Known today as Saint Augustine, a Christian theologian and philosopher who died in 430 A.D.

Avalon: Now known as Glastonbury, rumored to be the final resting place of Arthur in Arthurian legends. It is not known if Glastonbury really is in fact Avalon, but in this story, they are the same.

Badon Hill: Also known as **Mount Badon** or **Mons Badonicus**, an unknown place where a great battle occurred around 500 A.D. In this book the same placed is named differently by different groups. The-Saxon's use Badon Hill, the British call it Mount Badon, and Latin speakers referred to it as Mons Badonicus. The location used in the story is Liddington castle, but the actual battle site is unknown.

Balearic Islands: Islands off the coast of Spain, famous for the skill of their slingers.

Ballista: A large siege engine, designed like a large crossbow, that can shoot bolts hundreds of yards.

Bard: A professional storyteller, music composer, oral historian, and genealogist, often hired by a patron to praise that patron's family or deeds.

Barratus: Germanic war cry.

Basium kiss: A Latin term for an intimate kiss.

Beelzebub: A name used in the New Testament as another name for Satan.

Belgae: Tribe in southern Britain.

Berserker: A Nordic warrior who fought in a trance-like fury, often wearing only animal pelts.

Bifrost bridge: In Norse mythology, the link for travelers between Midgard and Asgard.

Bishop: A Christian church officer that had the care of multiple congregations to appoint, ordain and discipline priests and deacons.

Bint: British slang, a derogatory term for a woman.

Blaggard: a scoundrel.

Blooming: British slang, archaic form of bleeding or bloody.

Bollocks: A vulgar British slang word for testicles and can also mean something that is nonsense or rubbish.

Book of Kells/Kildare: A beautifully illustrated Bible from the Middle Ages.

Boudicca: Queen of the Iceni who led a revolt against the romans in 60 A.D.

Britannia: Roman name for Britain.

Brittany: A region of France, the Amorica peninsula, where a large number of British refuges settled during the fourth and fifth centuries, speaking a language similar to British called Breton.

Bugger: British slang for sex, or to can be used to tell someone to leave, as in "bugger off."

Byrnie: Anglo Saxon chainmail shirt.

Caesar Augustus: Julius Caesars' nephew, the first of the Roman emperors and was the leader of Rome during the time of the crucifixion.

Caledonia: Roman name for Scotland.

Caleva Atrebatum: A city in southern England, located next to modern Silchester, in the county of Hampshire, the capitol of the Atrebetes tribe.

Caliburnus: The Latin name for Excalibur, a word that means legendary sword.

Caltrops: Triangular spikes that are put on ground to impale the foot of horses and men.

Camalet: An alternative pronunciation of Camelot from the Middle Ages. In this story it is located at Cadbury Hill, an iron age fort that was reoccupied during the era of sub-Roman Britain, starting in the 400's. Pottery finds from the Mediterranean world make this one of the possible sites for Arthur's Camelot, near modern Yeovil in Somerset.

Camulodunam: An important city in Britannia, modern Colchester in Essex.

Cantii: A British tribe that occupied Kent.

Carissa Mater: Latin for dearest mother.

Carroballista: A smaller Ballista that is mounted on a cart.

Cataphract (plural **cataphractarii**): Fully armored heavy cavalry that originated in Persia, but used throughout Eurasia and the Roman Empire, like the armored knights of the Middle Ages.

Catuvellauni: Tribe in southeastern England in Hertfordshire, Bedfordshire, and Cambridgeshire, their capital near modern St. Albans at Verulamium.

Cernunnos: A Celtic god who had the spirit of a stag, his head adorned with antlers, who was the guardian of winter.

Chainmail: An armored shirt made of multiple metal links woven together to protect the wearer from edged weapons. The Saxon word for this is Byrnie.

Cheeky Bastard: British slang for a mouthy overconfident jerk.

Children of the Ash and Elm: An expression the Vikings used to describe themselves based on the Norse creation myth.

Children of the Oak and Mistletoe: An expression the Druids used to metaphorically describe themselves and the traditions associated with them, as they venerated both oak trees and ritually harvested mistletoe from them.

Christos: Greek for Christ, and the name that some Romans used to refer to Jesus Christ. Also known to the pagans as the Nailed God or the Dead White Christ.

Cicero: A Roman statesman, lawyer, scholar, orator and writer during the time of Julius Caesar who died in 43 BC. His philosophies were important to the founders of the republic of the United States.

Clinker built: A construction technique for ships, typically warships from

Scandinavia, where the edges of the longitudinal (lengthwise) hull planks overlap each other.

Codex: A book made of parchment with one side bound and written on both sides like modern books.

Colonia: A city founded by Rome as a community for retied legionaries. Former Roman Colonia in Britannia were Glevum, Lindus, Camulodunum in the east.

Commodus: A Roman Emperor in the second century who was infamous for his cruelty.

Compluvium: A square opening in the roof of a Roman atrium towards which the roof sloped and through which rain fell into an impluvium.

Concubinage (Concubine): An interpersonal and sexual relationship between a man and a woman in which the couple does not or cannot enter in full marriage. In Roman law, it was a quasi-marriage found in unbalanced couples, such as one being a free born citizen and the other is a freed slave. The woman called a **concubine**, had some legal rights but less than the legal wife.

Constantine The Great: The first Christian Roman Emperor who made Christianity the state religion in the Roman Empire.

Corinium Dobunnorum: A city in southern England, near Cirencester, county of Gloucestershire, capitol of the Dobunni tribe.

Contubernium: The smallest unit in the Roman Army, composed of eight legionaries sharing a tent. It was a close-knit group, sharing food, living space and equipment. Ten Contubernia formed a century.

Cornu: A Roman brass horn that was about three meters long and in the shape of the letter "G", used in the legions to signal the troops.

Corpse God: Norse nickname for Jesus Christ.

Coup de gras: A killing blow.

Cuirass: Armor with a solid breast plate and a back plate tied together.

Cunny: Vulgar British slang for female genitals.

Dagda: Celtic god and the primary deity of the Tuatha De Danann, a family of God and goddesses. He was associated with fertility, strength, abundance and order.

Danu: Celtic goddess of nature, fertility, wisdom, and abundance. She was known as the mother of the gods.

Daub and wattle construction: A building technique using woven branches and sticky mixture of mud, clay, sand, and straw to create weather-proof walls and buildings common to the British Isles.

Deaconess: A group of women who served in the early Christian church in a variety of roles, for both practical and liturgical duties.

Decurion: Roman calvary commander who led a squad of calvary, equivalent to an infantry centurion.

Demosthenes: A famous Greek orator and statesman for the classical era of Greece.

Deva Victrix: A city in western Britannia, now called the town of Chester, former home of the Legio XX, Valeria Victrix, the twentieth legion.

Dilemma of Achilles: In the Iliad, Achilles was given a choice by Thetis, his mother: going to the Trojan war would mean eternal he would be eternally famous but would suffer a premature death, while staying home would lead to a long and happy life, but his name would be forgotten.

Dobunni: A tribe in southern England.

Dodgy blighter: Dodgy means an untrustworthy person, and blighter means as contemptable, annoying, and worthless person.

Dogging: British slang for sex in a public place while people could potentially see you.

Domina: Latin for a female master over slaves and servants.

Dominus: Latin for a male master over slaves and servants.

Domus: Latin for a Roman house.

Doxy: A prostitute.

Druid: A priest of the ancient religion of the Celts.

Dumnonai: A tribe in southern England, what is today Cornwall and Devon.

Dun Guaire: Iron age fortress on the northeast coast north of Hadrian's wall, today known as Bamberg Castle.

Dunderhead: A stupid person.

Durnovaria: Town in Britain, capitol of Durotriges tribe, modern day Dorchester in Dorset.

Durocornovium: A small, abandoned village along the Calleva to Corinium road.

Durotriges: A British tribe in southeast Britannia.

Dux: A high-ranking Roman military commander over an entire province, a title that became Duke in modern times.

Ealdorman: Anglo-Saxon nobleman in charge of one or more shires.

Eboracum: The modern city of York, the largest town in northern Britannia and a provincial capital.

Eir: A Norse Valkyrie that heals the wounded.

Enfilade: A military tactic where missile fire is directed to an enemy formation along their longest axis to hit multiple targets at once, like lining up bowling pins in a line and hitting them from the side.

Equestrian: A nobleman from Rome, a step below the Patrician class, but still were wealthy and held important government positions.

Equites: Roman cavalrymen. It also refers to a minor Roman noble social class, the equestrians, equivalent to a medieval knight.

Ergi: A word for a receiver of unwanted homosexual encounters as the passive partner, despised by the Anglo Saxons as not being a real man, usually a slave or captive.

Eunuch: A man who had been castrated.

Feckin' eejit: slang for fucking idiot.

Fermanagh: A site in Hibernia where a powder made from rock was made that helped wounds heal.

Firebrand: A torch.

Folkvangr: A field in Asgard ruled over the Goddess Frea, a place where half those who die in combat go upon their death, similar and analogous to the concept of Valhalla.

Frea: Anglo Saxon goddess equivalent to Freya in Norse mythology, the goddess of love, war, love, and beauty.

Friesians: A Germanic tribe on the north shore of Germania and the Netherlands, located west of the Angles and Saxons.

Gangrene: A feared complication of wounds, an infection that rapidly spreads requiring immediate amputation for any hope of survival.

Gaul: Roman province roughly equivalent to modern France, whose native language was Celtic.

Gawping: to stare openly in a stupid or rude manner.

Geebag: Irish slang for a woman who is annoying.

Germania: Roman name of modern Germany.

Gladius: Classic Roman short sword used by legionnaires in the early empire, it was designed for thrusting with a sharp point and a broad blade with both sides having sharp edges.

Glevum: A town in western Britannia now known as Gloucester.

Great Conspiracy of 367: Historically recorded revolt in Britannia where an auxiliary unit on Hadrian's wall mutinied and let a Pictish invasion occur in coordination with other raiders, the Saxons and Hibernians, that led to chaos with roving bands of bandits ravaging the countryside for months until a Roman army was dispatched to quell the rebellion.

Greave: A piece of armor covering the shin of a lower leg, made of bronze or hardened leather.

Gobshite: An insulting term for a loud-mouthed idiot.

Gobsmacked: overwhelmed with surprise or shock.

Godi: A Norse pagan priest.

Golden Hind: In Greek mythology, a golden-haired deer sacred to Artimis, goddess of the hunt. In the Celtic world, a female deer represented femininity and gentleness. The combination of those two concepts is a part of this story but is not a historical association.

Goths: Germanic tribe that was the first to sack and occupy Rome in the fifth century.

Gravitas: The Roman virtue that denoted seriousness, giving one dignity and importance in the eyes of others.

Gwent: A Welsh kingdom that was founded at the former Roman town of Venta Silurum in southern Wales.

Haesta: Anglo-Saxon chieftain of a village.

Handfasting: An ancient Celtic wedding ritual in which the hands are tied together to symbolize the binding together of two lives.

Haruspex: A diviner who inspects the entrails of sacrificed animals to determine will of the gods and to tell the future.

Hel: A Norse Goddess, the daughter of Loki, who controlled a place of the same name, a version of our Hell, but a cold and underwater place.

Helots: Members of a class of slaves owned by the state of Sparta in ancient Greece.

Henbane: A plant that, when ingested, induces delirium, is said to be used by berserkers to induce a trance.

Hermod the Swift: A Norse messenger god, like the Roman Mercury, renowned for his quickness.

Hibernia: The Roman name for Ireland.

Hirdmen: An Old English word for a warrior in a royal household in the service of a king.

Homer: Greek author of The Odyssey and the Iliad.

Hypocaust: A system of central heating using a space under the floor with hot air from a furnace heating the floor which circulates to warm the room from below.

Iceni: A tribe in southeastern Britain.

Impluvium: The sunken part of the atrium in a Roman house, designed to carry away rainwater from the compluvium, sometimes a small pond or fountain.

Insula Manavia: Roman name for the Isle of Mann.

Isca Dumnonai: Capitol of Dumnonai tribe, modern day Exeter in Devon, was a fortress of one of the three roman legions in Britain, the Second Augustan Legion.

Isca Silurum: Also known as Isca Augusta, the headquarters of the Second Augustan Legion near the city of Newport today, in the town of Caerleon.

Isis: Egyptian Goddess that was also a Roman cult for women that was a competitor to early Christianity

Island of Mona: modern Anglesey Island, a Druid sanctuary destroyed by the Romans in 60 AD.

Italia: Latin word for Italy.

Jarl: A Norse word for chieftain, the origin for the title of an English Earl.

Javelin: A light throwing spear.

Jimson weed: A poisonous plant with anticholinergic properties.

Juno Lucina: Roman Goddess of women and childbirth.

Jupiter Optimus Maximus: The god Jupiter, the best and greatest, Roman god of sky and thunder, and the supreme god in the Roman pantheon.

Jutes: A tribe originally from northern Denmark, that settled during the Migration Period into Kent, the Isle of Wight, and Winchester.

Jutes land: Modern Denmark.

Knackered: British slang for tired or exhausted.

The Land of Fire: In Norse mythology, a hot, bright, land of fire in the south guarded by a fire-giant armed with a flaming sword.

Lindinis: A town in Somerset, home of the Durotriges tribe today's Ilchester. It is close to Camalet.

Lindum: Known today as Lincoln, A Roman Colonia south of Eboracum/York.

Londinium: Primary capitol of Roman Britain, today's London.

Ludis: A training school for gladiators.

Lugh: A Celtic god, known as son of the spear, a god of war and light and protecting travelers.

Luguvalium: A town at the western edge of Hadrian's Wall, today is the town of Carlisle.

Lysistrata: A Greek comedy written about the time of the Peloponnesian war.

Manica: Forearm protection used by gladiators

Marcus Aurelius: A Roman emperor in the second century, renowned as an author and a stoic philosopher.

Mare Brittanicum: The English Channel.

Mare Germanicum: The North Sea.

Mars Ultor: The Roman god of war was **Mars**, and Mars Ultor was "Mars the avenger."

Medicus: A Roman physician.

Meditations: A book of philosophy written by Marcus Aurelius.

Midgard: In Norse mythology, a name for middle earth, the lands where people live as opposed to the other realms, such as Asgard, where the gods lived.

Mithraeum: A place where the god Mithras was honored, usually a cave near water.

Mithras: The deity of a religious cult favored by Roman legionaries, a Persian god associated with the sun, light, and justice.

Mollycoddle: to pamper and overprotect.

The Morrigan: Celtic goddess of war, death, and fate, often depicted as a crow, she had a triple nature along with her two sisters Badb and Macha.

Mount Badon: See Badon hill, in this book it's the British pronunciation for today's Liddington castle.

Munster: The southernmost of the four provinces in Ireland.

Nailed God: Norse nickname for Jesus Christ.

Nicaea: the council of Nicaea in325 A.D. established the Nicene creed and standardize some of the tenets of the Christian faith.

The Night of the Long Knives: A probable historical event when a group of British nobles were massacred by Anglo Saxons in an act of treachery.

Nightshade: A poisonous plant.

Nithing: A Norse word for a despised person, a man who is nothing.

The Norns: In Norse religion, three blind witches who weave threads of fate on a magical loom that determined men's future.

Norse, Northmen, Nordic: The people of what is today Scandinavia and northern Germany.

Novomagus Regini: A city along the coast in southern England, capitol of the Regini tribe, today known as Chichester.

Novum Britannia: This is a term that only exists in this book but is a name we are using for the grand alliance of Britannia.

Optio: A rank in a Roman legion, second in command for a century (80 soldiers) under a centurion.

Ordovices: A British tribe in northern Wales.

Osculum kiss: A Latin term for a formal peck in the cheek.

Oculus: A circular opening in the center of a dome or in a wall.

Papyrus: Greco-Roman paper from Egypt, where our word for paper originates.

Parchment: Writing material made from the skin of an animal.

Paterfamilias: Latin for the head of the family, but under Roman law the dominant male who had life and death decision-making power for his immediate family and patrons.

Patrician: The highest class of nobility of the Roman Empire.

Pedo: British slang for a pedophile.

Pelagius and Pelagianism: A heterodox Christian theological position that holds that original sin did not taint human nature and that humans have the free will to achieve human perfection without divine grace; Pelagius was a Briton in the fifth century.

Phallus: Penis.

Philistines: A tribe in Israel mentioned in the Bible, regarded by the Jews as barbarians.

Picts: A tribe in northeast Briannia in what is today, Scotland.

Pileus pannonicus: A felt hat in Roman empire, commonly worn beneath a helmet or by itself.

Pilum: A heavy Roman throwing spear.

Plato: Ancient Greek philosopher from Athens, author of multiple works, including "The Republic" about how to bring about the greatest possible happiness in a city.

Plebians: The common people of the Roman Empire.

Plumbata: A large, weighted dart used by the later empire Roman Legionnaires as a miniature javelin.

Pommel: A knob or disc at the end of a sword handle that counterbalances the blade and keeps the hand from slipping off. In the equestrian world, a handle on a saddle.

The Pontes: The river crossing of the Thames, meaning the bridges, so it was thought a bridge crossed over to Church Island, and then a second bridge was sent from the island to the southwestern side of the Thames, between Caleva and Londinium.

Pugio: A Roman short knife with a broad blade, used for eating and self-defense.

Ragnarök: In Norse religion, the battle at the end of the world.

Ran: Norse goddess of the sea, storms, and the drowned dead.

Randy: British slang for someone who is horny and ready for sex.

Regini: A British tribe in southern England.

Retiarius: A type of gladiator who was lightly armored, who fought with a trident and a net, like a fisherman.

The Ridgeway: A pre-Roman road going east to west in southern England located along the ridges of hills just south of the main roman road from Corinium to Calleva.

Riedonum: The modern city of Rennes in Brittany.

Riothamus: A Romano-British general who led British troops alliance fighting a losing battle against the Goths. Called the king of the Britons in surviving Roman records, his actual identity was unknown.

The River Sabrina: The Severn River.

The River Styx: In Greco-Roman mythology, the boundary between the world of the living and the underworld of the dead.

The River Thamesis: The Thames River.

Rheged: a medieval Welsh speaking kingdom at the western end of Hadrian's Wall.

Rock of Cashel: A natural fortress in southern Ireland, the tradition seat of the kings of Munster.

Roman consul: The highest rank of Roman magistrates.

Roman Magistrate: A high-level elected officials of a Roman republic and empire.

Rubicon: A river in Italy that Julius Caesar crossed that irrevocably committed him to starting a civil war that ended the Roman Republic. When used in a sentence, it means going past the point of no return.

Sacrementum Militare and the Gladiatorum: The oaths to the gods pledging service to the emperor, the first given by legionaries, the second given by gladiators.

Sally Port: An entryway into a fortified place, designed with a series of secure gates to control passage and allow defenders of a castle to launch surprise attacks against besiegers of the fortress.

Salutem: A Roman toast equivalent to saying "cheers."

Sarmatians: Light horsemen and heavy calvary from the eastern steppes of what was Persia that were sent to Britannia by the Emperor Marcus Aurelius in the second century A.D.

Saxons: tribe from the northern German coast near Denmark that settled in Sussex, Middlesex, Essex, Wessex, and Northumberland.

Scallywag: a rogue.

Scotti: A tribe from Hibernia settled in northwestern Britannia in what is today's Scotland.

Scroll: The Greco-Roman book, the written word made of papyrus leaves glued together and read by unrolling.

Scutum: Roman shield used by legionnaires in early empire, it was large, convex, and rectangular.

Seax: The short sword most Saxons carried, featuring its sharp edge on one side.

Secutor: A type of gladiator who was heavily armored, carrying a short sword and a large rectangular shield, designed to fight a retiarius.

Sgian Dubh: Irish word for a small hidden knife.

Shag: British slang for having sex.

Shite: British slang for shit.

Silures: A British tribe in southern Wales.

Sol Invictus: Roman sun god, the name in Latin means "unconquered sun."

Spartacus and the Great Slave Revolt: A gladiator who led the most famous servile revolt in the Roman Empire, lasting two years from 73 to 71 B.C.

Sodding: British slang to express anger, contempt, or annoyance for something.

Spatha: A Roman long sword, originally used by calvary but eventually used by foot soldiers in the later empire and was adopted by the Germanic tribes as their sword of choice.

Spoons of Diocles: A surgical instrument invented by the Greeks that resembled a pair of salad tongs designed to remove an arrowhead from a wound.

Stoicism: Greco-Roman philosophy, espoused by Marcus Aurelius, taught that virtue, the highest good, is based on knowledge, the wise live harmoniously with the divine reason that governs nature, and are indifferent to the vicissitudes of pleasure and pain.

Sub-Roman Britain: Time period in history during late antiquity in Britain after the Roman legions left and before the Anglo-Saxons had fully conquered what is today, England, from late fourth century to early 600's A.D.

Suebi: A group of Germanic tribes, who in the Roman era lived the Elbe River region.

Sulis Minerva: A hybrid goddess combining the Celtic Sulis, goddess of healing waters, and the Roman Minerva, goddess of wisdom. She was the deity worshiped at Aqua Sulis (Bath).

Svien Hund: Old English for pigdog, a scurrilous insult.

Swiving: an archaic British slang for having sex.

Tacitus: A Roman historian who wrote about the conquest of Britannia during the reign of the emperor Claudius in the first century A.D.

Testudo formation: A legionary troop formation where soldiers formed a tight rectangle using their shield to create walls and a roof for protection from missiles.

Teutoburg forest disaster: A battle between an alliance of Germanic tribes that destroyed three Roman Legions totaling over 20,000 men in 9 A.D.

Thamesis River: The Thames River.

Thrall: A Norse name for a slave.

Theban Band: *The Sacred Band of Thebes* consisted of 150 pairs of select soldiers that formed the elite shock troops of the city state of Thebes. The contemporary historian Polyaenus described them as "devoted to each other by mutual love," fearsome warriors bound by sacred vows of fealty between two male lovers. This elite unit of homosexual fighters wiped out by Alexander the Great in 338 BC.

The Three Fates: Nona, Decoma, and Morta. In Greco-Roman mythology, they were three sister witches who personified the inescapable fate of man in their weavings of a thread of life. They were similar the Norns in Norse mythology.

Thunor: In Viking mythology Thor, the Germanic god of thunder, lightning and war.

Tinker: British and Irish slang for a gypsy.

Tintagel: A town in southern England in Cornwall, the reputed home of King Arthur.

Toff: British slang for a stylish upper-class person who is perceived to have an air of superiority.

Toga: A distinctive Roman garment for men made of white wool that semicircular and was draped over the shoulders and around the body and worn over a tunic. People who wore Toga's were considered civilized Romans and in the late empire were worn primarily for ceremonial occasions.

Toga Virilis: An article of clothing Roman youths was presented with in a ceremony when they were proclaimed to have passed from boyhood to become a man.

Tonsure: A haircut style that Christian monks wore. A Celtic tonsure was the front of the head was shaved, while a Roman tonsure the crown was shaved.

Torc/torque: A piece of jewelry, an open-ended ring of twisted metal that is worn around the neck. waist, arm or wrist.

Tosser: British slang for a stupid or unpleasant person.

Trials of Hercules: An expression referring to the series tasks accomplished by the Roman God Hercules.

Tribunus Primus: A high-ranking officer in the Roman Army. Tribunus Secundus and Tribunus tertius rank lower as the secondary and tertiary commanders.

Tuatha De Danann: The family of Celtic gods and goddesses head by Danu and Dagda.

Twat: British slang for female genitalia.

Twit: British slang for a silly or foolish person.

Urban Cohorts: Roman soldiers stationed in cities to fight fires and keep the peace on the streets.

Valhalla: In Norse religion, an enormous and majestic hall in Asgard, ruled over by Woden, where the Valkyries lead those who have died by combat to feast and do battle until the end of the world in Ragnarök.

Valkyrie: In Norse mythology, "chooser of the slain," a group of female figures who guide souls to Valhalla.

Vanir: Norse goddesses of fertility and wisdom, counterparts to the Aesir.

Velum: A writing material made of thinned cowskin.

Venta Belgarum: City in southern Britain, today's Winchester, in Hampshire County that eventually became the capitol of the kingdom of Wessex and

Alfred the Great. In this story, "Venta" will refer to this town, though other towns had the word Venta in the title.

Venta Silurum: City in southern Wales, near Caerwent, capitol of the Silures tribe near the mouth of the River Severn (River Sabrina).

Verulamium: City in southeast England, county of Herefordshire, capitol of the Cantullevauni, near St. Albans, north of London.

Vigiles: The policemen of ancient Rome.

Viroconium: A Roman town now occupied by Wroxeter in west-central Britannia.

Visigoths: The first Germanic tribe to sack Rome in 410 A.D., eventually settling in Iberia.

Vitus: A club made from a sturdy vine, a symbol of authority, that Roman centurions used to physically discipline their soldiers.

Wanker: British slang for an obnoxious idiot, associated with masturbation.

The Weald: A heavily forested and largely uncultivated wilderness, an area in southern England, south of London and north of the coast between the north and south downs. It was largely unoccupied in Roman times, but rich in minerals particularly iron, and crossed the counties of Hampshire, Surrey, West Sussex, East Sussex, and Kent.

"Wearing the purple": A Roman expression for the color associated with power and royalty, still in use as a ceremonial color in today's European royalty.

Welsh: Derogatory term for foreigners that the Anglo Saxons used for all the native people of Britain, not just what modern people today refer to as Welsh.

Wergild: A Norse term that translates to "blood money," a monetary gift as a penalty for taking a life to avoid a blood feud.

The Whale Road: A Norse term for traveling at sea.

White Christ: A Norse nickname for Jesus Christ. Also known as the Bloodless White Christ

Witan: The tribal council of elders that acted as an advisory body for the king.

Woden: The Old English pronunciation of Odin, the chief god of Norse mythology and head of the Anglo-Saxon gods.

Yggsdrasil: In Norse mythology, it is an immense and central sacred tree, and around it exists all nine worlds. Including our human world, which the Norse referred to as Midgard.

Xenophon: A Greek military leader, philosopher, and historian who led the retreating Greek mercenaries called "The Ten Thousand". His book "Anabasis" recounted the adventures of these warriors after the defeat of Cyrus the Younger in his failed attempt to claim the Persian throne in 401 B.C.

ACKNOWLEDGMENTS

First and foremost, I would like to thank my wife for putting up with me when I went into my own little world to write this trilogy. She is a saint in more ways than one, putting up with me being immobilized in the chair, ignoring the world around me as I wrote. My golf game has suffered, but my writing skills have improved.

Rebecca Jaycox, my editor, who is from our area of Missouri that I had met when she was just a teenager playing tennis, had the amazing patience to do three edits for me, and in doing so she taught me how to write. This could never have come together without her. There are no words I can use to thank her enough.

As for my beta readers, Paul Watkins was an old family friend who only read a couple of chapters, but his observations make me re-think how to flesh out the book's characters. My college buddy Beta reader, Beth Hoff, helped with the glossary and reminded me to tone down the language. Sandra Wise, my other Beta reader that I found on Good Reads, also graced me with helpful comments and ideas. Paula Hall Duckworth, a relative though complicated marriage ties, did my final edit during her Beta read to give it a more professional feel.

Rebecca referred me to her British friend Molly Phipps, and her work on the cover art for the book was simply breathtaking. She also formatted the books. Hail Britannia! She in turn referred me to Ricky Gunawan in Indonesia, who made the amazing map. Thanks go out to all my co-workers who put up with my going into my cave at work to write and then having to pull me out see patients. Also, thanks to Janeen Olmos, who helped counsel me into a healthier mindset and taught me about EMDR.

The authors that inspired me include Bernard Cornwell, James L Nelson, Wayne Grant, and a host of others. The book that first got me hooked on the Viking world was Frans Gunnar Bengtsson's *The Long Ships,* written in 1941. I was inspired to read it after watching the movie of the same name, and it turned out the two works had nothing in common, but that literary work got me enthralled with the Norse ever since. As for Roman Britannia, Rosemary Sutcliff's trilogy about the ninth legion, written in the 1950's, still fascinates me.

During the COVID pandemic, I listened to a podcast narrated Purdue University's Dorsey Armstong and her series of lectures entitled *King Arthur, History and Legend.* This can be still found on Audible as a part of the Great Courses series, and it got me interested in exploring the historical King Arthur, and ultimately this trilogy. Her academic journal, *Arthuriana*, is a wonderful resource.

My family and friends and been so supportive during this entire process, and I would have to add another few thousand words to thank them all. Next up: the Conquest of Mexico, featuring La Malinche, Bernal de Castillo, and a host of others.

ABOUT THE AUTHOR

JOHN FITZ is a practicing Ophthalmologist, and this is his first published work. Living in Southeast Missouri with his wife in their recently built hobbit house (see BrynDerwenBurrow.com), he has numerous hobbies besides writing historical fiction, including golf, fly fishing, playing bridge, hiking, listening to Celtic music, and collecting military miniatures and other militaria. He enjoys walking his two dogs and tolerates his two cats. He enjoys the company of a blended family of five children, their spouses and significant others, and his hopefully ever-expanding cadre of grandchildren.

Find him online at:

JOHNFITZAUTHOR@GMAIL.COM

JOHNFITZAUTHOR.COM

www.ingramcontent.com/pod-product-compliance
Lightning Source LLC
Jackson TN
JSHW022049140126
96714JS00004B/14/J